# Out of Eden

Also by Kate Lehrer:

*When They Took Away the Man in the Moon*
*Best Intentions*

# Out of Eden

## A Novel

# KATE LEHRER

Harmony Books · New York

Published by Harmony Books, a division of Crown Publishers, Inc., 201 East 50th Street, New York, New York 10022. Member of the Crown Publishing Group.

Random House, Inc. New York, Toronto, London, Sydney, Auckland

http://www.randomhouse.com/

Harmony and colophon are trademarks of Crown Publishers, Inc.

Printed in the United States of America

Book design by June Bennett-Tantillo

Photo composite by Deborah Lil

Library of Congress Cataloging-in-Publication Data is available upon request.

ISBN 0-517-59956-2

10  9  8  7  6  5  4  3

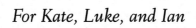

*For Kate, Luke, and Ian*

# Out of Eden

Let us not then suspect our happy state
Left so imperfect by the Maker wise
As not secure to single or combined.
Frail is our happiness, if this be so;
And Eden were no Eden, thus exposed.

—John Milton, from *Paradise Lost*

# Prologue

Did the women build all of this? The willows, the pond—were these a part of their grand scheme?

Not so long ago on the high plains of western Kansas, tucked among wheat fields and sand hills, stood two identical houses, demanding notice, exacting respect. Their still graceful shapes remain cradled in a hollow, but the wood is now stripped of paint, the roofs and windows in disrepair, one front door ajar. The rotted walkway in between tantalizes with its boarded-up entrances, board upon board—the only secured portals in either house. Does this walkway provide a clue to secrets long forgotten? There should not have been so great a toll on such a dream, for they had stood tall and proud, these twin sentinels against the night.

Like ancient cities now in ruins, no longer rampant with avarice and aspiration, their mysteries are left for later generations to ponder, to encounter from their own dimension in time and place. Since the pettiness of the human heart is matched only by its bountifulness, the questions are always the same: What inspires? And what destroys?

# Part One

*1* In opera as in love Lydia liked beginnings best. Before performance intrudes on expectations or transitions lead to tedium, she envisioned a flawless evening, a flawless union. Anticipation, of course, assumed flawless first notes in the music and the company. At such moments one could imagine a life without longings.

She had willed 1880 to be a good year, and now, only one month into it, she felt a resurgence of life, a banishment of emptiness. Looking down at the array of golds and reds and purples reflected in the gilded walls and boxes of the Paris Opéra House, and hearing the voices of the singers in perfect harmony, Lydia foresaw such pleasure awaiting her here in Paris that she wanted to laugh out loud.

She had the good fortune to be staying with cousins who actually knew people. Until she began this extended visit to France three months ago, she had never realized her Jackson relatives were capable of introducing her into such a world. Just in the brief season she'd been here, she had discovered more nuances—in ideas, in colors, in taste—than she'd encountered in New York in a lifetime.

At home she had chafed under the constraints of her very proper life of tea parties and suppers and the endless stream of complacent chatter, and neither her early marriage nor her equally early widowhood had changed the monotony of that comfortable, privileged existence. Now, though tea parties and suppers abounded, they took on different hues here, as with these shimmering golden voices tonight.

Good fortune, however, had its demands, and delight in listening eventually gave way to basking in the attention of Baron Gabriel de Rochefort. But at the same time she felt uneasy. Why would a member of the French aristocracy be pursuing her, an American widow? Why not one of the French beauties saw around her? Although aware that she was considered quite comely, she had never felt entirely confident of her charms, a hangover from her childhood.

What did the baron expect of her, she wondered. A mere flirtation? Or was it possible that it could lead to marriage? Enjoying her independence, she hadn't truly come close to involvement with another man since her husband's death. The thought of marriage to a baron made her a little giddy.

Until now Lydia had found the notion of royalty slightly offensive. Even now, despite her current infatuation with all things French, there was more consciousness of class here than made her comfortable. She shuddered to think what life must have been like for the French before their revolution.

In both America and France, Lydia had noted an unseemly drive to get ahead, to do the "proper" thing, to promote stifling ideas about marriage and family. She suspected these ambitions conflicted with one another, but such confounding thoughts were easy enough to dismiss when sitting in the front row of Baron Gabriel de Rochefort's box.

Almost imperceptibly she allowed the toe of her emerald satin slipper to show beneath her skirt ruffle, although she'd never understood why men found a clothed foot so exciting. When the baron leaned forward, ostensibly to hear better, his light breath pulsed gently on her neck. To be closer to him she pressed against the back of her chair.

In spite of her rebellious streak, she was both ashamed and alarmed by such bold feelings. Like those who are convinced of the constant presence of danger, she was most comfortable when she was most in control—of situations and emotions. Nevertheless, she continued to strain her body toward his. Even with her late husband she had never acted this way; but then, never before had anyone so admired her, so focused his attention on her. She would have been surprised and pleased to know that men considered her to be a woman of lively and restless intelligence; her spirit daunted most men, French as well as Americans. Neither her eyes nor her manner concealed her willfulness. Nor had anyone taken the time to teach her to hide her formidable drive, which presented itself as an assuredness that, in reality, eluded her.

Lydia knew full well that, for a woman in any country, distinction, save that of virtue, was not always trusted. Thus, more than she could readily acknowledge, she felt grateful to as much as drawn to this man who accepted her on her own terms—*almost* on her terms.

Since she couldn't ignore the obvious fact that the French were not going to be interested in, much less accepting of, a potentially impoverished American widow of twenty-five, no matter how clever she proved or how "good" her family, she had engaged in a bit of subterfuge that she considered part of her lark. While she might deplore Parisian snobbery, she did want to experience the pleasures of this particularly elegant world.

The difficulty was one of inheritance; hers was quickly running out, as was her brother's. But the economic forecast had begun to improve in America, and she trusted entirely in her ability to survive.

She wasn't so sure about her brother. Samuel's dreaminess, his unparalleled correctness, worked against him. He was ill-suited for most endeavors. And now he'd married a woman with not one whit of irony in her pretty little head. All that earnestness and proper-young-lady posing drove Lydia to distraction, although she tried hard to retain her sense of humor and to keep her proprietary feelings toward Sam in perspective. But here was a man who loved to spend hours discussing literature, history, the latest scientific theory, and his wife seemed to have no interest in books or ideas at all.

Unfortunately, May did share Samuel's strong tendency toward conformity—a reaction, Lydia suspected, against her own defiant nature. Her gentle brother never openly challenged her, but he knew his conventional behavior was most annoying to her. As was his recent talk of moving west to find better opportunities! She knew he wasn't fit for that kind of life. If she did marry Gabriel, she would persuade Sam to move to France. She was sure he could be happy here.

Lydia—lost in the music and her thoughts didn't notice the end of Act One, until the baron touched her shoulder. "Are you as entranced as I am?" she asked quickly, to cover her inattention.

"I'm entranced by *you*. Your voice puts the singers to shame." It was a lovely sentiment, but Lydia, being a modern woman, did not wholly believe in sentiment. She hadn't up to now, anyway.

Flattery was pleasing, she'd concluded, but not seductive. To be seductive meant paying close attention to the nuances of a woman's movements and taking time to interpret their meaning. Possibly that was why she'd never been seduced by an American man. Even after she and Herman married, he had never seemed at ease when she was around. If only he had died a hero's death, instead of falling off a horse while chasing a fox!

If the Jacksons were discreet, however, none of the French would know she'd married a man who loved his liquor too much. She wasn't terribly worried, for her cousins had been nothing but wonderful to her, urging her to come here to cheer herself up after her husband's death and her brother's unfortunate marriage. They had gone so far as to ensconce her in their apartment, introduce her to French society, and depart soon after for England. Nevertheless, if she had to keep up the masquerade of wealthy American heiress much longer, her fortune would be depleted sooner than she expected.

Realizing she'd lapsed into reverie again, Lydia hastily turned to the baron's cousin Isabelle, who confided that she had come tonight only for the gossip. Lydia laughed. Although she loved the music, she, too, became restless after sitting still so long.

Isabelle had made two debuts—only two were allowed—before acquiring the label of spinster. To some extent her situation arose from her coarse features and slightly askew right eye, which appeared, disconcertingly, to be gazing over one's shoulder. Despite her looks, Isabelle moved about Paris with serene self-possession and with no outward sign that she wished her life to be other than it was. Lydia could hardly imagine possessing that kind of confidence.

"Isabelle never bothers with people or events that don't amuse her in some way," Gabriel had told her once. So Lydia had been pleased when Isabelle took a liking to her and introduced her to the baron.

Now, to Lydia's disappointment, he excused himself to "pay respects to some older ladies," adding, "Be assured I shall return to the two of you as soon as possible." In deference to Lydia, he had "*vous*-ed" both women, but she'd already won the more familiar *tu* for herself in private.

As he left, she concentrated on Isabelle and her banter: "Do you think *anyone* here comes for the music? Besides, I've nothing to lose by speaking my mind. No one dares leave me out, for I'm the reposter of too many a confidence."

Isabelle had stayed in Paris when the Prussians shelled the city into submission, and even afterward, when the Communards turned their fury on the nobility and the Provisional Government for negotiating the loss of Alsace-Lorraine. After the workers, intellectuals, and artists burned and pillaged the very city they'd been trying to protect, rumor had it that Isabelle had persuaded the mob to spare her family home as well as her life. The women who told Lydia these stories had also told her that Isabelle wouldn't speak of that time or those events.

Lydia decided to prod discreetly: "I still can't get over how Paris has revived. Our War between the States has been over longer, but our country hasn't recovered as quickly or with such spirit."

"I suppose, but the Third Republic is so boring. So . . . so respectable," Isabelle lamented.

"I think wars and revolutions make people hunger for pleasant times," Lydia said. "They look to possessions for assurance and to their families for comfort."

"Comfort begets smugness, wherever you are," Isabelle said, harking back to their first conversation when they'd discussed the tediousness of being a woman in society and the constraining sense of propriety, which existed even in America.

Sitting in their red upholstered opera box, they once more debated escapes with Lydia arguing for challenge and engagement, while Isabelle continued to desire a less strenuous, more metaphysical quest.

"The danger with quests," Lydia said while observing Gabriel charm others, "is that if we do find answers, the knowledge will be too great to bear—be it God, or nature, or something inherent in ourselves."

"Precisely why we must proceed cautiously," Isabelle answered in her unhurried manner.

"At any rate," Lydia confessed after reassuring herself that Gabriel was only being polite, "the delights of Paris have happily distracted me from more serious endeavors."

Isabelle nodded, for, like Lydia, she accorded even mysteries and meanings a certain irreverence.

It was then that Lydia noticed her most attractive, most clever escort flirting with another woman. "That shrew," Isabelle murmured, referring to the Comtesse du Gramont, a handsome, older woman. Lydia wasn't so sure, for she saw a strong physical resemblance between herself and the comtesse, whom Isabelle continued to denigrate as they watched her toss her head to the side like a girl.

"Well, be assured that woman is not entertaining out of love for her daughter. That woman has never loved anyone."

The comtesse was to be their hostess after the opera, for a late-evening supper welcoming the comtesse's daughter, Charlotte, back to Paris. As Isabelle talked, Lydia adjusted her opera glasses to bring the comtesse into focus and was relieved to see the woman's skin and her hair color, more yellow pearl than white, had held up well. Some women as light-complexioned as the comtesse, and Lydia herself, wrinkled pitifully early. Until now she'd always considered her own eyebrows too heavy, but the same feature worked well on the comtesse. Gratified, she turned her attention back to Isabelle, who was still recounting the daughter's plight.

The comtesse, suffering from a rather hearty dose of jealousy, had stowed the young and beautiful Charlotte in a convent for a while, before sending her on to Britain and Italy. Recently, however, when her parents' marriage dissolved, Charlotte had gotten revenge by siding with her father, even choosing to live with him for several months against the express wishes of her mother.

"Look, there's Charlotte," Isabelle pointed out, letting excitement slip into her voice. "She's making a grand entrance, arriving as the members of the Jockey Club come in. By arriving at an inappropriate time, she's up-staged them, and this will really infuriate the comtesse."

Jockey Club members always appeared only in time for the ballerinas to perform, but Lydia suspected the comtesse's daughter's arrival was not particularly calculated. Nor did Charlotte's solo entrance appear so grand to Lydia, who observed a very erect young woman, dressed in an elegant but simple, high-necked cocoa-brown satin dress that exactly matched the color of her hair. As she leaned forward to kiss her mother's rather puffy, unproffered cheek, she smiled.

The smile was too forced to be beautiful, but the girl's cheekbones and high breasts would serve her admirably over a lifetime. Lydia noted a slightly receding lower lip, but otherwise, Charlotte's features—a small, beautiful nose and dramatic brown eyes—came close to perfection. Lydia could sympathize with the comtesse for wanting to keep this lovely young woman hidden away.

Isabelle began whispering the details of the family's scandal: the comtesse's husband had left her for a not-so-attractive, not-so-young, not-so-wealthy woman, and the couple had retreated to his family's run-down estate in Normandy, a veritable backwater. "My dear, the woman was hardly worth being kept, let alone leaving a marriage for," Isabelle explained. "Quite unheard of, really. I mean, there are so many perfectly good mistresses around."

Lydia laughed with Isabelle, but lost interest in the parents' intrigues as she watched the baron shift his attention from the comtesse to her daughter. With her arrival, Gabriel's face had softened. He seemed easy, even familiar, with Charlotte as she said something that made him throw back his head with laughter.

Suddenly the glittering spectacle of the Paris Opéra—seemed to mock her every movement. Who did she think she was to enter such a scene, to think she could be a part of anything so splendid? Why would a baron be interested in an American woman with nothing to offer? And all this gold—another heaviness to wear. It constrained as well as excited her. More perhaps; and she had grown weary of constraints.

"I have a dreadful headache," Lydia pleaded and resisted all entreaties to wait for Gabriel or let Isabelle accompany her, agreeing only to borrow their carriage. Lydia kissed her friend on the cheek, and Isabelle patted her hand comfortingly.

This was what people meant by the phrase "sick with jealousy," she thought as she hurried down the great, sweeping marble staircase, praying with each footfall that she would not see Gabriel. I am in love, and I am jealous. If this is what I can expect, I want no more of either emotion.

———•◦•———

Once in her room she accepted a glass of warm milk and asked the maid to help her undress. As soon as the servant closed the door, Lydia began to pace. Her rage—at herself and him—escalated until she finally hurled her glass into the fireplace, sending drops of milk skittering across the coals and running down the fireback. No sooner had she gained a certain satisfaction out of that effort than her fury gave way to despair. She had never understood love or passion and maybe she never would. Maybe she was destined to spend her whole life without experiencing either. Worse, she wasn't sure she was brave enough to risk more, though she had always thought of herself as having courage.

Now she was frightened. Was that why she had run away tonight? What exactly was happening to her? She'd been unfair to the baron. He hadn't done anything; yet she'd ruined both his evening and her own. She'd been happy; then suddenly she'd lost control—all because Gabriel de Rochefort was enjoying the company of another woman. What was happening to her?

When someone knocked on her door, the intrusion restored her anger. "What is it?" she demanded. Gabriel had flirted with others. He had ignored her feelings. But now she was told he had come to see her and would stay until he did. Although Lydia enjoyed the idea of his sitting downstairs all night—and she knew he would—she also realized the impropriety of the situation. There would be talk.

"Tell him I can't see him." Lydia told the maid, hurriedly removing her nightdress as she decided which dressing gown most became her. She would appear for a few minutes. That was all.


"My poor darling," the baron said in English as he caressed her hands between his large ones. "Why didn't you wait? I can't have you leave like that. How naughty!"

She liked it better when he spoke French; the words didn't sound so silly in French. He looked a little silly himself, she thought, standing there apparently ready to devour her. Even sillier was her own desire to return the look. Poetry hadn't prepared her for this man.

"Such a headache," she mumbled.

But he was excellent at relieving the pain of headaches, he countered, boldly addressing the cleft between her breasts.

"I only need rest now. Really." Her voice was shaking, his ardor having affected her unreasonably. She must get out, she knew, for she wanted more than anything to continue to display herself. She had never been so light-headed, so aware of herself as a sexual being, and she reveled in the excitement even as she scorned her feelings as ridiculous. Already, of course, it was too late for caution.

To Lydia's embarrassment, Gabriel was the one to break the tension. She could have remained like that all night and understood, for the first time, how ill equipped she was for romance. What was happening to her was worse than a bad fever and much more dangerous.

When he said he would see her the next day, Lydia could only nod her head in assent. "You're unlike anyone I've ever known," he said, encircling her wrists with his long fingers and pressing his lips against her forehead. Before Lydia had time to respond, he turned to go.


After changing back into her warm, serviceable nightdress, Lydia banked the coals and nudged two of the larger shards of glass toward the fireplace. This time she floated to bed.

Too exhilarated to sleep, and too exhausted to do anything but lie there, she stared for a long while at the cherubs painted on the inside of her canopy and scolded herself for being so foolish at the opera. Maybe the baron did love her; certainly she had never felt more loved or desired in her life. Why must she always assume the worst? Why did she look for the irony in every romantic glance, every foolish, tender gesture? For once, why couldn't she satisfy her need for security and for romance instead of sacrificing both? At the very least, she should let herself enjoy this new experience in the same way she enjoyed Paris, find out what might develop if she gave herself and the baron a chance.

Her behavior had been absurd, though love *was* worth a jealous rage now and again. She would pay that price.

In the morning she would write to Samuel. "Sam, dear," she'd begin. "I think I am falling in love." Either that or I'm going a bit mad, she decided. "If that is what it is, I want you to meet my baron." If indeed he was "her baron." She smiled contentedly. She supposed she would find out soon enough.

2 Charlotte Duret stepped barefoot onto the stone balcony and
stretched out her arms to receive the city at dawn. She'd been
gone much too long.

"My Paris," she called out to no one in particular, though
the night-soil man, beginning his rounds, looked up, startled.

Last night, on her return, darkness had veiled the city. The morning,
however, her first in Paris in two years, dazzled her with its deep grays,
luminous pinks, and pure blues, all bathed in a light frost. On such a
day, surely Maman could not be in a bad mood, Charlotte told herself in
an attempt to assuage her sense of foreboding.

At the opera Charlotte had been surprised and pleased at how well
her mother behaved toward her—distant, yes, but that was to be expected.
Arriving late had been the right decision, after all. With her mother one
could never be sure, but the comtesse tended to treat Charlotte better in
the presence of others.

As Charlotte wiggled her bare toes on the cold tile and wrapped her
thin arms around herself, she sensed Odile behind her, even before she
heard the whoosh of the heavy satin curtains opening, and anticipated the
gentle scolding.

"Mademoiselle! Out here in your nightie for all the world to see! And
no slippers! You'll catch your death! After such an evening you should still
be sleeping. Without proper rest, your face will grow old, and no one will
say how beautiful you are. No men will vie for your hand in marriage."

Charlotte turned, laughing, and put her palm on the other woman's
cheek. "For as long as I can remember, you've been threatening me with
spinsterhood, Odile."

"For as long as I can remember, you have been too headstrong for my
warnings to have an effect."

Odile returned to her room to fetch Charlotte's dressing gown and
slippers, and her ward dutifully, even gratefully, put them on.

"How is Maman?"

"She's going out more than ever. She is still a handsome woman with much to occupy her time."

"I know that, but how *is* she?"

Odile gave her a sharp look. "How would I know, Mademoiselle Charlotte? She does not grieve in front of others. She does not mention your father, but . . . I think you must watch yourself."

"No need to remind me of that." Charlotte pulled the robe more tightly around her. "So what gossip have you heard about last night?" Charlotte teased, allowing Odile to herd her back into bed.

"You flirted with everyone, but showed no special favor to any of them, though both Baron de Rochefort and Comte de Rohan are clearly in love with you."

"Baron de Rochefort is clearly in love with any woman who catches his attention. Since I haven't been here, he has not had time to become bored with me," she said as Odile smoothed and plumped the pillows behind her.

"You're too harsh in your judgments."

"I'm realistic in my judgments!"

"I'll make a fire before you come down with a chill."

"I won't catch a chill on such a gorgeous day. Don't be silly!"

"But you're cold," Odile said stubbornly, her square face set in lines of disapproval.

Charlotte pulled the covers up around her neck and denied it. "I *am* ready for my coffee," she added, knowing Odile expected her to go back to sleep. Though Odile didn't reply, she managed to sulk around the room for several more minutes before taking her leave.

While Charlotte had missed Odile, missed her more than anyone else, the independence from her protective tyranny had been liberating. Odile still thought of Charlotte as a naughty twelve-year-old, and what her mother didn't censure, Odile did.

Charlotte had truly missed Odile during her visit to Papa at his family's estate near Rambouillet. Since Audrey, his mistress, couldn't join him there immediately, Papa had asked Charlotte to help him set up his new household. Outraged, her mother had forbidden her to take Odile along. "For all I care, you and your father can starve, but I will not allow a servant in my household to live in poverty!" her mother had screamed. "If you think, my fine lady, that your father can support you *and* a mistress, you are wrong. And you can be sure he will not choose you."

But Charlotte and her father had done very well without the grand house and swollen staff and endless parties. She had enjoyed their informal arrangement and basked in her father's gratitude and love. Maman was wrong to protest Charlotte's devotion and loyalty to Papa, for it didn't mean she wasn't loved also. A daughter should not be forced to choose between her parents, Charlotte thought, although she could understand why her father had left.

A marriage with no soul—that was what he'd had with her mother. They had nothing in common. She did not understand him, nor he her. He could please her mother no better than Charlotte herself could, and Maman was not bashful about letting either of them know how she felt.

In spite of her mother's carping, Charlotte had been a good daughter. Only on this one visit to Papa had she ever defied her mother, and to Charlotte's astonishment, the world had not collapsed under the weight of this act of disobedience. On the contrary, she had never felt freer, more wholly her own person. Those months alone with her father had been the best in her life, like a holiday from reality.

At Maison du Val Bleu the two of them rode together every morning. They hunted; they explored the countryside. They ate simple meals and played board games until dawn. Whereas before she'd hardly functioned without servants—both Odile and her mother had seen to that—with her father, she reported to no one.

Even after Audrey's arrival, Charlotte reveled in her newfound freedom. Though sometimes she'd felt that she was in the way, no one had tried to tell her what to do. She admitted also to the sweet satisfaction of having her own way—for once—with her mother. But she would make it up to Maman, starting this morning. Her mother loved her.

And she would make it up to Paris, too. She would attend its balls, partake of its enticements. She would indulge its most vain and glorious self, for she, too, felt vain and glorious . . . and drowsy. She fell asleep before Odile came back with her coffee.

In the garden room ferns and palms and morning glory vines devoured the warmth of the winter sun at midmorning as light poured through the glass ceiling and was reflected off the alabaster statues of Cupid and three Roman goddesses. A table draped in sky-blue damask stood in the middle of the room, and an equestrian bronze presided over the center. A gilded chair upholstered in pale green silk, the same pale green found in the lightest shade of the nearby clematis vine, had been placed next to the table, and sitting in it was Charlotte's mother.

Resplendent in a blue satin robe—the same blue as the damask cloth, the same blue as her eyes—she did not look up when Charlotte entered, but continued writing.

"Thank you for the lovely party, Maman. Did you enjoy your evening?"

"It is not the function of a hostess to enjoy herself while attending to her guests," the comtesse replied, still without looking up.

Charlotte wished she would. Until her mother looked at her, Charlotte had no way to judge the temper of the day, no way to know whether to cajole or tease or settle for subservience. Emboldened by her time away, she decided to remain firmly cheery, no matter what her mother's mood dictated.

"Well, I enjoyed your company, Maman, and I believe everyone else did also. You sent your guests away in a most agreeable humor." That last remark sounded silly. She'd begun to prattle, she knew, but now at least she had her mother's attention.

"You must do something about your hair and your clothes," her mother said in a cool voice. "That American woman was better-dressed than you. The men paid attention to her, not you. An American! And she's getting on; she must be at least twenty-five."

Charlotte blushed and stared down at her hands. Now it was her turn to keep her eyes averted. She shook her head. "I don't remember her."

"She left early, but not before everyone noticed her style." The comtesse rose out of her chair and came to stand in front of Charlotte. Even when both were standing, the comtesse, regal bearing aside, towered over her daughter.

Charlotte, with her father's small, dark features, sometimes felt she'd have fared better with her mother had they looked more alike, but she knew it would not do to say so. Indeed, she had received many compliments last night. Charlotte had been pleased with her appearance, had felt a newfound confidence on her return and assumed that must be what others responded to also.

She was a vain creature, she admitted it. She loved the compliments and the flattery, took them as her due. None of that counted now, though, for with one sentence her mother had shattered the self-esteem bestowed on her by others.

"Maman, why do you say such things to me? Your own daughter!"

"Who else will tell you? This is for your own good. Otherwise you will never find a suitable husband to provide for you, and, my dear, you are going to need one soon."

Her mother dug into a bowl of peeled green grapes until she found one to her satisfaction, but she didn't offer any to Charlotte, who, with effort, said simply, "I don't understand."

She didn't want to get into another conversation about her need to find a husband. Long ago she had made it clear she would never marry a man who was not of her own choosing. She had spent her life observing two people locked into the hostile, lonely land of matrimony. If only her mother could admit it, the union had worked better for her husband than for her. As wonderful and kind as Papa was, he had paid his wife scant attention. Charlotte understood that and therefore understood the root of her mother's unhappiness.

"Maman, I will try to look prettier for you as well as for my future husband. I will also try harder to find someone who pleases us both." She shifted position, for the sun's rays stung her eyes.

"No one can please you. Your Papa ruined you—talking about ideas, treating you like a son! That haughty air of yours would repel any man. A little aloofness can be a beneficial exercise, but you behave condescendingly toward men."

"*Oui,* Maman, I am too hard to please. I'll do better." Charlotte made the last remarks with what she hoped was the proper amount of humility. With luck her mother would now dismiss her, and they would avoid altogether any talk of her father. As bad as this session had been, it could have been worse. Charlotte was aware of that.

"You *will* do better, young lady, for I am removing your feeling of superiority once and for all. You think I don't know what you and your father say about me?"

"I don't understand," Charlotte once again replied. "We never . . . I never . . ."

"Ha! Condescension pervades this house like a presence. I no longer have to put up with your father's arrogance, and I see no reason to put up with yours either."

"I'm sorry if I have ever given you a moment's unease about my feelings for you. I love and respect you very much. I will try to make sure this never happens again."

"You still don't understand, my dear. *I'll* ensure that it never happens again. You are to leave my house and my life. You are no longer my daughter." The comtesse's voice had gone flat, but the hollow in her neck pulsed fiercely.

"Maman!" Charlotte jumped up and rushed to her mother, but the comtesse pushed her away. Charlotte shook her head. "I don't understand. Last night you gave a party in my honor, to welcome me home. What has changed since last night?"

"Nothing at all."

"I don't understand. Why did you change your mind?" Charlotte repeated.

"I did not change my mind."

"You mean you knew this last night? You gave me a party *knowing* you were going to say these things to me? Oh, Maman, how could you? Don't be so unforgiving. Do not make us this unhappy. I beg you, Maman." Charlotte, now sobbing uncontrollably, lurched toward her mother again.

The comtesse raised her arm, then swung it hard across Charlotte's face. For one silent terrible moment, the women stared into the depths of each other's darkness until the comtesse barked: "Go to your father. Let him provide for his precious daughter."

Charlotte made no more protest, cried no more tears. Never again would she be a supplicant. And if she didn't die, she would be free.

3

A false spring was not to be trusted, for late March frost killed early-blooming flowers, Madame Martin informed Lydia. Then, spotting Charlotte Duret on a path in the Tuileries, the talkative Madame Martin ordered her carriage driver to change directions.

"You must meet her. She was your only rival until her mother disinherited her," she said and rapped her own knuckles with her dark red fan, the way she always did when she'd been too forthright—tactless, some would say. "She'd be destitute if her grandmother hadn't taken her in. When the old woman dies, I don't know what will happen to the child."

Lydia Fulgate tsked appropriately, although she wasn't the least bit interested in Charlotte Duret's plight, except as it concerned Gabriel de Rochefort. Though he'd assured her there was no one else, she needed to satisfy herself that he wasn't involved with Charlotte, or with that other woman she'd seen him flirting with at Madame Martin's recent soiree. Both occasions had caused her to suffer intolerable emotions, the kind she refused to dwell on. In the light of dawn, she had realized just how frightened she'd been by those strange impulses. It was no wonder she had always held love at arm's length! Since then she had worked hard at both encouraging the baron and keeping him at a slight distance.

"I'm sure you'll find Charlotte amusing," Madame Martin said as the carriage approached the slender young woman. Charlotte Duret might be destitute, but she comports herself like a queen, Lydia thought as Madame Martin began scolding her for walking alone.

"Maman spoke well of you," Charlotte said to Lydia. She blushed and laughed, then added, "Before we stopped speaking."

Madame Martin, having donned a full-dress-funeral face for Charlotte's benefit, appeared at a loss for a response to the irreverent mention of the unmentionable, for it was hard to offer pity to someone who laughed at her own predicament.

"At any rate," Charlotte continued, "Maman advised me to be

more like you, and I can see she was right. You are as beautiful as everyone says."

The words and smile beguiled Lydia. "I'm good at subterfuge," she responded. "Anyone can do wonders with a pleasant enough face, and that's all it is. You, on the other hand, have exquisite features."

"I hope you're not alone in this opinion," Charlotte replied, clearly not caring one way or the other about the opinion or her beauty. "Now that I'm impoverished, I must resort to something, mustn't I, Madame Martin?"

For the second time, Madame Martin rapped her own knuckles but said nothing offensive and hastily explained that Madame Soliel was expecting her. She offered to drop Charlotte and Lydia somewhere. Without consulting Lydia, Charlotte told her they would walk.

"*Nobody* walks."

"The day is lovely, and there's no mud." This time Charlotte did look to Lydia for confirmation, which she grudgingly gave, more to spite Madame Martin than to be polite.

Lydia hoped her annoyance didn't show, as the shiny carriage pulled out of sight, but what did she and Charlotte have to say to each other? As delightful as Charlotte appeared to be, she was a rival. Thus, they would simply waste each other's time, for they couldn't be friends.

As if Charlotte had read her mind, she asked: "Do you mind walking with me?"

"A little," Lydia admitted, "but I wouldn't give Madame Martin the satisfaction of knowing it."

Charlotte clapped her hands with delight. "Are all Americans as refreshingly candid as you? I've never had an American friend before, and I'd like to know you better. I've spent too much time out of Paris these last few years, but now that I'm back, I'm feeling bold, and I sense that you are, too. Or do you think we're too much the competitors to be friends?" She said all this in a breathless rush, making Lydia feel years older and even a little protective. "We do seem to attract the same men," Charlotte went on a little nervously.

For the first time that afternoon, Lydia produced an authentic smile. She would certainly like to have a friend right now. As wonderful as Paris was, she was unsure whether she would ever get to know anyone intimately. She'd begun to think she might always be an outsider. Lydia was lonely.

Turning her full attention on Charlotte Duret, she saw that her large brown eyes, quick and curious, kept her from being as seductive as she was beautiful. Though Charlotte's smaller frame and imposing posture made her appear taller, they were about the same height, Lydia realized, but other than that they were not physically similar. And Charlotte seemed so ladylike, not at all the nonconformist who balked at overrefinement.

"Why *do* we attract the same men?" Lydia asked out loud. She blushed at her own blunt question to this stranger, though Charlotte herself had been overly familiar.

When Charlotte suggested they try to solve the mystery, Lydia consented, adjusting the brim of her favorite hat—deep blue with saucy ink-green feathers.

"Shall we talk first of ourselves or of our conquests? And would you prefer to speak English? I have an English friend and I've spent time in that country." Charlotte assumed a conspiratorial air as easily as if they were sisters.

For the second time Lydia smiled without self-consciousness. "French is best for me. I've studied it a long while and took a tour here when I was a schoolgirl, but I still need the practice. And let us speak of suitors, by all means." Lydia, of course, was interested in only one of them; the others she saw as a means to pass the time not spent with Gabriel and as a way to make him a little jealous.

"Philippe Richet?" Charlotte asked. "Or is he too boring? Perhaps Comte de Rohan?"

Lydia gave a halfhearted assent, and they began to exchange caustic opinions about the men they knew. Lydia was not sure whether to be flattered by or wary of this young woman who thought nothing at all of confiding in a stranger—a characteristic that was more American than French. Lydia feared the girl was either very naive or very desperate, but found herself responding more candidly than she was accustomed, and this openness felt good. She felt she might be ready to test herself in the waters of real friendship, now that she was dipping slowly into treacherous whirlpools of emotion with Gabriel. In New York she had always relied on her friend Anne, whom she'd known her whole life. As a result, she hadn't had the inclination or the need to reach out to others, although even her friendship with Anne was based on a mutual regard for reticence.

"Gabriel de Rochefort and the duc de Mont-Orient are quite in love with you," Charlotte finally said as she looked at Lydia and smiled. "I think they must first fall in love with your eyes. That deep gray-blue is memorable. I've never seen eyes like yours."

Genuinely moved by the compliment, Lydia thanked her, but hoped to steer the conversation back to the baron. "I expect no one is really in love with my eyes or with me."

"Since I suffered reduced circumstances, I only hear these things from friends; I haven't seen Rochefort or Mont-Orient," Charlotte said matter-of-factly.

"Then I shall not see them either," Lydia responded loyally. At any rate, she now realized that she and Charlotte weren't rivals—a relief. "I've no interest in fortune hunters."

"Oh, those two men strike me as no less honorable than most."

Satisfied that it was rumored Gabriel loved her, Lydia could now comfort Charlotte. "All of Paris is in love with *you*," she said magnanimously.

"Then all of Paris is dwindling," Charlotte replied and laughed.

They walked on as afternoon sun gave way to early evening light, examining geraniums and pansies in window boxes, watching the brisk pace of silk-gowned women in carriages making late afternoon rounds. Nannies strolled past with small children in starched clothes. The sounds of birds mingled with smell of wisteria and hyacinth. White cloud puffs, inviting enough to dip your face into, drifted over the rooftops and spires. With the same effortlessness Lydia and Charlotte strolled along the streets.

Lydia knew she must get home, of course, but she'd seldom so enjoyed an afternoon.

"I'm beginning to think Maman was right about me in one respect: I am entirely too hard to please. When I find a man who interests me, I try to imagine what life would be like with him. I picture us in romantic situations—walking in the woods, enjoying a concert together, kissing after an absence—but invariably I come around to seeing us as Maman and Papa, shouting, crying. Then I despair of spending my life that way."

Charlotte shook her head. "I sometimes think we'd be better off without men. I hate this business of looking for a husband. I think I should hate having one all the more. Either we're madly in love and we get hurt, or we're not in love and we treat each other like chattels. I'd rather be a courtesan than a wife. They have more independence."

"Charlotte!" Lydia said, grinning.

"What I say is perfectly true."

Lydia sighed. Romance was costly; so was marriage. One had to be pleasing and accommodating even in the best of worlds. Sometimes the independent part of her just wanted to smash the ingratiating part. For Gabriel she was willing to conform more, but still . . . "If one chooses an even-tempered, responsible husband—"

"But Papa was all that, and he made Maman unhappy," Charlotte said, interrupting, a small furrow forming between her brows. "She's difficult, but I understand her frustration."

For the first time Charlotte seemed to censor herself and refocused the subject. "Did you find marriage at all appealing?" she asked. "If that's not too impertinent a question."

"I had a devoted husband. I was lucky."

"And did you love him?"

"I don't know," Lydia answered, a little too sharply before relenting. "I was very young, and he seemed very mature. I'm not sure what I expected, but we were married less than a year."

This response emboldened Charlotte to ask quickly, "And in bed? Is that agreeable?" She blushed and apologized. "Odile, my maid, explained some of the facts to me, and what little information I have came so late that I can't ask friends. I couldn't bear to have *that* gossip spread in Parisian parlors!"

"And you think I won't spread the news because I'm an American?"

"I think you won't because you are the first person I've ever trusted other than Odile, Grand-mère and Papa."

"You don't know me."

"I feel I am beginning to know you very well," Charlotte responded simply.

Lydia stopped walking and turned to face her companion. "It is much like a kiss, once one gets used to it. Kisses are better but it's not unpleasant."

"How long does this getting-use-to take?"

"The first time hurts, so you must tell your husband to be gentle." Lydia leaned in closer to Charlotte. "All I was told was that something mysterious and intimate would happen on my wedding night. I was so frightened at the idea of sleeping with a man that I wore pantaloons, a petticoat—everything!—underneath my nightgown." Remembering her excessive modesty, she laughed, then instantly regretted revealing so much. It wasn't at all like her.

"I would like best to be held," Charlotte confided, and Lydia agreed.

Again they walked in silence. The streets were becoming more crowded now as men left their offices and the cafés began to fill. I really must go, Lydia thought, but again she made no effort to disengage herself.

Charlotte shook her head. "This business of being a woman is so confusing: one is not supposed to know certain things, one is not supposed to *do* certain things. What if we don't want to marry at all? Or have children? Does this make us less feminine? I like some of the same activities men like, and so do a good many women I know. I don't consider such women masculine; I consider them interesting."

"Yes!" Lydia agreed, grabbing Charlotte's arm. "We have to do more than we're told we can. I've never believed we're helpless for a minute, or I would have suffocated long ago. Marriage, for instance, should be something we enter into because we choose to, not because we ought to."

"But if one is without funds . . ." Charlotte turned to Lydia. "In America are there adventures and husbands?"

"There are not that many husbands in the part I come from, and the South is even worse. A whole generation of young men on both sides died in the War between the States and many of the survivors are moving west because of a bad economy. Unfortunately, my brother plans to do the same," she said and grimaced.

"Then perhaps we should move to this mystical West."

Lydia considered the question in silence. Until Gabriel came along, she'd entertained all kinds of ideas. As she went about the rounds of parties in New York and embarked on her travels to Virginia to visit relatives, she'd experienced boredom verging on apathy. She'd felt the West's pull after reading romance novels and magazine stories that brought its prairies vividly to life, but it seemed too remote a place for a woman alone. As dissatisfied as she'd become with her life, she knew herself to be a social creature. While she took few into her confidence, she took many into her company, a not unsatisfactory compensation.

Charlotte smiled. "I want to see the wilderness of the western United States. Maybe I should meet your brother."

Lydia shook her head. "Too late. He recently married a totally unsuitable woman—at least, his big sister thinks so." They both laughed. "I'm a little jealous," she admitted.

"You will miss him very much, if he moves there," Charlotte said softly.

Suddenly Lydia found herself pouring out her feelings about Sam and their situation. How their parents had little time for anyone but each other and their social activities. She'd wanted somebody to care for her, pay attention to her, instead, she had become Sam's mother, even before their parents' early death. She cared too much about him, worried too much about him but it was an old, old habit.

Lydia looked at Charlotte, who seemed so attentive and understanding that she continued. "Of course, now that he's married, our relationship is not the same at all, but I could accept that if he just wouldn't go to Kansas."

"Maybe he'll change his mind," Charlotte said, trying to console her.

"Only if our coffers swell." Lydia brought the conversation to a halt. She must not be so indiscreet. Already she'd exposed herself more than she ever had before, and she surely wasn't going to explain how much more necessary money became to her every day as she kept spending exorbitant sums to keep up appearances. Since widows were frowned upon if they wore anything more ostentatious than modest black onyx, she'd even considered pawning her few pieces of jewelry, most of which had been her mother's; but she was reluctant to part with a single small stone, since jewelry and a love of reading were about all her mother had ever given her.

"Besides," Lydia finally continued, going back to the subject of Sam, "he's been told that Kansas is a paradise—a very foreign paradise, I should think—and a part of him craves the excitement of such a life."

"If I were he, I would, too." Charlotte conceded. "Were it not for my papa, I believe I would go to Kansas right now. I mightn't need a husband at all. And if I did, I'd look for a vigorous westerner. With my fellow countrymen, I'm afraid of catching the pox."

Lydia looked alarmed. "Is it so bad, do you think?"

"That's what I hear, though we respectable young women are forbidden to hear anything, let alone speak of it. Parisian men are the worst." Charlotte's ivory fan with its hand-painted nightingales tapped Lydia's slender hand. "That's why one must be careful in choosing a husband. If he has been too much of a scoundrel, then I say pass him up."

Lydia wanted to ask about Rochefort, but she couldn't bring herself to pose the question. She was much more a young woman of her time than she would have cared to admit.

When they parted, both women agreed to be in touch soon, but their talk had unsettled Lydia. On the one hand, she didn't know when she'd enjoyed anyone's company more; on the other, she wasn't given to sharing the kind of confidences Charlotte Duret had extracted from her. Better to keep one's own counsel, she'd always believed.

But why was she brooding? Gabriel would be waiting to take her for a ride. And he loved her; Charlotte had heard as much. Surely he didn't have the pox. How could anyone so splendid catch anything so appalling? But, against her will, Lydia suddenly saw that splendid man maimed, then blind, then mad.

Another moment passed before she could laugh at her own silliness. Rochefort was the picture of health, and she refused to believe one could have the pox for years without knowing it. She should explore the subject further with Charlotte after all. She might go so far as to divulge her feelings about Gabriel. She trusted her new friend to protect her secret.

This lovely, buoyant woman was worth the risk, the plunge, as much as Gabriel was. When one stopped to think about it, fortifying oneself against loss was an impossible task. She might just as well learn to open herself to the world. That had happened anyway, and it was such a relief, such a delight, to have found someone she could confide in.

As she hurried on to her rendezvous, her supple calfskin boots clicked to the rhythm of the verse flowing from her happiness: " 'With their triumphs and their glories and the rest! Love is best.' Oh, love is best!"

4 She wished she hadn't allowed the baron to come into her quarters, and she wished he hadn't persuaded her to sit on the sofa beside him. Tonight's concert had gone on too long, and she was out of sorts. Gabriel was too superficial, too flirtatious to suit Lydia. She didn't want him to think she was the least bit jealous of the woman he had spent the evening charming. Lydia had to admit she had been pretty, that woman with the milky blue eyes and hair the color of cinnamon, whose name was Marceline and whose seductive nature matched his.

"You're so quiet, *ma chérie*. Perhaps another headache?" Gabriel asked, placing his fingers on the back of her neck.

"I feel fine." She pulled away from him without appearing to and began straightening the needlepoint sofa pillows. In a softer tone she added, "It's been a lovely evening." Lydia could not be unaffected by his behavior around other women, but she was learning to conceal the hurt.

"If you lean back in my arms, the evening will be even sweeter," he suggested.

She submitted and at once regretted it. Superficial or not, flirtatious or not, he smelled good and the warmth of his arms reassured her. Though she averted her face so he couldn't kiss her, she found herself relaxing into his embrace.

"Shining silver buttons," he said, touching the one at the bottom of her gray-green jacket. "Pretty shiny buttons all, and I am jealous of your maid's having an opportunity to close them for you."

Giving in to his silliness, she smiled and replied that she buttoned them herself.

"How many buttons are there?" he asked.

"I have no idea," she replied, entwining her fingers, primly now, in her lap.

"One . . . two . . . three . . ." He began counting and rubbing her buttons from the bottom. "Four . . . five."

At first she thought he might try to undo them, but once reassured that he was simply counting, she let him continue. As he approached her breasts and his hands didn't stray, she allowed herself to enjoy his funny romantic notions.

Since that time in her rooms, she'd become wary of intimate encounters with him, constantly reminding herself that an affair was out of the question, for, if he meant that much to her, and that was more and more the case, then they should marry. Besides, when her rational side functioned properly, she knew romance was only for schoolgirls and the very wealthy.

When he got to the buttons securing her high collar, he lifted her chin gently to finish counting. "Twenty-three, twenty-four, twenty-five," he intoned. "Twenty-six," he finished and kissed her. Boldly he began flicking his tongue in and out of her mouth, and to her amazement she responded in kind. She had never been so brash.

When she finally drew her mouth away, he began counting backwards. "Twenty-six, twenty-five, twenty-four . . ." This time he undid the buttons. "Eighteen, seventeen . . ." He slipped his hand under her jacket and across her breast.

"Gabriel, the servants! Someone could . . ." she began protesting. At another time she might have been weak enough to allow him this liberty, but her small breasts would make a pitiful showing compared to Marceline's ample bosom. Everything about that woman had been lush, like some overgrown, half-wild garden, and Lydia was not about to compete tonight with all that fulsomeness.

Gabriel responded by rising from the sofa, locking the parlor door, and drawing the curtains.

"Now, where were we?" he asked, his tongue finding her mouth again, his hand slipping this time under her chemise and rubbing the silky skin of her breast. He took a long while fingering her nipple before he leaned over to kiss it.

"Oh, Gabriel, you mustn't," she said, pressing him to her. What a fool she'd been to think she understood what making love was all about! "No one told me . . ."

"What, *chérie?*" he murmured.

How could she explain that, before him, she hadn't thought a woman capable of such appetites. As grateful as she was excited, she kissed his temple, his neck, his earlobe.

The poetry began in her head: "Shall I compare thee to a summer's day? Thou art more lovely . . ." but the lines stopped abruptly when she felt his other hand slide under her crinolines and onto her thigh. Without thinking, she spread her knees. Suddenly he was touching her sex and she felt her liquid response.

"Gabriel!" She tried to push him away, but he grabbed her hand and placed it between his legs where she could feel his own sex, swollen and ready.

When he turned his attention momentarily to unbuttoning his britches, she rapidly began to calculate her options. Who would protect her other than herself? If she let him have her, he would not marry her. Then again, she reasoned as her hips began to move along with his unextricated hand, if she got pregnant, he would *have* to marry her. But she had never conceived with Herman, and was this moment of lust really worth giving up a marriage that promised such pleasure? This last thought had the needed effect, and not a moment too soon.

Before Gabriel had undone his last button, with some effort she removed his hand from under her skirt and, for good measure, crossed her legs. When he finally realized she meant this love play to end, a look of dismay crossed his face, endearing him to her that much more.

Not quite sure yet of the rhythms of French courtships, she was confident of her power to move things along. A late spring wedding would take them out of the city together for the summer. With a little more ingenuity and the help of Gabriel's money—if he wasn't brilliantly wealthy, his inheritance, she was sure, would suffice—she would talk Sam into settling in Paris. Then she could surround herself with those she cared for—Gabriel, Sam, and Charlotte. And why not Anne as well? That way she would have her own small universe exactly as she wanted it and never have to feel lonely again.

She laid her head on Gabriel's chest and had to restrain herself from telling him how blissful their marriage was going to be now that she was no longer such an innocent. She rubbed his knee with her fingers. "Not to worry, darling," she reassured him. "It will be ever so much better if we wait and have it last forever." He appeared more resigned than happy.

5 Lydia felt foolish as she walked up the steps with pastries for Charlotte. She'd brought them because she wanted to reach out to her new friend, to be of some help, and all she could think to do was what her own grandmother had done in times of bereavement: take food. She had no idea, however, of what was and what was not appropriate in France. She intended to make it clear that she understood how presumptuous it was of her, to be calling so soon after the death of Charlotte's grand-mère.

When her own granny had died, there was a long period when she could hardly bear to see anyone. Her grandmother had suffered in pain for hellish months, and Lydia, then seventeen, had tended her faithfully as best she could. Although theirs was not a confiding family, she and her grandmother shared a closeness. Granny had listened. Granny cared.

Her own parents' death two years earlier had been such a shock that she barely remembered that period in her life, had little recollection of mourning. Her parents had the bad luck of visiting in Saratoga when a flu epidemic struck there. Suddenly they were dead, and Lydia hadn't even known they were sick. All she really remembered of that time was an even more powerful sense of responsibility for Sam, a redoubling of her efforts to look after him. By the time the shock wore off, she could almost convince herself that she didn't miss those two always scarce presences in her life.

With the loss of her grandmother, however, Lydia gave full vent to her feelings, and, for the only time in her life, she couldn't cope with her grief. Her aunt Bea had come from Boston to stay with her and Sam for several months. Until then she'd spent little time around her unconventional, headstrong aunt, because the family already considered Lydia too much like her for her own good. But necessity and Aunt Bea had taught her how to survive, and now maybe she could help Charlotte do the same.

Charlotte appeared at the top of the polished stone stairway wearing a simple black cashmere dress, all quite proper, except that unmarried young women didn't wear cashmere. Extravagant taste was thought to scare away prospective husbands. Lydia admired this small act of defiance.

"I thought I heard your voice," Charlotte said, looking pleased.

"I was leaving sweets, but I didn't want to disturb you," Lydia explained, although Charlotte seemed genuinely glad to see her.

While thanking her profusely, Charlotte whisked her into a gloomy sitting room filled with dark furniture. "This isn't the most pleasant place in Grand-mère's house," she said apologetically as she closed the door behind her. The room was her only escape from her grandmother's four sisters, who had perched themselves around the house and were quarreling with each other—their favorite sport. Charlotte laughed, but Lydia felt she might just as well have burst into tears.

To Lydia's delight, Charlotte began teasing her about Gabriel's fascination with her. Evidently everyone now knew of his grand passion for "the American," and, as usual, Lydia was comforted by this information. Inexplicably, it always meant more when she heard it from someone other than the baron himself.

Although Gabriel was forever declaring his love, on some days she didn't quite believe him. On those days she would frantically engage in all sorts of activities—paying calls, taking carriage rides, purchasing books or pictures—anything to take her mind off her fear that she might not be able to establish her new world after all. Her disciplined decorum, had become useless to her.

With an effort, Lydia started to listen to what Charlotte was saying about her aunts: "They become more and more extravagant in their pity with each passing hour since my grand-mère's death. 'Oh, poor dear, what a shame for you.' Imagine!" Charlotte now stood with her fists on her hips, perfectly capturing the tone and look of all those Parisian busybodies.

"Naturally, Maman's coming to the funeral and not speaking to me helped confirm that hope. Their only disappointment is that their 'poor, dear nephew,' my papa, is too sick with a fever to come mourn his maman. My papa had a very wise fever, I think!" She was trying to maintain a light tone, but her grandmother's death had been an even larger blow than she'd expected.

Charlotte had been paying a call on Isabelle, who had been speaking of the comforts of routine, when a servant interrupted. Without waiting to be announced, one of Charlotte's least favorite cousins had trailed in behind the servant. The woman, dressed in black, had worn the solemn, self-important look of someone who relished delivering bad news. "Forgive me," she'd said to Isabelle as she put an arm around Charlotte, who felt diminished by the gesture.

So it has happened, Charlotte had thought with an unseemly calm. My grand-mère is dead and I am poor. What a pity for us both. She touched the fallen petal of a fiery pink rose and took comfort in its yielding softness.

Isabelle, too, became oversolicitous as Charlotte folded away her stitching and gathered her parasol. I will not cry, Charlotte had vowed. They would think I wept for myself, and they would be right. Her grand-mère deserved better.

"I shall miss her," Charlotte had said quietly and to no one and set out to mourn a death, and to celebrate a life well lived.

But today Lydia had come, and Charlotte could hardly contain her excitement over the visit. Though they occasionally called on each other in the afternoon, Charlotte liked it best when they met coincidentally, for the lack of intention relaxed them. Much to Charlotte's disappointment, however, the spontaneous, confidential tone hadn't recurred, although they laughed easily together and enjoyed each other's company. This afternoon Charlotte felt especially protective of Lydia, who was too vulnerable, too . . . American for a man like Gabriel de Rochefort.

Until Marceline de Saint-Antoine was announced, Lydia had not been thinking about Gabriel. And as she came through the door, Lydia, remembering how she and Gabriel had flirted together at the opera, felt herself go limp.

"Have I interrupted?" the voluptuous young woman asked without the slightest sign of apology in her voice.

"I'm lamenting the vice of solicitude," Charlotte answered, embracing her latest visitor.

"Solicitude toward you or others?" The word "you" landed lazily on Charlotte's right cheek, "others" on her left, as Marceline took note of their surroundings.

"Are we forever relegated to this hideous room? When are those vultures upstairs going home?" These words came with such rapidity that Lydia had a hard time following the conversation.

"Not until they're satisfied that I'm as destitute as they hope I am." Charlotte still had Lydia's basket of pastries hooked over her arm and now offered a treat to Marceline, who daintily picked one up, examined it as if it might be an insect, then popped the whole thing into her mouth.

Lydia found herself liking this impudent charmer and she noticed that Charlotte responded to Marceline with the same ease. These women were all so easy around one another, Lydia thought enviously, and easy with themselves. Of course, there was a long tradition in France of powerful, intellectual women, but she sensed something else, too. Each was proud to be a woman. Even now, in the throes of love, she didn't possess their kind of sexuality which spoke of powers known only to them, and she wanted that more than anything.

"And what do you think?" Marceline said, turning abruptly to Lydia, whom she'd only met in passing on the evening she had captivated Gabriel. "Do you wager that our Charlotte is destitute?"

"Don't be rude, Marceline," Charlotte interrupted, "Lydia is not one bit like that."

"Then I apologize," Marceline said, holding out her hand. "I understand you're to be congratulated for capturing the most charming of scoundrels. The baron has no money, of course, and he is fond of saying, 'We must regild the family coat of arms.' "

"Stop it, Marceline!" This time Charlotte turned to Lydia. "Forgive my friend. She doesn't mean to be rude."

Lydia and Marceline locked eyes. "Yes, she does," Lydia said quietly.

"Madame Fulgate is right. I most certainly do. I think my way is much better than all this hideous politeness the vultures upstairs and our so-called friends hide behind. I don't like relinquishing the rogue baron's attention—not that I had much of it in the first place—but I mustn't be a poor loser. For the second time you must accept my apology. If I ask another of you, feel free to pull my hair." Marceline smiled radiantly, and Lydia found herself smiling back at this woman who had insinuated herself into the loftiest reaches of French society.

She was known to keep company with artists and writers, including Victor Hugo, and in this way had come to the attention of that element of the aristocracy who flirted with the world of ideas. Lydia had heard that Marceline was considered somewhat of an enigma, acknowledging only that her family came from Bretagne and had left her enough money to live comfortably. Not everyone believed it was her family who had done the providing.

Marceline patted a faded love seat with the same quickness of movement she used in her speech and instructed Charlotte to sit by her while she quizzed Lydia about America. A liveryman of hers named Will was moving to Montana. Remarkably she managed to appear indolent and birdlike at the same time as she spoke of how much better his new life sounded compared to the tediousness of the one she herself led.

"I agree with you," Charlotte said. "My life in the country was liberating while this city, though I love it, has become more and more confining and pretentious. So many rules, so rigidly enforced. All this nonsense about catching a husband. All this . . . this *unnaturalness.*"

"Compared to New York, this city is free-spirited," Lydia countered. "In New York we've *many* more morally superior people."

"How awful! But tell us about where Will is going," Marceline insisted.

"Well, the West is supposed to be the land of milk and honey. A place where the earth is fertile and anything will grow. The land is so cheap that empires can be built on small investments."

"Of course, that's why the French of all classes go to America—though some go to escape punishment for a crime."

"In which case, I'll warn all my friends to beware of French criminals," Lydia answered lightly. That the French seemed so taken with themselves in all things sometimes amused Lydia, but sometimes it annoyed her, too—as fond as she was of them, and as intimidated by them.

"You see, Charlotte? Your friend Madame Fulgate handles my rudeness beautifully."

"But how does one get to the West?" Charlotte asked.

"Will says that once you're in America, all you have to do is get on a train and go there. He showed me a railroad brochure. Could this be right?"

"I don't think it's quite that idyllic," Lydia sighed, "but my brother is planning a similar move and is very excited about it."

"If he were my brother, I would insist he take me with him." Marceline stood and stretched. "I'm now going upstairs to ask those aunties of yours, Charlotte, when, if ever, they plan to leave. If their answer is not satisfactory, next time I'll bring us good cigars, and we will *smoke* them out," she said, getting up with the same abrupt movement she'd used to sit down—though once down she had slouched as if she never planned to rise again, Lydia noted.

Marceline kissed Charlotte on both cheeks and shook hands again with Lydia. "If you do find out how our Charlotte is going to manage, please let me know. In case it's good news, I plan to be more respectful of her and her new American friend. I'm sure I'll like you for the same reasons she does."

At that moment, Lydia could not imagine what those reasons could possibly be, and she hoped Marceline didn't think she was here to fetch another piece of gossip. These days everyone was speculating as to just how much money the grand-mère had left Charlotte, and the speculation ranged from a fabulous fortune to absolutely nothing.

"I'm fine," Charlotte said to Lydia as soon as Marceline left the room, "though I don't yet know how much Grand-mère left me. If it isn't much —and I suspect it's not—I shall go live with Papa."

"I won't tell anyone," Lydia assured her.

"That's why I told you. I trust you, as you already know."

Thinking of Gabriel, Lydia now understood exactly how quickly unexpected intimacy could arise. As she started to leave, Charlotte linked arms with her and thanked her for coming. Struck by that forlorn face, most telling in the trusting eyes, Lydia confessed her own feelings of loss since Sam's marriage. "He's now close by, in England on his honeymoon, and though Gabriel is attentive, I sometimes feel completely alone."

"I'm so sorry—"

"No, no," Lydia interrupted. "Everything is going to be fine for me, as I am sure it will be for you. Fortunately you have your father."

"Yes, I do," Charlotte said, brightening, "and you for a friend, but I hope Gabriel de Rochefort doesn't monopolize all your time."

"You need not worry," Lydia smiled.

"Well, he mustn't make love to you until he promises to marry you and vows not to see other women."

Lydia wanted to laugh at her friend, who looked so much a child, lecturing her as if she were a child, too. "He doesn't see other women," she answered lightly. "And he does want to marry me." At that moment she believed both statements with all her heart, her faith in Gabriel renewed.

"Then he has proposed!" Charlotte hugged Lydia.

"It is understood."

"Of course."

*"Of course, I want to marry you," Gabriel had told her one night while sitting in her dining room. She'd been standing in front of him as his hands fumbled with the buttons on her blouse. Soon his head followed the path of his hands, for she now allowed him this privilege, and she had quite forgotten to pursue his proposal—well, not exactly a proposal—until the next day. When he assured her he'd meant it, she'd become calm, happy, her jealousy all but disappearing. Alas, the jealousy had come back but not, so far, the proposal.*

Lydia promised to return for tea two days later, but she almost wished she could stay and tell Charlotte all about him—about how special he made her feel, about how hard it was to resist his sexual appeals, about how she wanted to be his wife. But does Gabriel love me? she wondered, just as Marceline de Saint-Antoine, her curls bouncing, reappeared at the door.

"We've got to get Charlotte out of this house. It has depressed me, and I've stayed only an hour. You both must come with me to Madame de Loynes's salon. Her notions will be more to your liking. At the first opportunity I'll sneak you out of here, Charlotte, and you will join us in an adventure."

By the time she uttered her last word, the rash young woman had tripped down the front stairs and disappeared once again into the mist of the early evening gaslight.

6 "Do you think she looks like a Charles?" Lydia asked. They were rescuing Charlotte from proper mourning by disguising her so they could take her to the carousel.

"But of course," Marceline replied as they turned their creation around for a critical look. As usual, Marceline was a study in contrasts, Lydia noted: quick and birdlike one minute, yawning and lethargic the next.

"There will be many people at the carousel," Charlotte argued, "and it's against the law for a woman to be caught wearing men's trousers."

"You look like a Charles to me," Lydia assured her. "With you as our escort and protector, we can go to many more places, and you can enlighten us on what it's like to have the freedom of a man."

"Lydia, your cousin Monsieur Jackson has exquisite taste and a convenient size," Marceline said, scrutinizing Charlotte once more.

"He has French taste," Lydia answered, happy that Marceline had used the familiar *tu* with her for the first time. "My cousin also has an abundance of costumes."

Without a word, the three women looked at each other, smiled, and spent the better part of the next hour undoing hooks and buttons on the dresses, bustles, and corsets that Lydia and Marceline wore. As they pinned their hair under top hats, Charlotte looked around her cousin's room, as if she'd only just noticed it. "I would say your cousin has an eye for detail, too."

"His wife has that. Unlike most Frenchmen, American husbands leave the decoration of houses to their wives."

"I should want to decorate my own house," Charlotte said.

"Then marry some old man who is dotty for you," Marceline advised her, causing Lydia to wonder again just where her money had come from. An elderly man might be the answer. However, Marceline had impeccable taste, and none of the characteristics of the nouveau riche. She was also,

Lydia had decided, either very secure or very reckless, for she was willing to break rules—like rescuing Charlotte from mourning by disguising her in trousers. Now, suddenly, here they all were dressed to roam the city.

What life could be more interesting and exciting than mine? Lydia wondered as they made their way through the festive crowds that had turned out to watch the last day of the *concours hippique,* a large horse show. Lydia vaguely recalled Henry James in the *New York Tribune* likening it to an elaborate circus, and she was inclined to agree with him.

The event had been going on for weeks, and this was the culmination, the final pageant. The inside of the Palais de l'Industrie had been turned into an arena embellished with all the trappings of a medieval court. The duchesse d'Ugès, a Royalist to the core, had condescended to sit in the midst of the Republican court. "She's master of the hunt at Rambouillet, close to my father's estate," Charlotte had said, pointing out the tiny figure, "and someone I admire enormously. After her husband died, she set up her own champagne business. She's in her sixties now, yet she still serves as president of the Union of Women Painters and Sculptors. She also races horses, which she rides herself, winning blue ribbons in the process. She can handle the reins of a six-in-hand better than most men!"

A military school provided entertainment and color with its beautiful horses and gorgeously cloaked cadets. According to Charlotte, there were not as many soldiers on the streets nowadays as there had been a few years earlier under Napoleon III; but even now the French took pride in their country's display of military wealth and competence.

Charlotte kept whispering how marvelous the horses were and how happy she was to be here. "I've not seen such beautiful horses since the siege."

"There have been no good horses in Paris since then," Marceline said to Lydia. "We Parisians ate them all."

"Can you imagine such a thing? Eating our own horseflesh!" Charlotte reared back, as though repelled.

"Had you been here, you would have, too—and worse," Marceline retorted.

"Were you here?" Lydia asked Marceline, hoping the answer would lead to some fresh revelation.

"You didn't have to be here to understand the suffering," Charlotte replied, "and I shouldn't make light of such a terrible time." She turned to Marceline. "You're right: I would have eaten a horse. I'd have eaten a rat or a monkey at the zoo, the same as everyone else."

Marceline shrugged and then, addressing Lydia, replied, "As Charlotte said, you didn't have to be here."

"Look at me," Charlotte said. "Only a short time back in Paris and I'm quickly becoming as complacent and supercilious as the rest of society."

"It takes constant vigilance not to." Marceline answered with a conviction that revealed an acute sensibility behind her usual cleverness.

Charlotte drew close to them. "We've forgotten to whisper, so we should move to a new spot. Our voices have already turned a head or two."

At that moment two lines of horses bearing red-coated cadets trotted smoothly by, and Lydia looked around admiring the aura of prosperity emanating from the festive crowd. "I still can't get over how quickly the French recover," Lydia said.

"We forget, but we don't forgive," Marceline reminded her, pointing to a group of German tourists. "They would have done well to stay home. There is no Frenchman in this crowd who doesn't hold them in contempt."

"Those Germans will have their pockets picked before this event is over," Charlotte assured them, hitching up her black trousers.

"Ours will be picked, too, I'm afraid," Lydia said and cast a glance toward her own.

"Then let's find a café for protection and excitement," Marceline suggested. "Three young men on the town—why not?"

Lydia looked down at her cousin's tailored pin-striped jacket and laughed. "Why not, indeed!"

They chose Tortoni's because it was fashionable among artists and writers; and, in order not to be expected to remove their top hats, they chose to sit outside.

"There's Zola," Charlotte said in a low, conspiratorial voice, and she told of the night her papa took her to supper with him and other writers. "All night Turgenev and Flaubert talked of how artists shouldn't marry because women use up vital energy necessary for the creative process. I kept wanting to say, 'And what kind of energy do you think a wife gives up?' "

Marceline nodded in agreement. "Madame de Loynes believes the only way any woman can remain independent is to marry her lover."

Lydia blushed. She was, she realized, not quite as French yet as she liked to think, nor could she imagine how marrying Gabriel would make her more independent in any way other than financially, for she became more emotionally dependent on him daily. To change the subject, she said, "Tonight we get to go where we want. We can wander all night if we like. Drink beer and smoke cigars as we please." They had taken Cousin Jackson's cigars as well as his trousers.

"And we don't look nearly as ridiculous as those preening men over there. I'm glad I'm not a man," Marceline said.

"I think I'd like being a man for a while," Charlotte responded, propping her chin in her hand and looking dreamy. "I would be in the cavalry and ride horses all day and not have to pay tiresome calls or receive tiresome callers."

"Or worry about pleasing others," Lydia contributed. "It's this need always to be charming that I hate."

"I refuse," Marceline said. Tonight she carried herself like a general.

Lydia replied. "I'm in a constant battle with myself, for I want all the world to love me, yet I somehow manage to offend. I sometimes think it's best to be a fetching simpleton."

"*You*, a simpleton!" Charlotte said indignantly.

"Not only do you think, you *feel*," Marceline added. "I'm quite envious, really. You have an energy that—"

Lydia interrupted with a laugh. "Some people call it bossiness—or worse!"

"Well, they're wrong," Charlotte answered, "and the next time anyone says that, remember you have two friends here who will take them on and love you no matter what you do."

"Yes, absolutely," Marceline added, sealing the contract with her lovely mischievous eyes.

Overcome with affection, Lydia dabbed her eyes with Cousin Jackson's handkerchief as a waiter served them beer. They all remained impassive until he left their table, at which point they grinned triumphantly and planned a return performance.

"Next time let's be even more adventuresome," Lydia urged, feeling rejuvenated. Although she had Gabriel and experienced life intensely, she had to admit there were times when she longed for something more, excitement of another order, a throwing off of the shackles of her very way of being—so vague a dream that she couldn't grasp it.

"I wish your cousin's boots fit me better," Charlotte complained. "They're rubbing my ankles."

"I'd prefer boots to a corset any time," Marceline countered. "And to think of the time we'd save by not changing dresses all day. My life consists of getting into and out of one boring dress after another."

"If we were men we could spend all our time in cafés and marry beautiful, rich women who would never bother us," Marceline whispered.

Lydia laughed along with the others, but her feelings about marriage were no longer theirs. Unarticulated dreams or not, she wanted to marry Gabriel. She only wished marriage wasn't becoming a necessary expedient. Without question she had to replenish her coffers, and she now realized she'd come to count on the baron's money to enable her to rescue Sam, too. She needed a little more patience, though she could not waste too much more time. Having her plans contingent on someone else's decision had always agitated her, never more than now.

In their enthusiasm they hatched a new plan: Marceline would take them to Madame de Loynes's Friday evening salon. Since Charlotte still had to observe mourning, this time she'd go disguised as a young provincial poet.

Charlotte reminded them that she couldn't wear her top hat inside. This problem caused a few minutes of anguished discussion until Marceline came up with an answer. "We'll buy you a beret and *that* you can keep on. Madame de Loynes indulges artists and writers in every possible way; she must or she knows they won't come. It's because of them that the discussions are never boring."

Charlotte smiled. "Nothing can be as boring as what I'm accustomed to."

Lydia was already looking forward to meeting Madame de Loynes, who was known to be the epitome of charm. Although from humble origins, she'd managed to establish one of the most formidable salons in Paris, even winning acceptance from the oldest of the aristocrats from the ancien régime. Lydia wanted to observe her style. She wanted to learn how to be a part of Paris.

7 So this is the beloved Sam, Charlotte thought as Lydia's amiable, sandy-blond brother leaned across the dinner table. He wore the same sort of mustache, only slightly shorter, that every man in France sported these days, though he'd stopped short of the omnipresent goatee. She was glad he didn't have one. Speaking with great conviction, he was asserting that Mr. James Garfield should be president of the United States. He mentioned civil service reform and protective tariffs, his manner that of a man who lived in the service of the good boy he was raised to be. This air about him, this moral rectitude, coupled with a natural reserve, made him appear more opinionated than he actually was.

Charlotte found him a little too fine-tuned. Not bad looking, she decided, but without Lydia's extravagant paleness and indomitable vitality. He was not entirely without appetites, though. Samuel clearly relished the sumptuous meal and the lively conversation, and he had enjoyed every play, concert, and ballet he and his wife had attended in London. His interest in politics seemed no less fervent.

"New York is hopeless," he was saying. "Nobody there gives two cents for the real issues. All they care about is who has the best chance of winning."

"It's the same here," Charlotte replied. "After all the fanfare trumpeting our new government, these leaders aren't really so different from the old ones. They speak of 'enlightened self-interest,' but all the politicians care about is themselves and their own party, not the country as a whole." She hoped he had an easier time understanding her French than she'd had following his English. A few seasons in London had made her fairly proficient, but when it came to actually using the English language, Americans weren't the British, she was discovering.

According to Lydia, the couple, discovering that May was pregnant, had cut short their European honeymoon and arrived in Paris weeks sooner than expected. Both the surprise visit and the baby announcement dismayed Lydia, and she had urged Charlotte to dine with them. "You have to dress at my cousins', anyway," she reminded her, for this was the night they had planned to go with Marceline to Madame de Loynes's salon after dinner, Charlotte, in her poet disguise.

At Sam's insistence, Lydia had decided to continue with their plan. "If your brother and his wife see me in the Charles costume, they'll be scandalized by our behavior," Charlotte had protested, not too vigorously.

"So let them."

So Charlotte sat at the table dressed again in Cousin Jackson's meticulously cut suit, and they were, properly scandalized. May was proving herself especially tiresome with her overlong complaint of the taxi strike afflicting Paris, taking it quite personally.

Ignoring his wife, Sam asked Charlotte to tell them about the salon that she and Lydia were to attend later. Obligingly, Charlotte described their hostess for the evening, Madame de Loynes, as a bottle washer in a provincial champagne factory who had come to Paris to seek her fortune. She told of a young lover dying and leaving the impoverished fifteen-year-old damsel his inheritance, then told of her eventual marriage to a count. With humor, she related how Madame de Loynes had agreed to an annulment only if she retained his title and had then refused to use it.

Upon hearing that this embellishment of the young woman's charms had given her easy access to the grand houses of Paris, Sam laughed—an earthy laugh, for he delighted in hearing that seemingly impervious French circles were as susceptible to a clever ruse as any others. That royalty, Republicans, artists, and politicians now flocked to the woman's house pleased him even more.

Charlotte liked seeing him relaxed and liked it even more when he finally said with a grin, "I never thought I'd meet someone so much like my sister but at the same time so *French*." At that, all four of them laughed.

At the mention of the French, May launched into another monologue, this one on the excellence of Paris fashion. Finally she turned to Charlotte: "French clothes are uncomplicated, like the French, aren't they?"

Possibly to silence May and smooth over her remark, Sam put aside his dessert spoon and said that simplicity was based on refinement of line; and the refinement applied to both the fabric for dressing and living. As Charlotte listened intently in order to grasp his meaning, he began addressing his remarks solely to her.

This French simplicity was the opposite of crudeness, he explained, and required an educated instinct for what worked and a discerning eye. "It requires someone like you," he finished, a look of discomfort and confusion gradually settling on his face.

May looked as confused as he, but rallied by asking with more than a little smugness, "Aren't I lucky to have such a clever husband?"

Sam, however, did not appear to be reveling in his cleverness. As he took a drink of the fine wine Lydia had served, Charlotte found herself confronted by those remarkable eyes, as extraordinary as Lydia's, the same color exactly, only softer and less readable. To be sure they weren't young eyes and probably never had been, she decided, hoping no one else noticed the unadorned admiration that momentarily passed between them.

Abruptly Samuel asked Charlotte if she'd ever visited America.

"No, but I'd love to someday. It would be quite an adventure— though not, of course, on the order of your upcoming move west." Charlotte fingered her bow tie.

"We most certainly are not moving west or anywhere else," May answered promptly. "The whole idea was preposterous even *before* our lives changed." The "before our lives changed" was one more of May's euphemisms for her pregnancy. "A preposterous idea," she repeated.

"I hadn't understood that the move was completely off," Lydia said, looking at Sam.

Sam, eyes lowered, only nodded as he proceeded to slice his cheese. Charlotte looked from Sam to Lydia, whose face registered no emotion. Having made no secret of wanting him to forgo the Kansas move, she should have been elated by this last news, but if she was, she was keeping it to herself. Perhaps she didn't want to side with May. As Charlotte sat there observing the two women, she'd become acutely aware of the differences in their personalities and temperaments and had no doubt that each equally attracted and repelled Sam, who shifted his focus from one to the other. A very dangerous commodity, this conflict he was playing with, and she was glad she wouldn't be a witness to that drama when it erupted.

He had changed the subject. He was asking her a question: "Are you as fond of poetry as Lydia is?"

"Probably not," she answered truthfully, explaining that she would pretend to be a young poet this evening simply as a convenient way to blend in with the other guests at the salon. "Who is your favorite?" she asked, helping him to keep the conversation on more neutral footing.

"Dante," he answered promptly. "He was a true medieval thinker . . . knew right from wrong. Unlike many morally vapid poets today, Dante had passion, conviction. He believed man was responsible for his actions. He would have hated today's materialism and blandness."

"Why, I feel much the same way," Charlotte said, sensing another spark between them.

Apropos of nothing, May had begun to lament on the high price of theater tickets in Paris as compared to London. Her complaint sounded rehearsed, especially coming from someone who hadn't yet attended a play in Paris, and Charlotte suspected the bride of practicing a routine to be performed frequently once she arrived back in New York.

"You sound just like your mother!" Sam suddenly interrupted her. Trying to make light of the impetuous comment, he then smiled, but the tone had been unmistakable.

May looked stunned. "You've never mentioned that before," she answered dully. Much less spoken to me in that tone, her look implied—as did his own stricken expression.

He looked trapped. As if he had just realized that marriage and his wife's pregnancy had sealed him into the wrong fate. His naked misery caused Charlotte to turn away.

But when the time came for her and Lydia to leave, she surprised herself—and Lydia—by asking Sam and May to join them. This was mischief, of course, though what was the harm in shocking this very conventional couple once more this evening? Hadn't that been Lydia's intent all along? Else why the insistence on the Charles charade this particular night? Charlotte reasoned.

Immediately, Sam accepted the invitation. Only then did he glance quickly at his wife, who looked appalled, and replied that she was much too tired for an outing. Her remark caused him to apologize for not first consulting with her. His impetuosity, not to mention his earlier behavior, had disconcerted him. Now May was insisting he go and he was resisting.

Wisely, Lydia did not intervene in the dispute, but Sam kept glancing in her direction. Charlotte suddenly realized that Lydia intimidated her brother. He's pulled between her and May and guilty about both, she thought.

She could understand May's hurt feelings and regretted having precipitated this situation. She brushed a crumb from her trousers. "Perhaps we can all go out together another night," she suggested, turning to open the door.

He is attracted to me precisely because I am May's opposite, Charlotte concluded, understanding that this would someday cause him trouble. May would never be enough for him.

He hesitated only a second. "You know, I think I will come," he said, to his new wife's obvious surprise.


While Sam saw May to their quarters, Lydia put the final touches to Charles.

"Now you understand why I'm so disappointed in his marriage," Lydia whispered as she stuffed some recalcitrant strands of hair under Charlotte's beret. "May really *is* like her mother. It's never dawned on either of them that they don't have to follow every little rule of correct conduct. May is not a perfect wife for Samuel. She's simply not his equal."

Charlotte was not so sure that Lydia would be any more pleased if May had been his equal. Throughout the evening she'd behaved more on the order of a mother giving up her only son than a sister in the throes of her own love affair. To be fair, she'd confessed her problem, could laugh at herself about it; but Charlotte realized she still had a lot to learn about her friend.

*8* Madame de Loynes's house was a disappointment. Charlotte found it gloomy and weighted down with massive, pretentious furniture, huge pedestrian portraits of an invented family, and tawdry souvenirs from the 1878 Exposition. One would never suspect that such a proper bourgeois residence regularly received Manet, Degas, and a host of other disreputable and nonconforming artists.

When Madame de Loynes pressed Charlotte's hand and looked directly into her eyes, Charlotte understood why men fell in love with her. Even Marceline became docile in her company. As Charlotte made a deep bow and kissed the proffered hand, she regretted not having met this woman long before. However, it was Sam's arm their hostess took as she led them to meet her current lover, twenty years younger, and Verlaine, a fellow poet for Charles.

Though he did not appear to be particularly at ease, Sam had obviously decided to enter into the fun of the evening and set about charming Madame de Loynes, who accepted his graceful effort. When she smiled at him, he responded with a quick, shifting movement of his shoulders, much looser than Charlotte had thought possible. Obviously he and Lydia, in their separate ways, shared the same zest for life, though hers was manifest while his was submerged. Clearly there was a lot more than propriety in Samuel Benson's body, a lot of facets to his character that she would never know. Anyway, at that moment Charlotte had other interesting matters to occupy her.

She was finding Madame de Loynes's young lover easy to talk with but was unsure of what, if anything, to say to Verlaine, when Madame de Loynes insisted on leading them over to meet another group of men. As they were led away, Charlotte heard Verlaine begin an attack on him while he in turn was attacking Victor Hugo. Charlotte was stunned and amused to see so many factions in so many fields who were known to be so violently opposed to each other. As she and Lydia sometimes joked, the French took their dramas, on stage and in life, very seriously, and considered both better than they were.

Lydia, too, appeared to be captivated by the scene. "With emotions this high, I don't think such civilized discourse would be possible in my country," she said, turning to their hostess.

"We're an old country and have had a long time to practice vehement disagreement on everything in order to maintain a proper level of passion," Madame de Loynes responded. "We French don't like compromise, and the more insignificant the issue, the better. Meaningful attachments are too costly."

Lydia smiled and was prepared to continue the discussion, but Madame de Loynes had afforded her more than the five minutes of allotted attention she usually bestowed on women and lesser grandees. With great charm and determination, she withdrew from their little group as an acolyte of Mallarmé's joined them.

Discovering that Charles-Charlotte was a poet, he attached himself and began lecturing on the need to find the wellspring of his creativity. Lydia and Marceline exchanged amused expressions and left her to join another group close by. Annoyed with them and the pretentious poet, who was going on interminably about wellsprings and essence, Charlotte finally told him that she didn't think anyone understood what the search led to. "I mean, do you honestly know what *essence* is?"

When he looked at her as if he considered her an imbecile to ask such a simple question, she didn't shrink, but instead of waiting for an answer, continued: "Mallarmé says that essence can't be named, that all we can do is suggest images and that the constellation of images is essence. I myself would like to believe that underneath the constellation is a wellspring, an essence that can be picked up and handled." She was warming to her subject, although the necessity to keep her voice an octave lower than usual was beginning to exhaust her. "In fact, I see the process of discovery more as a shedding of one's skin. Call it my soul and give me more than a cluster of images to define it."

The young poet began to laugh condescendingly. "Terribly commendable of you, if a trifle naive," he responded and began another lecture about descending into the depths of life to one's wellspring, citing Verlaine, who had accompanied Rimbaud on his quest.

Charlotte countered that Rimbaud had given up poetry and Verlaine had renounced poetry when he ended up in prison to pay for his experiment. "In fact," she finished, "isn't it true that Rimbaud has stopped looking inward and gone out to explore the world? I don't believe that plunging into the depths of despair and lassitude will do any more to help us find out what we're about than going out to confront the world."

"Really? Such silliness and from such a delightful boy! I could teach you much, you know." He raised his hand to touch her cheek, and instinctively she drew back. "Though I'm not sure you're educable."

"Not as a poet, perhaps," she answered, trying to contain her anger, "but as a human being I most certainly am."

"That too is in doubt," he returned scornfully.

Suddenly Sam, who'd been listening intently, broke into the argument. "Sir, I don't presume to follow all this discussion, but it does appear that the la . . . uh, gentleman has a point. You are being entirely too patronizing toward this charming . . . uh, young man."

Charlotte began shaking her head vigorously by way of cautioning him to be careful. Sam evidently realized he'd gone too far, and his face turned bright red, a reaction—along with his initial one—that Charlotte found engaging. When, in his confusion, he took a step backward and bumped against a waiter's tray, he had her heart.

A bottle of vintage plum brandy and several cut-glass snifters crashed to the floor. The look of utter confusion and dismay on Sam's face struck her as dear and at the same time made her want to laugh aloud. To stop herself, she quickly stooped down to pick up the broken glass. Sam just as quickly followed suit; almost as quickly, he brushed against Charlotte's head, knocking her beret askew. Several locks of her long hair fell about her ears, which he tried to fix hurriedly with his hands, his distress now palpable to the entire room.

Seeing the situation as a ridiculous farce that wouldn't end, Charlotte could no longer contain her laughter, and so she doubled over, pretending to cough . . . but of course—a coughing fit!

She reached for Sam's arm and pulled him toward her. "Whisk me out of here and don't let anyone stop us," she whispered between gasps.

Sam practically swept her toward the door. "We'll meet you at the Jacksons'," he called over his shoulder to Lydia, who, along with everyone else was staring at them. "My apologies to our hostess," he added as he bolted down the steps toward a taxi some other guest had hired for the evening.

Literally heaving Charlotte into the carriage, Sam scrambled in beside her, and the cab lurched away as they began howling with laughter at the absurdity of the situation. "You were magnificent!" he said and imitated her cough and jerking motions.

"And *you* could star in a Feydeau farce. Your timing was superb," she answered.

"*Our* timing was superb—and ridiculous."

"Ridiculous," she agreed as they swayed from side to side, their exhilaration palpable.

The horses galloped at near runaway speed, and the carriage—a run-down contraption with a smell to match—pitched them into a tangle. They began to laugh again until Sam looked down to find his arm against her breast. Both quickly attempted to pull back, and just as quickly their laughter dissolved.

"My God, what's wrong with this driver?" he asked as they quickly extricated themselves. He had sobered, but there was no denying his excitement, which seemed to make him angry. Unfortunately his somber mood, his anger, his excitement—her own, too—struck her as so hilarious that she started laughing again, lightly rapping her fists on his chest.

"I'm sorry to laugh like this," she finally gasped, tears streaming from her eyes. "We must have a novice driver substituting because of the"—she broke into another laugh—"because of the strike." The word "strike" sent her off once more.

"Stop it!" he cried out, shaking her shoulders. "This may be funny to you, but it's not to me. I've disgraced my family, and you sit there laughing like a . . . a madwoman," he said in a choked fury.

She wiped away her tears with the back of her hand. "I'm sorry, truly I am," she replied, trying not to smile or, worse, laugh again, for she was sorry. He was such a lovely man. After a few silent minutes Sam apologized.

"There's no need," she told him, "I've behaved very insensitively."

"This isn't your fault. I shouldn't be here. This situation has gotten out of control."

"Our driver has calmed the horses," she pointed out, as if this would comfort him. She didn't want him to leave Paris so soon. Lydia would be upset, she told herself.

He began helping her push her hair under her cap. "I really never yell."

"You didn't now either."

"The same thing."

She touched his fingers as he tucked up the last lock of hair. "Not at all," she answered, looking straight into eyes so like Lydia's.

Then without warning he ran his hands slowly, carefully down her body. Once. Then, asking her forgiveness, he drew back, called to the cabbie to halt, paid the man to take Charlotte the rest of the way, and fled without a backward glance. The horses trotted on without incident, but she hardly noticed, or cared.

By the time Lydia and Marceline returned to the Jackson residence, Charlotte had composed herself. Mollifying Lydia took longer, for she only gradually began to see humor in the situation, including the raucous carriage ride home. Of that one perilous moment Charlotte, of course, didn't speak.

Since Lydia kept looking for her brother, Charlotte had to explain that he'd felt humiliated and needed time alone, and tactfully let Lydia know that he wanted neither commiseration nor female solicitude. Marceline proved to be such a help in bringing Lydia around that when Sam did return, she didn't rush to him or seem hurt when he didn't bid them good night.

In fact, Marceline, in great good spirits about the whole evening, suggested the three of them go to a café. "Everyone will be out on this balmy night. And we'll have our Charles with us."

"Charles has had sufficient excitement for one day," Charlotte replied, grown weary now but also reluctant to leave her friends' company. She didn't want to think about what had happened in the carriage.

It seemed impossible that this could have happened to her—a married man, and Lydia's brother at that! She would sooner betray her own beloved father than her dear friend Lydia, who had shown her such kindness and understanding.

Rather than leave her little band, Charlotte, still dressed in trousers, lounged on the sofa, listening to the other two recount the evening from their perspective. "You were most wonderful in your arguments," Lydia assured Charlotte. "I kept listening with half an ear while trying to talk with that terrifying-looking artist."

"I listened, too," Marceline declared. "You were holding your own better than most could have against that arrogant idiot."

"But could the pompous fool be right?" Lydia asked. "Is there no soul, no substance?"

"Well, there is mystery in us that we can't readily see," Charlotte answered, thinking not in the abstract at all. "Maybe we can explain mystery only through suggestion. In that sense he was right, but he was so disagreeable that I wasn't about to concede him any points."

"As for me, I believe I have another person wandering around in here, but not necessarily a better one," Marceline said before yawning.

"For me it's not so much another person as a distillation of the one that walks around and smiles and says, *'Merci, monsieur.'* " Lydia mimicked herself, causing Charlotte to laugh and ask, "But how do we find this distillation?"

"Emerson thinks we do it by returning to nature."

"Better than through orgies," Lydia quipped.

"However we find it," Marceline interrupted, becoming serious, "we have to reject the shelter of polite society."

"Verlaine?"

"Only when he chooses, which is seldom. He's created his own world, as did Thoreau."

Charlotte sighed. "Horses provide my escape."

"I'm thinking not so much of an escape from my daily self as of an excavation for my real self," Lydia persisted, "which is what Charlotte was talking about earlier."

"Again, you see, Charlotte, I've underestimated our American friend, who has made the proper distinctions better than we much more subtle French."

Lydia confessed regret that she didn't have even half the learning that the two of them had.

"But you have a head filled with lovely whiffs of dreams," Charlotte returned affectionately.

"And enough facts to determine what you want," Marceline said as she pulled Charlotte up from the sofa. "That's quite enough, even without counting Gabriel."

"Perhaps, Lydia, you should lend me some of your secrets, for I have to leave for Papa's tomorrow."

Out of consideration Lydia and Marceline expressed no surprise at the suddenness of the announcement, nor did they ask whether this was a visit made out of need.

Charlotte herself had not decided to leave Paris until that instant. All that mattered to her was that for one moment, had Samuel Benson asked, she would have stayed in the cramped, smelly cab with him forever.

*9* Lydia glanced around the restaurant in the Bois de Boulogne, then looked through the open windows to the tables set on the wide ribbon of lawn. Isabelle nudged her. "He told you he'd be late."

"But we are late," Lydia reminded Isabelle, who was wearing an enormous bustled yellow skirt—"to keep the air circulating underneath," she'd stated.

"We'll never be as late as my cousin. Come, let's enjoy ourselves. We know half the people dining here."

As they were led by the maître d'hôtel to a window table, Isabelle and Lydia gave themselves over to the pleasantries of their fellow diners. The dinner had been an impromptu affair, suggested by Isabelle as relief from an unexpected heat wave. "Believe me, it will be much cooler in a park filled with shady trees and a lake," she'd assured Lydia, who embraced the idea immediately.

In the city the limestone buildings and asphalt streets combined to increase the sun's misery. But while others moved up their summer plans —almost everyone who could escape would be gone by the end of the week—Lydia was content to idle away her time in sidewalk cafés, since neither Gabriel nor Isabelle had left the city yet. Only occasionally did Lydia regret not having joined her cousins in Biarritz—a "still fashionable summer place," they had assured her, "even without the empress Eugénie to liven it up."

On this evening, however, she was glad to be in Paris still. Here, away from the city, the light summer air whispered its way around the diners. Lydia's contentment was almost complete, although she and Gabriel were no closer to agreeing on a wedding date. He kept promising, but his assurances were not quite enough anymore. In fact, Lydia had begun to wonder if *he* was enough, if possibly she should just accept that this was one grand lark and enjoy it for what it was.

"Wake up," Isabelle teased. "Madame Martin is coming our way, and as usual, she'll ply us with much speculation and no facts."

"She looks delighted with herself, as if she's delivering a present to us," Lydia said.

"Just so it's not a long one."

As Madame Martin approached the table, they made an effort to contain their laughter.

Charlotte's grandmother, they were quickly informed, had left her a fortune after all, and she was sharing it with her father. "It's more than he deserves," Madame Martin continued. "I mean, if he'd had the strength of character to stand up to his wife, neither he nor Charlotte would have been in the financial straits they've found themselves in. He should keep a mistress like a normal man, but he never was disciplined. Not bad, really, unless weak classifies, and sometimes I think it does."

As Lydia listened, she noticed Gabriel out on the lawn, speaking to a small group of strollers, and felt a surge of well-being. "I'm happy for Charlotte," Lydia said as soon as she and Isabelle were alone again.

"We have to hope Madame Martin knows what she's talking about," Isabelle said as she scanned the room for familiar faces. "Isn't it amazing how otherwise perfectly sensible people tend to pack into the smallest possible space? Is it our preference for the anonymity of a crowd or our fear of missing out on these trivial transactions?"

"Don't be too hard on our need to feel included," Lydia bantered. Then she spotted Gabriel again, still on the lawn and in a conversation with Marceline, who had come with another party. This time Lydia decided to go fetch him.

Dusk was fading into darkness, and Marceline had sat down with a group of their friends. Gabriel, however, was nowhere to be seen. Lydia waved to her friend and left the restaurant to search for Gabriel, who was probably looking somewhere for her, she reasoned. In a more secluded part of the garden, she spotted him sauntering arm in arm with another woman—thick-waisted, this one. They disappeared behind a hedge, and Lydia circled around the terrace and then around the lawn to the hedge. She felt only slightly ashamed of herself for spying on them.

"Fifteen, fourteen . . . thirteen," she heard him say and would have sooner caught him in bed with somebody. To use their own intimate joke as if it were of no consequence!

"Twelve . . . such tiny little buttons to protect such treasures." And Lydia just knew they were large treasures.

"Don't be naughty," she heard the woman say with an American accent not unlike her own. "I mean it," she said without conviction.

Angry and afraid to hear more, Lydia stepped around the hedge. Becoming aware of her, the couple pulled apart but stood there saying nothing. The woman was older than she, and Lydia thought she looked familiar. Then she knew why: she was the American heiress who had just arrived from Pittsburgh.

Lydia whirled and began to run—away from them and toward the edge of the park. She had to get home. Someone was running behind her, and she prayed it wasn't Gabriel.

But it was Marceline who caught up with her. "Don't be foolish, Lydia. You mustn't hold Gabriel's flirtations against him. This is the way he is. He likes women. And why not? You musn't be such a child about these things if you wish to marry a Frenchman."

"You don't understand. He played our own private game with her. He was doing the exact same . . ." She muffled a cry with her fist.

"Oh, men are unoriginal creatures. They use the same tricks on all of us."

"I hate him, Marceline! He's made a fool of me."

"Naturally. But by next month you'll have quite forgotten this. Go home, have a good cry and wait until the light of day to judge what's happened." She began to tidy Lydia's hair and examined the scratch on Lydia's arm. "You snagged your skirt on the bushes, too," she said. "I'll get my carriage for you and explain your departure to Isabelle. No need for you to go back inside."

Lydia nodded mutely, for somewhere under the hurt and anger, the inevitable return of pride had begun.

10  As soon as she saw Audrey again, Charlotte knew she shouldn't have come back to Maison du Val Bleu. But of course she'd already known that. Had she not felt so desperate, she would never have come in the first place. Nevertheless, she had managed to forget just how miserable she'd been during those last few weeks spent with Audrey and her father.

Audrey had been perfectly lovely to her, and that was the trouble. Audrey was perfectly lovely to everyone. She walked through life untouched, unmoved. Her serenity unnerved Charlotte, but Papa clearly adored the woman. While he continued to be his easy, teasing self around Charlotte, he changed in every other way once Audrey appeared, filtering his emotions through her large, vague eyes. He became a man who ceased to breathe his own air.

Then Charlotte saw him, his mustache impeccably groomed, his slender, firm body clothed in a superbly tailored suit, even in the country. He hugged her and called her his pretty lamb, his sweet one, his precious cub, said he loved her with all his heart, said she must never leave him again, said she was his own dearest pussycat, the same as when she was a child. In that moment Charlotte believed everything he said and forgave him everything he'd done. She felt encouraged about presenting him with her plan.

"And how is Paris these days?" he asked, his dark eyes and slender frame reflecting Charlotte's exactly; if anything, he had more energy, quicker movements.

"Who is hurling accusations at whom? Are any amusing stories being bandied about? Do my friends speak of me?"

Charlotte laughed and squeezed his arm. "Overnight the Parisians forget about their hardships, but forget you—never!"

"As it should be," he said, looking satisfied. "And how is your maman? Does she hate me as much as ever?"

"She hates us both, Papa."

"My poor *chérie,*" he said, "You are so brave for me."

Once more he clasped Charlotte to him, and Charlotte regretted her response. She had not intended to beg for sympathy.

"No, not brave." She pulled away and smiled—his smile, the one he used when he was being charming. "I'm out to conquer life."

"You will conquer many hearts, of that I am sure. Won't she, Audrey?"

Audrey, who had been watching them, nodded and smiled. "Perhaps Charlotte would like to freshen up and rest a while. You'll wear her out with your questions, my own love. She will be staying for a while, after all."

"I'm fine," Charlotte answered. "I haven't come all this way to rest." She noted just then how tight Audrey's smile was, the perfectly lovely one.

"Then do come in and sit down."

"And how thoughtless of me, little one!" Charlotte saw that her father addressed Audrey and not her. "What can we get you to drink or to eat, dear Charlotte?"

"A cup of tea will be lovely," Charlotte answered, as much to get rid of Audrey as anything. When Papa turned to her, however, Audrey just stood there, refusing to move.

"Why don't you have Adolphe bring us all some refreshments?" Audrey suggested, catching her father off guard. And Papa, who had no domestic abilities, went to fetch the servant.


Over dinner Charlotte told of the new plays, the new affairs, the old hatreds. She described in detail the state of the opera, the state of the public gardens, the state of Parisian society in general and of their small clique in particular. She made him laugh at what she called "acquisition fever." "Everyone has gone crazy buying possessions—land, houses, coaches, dresses." Her father could not get enough news, and appeared to enjoy even tidbits about his wife. His enthusiasm was contagious, to Charlotte at least, and the more he encouraged her, the more stories she told him, as always.

The two of them so dominated the conversation that Charlotte almost forgot Audrey was with them—and began to believe that she could accommodate herself to the household, could stay here indefinitely, certainly until she found a husband who truly suited her.

By now she'd persuaded herself that the fleeting interlude with Sam was just an aberration, to be dismissed without further contemplation. They had simply been caught up in the prank.

In any case, few could or would suit her after Papa, especially on occasions like this. Never had she loved him more than now as he brought her out, made her feel special—his special star, another pet name for her since childhood.

When he asked, "But *who* has asked about me, *chérie?*" her eyes filled with tears at his touching vulnerability. As he must know, if he thought about it for a minute, Parisians were much too self-absorbed to let their curiosity stray far from those within their vicinity.

As she prepared to lie, Audrey spoke up: "Darling, isn't it time for us to go to bed? You have all week to ask Charlotte questions."

Charlotte looked to her father to insist that a week would not be nearly long enough; a year would be more like it. But he did not protest that his daughter could not possibly retire so early. Instead, he jumped up, all concern, apologized to Charlotte, kissed her hands, her cheeks, expressed his great love, his gratitude, his joy at seeing her; but somehow, after all the breathlessness, the expenditure of energy, she still found herself alone in her room.

So she would have to fight for him—her own father! But if that was the case, then fight she would. Hurt as she was that such tactics were necessary, she had no doubt she would win. He was already bored with his life in the country, and soon he would be just as bored with his mistress. What a terrible predicament he'd gotten himself into because of that woman! Charlotte could not understand why. Or why he had let Maman ruin his own daughter's life. He could have stopped it or stopped Maman.

But she was not being fair to him, for he'd explained that the money was really Maman's to begin with and he felt he had forfeited his right to it when he left. In his own way he was honorable. She snuggled down into her pillow. Her mother was probably right to say men were hopeless idiots. At times, anyway.

Charlotte spent the next few days devising a calculated strategy to beguile both Papa and Audrey. In the early morning she and her father hunted game; in the afternoon, they rode. The old closeness between them settled in as they basked in each other's presence. But she also feigned interest in the smallest detail of his and Audrey's various endeavors together—modestly decorating their house, planting a flower garden—and she made herself helpful around the house. Nothing else was said about her leaving in a week.

She had already begun to imagine how her father and Lydia would get along; perhaps she'd invite her friend to visit soon. Charlotte knew her papa would adore the beautiful American, and Lydia would be so pleased with him. He and Lydia might fall in love—stranger things had happened—and then the three of them could live happily ever after. Charlotte could easily spend a lifetime with the two people she loved most. Yes, she already loved Lydia, new as the friendship was. In Lydia, she had found a like-minded companion, a respected confidante, and a true sister.

During the second week of her stay she mentioned Lydia to her father when they were alone on one of their many walks through the gardens. The early summer poppies and daisies were only beginning to come into bloom, but the trees and shrubs had the lushness of warm mornings and rainy evenings about them. These walks were favorite times for Charlotte, and today, after describing the beauty, the humor, the candor of her friend, Charlotte ventured to add, "I should like to ask Lydia here to meet you, Papa."

"By all means, *chérie*. I must meet any creature who charms you in such a way. On your next visit she shall come with you. Next month would not be too soon for me! I miss you so when you are gone."

Now is the time, Charlotte decided and gathered her courage and her breath: "I don't have to leave, Papa. With grand-mère dead, I'm free to stay with you." Charlotte felt the words thick on her tongue. She and her father had stopped by a stream that ran not far from the house and Charlotte watched a frog make its way across the rocks.

"Ah, darling one, I'm afraid your maman would not hear of it."

"You don't understand, my maman will not hear of *me*, Papa." Charlotte stared at a stone between her father's shiny boots and had a sudden urge to smash it. He moved to her side and put his arm around her shoulders.

"She doesn't mean it. You must go back. Make up with her. She is your mother and important to your future."

Charlotte stepped away from him. "I cannot—I will not—go back. Nor will she accept me. She is my past. You are my present." She hated herself and hated him for making her say these things. "I'll be Audrey's friend, too." Oh, God! she thought. Why was she humiliating herself like this?

"The problem, my darling," he said, taking her hand, "is that Audrey cannot be your friend. Silly woman that she is, she is jealous of you." Charlotte watched her father preen in the knowledge of his lover's jealousy, and in those few seconds of preening, her heart closed against him. "I will always welcome you—Audrey will also—but to live here"—he lifted his arms and shrugged—"it is impossible. And for you, too. You would see soon enough, *chérie*."

She bent to pick up the stone in order to give herself time to compose her face. "I will trouble you no more," she said and turned away. Not wanting him to see her cry, she broke into a run, and though he called after her, he did not try to catch her.

Audrey had the grace to disappear during the unseemly period of packing and crying and Papa's pleas for understanding.

"I was never God, my precious cub. You expect too much of me. I love you. I still want you by me. But the two of us alone together? That's no life, for either of us."

Through all his appeals, Charlotte continued to pack and cry, but she did not speak to him until finally she could be silent no longer. "How dare you send me away? How dare you!" she said in a voice choked off by the constriction in her throat.

"It is for your own good, too, *ma chérie*."

She slammed her trunk shut. "Stop condescending to me."

"Forgive me. I don't mean to," he said, his head bowed.

"You've betrayed your own daughter's love. You taught me the charms of life and now you are sending me out into a hostile world." Her body trembled with rage. Raising her arms, fists clenched, she howled from deep pain, "I have . . . no family!"

"Charlotte, Charlotte!" he cried out and tried to comfort her, but with one violent jerk, she slapped him across the face.

"Leave me," she said, her voice calm now. As he started to speak, she added, "I mean it."

Without another word, he left.

A few hours later and moments before her carriage started down the path, he climbed in beside her. "I cannot let you leave like this," he said. "I cannot bear to lose the devotion of my daughter. I cannot bear to lose you."

Charlotte stuck her head out the window and called for the driver to stop. "You have a long walk back as it is," Charlotte stated flatly. "You must go."

He hesitated, then climbed out, but grasping her hand through the window, he entreated one more time: "Believe me, you will someday thank me. I am not perfect—the worst sin I have committed is to let you think differently—but on this matter I am right."

"And you believe me," Charlotte responded, "you have orphaned me."

*11* Lydia nursed her wounds in private. When Gabriel sent word by the chambermaid that he planned to camp outside her door, she merely shrugged, no longer amused by his ploys.

For two weeks she cursed Gabriel and herself. For two weeks more she wallowed in anger, grief, and self-pity. But it took longer to face her own complicity in the betrayal: from the beginning she had assumed that Lydia Benson Fulgate had no value other than that of a pleasing and wealthy ornament.

In spite of all the hints to the contrary, she had duped herself into thinking she was special enough to change Gabriel de Rochefort. She alone had conjured up the dream of a happy solvent family that included Gabriel and Sam and May. She alone had allowed her emotions to get out of hand, had turned a lovely lark into something else entirely. Gabriel had merely indulged her in her whims, and his.

She finally read Gabriel's letters imploring her to forgive him, confessing his love, asking for her understanding and patience. Then she arranged them in the fireplace, lit a match, and watched them turn to ashes.

During the long days and nights she had come to understand how little suited she was to the way of life that Gabriel augured. He was available to the highest bidder; even her pretty face hadn't really mattered. Again, she faced the terrible truth that she had known it all along. Why else had she spent money so freely? She had been shameless in her need.

And her need was great. She had succumbed to romantic illusions because she wanted to believe that this marriage would satisfy her deep craving to love and be loved, and she had assumed this was possible if she willed it to be so. But no more. She now knew she could not pay the price pretending would exact.

Thus, she mourned her loss—all her losses, a lifetime of them. Each one, it seemed, compounded all the others and made them fresh again. Maybe Marceline had been right that she expected too much of the world. Yet even as she questioned the fierceness of her pride and anger, she began to sense a freedom born of her resolve. She was emboldened by the knowledge that her desperation had a limit beyond which she would not trespass. She began once more to trust in her ability to discover a future that would not let her live life on her own terms and to the best of her ability.

After the worst of her melancholy passed, and as soon as she felt she could remain reasonably composed, she chose her prettiest summer dress, a light blue silk trimmed in white eyelet, and a white hat with blue ribbons, and prepared to pay a call on Isabelle.

During this period she had faithfully written Lydia notes in which she spoke of their friendship and did not mention Gabriel at all. Because of her indolence, she wrote, and her inability to face the summer hordes, she had remained in the city, and would Lydia please come to call when she felt like it? At last Lydia felt like it.

They sat on a wrought-iron bench near a fountain in Isabelle's garden, their parasols protecting them from the afternoon sun.

"My cousin says I'm to convince you that he loves you and is in agony," Isabelle told her guest.

"Keeping his options open, is he?" Lydia asked lightly.

"Of course, but he also says he loves you."

"And does he often feel this way about women?" The sound of the splashing water and the play of sunlight on its puddle comforted Lydia.

"Of course."

"And do you always convey his message?"

"I did not come to you, did I?"

They talked awhile longer of their friends. Neither had heard from Charlotte, and Marceline had vanished entirely. Then Lydia said her good-byes, turned toward the garden gate, stopped, and turned back toward Isabelle.

"Would he have married me?"

Isabelle shrugged. "Who knows? At the moment he's wild about you."

Lydia turned to go again, but this time Isabelle called to her. "Lydia, have you plans for the rest of the summer?"

Lydia shook her head. "My original plan assumed marriage this month. I haven't seemed able to move beyond that," she confessed.

"Would you care to join my family in Dieppe? There'll be lots of picnics and parties, mostly with old Royalists who didn't like the Empire any more than they like the Republic. But they're an undemanding sort."

"Will he be there?"

"No. He's on his long-discussed and laboriously planned trip to Italy."

She turned back to Isabelle to kiss her cheek. "Then I will come. He did not tell me about Italy."

"He never tells anyone everything," Isabelle explained, summing up her cousin for Lydia.

"Yes. But you knew about Italy."

*12* Charlotte arranged the heavy silk shawl covered with pink and purple peonies around Lydia's shoulders, and Lydia twisted this way and that, scrutinizing herself in the mirror.

"I feel so extravagant swaddled in all these flowers. October blows outside, but in here it's spring," she said.

"The flowers make your complexion glow, but they also reflect your inner spirit."

Lydia looked in the mirror again. "Do you really think so? My inner spirit?" She plopped herself down on the floor, petticoats ballooning around her. "Lately I've more resembled a patch of withered weeds, inside and out."

"That's why you must have my grand-mère's shawl—to help you rediscover your exuberance."

Lydia smiled and nodded, but tears filled her eyes. "It's a joy to have you back. So much has happened. I'm better now, but I've been so miserable," she confessed.

Charlotte, joining her friend on the floor, put an arm around Lydia's shoulders and gently shook her. "I'm glad Rochefort is gone. Better the heartbreak now than with a child in your belly or pox in your body. Don't look so shocked. I'm only speaking the truth and you know it." Charlotte dug in her pocket for her lace-trimmed handkerchief, which she gave to Lydia.

"I just don't understand, Charlotte. I just do not." Lydia interrupted herself long enough to blow her nose. "Nobody else has ever treated me so . . . tenderly, so attentively. Once he counted the buttons on my dress— to know more about me, he said, but then he . . . he . . ." Lydia couldn't finish.

"He was trying to seduce you," Charlotte said matter-of-factly, then looked at Lydia's stricken face. "No, no. I don't mean just seduce you. He loved you, of course. I mean he wished to seduce you into loving him more."

"He didn't love me. I finally faced that, but I wish he had seduced me! He made me feel more alive than I ever have in that way. As it is, I ended up denying myself and for nothing. I might as well have gotten *that* out of it."

"This doesn't sound like you, but I admire what you're saying."

"Well, I've concluded that men are dangerous and that we women mustn't allow ourselves to be victims. We have to assert ourselves sexually, the same as men do. Why not make love for the pleasure of it? That's what men do."

Charlotte smiled and swung around to face Lydia. "In this case, you might have gotten a lot more than you wanted. You can't afford to have an experience with a man who has a flaw as excessive Rochefort's."

Lydia laughed. "Disease—to go back to your obsession."

"For good reason."

"All I know is that I don't want to go through this again. The truth is that Gabriel was never mine, although I did my best to believe he was." She smiled at Charlotte. "I've vowed never again to let a man humiliate me like that."

"You were wise to break off with him instantly."

"Some instinct for self-preservation saw me through," Lydia replied and patted Charlotte's arm. "What I want now is to cleanse myself of everything—hurt, jealousy, deceit."

Charlotte nodded. "We should purify ourselves."

"Maybe we should do without men altogether—except that my money is going to run out. Be very thankful that hasn't happened to you."

"How do you know it hasn't?"

"Everyone knows your grand-mère provided well for you—much to your mother's consternation, I gather."

Charlotte rose from the floor and smoothed her skirts, the little peplum of her jacket accentuating her tiny waist. "Everyone knows what I choose to let them know. The truth is that Grand-mère provided as well as she could, but that isn't quite well enough." Charlotte put her hands on her hips and gazed down at Lydia. "Do you swear to keep a secret?"

"Swear," Lydia answered with her right hand over her heart.

"I got one hundred thousand francs, which will have to last me the rest of my life—or until I find a rich man."

Lydia computed quickly in her head. That came to even less than she herself had. "Oh, dear!"

"Yes. Oh, dear."

Lydia scrambled up to her feet, and put her arm around Charlotte. "I'm so sorry. And here you are comforting me, giving me your grand-mère's shawl. You have too generous a heart."

"Not generous at all. I like you. When you care for someone, giving isn't an act of generosity, it's an act of satisfaction."

Lydia nodded and stared at Charlotte in the mirror. Suddenly she spun around, took hold of Charlotte's hands, and pumped them for emphasis as she said, "I may now have the most marvelous idea for the most spectacular adventure of our lives!"

Charlotte smiled. "I've seldom seen you so excited."

"Shall we take a walk?"

"Only if you promise to tell me your idea."

"Once we're outside—and I shall wear my shawl," Lydia said, twirling in front of the mirror.

"You should wear your cloak, too. It's a nippy day."

Lydia started to comply, then changed her mind. "No. I must toughen up. You must, too, if we're to have our adventure."


"What adventure?" Charlotte asked as they made their way along a path in the Tuileries. She had chosen to wear a fine wool cloak and was far more comfortable than Lydia.

"Well, as you may remember, Sam was considering going west."

"I remember," Charlotte said with only a small catch in her voice.

"Well, after much investigation, he decided that Kansas offered the greatest opportunity—virtually unlimited opportunity. For only a few dollars a settler can get one hundred sixty acres of land!" She explained that she and Charlotte could stake separate claims. Then they could build houses next door to each other and pool their land, giving them three hundred twenty acres in all.

"My, that's a lot of land, but what would we do with it?"

Lydia cocked her head to the side, considering the question: "You could ride horses. A cousin of ours from England has moved west with a group of his friends—second sons, most of them. They've set up country estates just like their family's and at a fraction of the cost. They hunt and fish." Lydia stopped and looked around.

"We could have gardens like these with flowers blooming year-round. And our friends could join us. We could live a very fine life and control our destiny."

"And we would be rid of all the moralists who make us feel we've sinned by not seeking a matrimonial commitment to any man who'll have us."

"We would be in charge of our lives."

"And no men?"

"No men," Lydia agreed. "*We* would be in charge."

Charlotte shook her curls emphatically. "I'll never want a husband, but I do miss Papa terribly. He'll not miss me so much. He'll hardly notice I'm gone, no matter how he protests." Now it was Charlotte's turn to have tears in her eyes.

For a few minutes the two women walked in silence, listening to the cadence of horses' hooves, and Lydia worked out her next thought. "We aren't poets or artists or musicians, but our own lives are a creation of sorts. Can't we re-create ourselves?"

"Yes, of course, and in doing so we'll satisfy that incomplete feeling you talk about with a more authentic life," Charlotte said.

After pondering her next words, Lydia continued. "So we shall cleanse ourselves of our old ways . . . lose our present selves. Go where people live free of convention."

"Such communities exist in Kansas?"

"Oh, yes!"

As the late afternoon traffic trundled on, the clouds thinned and a gauzy sunset lighted the Paris rooftops. The women paused in admiration; then Lydia smiled at Charlotte and said in a voice filled with excitement, "On the plains, I've heard you can see for miles and miles."

"But your brother will not be coming," Charlotte said, needing to be absolutely sure that Samuel wouldn't disrupt their new paradise.

"Of course not. But no matter," Lydia replied brightly. "We'll be fine on our own."

"Shall we ask Isabelle to join us? From what you say, I think she'd like this place."

"As soon as we're settled, she'll be the first one we invite to come join us. We'll invite everyone who is dissatisfied with all this falseness," Lydia said expansively and took Charlotte's hand as they continued walking. "In Kansas, we'll either discover our essence, as you call it, or we'll create one. How about that?"

Charlotte laughed. "We'll be independent!" she practically shouted.

Lydia turned to her: "You once asked me what it meant to be a woman. Now we can find out."

13 Lydia tapped her foot to the sound of violins coming from the ballroom and watched the swirl of dancers gliding by. This was the "proper farewell party" Marceline had promised them in her note. Indeed, it was that and more. They would, she'd declared, leave Europe with their heads high and the rest of Paris envious.

If the rest of Paris wasn't exactly envious, it was respectful and admiring; it was also uncomprehending. Charlotte and Lydia, however, had become more convinced of the rightness of their decision with every passing day.

Now as she gamely parried with the comte de Rohan, Lydia had never been more sure of their choice. She only wondered how she could possibly have considered this man worthy of her attention—or any of the other men here in this gilded and candlelit room, for that matter. Because she and Charlotte had stayed away as much as possible from social gatherings of late and had given their days over to planning their adventure, this world already had begun to feel remote.

To help pass the time until their departure, they'd also had dresses designed and made for another kind of life, and they had perused the shops on the rues Le Peletier, Lafitte, and Taitbout searching out china bric-a-brac—Lydia's passion. She was especially fond of statuettes of the

Olympian gods—supposedly Dresden and supposedly eighteenth century, though Charlotte professed to having doubts about their authenticity. Together they sought out such treasures in as many crannies as time and energy would allow.

Just as the comte was ready to launch into another story of his summer away, Marceline swept by looking for someone, and Lydia blew her a kiss. "A wonderful party," she mouthed. Under the comte's drone, Lydia could hear Charlotte lecturing a baffled Madame Martin: "Do you realize that everything in a woman's life is a symbol of something else? Our clothes, our houses, our carriages, even our accomplishments are for others to see, to make us more agreeable to society or to our families. From now on, the symbols will relate only to what pleases us." For once, Madame Martin had no reply.

Eventually Charlotte signaled, and Lydia began threading her way through well-wishers to Marceline's library. Their hostess and Isabelle were to join them for a private moment, which Lydia and Charlotte had been impatiently awaiting. While Marceline and Isabelle had been invited to join the adventure as soon as feasible, neither had really done more than express polite enthusiasm. Since they had only just now returned to Paris from the summer holiday, there had been no opportunity before tonight to make a persuasive case.

"We have the weather in our favor," Lydia told Charlotte as they waited in the library for their friends. "As damp and cold as it's been these last few days, they'll be delighted to join us in a land of sunshine and crystal-clear skies."

"Let's first urge them to come for an extended visit; the idea of a permanent move may be too frightening."

"We should give them our romance novels about the West," Lydia said.

"They wouldn't take the time to read them in English."

As if on cue, Marceline entered the room and began lamenting their withdrawal from the winter social season. "It's selfish of you to leave. Already everyone here is tedious, and without the two of you to liven up my evenings I'll be forlorn."

"Marceline is right; we'll miss you," Isabelle said, locking the door behind her. "But don't believe her entirely. She thrives on the gossip of the afternoon rounds and the flirtations that come with the evening."

When Marceline protested, Isabelle smiled and agreed that they wasted a lot of time on the most superficial of pleasures and comforts. She paused, and had anyone else remained silent for so long, all three would have begun commenting. For Isabelle, however, one waited.

"Last week I used opium to relieve the discomfort and tedium of the long carriage ride back into the city."

"What a good idea!" Marceline said and adjusted the shade of the table candle.

"Not really," Isabelle said, obviously disappointed not to have caused more of a stir with her revelation. "It only served as another escape in a half-lived life."

Lydia and Charlotte looked at each other, and Charlotte tipped her head a hairbreadth forward, all the cue Lydia needed. "But your complaints," she said, "are part of the reason we're going to Kansas. Certainly we've had our disappointments, but this move has to do with more than those. We're shedding all the debris that keeps us from doing what we want."

Now Charlotte took over. "We don't want to depend on anyone but ourselves, and Kansas offers us that chance. We can discover what it really means to be a woman and, in the process, liberate ourselves from other people's definitions. We can be free!" she declared in a great burst of enthusiasm.

Marceline stretched luxuriously. "That's an even better idea than opium. Imagine finding things that speak only to me, that please only me . . ."

"That's right," Lydia agreed. "We're going to simplify the way we live. We'll find excitement in daily lives well lived and decent people who won't bore us, including a few of our friends—if they'll come," she said.

"I'll come for a visit," Marceline declared. "Here, I admit, I am too . . . too French, but in Kansas I might have a chance to discover in myself something worthwhile."

"You'll have all the chances you want," Lydia assured her, "an infinite number of chances."

"Be careful, Marceline. They're also giving up men," Isabelle teased. "For me, that's of no consequence, but for you . . ."

"Men are hardly the be-all and end-all of my life," Marceline retorted sharply.

"When I was growing up, I remember my aunt Bea telling me about a movement called the cult of single blessedness," Lydia said. "They believed that matrimony is usually a master-slave relationship, and rather than endure that, or settle for an unacceptable husband, a woman is better off to remain single and devote her life to good causes and ideas."

"I agree that women are better off single," Marceline said, "but I wouldn't want to devote my life either to a husband or to the world. I don't see much difference."

"Are you saying," Isabelle asked, "that in America there's an acceptance of single women?"

"Not so much as there was before the War between the States," Lydia admitted, "though I'm sure the western settlers will be open-minded."

"I hope so. The French have become impossible," Marceline said and made a face. "They would have us all in a marriage or a convent."

"The beauty of living in Kansas is that we won't have to renounce the world; instead, we can create one that suits us," Charlotte said.

"Then prepare for our visit as soon as possible," Marceline said, and Isabelle seconded the suggestion.

The four women formally curtsied to one another and proceeded out the door, catching up their satins and velvets and crinolines as they descended the staircase. At the landing, Marceline paused, asked a waiter for wine, then clapped her hands for the crowd's attention.

"To Kansas," she toasted holding her glass aloft, "and an infinite number of second chances!"

"To Kansas," the whole room roared, amid the clinking of crystal.

# Part Two

14

Shivering, Charlotte slammed the door to their hotel suite behind her and rubbed her numb hands together. "Chicago is the coldest place I've ever been in my life," she said to Lydia, who was swinging two sticks resembling small baseball bats over her head. Some renegade doctor had recommended strenuous exercise for women, prompting Lydia to purchase these Indian clubs to strengthen their bodies. Lydia also believed these exercises would help them redefine womanhood and test their limits. So far, Charlotte was more amused than convinced.

While Lydia began touching the weights to her shoulders, Charlotte rang for tea, then went back to warming herself in front of their parlor's small fireplace. The room wasn't large, but it contributed to their contentment, its every surface covered with the books and papers relating to their new venture. They had finally decided to settle in western Kansas, having learned that the land in that area was less settled and cheaper.

That they were in America at all still seemed like a miracle to them; and, like new lovers, they spent hours remarking about the wonder of two particular people encountering each other in such a particular way at such a particular time. Already they had come far together—first, their crossing, then New York, and now Chicago. Because they were eager to start their new life, they had crossed the Atlantic during a severe early winter storm. Although they had sometimes felt queasy and shaken, their spirits never flagged. "We are toughening up," they told each other. Charlotte was certain she would never again experience the euphoria of that ocean crossing, what with the promise and risk of their undertaking a vivid reminder every day at sea.

"Just wait until we get to western Kansas. That's when the adventure will truly get under way," Charlotte said, once they'd brought themselves to the present moment.

"Now will you take off your coat?" Lydia asked, putting down her exercise equipment and retrieving the tea tray from the porter.

"Not yet; this city has turned me into a permanent icicle. These winds are brutal." Charlotte hugged herself. "But I shouldn't complain, since Chicago is the *northern* gateway to the West." Frank Bailey, a man they'd met through mutual friends, had told her that.

"Do you want to go back to New York?" Lydia asked. Since they had come here to buy supplies, they could, if they wished, spend the rest of the winter in New York and travel to Kansas in the spring to buy land and supervise the building of their houses.

Charlotte considered for a moment. New York, which had neither the elegance of Paris nor the adventurousness of the New World, had disappointed her. Everyone in Lydia's circle, with the exception of Anne Cunningham, was a little too predictable, a little too straightforward—too earnest, as Lydia herself described them. The people in Chicago shared this American earnestness, but they laughed more and didn't seem to take the world or themselves as seriously as the New Yorkers.

She hadn't yet told Lydia that Frank Bailey had invited them to tour the "city's lifeline," as he called it. Lydia did not approve of Frank. "Boorish, overbearing, and uninteresting," she said. With the exception of her brother, Lydia liked men to be complicated, but Charlotte felt that her life was complicated enough already. Besides, men hardly ever yielded much of what was going on beneath their surfaces.

"Char-ro-lotte? Chaaaar-o-lat-ay?" Lydia trilled.

Charlotte turned away from the fire to discover a bemused Lydia.

"Is the question so hard to answer?"

"Question?"

"Do you want to go back to New York?"

"Oh, no, *chérie*. You cannot want to be around your brother's nest when the petite bird is hatched."

Lydia laughed, so Charlotte quickly continued. "Besides, Chicago is the city of the future. We must study it so that we may be of the future, too. Here we can better prepare for Kansas." And besides, she wanted to add, Mr. Bailey has offered to squire us around next Wednesday.

"You've been digesting too much Chicago boosterism." Lydia teased, but she did look relieved.

"Mr. Bailey has made me a believer."

"Mr. Bailey?"

"You remember—the man who made windmills of his arms." Charlotte imitated him, and Lydia laughed again. "I ran into him on my outing today, and he has quite kindly offered to show us the city's infrastructure."

"What's that?" Lydia asked as she picked up her weights and handed two more to Charlotte.

Charlotte shrugged. "We'll find out next week." Together they flung their arms out and brought them back to their chests. "I hope you don't mind."

"Of course not," Lydia answered quickly. "We should take advantage of all educational opportunities, even from the likes of Mr. Bailey."

"*Exactement!*" Charlotte responded with perhaps a bit too much enthusiasm. But she had so liked him. He had the most definite manner of anyone she'd ever known. He declared the French more fun than Americans and more cynical; dismissed the eastern United States as too earnest, too decadent, too ready to ape Europeans; and anointed Chicago the gateway, the crossroads, the future.

Finally warm, Charlotte began to untie her cape and only then remembered Isabelle's letter. "But I have a treat," she said, rummaging in her pocket. "Isabelle has written."

"Oh how lovely!" Lydia said, before growing anxious. "She's still coming, isn't she?"

"A *treat*," I said. "Certainly she's coming—Marceline, too—possibly by summer. Read for yourself."

Charlotte came to sit on the footstool in front of Lydia, who smiled as she read, devouring the words and with them their friend's warmth and good humor. Isabelle and Marceline had been practicing their English, had even gone to England for a month to see if they would like America. When Lydia read this aloud, she and Charlotte burst into laughter. It would be a merry group, of that they were sure, especially with Anne Cunningham added.

On Charlotte's last day in New York, Anne had taken her aside in the Bensons' drawing room and confided how pleased she was that Lydia was moving to Kansas. "She needs a new life for herself. I'm very happy that she has you and her dream of Kansas."

That sojourn in New York had not been good for either of them. Sam had been away on business, and Lydia was crushed because of it. The business was urgent, May had said, but she appeared puzzled by his absence. Charlotte wished he hadn't bothered to disappear. Whatever had passed between them was over. Anyway, she had planned to make herself scarce, by pleading ill, if necessary.

In fact, after three days of polite smiling, she did feel ill. Then she finally met Lydia's old friend Anne at tea. Immediately she took to this quiet, severe woman with sparrow-brown hair and wise hazel eyes, who looked ill herself.

A woman of great integrity, Charlotte decided on their first meeting, even before Anne did much more than respond to May Benson's tiresome monologue. But when May began questioning her guests about Kansas—"You must tell us more, Charlotte"—Anne had been very encouraging. At that point Lydia hadn't been in the room and Charlotte had felt at a particular loss, not knowing what kind of response was called for. However, with Anne helping her with the English phrases and praising her fluency, she'd quickly warmed to her topic.

"Our worlds," Charlotte remembered saying, gesturing to include everyone, "provide only . . . spiritual ennui. We have no real purpose other than to acquire, marry, and propagate. . . ." She had hesitated, wondering if she'd gone too far, but Lydia had rejoined them and now nodded reassurance.

"In Kansas we shall find those who have dedicated their hearts to the soil and seek something other than conventions." Having never given such a long answer in English, though she'd been practicing for months, Charlotte again had looked to Lydia and this time received a beaming smile.

"Like Aunt Bea?" Anne had asked Lydia.

"We call them queen bees," Charlotte put in, pleased with herself, though their laughter puzzled her until the mistake was explained. Again, they discussed the cult of single blessedness, which May declared to be nonsense. Anne responded, yes, of course, it was. Why should a woman devote herself to good works any more than a man did, simply because she didn't want to marry?

Charlotte had then given Lydia an almost imperceptible glance, meaning they should try to recruit Anne. She *was* as wonderful as she seemed and she did look open to the adventure.

Oh, such a dream of Kansas, Charlotte thought as she studied Lydia's face, intent on Isabelle's letter. Wisps of her pale blond hair fell in spirals about her face, which could easily have been mistaken at this moment for that of an eighteen-year-old. We miss our friends, but we do not need them, Charlotte decided, for only on our own, without the accoutrements of the past, will we find out who we really are. Now that she had no maman or papa to please and no friend around with set expectations of her, she was free to find her own shape. Sipping the hot tea by the fire, she could almost feel her own outline emerging. Patiently she waited for Lydia to finish the letter.

*15* Frank Bailey had insisted they return to their rooms for warmer clothes before he would even hear of their accompanying him around the city. Both women had blushed when he instructed them to put on heavier undergarments—"all those things that go beneath your pretty skirts." They did as he suggested, though, and while neither felt attractively dressed, both found Chicago's ruthless winter winds more bearable than at any time since their arrival.

Which was just as well, since the first item on their itinerary was a walk around the waterfront to watch the boats loading lumber and farm implements and unloading bushels of wheat and bolts of cotton. Men shouted to one another, ropes groaned, bails slammed against decks, and chains clanged as accompaniment. Now and again a gust of wind off the lake would wrench a crate from someone's arms; then curses rang out, punctuating the thud.

As one particularly strong gust swept through, Lydia and Charlotte clung to each other and to Mr. Bailey. "Believe it or not, this is considered a mild November in Chicago," he told them, "otherwise we wouldn't see this shipping activity. Nothing moves once the ice forms. This year we've been lucky."

"Is Kansas this cold?" Charlotte asked him.

"Not *this* cold. It's south of here and doesn't have the wetness from the lake. But that's a mixed blessing. Kansas can be awful dry," Frank Bailey said and smiled at her. "You'll be cold, though, so I'm taking you two shopping. As fetching as you both look, you'll never last a winter in those duds."

While Lydia was inclined to agree with him, she resented the condescension in his voice. Abruptly she pulled back from the warmth of his huddle.

"All this *energy*," Charlotte said, gesturing toward the ships. She also pulled away, but more gently. "Paris recovered quickly from its devastation ten years ago; but, you've recovered just as rapidly from an equally destructive fire."

"You ain't seen nothing yet," he said; then quoted from a recent editorial proclaiming Chicago a city ordained by God and nature and, therefore, immune to decay. "Come on. We've just begun to tour this town." Flinging his arms around them, he marched them up the cobbled street, away from the water and toward rows of iron and steel buildings. Both women were relieved to get away from the water and its wafting spray.

"These are the tools that will shape the boards that will form the houses that Lydia and Charlotte will build," Mr. Bailey said as he led them through the cast-iron doors into a maze of tools.

"Our houses will not be so humble as Jack's." Lydia replied and laughed at Charlotte's puzzled expression. "Mr. Bailey was paraphrasing a nursery rhyme."

But this town is surely not a nursery rhyme, and its brilliance is hard-edged, utilitarian, aggressive, Lydia thought, having noticed the ubiquitous cast-iron steps and entrances to all the buildings. Inside the warehouses, clerks and buyers milled around amid much writing of lists and taking of inventories. She had never in her life seen people so busy, and she appreciated even more that she and Charlotte were not going to a place possessing this kind of drive. In Kansas, the people would surely slow the horses down long enough to find out why they were riding in the first place.

"Throughout the city, there are places like this, which sell to outlets all over the prairie and plains. In some of these buildings they make the stuff; in others, they sell it. Fortunes are made in these farm tools. The McCormick harvester alone has earned several fortunes. It's part of the farming revolution in this country."

Until that moment Lydia had not so much as heard of the possibility of a revolution in farming, but she certainly was not going to tell that to this Mr. Bailey.

"Oh, Lydia," Charlotte said, looking stricken, "how shall we know what to buy? We have none of this on our lists. None!"

"Well, unless you intend to put up your house with your own hands, you won't need to own all this," said Frank Bailey. "I'll box up the implements you might find useful. My compliments."

Bailey's largesse irked Lydia. He would acquire her and Charlotte if he could, and turn them into something else entirely. The habit of good manners, however, was hard for her to break. "That's very generous of you," she replied politely, "but we insist on paying—after we've approved the list, of course."

"Of course. But since I'm part owner in this enterprise, these items cost me next to nothing. The freight I'll leave for you to pay. You'll find shipping costs are going to cut into your budget, however extravagant it might be."

"It is not extravagant by any means," Charlotte answered. "So this is your business?"

"One of them. That boat we watched was part mine, too. This city is filled with endless ways to make money, and I try them all. I am unable to resist the promise of a new bounty. Now, before we have lunch, I have one more sight to show you, and you won't have to get out of the carriage."

Their next stop turned out to be the lumberyards. As far as the eye could see stood the stacked towers of white pine boards, city block after city block of them.

"And these are the boards that—"

"Will build the house that Jack built," Charlotte finished. She felt she was making great progress with her English—not only in understanding it but also in speaking it colloquially. Both she and Lydia were working on this last part, for they had noticed that in Chicago, the language was less formal than it was in New York. By the time they got to Kansas, they hoped to fit in easily. Pleased with herself, she smiled at Lydia, then at Mr. Bailey, who smiled back.

"But you are very wrong, Mr. Bailey," Charlotte was admonishing him in her most charming French lilt. "The Jacquelines will build the houses. Not Jacks. That is the point of our enterprise. And we shall build not one house, but two."

Frank Bailey made a pretense of doffing his hat. Just then they rounded a corner and caught the wind tunneling through the lumber fortress.

"We will each have our own house," Lydia explained.

"Yes, identical houses, sitting side by side, connected by a walkway so we can come and go as we wish," Charlotte added. "Both houses will be filled with beautiful objects—from France, of course, but not from our past, only our tomorrows. Everything will belong to our new Kansas life."

Frank Bailey shook his head and laughed. "It's mighty hard to see you two on the plains of Kansas. What'll you do?"

"Why, we shall ride beautiful horses and cultivate our gardens and search for our purest selves. We'll invite all our friends to join us, of course, and they won't have to depend on men, either. No more unhappy marriages. No more broken hearts." She paused, then added. "You are a friend, so we will make an exception of you."

Lydia scowled at Charlotte. "We plan to raise sheep, Mr. Bailey."

"And we will seek out a larger community that shares our desire for a simpler way of life. Now we are so smothered by overrefinement that we feel nothing intensely," Charlotte explained.

At that moment, however, Lydia felt intensely her dislike of this prying man and her exasperation with her friend. "Nothing except, of course, the personal betrayals—large and small—that mar every life," Lydia offered gaily.

"I know I talk too much," Charlotte said by way of apology, "but I trust Mr. Bailey."

"That trust is not misplaced, I assure you," Bailey said. "On the other hand, Mrs. Fulgate here trusts no one."

"That's ridiculous. I most certainly trust Charlotte."

"No, you don't," Charlotte rejoined, catching them both off guard. The two women stared at each other in painful silence until Frank Bailey adroitly stepped between them.

"Trust is a nebulous concept at best," he said, trying to smooth out the developing tension. "People put too much store by it and use the lack of it to justify their own mendacious ways. Speaking of which, I'll now take you to our Wall Street, give you a proper meal, and try to persuade you to seek your fortune in Chicago." This time he looked at Lydia. "If I don't, I'll give you my two cents' worth on raising sheep, and I promise to make sure the pine you receive is seasoned and dry, which is not always the case these days."

As they passed back the way they'd come, the waterfront still teemed with life and the streets around continued to fill with people, but Lydia no longer sensed the energy generated by all this commotion, and the smell made her want to gag. She was sorry she'd accepted the invitation. She'd known better. Bailey radiated the kind of sexual energy that could only spell disaster for those women who got too close. Even before Gabriel, she would have recognized the signals. Yes, that's what it was about this man that made him so uncouth, for he refused to hide his sexuality, dared you to ignore it, taunted you with its power. See, it's hardly mine, his body boasted. How can I control what's hardly mine?

Why wasn't Charlotte put off by him? She was no fool in these matters. Well, in the future they would stay away from Frank Bailey. Rifts healed, though this was their first. The wind stung Lydia's eyes and filled them with tears. She knew Charlotte felt as bad as she did. Why else had she confessed to being too tired to eat?

"I never knew there were so many people and trains in Chicago," Charlotte said as they waited in a line of carriages for yet another train to go by.

Lydia hadn't known about the trains either, though she didn't want to admit it. But rifts heal.

## 16

Before Charlotte awoke she smelled the coffee and, for one blissful moment, thought she was in Paris. But the woman standing over her with the tray bore no resemblance to Odile. In fact, Charlotte so disliked her, she couldn't remember her name; and all this—forgetting the maid's name, not seeing Odile, the gray light of another Chicago morning—made her extremely cross.

Of course, Lydia was right: Odile would have been homesick all the time. Lydia had found a servant who could easily have seen after both of them and saved them money, but the woman had run into her own bad luck with a Frenchman and had remained in New York to have her baby.

So Charlotte and Lydia had hired two young women, after all—one named Sally, who never said a word, and Norah, who had reluctantly agreed to move to Kansas. Sullen and pretty, she seemed to resent doing every little thing. Only if Charlotte asked would this woman consider opening the curtains. The coffee was often tepid and the milk not warmed. Norah would set the breakfast tray on the far side of the bed and leave the room in darkness, except for that chilling gray light that filtered through the slit between the curtains.

Propped up on her side, Charlotte poured herself some coffee, then added milk, gratifyingly warmed, and miraculously got a taste of strong French coffee. She lay back on her pillows, eyes closed, taking sips, inhaling the dark-bean aroma and experiencing, for the first time in weeks, a sense of well-being.

Although she and Lydia had had no more misunderstandings, Charlotte knew she hadn't been good company lately. She couldn't seem to cheer up. On some blustery winter days when the night came all too fast, she thought her chest would split open. In spite of Lydia and their new life together, she missed her own room in Paris and the stream that ran along their allée in the country and the tenderness of Odile and the funny faces that Papa sometimes made. Thinking of him brought tears to her eyes and ended her sense of well-being as her coffee grew cold.

"May I come in?" Lydia asked as she poked her head around the door.

"But of course," Charlotte answered and managed a smile. Lydia tugged at the rope until the curtains parted. Poor Lydia having to put up with such a miserable companion. As she had done every morning recently, Charlotte resolved to make more of an effort to smile, to talk, to be more enthusiastic about their plans.

"Do I have you to thank for this treat?"

Lydia's face broke into a pleased grin. "Is the coffee really good? I thought so. I made it myself, you know."

"*Chérie,* how clever of you!"

Lydia nodded proudly. "I discovered that one of the hotel's serving girls is French, so the other afternoon I stole into their kitchen and had her teach me how to make a proper pot of coffee. I planned to surprise you after we got to Kansas, but lately you seem so sad. . . ." Lydia's voice trailed off, as did her eagerness.

"I'm sorry," Charlotte said, near tears.

Lydia rallied. "How can you help it? Everything is so strange and new and, right now, not much fun. But you'll see. Once we get to Kansas, things will be different."

"I know that, sweet Lydia. And, except for the cold, I enjoy Chicago, honestly." Charlotte sighed. "I think my melancholy is to do with Papa." Tears came to her eyes again. "We've always been such friends, and then I left so angry. Until now the anger has kept me from missing him, but . . ." She blinked away the tears. "Once a day I think I must write him a letter to apologize. Then I ask why. He is the one who sent me away. I lose most of my inheritance, I lose the protection of Maman, and what does he offer? Nothing. He's too enamored of Audrey to think of anything more serious than sex."

Easing herself onto the bed beside Charlotte, Lydia began stroking her friend's forehead. "I understand how you feel. I do, Charlotte. I only wish you'd told me sooner how sad you were. We could have talked about this, come up with a solution."

Charlotte shook her head. "You cannot talk away abandonment."

"But your father still loves you," Lydia insisted.

"He is worse than Maman. I hurt Maman, and I had to pay for it.

But I protected my father, and I am paying for that too." Charlotte burst into sobs and Lydia took her in her arms.

"Don't cry, sweet Charlie." On hearing Lydia use her favorite term of endearment, Charlotte began to cry all that much harder. Lydia kept trying to reassure her: "You'll be happy again in Kansas, you'll see. You'll be fine very soon. We'll be so busy with the houses and gardens and sheep. Think how much fun the sheep will be."

Charlotte disengaged herself from Lydia's bosom where she'd been sobbing and smiled, not at the reference to sheep but at the notion of Lydia offering sheep as a cure for homesickness.

"You must talk to me," Lydia said as she smoothed Charlotte's hair away from her face.

"I didn't want to worry you, and I know I'll be fine again soon, when the winter is over. I've had too much time to brood. Honestly, I hadn't expected this melancholy."

"It's perfectly natural, but you mustn't let things build up."

Charlotte hesitated, then blurted something out that had remained unspoken until now. "I would like Frank Bailey to be our friend."

"But he is already your friend."

"I want him to be *our* friend. I want us to share everything."

Lydia forced a smile, "I can't be friends with a man like that."

"He's precisely the kind of person we should befriend because he isn't a calculating, hypocritical gentleman. He is a member of the new order, and it's the old one we're trying to escape. Besides, Lydia, we can use his help. We know nothing about sheep, and he arranged for us to meet that nice sheepman and that other man who taught us about fences. Also—"

Lydia threw up her hands. "For goodness' sake, that doesn't mean Mr. Bailey has to be *my* friend. I thanked him for his help."

"Grudgingly."

Lydia began another defense, then stopped and shrugged: "Grudgingly," she admitted.

"He has offered to come with us and help us get settled in Kansas." Charlotte thrust out her palm. "Don't look like that. I've already thanked him kindly and told him no. I explained how important it is to us—to both of us, Lydia—to be independent. I told him that we do not need men for financial or emotional support. I said that the decisions about our houses are too important to share with any outsider, no matter how much we value his judgment."

Lydia sat down in a chair by the fire, her hands to her face. "I feel awful, Charlotte. I have doubted you. I'm afraid our new life won't be enough for you—that *I* won't be enough. For that matter, why shouldn't you be lured by some other kind of exciting and glamorous life? The truth is, under all my bustle and bravado lurks a woman who can't imagine anyone could care about her, much less want to spend time with her." Lydia turned her wry smile back on herself. But enough of that," she said, throwing back her shoulders. "I've made you miserable, and I'm sorry."

Charlotte shook her head. "No, *chérie*. My parents made me miserable." She got out of bed. "But they are my past. You are my present, and Kansas is our future." She smiled and lifted Lydia's face in her hands. "I already feel that we've changed." Charlotte gave a little smile. "I suppose I thought this would be one big lark, that the past and its ghosts would vanish instantly. Well, the past hasn't disappeared so easily, and this is not always going to be a lark, especially if I continue to haul my old self around. I know already, though, that I'm stronger for facing up to the problems, as well as the solutions."

"And you said yourself that our old selves are changing," Lydia added encouragingly.

"Yes, but my old self is sometimes awfully recalcitrant."

"Write to your father," Lydia said.

"I do write Papa—about Chicago, about New York, about you. I can't write more."

"Yes, you can. You shouldn't apologize, but you must say you love him, for that's the truth. No matter what else you may feel—anger, hurt—you also love him, and he must know that. So you both can heal."

Charlotte brightened considerably and began piling her dark thick hair up on top of her head. "You're so wise, Lydia."

Lydia was pleased to see the young girl come out again in Charlotte, who was never so charming as when she was the delightful child. "Don't forget, Charlie, you will have a house—the most glorious house in the world. Also," Lydia added in a burst of generosity, "we'll invite Mr. Frank Bailey to dine with us this very week. And I'll ask his advice on all manner of things—cows for milking, chickens, pigs. You see? I did listen: he said hogs were very profitable because you can feed a lot of them on very little land."

Charlotte held her nose. "Peu," she said and they both laughed. She knew she'd struck just the right pose to make her American friend happy. And Charlotte regretted only a little that it was sometimes necessary to strike a pose here, too.

She smiled pleasantly while experiencing another acute twinge of longing for Paris.

*17* As the purple and amber of the evening sky gave way to the burnished amber of sherry and the smoky amber of lighted chandeliers, they relaxed around one of the cozy fires, crackling for the guests who sat in the shelter of the huge green palms scattered throughout the Palmer House lobby.

Such a civilized, comforting ambience, Lydia thought, and if the other guests had spent their afternoon as she and Charlotte had, they, too, would need all the sherry and illusion the hotel could provide. A hideous, blood-soaked afternoon they'd had, but the afternoon had eventually ended, and now they relaxed with the sherry and Frank Bailey.

As Lydia had promised, they'd invited Frank Bailey to dine with them; he had reciprocated with an invitation of his own: a visit to the stockyards. "You need to understand what will happen to your sheep and your hogs," he'd said. In their naïveté, they had agreed with him, for they would soon leave Chicago and they wanted to take advantage of every learning opportunity.

Lydia had suggested that they go to the stockyards and then come back to the hotel for dinner, allowing time for them to change into evening dress. And he had let them go on with that absurd plan, knowing full well that dinner would be the last thing they'd want that evening.

They had started with the Exchange Building, a large limestone business center, housing, and among other amenities, a bank and telegraph operation that gathered information about livestock from all over the world. He showed them its impressive great hall, furnished with comfortable upholstered chairs for the well-dressed men milling around, talking in groups, or slouching against walls.

"Those cattlemen will have more control over your future than you care to think about: they help decide prices, disseminate information, and set standards—minimal as they are," he told them as they walked through the rooms and halls replete with polished wood. "Given half a chance, they try to avoid facing the other half of their business, which is adjacent to this. But first we'll go to the top of the hotel next door to get an overall view."

From the hotel's cupola they surveyed the scene: thousands upon thousands of animals—cattle, hogs, sheep—herded into pens. "Even from up here you get a powerful sense of so much *life* down there. It's hard to believe that soon all those animals are going to die. From here it's so abstract," Charlotte said.

"You're right," agreed Frank Bailey. "Now look to your left at that pastoral scene with its well-tended fields and handsome barns—the kind of life you're looking for, and seemingly remote from what's going on below us." He pointed toward a tranquil body of water on their right and turned them around by their shoulders to view the newly sketched outline of the city of Chicago.

"Impressive," Lydia commented, as he moved them toward their next lesson—the sheep inside another building.


"A lot of people still like their sheep butchered close to the final destination," he explained as they walked inside the arena housing thousands of woolly animals, "but with the new refrigerated cars, its getting more convenient to kill them here." The acrid odor of feces and damp wool once and forever did away with any surviving romantic notions Lydia had of pastoral life.

"Come on," he commanded. "I'll show you how to choose a sheep."

As they went about examining eyes, ears, flanks, and tails, Charlotte looked ready to throw up, but Lydia thought passing out would be the better course, more seemly in front of Mr. Bailey, who appeared indifferent to the whole proceeding as he also gave them a lesson in assessing the price of a lamb, the later price of mutton, and the cost factor between purchase and final destination.

"These yards are de rigueur for all visitors to Chicago. The world's most delicate young women come through here to experience the horror of their lives," he told them as they prepared to go into the slaughterhouse itself.

No delicate young women they, Charlotte and Lydia armed themselves as best they could. Charlotte took Lydia's hand and whispered consolingly that she'd watched animals slaughtered and quartered all her life. "If you let only your curiosity operate, you'll be all right."

But Lydia was not all right, and neither was Charlotte. Although by now they'd become more or less accustomed to the stench, this room wreaked of a foulness of both odor and sound that the other hall had not prepared them for. As they clutched each other's arms, Frank Bailey continued to talk—of the markets at the other end, of the sturdy hands of the butchers. "Imagine the skill," he said of the men whose mustaches and hats were splattered with blood.

"One day soon I'll show you the miracle of refrigerated boxcars. They're the babies that make this efficient killing possible. Then we'll go watch them excavate the ice."

At that moment, Lydia could not imagine ever wanting to see anything else remotely connected to this place, and she wished he would stop talking. His voice only added to the frightful din surrounding them. The sounds are the worst, she decided as she tried not to breathe.

Charlotte looked miserable, for seeing and hearing one animal die had nothing to do with what went on here. She, at least, was managing to ask questions from time to time. Lydia, determined not to faint or to vomit, applied all her energy to affecting an air of nonchalance. While she was not as good as Charlotte at subterfuge, she could manage a pretty fair imitation.

Trying her best to shut out all sensation, she didn't know exactly when she became aware of the ooze around her feet. When she could no longer ignore it, when she felt her ankles grow moist, she looked down.

Her shoes were soaked in blood. Blood ran ankle deep. Blood ran from tables to floors to aisles.

To steady herself, she continued to grip Charlotte's arm with all her remaining strength. Charlotte continued to engage Frank Bailey in conversation. In a few minutes, however, she squeezed Lydia's arm in acknowledgment of their plight; and Lydia filled with pride for her friend, if not herself. One of them had passed the test.

If she ever did get out of here—a doubtful proposition, with the exit being an eternity away—she vowed she would kill Frank Bailey. Charlotte, already a good shot, would teach her to be a marksman, too.

"Would you care to see the hogs?" he asked as soon as they stepped outside into the now heavenly cold, windy, cloudy day. "We have plenty of time before we eat."

"You did that to us on purpose!" Lydia accused him. "It was a horrible experience *and* you ruined our dresses and our shoes and our stockings."

"I told you to wear old clothes."

"We don't *own* old clothes!" she shouted. "We gave them away."

"Perhaps we'll not bother with hogs today," Charlotte said calmly. "At any rate, we aren't going to raise many."

But Lydia was too angry to calm down. "You knew what you were doing to us. You knew!"

"I assure you, I'm not a sadist. I have other ways to amuse myself, but you need to understand the process. A farmer can't afford to go around in a sentimental haze. You will raise sheep to slaughter, I would remind you. Might I point out that you and nature have a much better chance at 'harmony,' as the two of you call it, if you understand that you are also a destructive force—not completely and not primarily, but don't forget that part of yourselves. If you do, the idyllic scene you envision will rise up swiftly and knock you down. Then your contrived innocence will be worse than useless to you."

The clouds had disappeared in time to reveal a resplendent sunset, while Charlotte and Lydia sipped full-bodied sherry with Frank Bailey and watched the fire's embers spark up in glory. Only a few hours earlier, Lydia had scorned the fussiness of the decor, the large potted palms, the highly polished marble floors, the enormous Oriental rugs, the frivolous dress and manners of fellow guests. Now she felt comforted by them, reassured by old habits, old conventions. She almost forgave Frank Bailey his transgression of being right. Resolving to be amiable, she asked if he'd spent much time in Kansas.

"Enough to know you can't be sentimental about the people or about the land."

"By their very circumstance, the people of Kansas will not be at all like these Chicagoans," Charlotte said, indicating with her head the well-dressed hotel guests.

Frank Bailey raised his eyebrows. "These people may be kinder and more honest. Who knows? Remember, a man might act simple, a man might talk simple, but that don't make him simple. Any time you put railroads and land grants together, you're going to find scoundrels abounding. Watch yourselves."

"We're not looking for simple people," Charlotte corrected him. "We are looking for simple lives."

Lydia wished Charlotte would not reveal their personal goals in front of this man, who didn't take them seriously enough. He, of course, found her remark delightful.

Frank Bailey ordered more sherry and they sat there taking in the murmurs of the not-so-simple guests, soothed by the gaslight's flicker, by those tranquil palms, by the taste of the sherry, and by the knowledge of having survived the afternoon intact.

In a quiet, more relaxed voice, he spoke again: "It's important for you to know that in Kansas there are underground springs. You don't see any clues and you can't find them easily. But they're there in a drought."

"Like our essence," Charlotte said, turning to Lydia and mocking her own analogy.

Lydia, ignoring her, was gratified to hear of the presence of underground springs. She'd read of a great subterranean flow through the region and so suddenly she was feeling more benign toward Mr. Bailey, who was a good teacher. It satisfied her that his respect for them had grown.

And she and Charlotte would leave Chicago soon. They could afford to enjoy this evening with him. In fact, they had all finally become sufficently tipsy from the sherry to anticipate their evening repast.

*18* Lydia and Frank Bailey continued to argue, but Charlotte soon began to understand that they enjoyed their sparring, and she relaxed around them.

Mr. Bailey had shown them everything, from how to string barbed wire to how to read a financial sheet and a racing form. "The more you know, the less vulnerable you will be," he asserted.

He had given them gentle moments, too—Lake Michigan at sunset, a ride into the tall-grass countryside. "This is not the way your land will look, though," he explained. On another evening, at a splendid concert, he'd cautioned, "This is about as far west as this kind of music travels."

As the time came closer for Charlotte and Lydia to travel west, they turned into whirlwinds, some of their activity necessary, some of it a release of nervous energy. They consulted with financiers, builders, farmers, ranchers, farm-implement salesmen, real estate agents. They read and reread books on every conceivable aspect of the West.

Their favorite reading material was a tract on western Kansas by a Mr. L. D. Burch, published only two years earlier. He claimed to be uncertain about the agricultural possibilities—not a matter of great consequence to Charlotte and Lydia, sheep being their primary concern—but he declared that western Kansas combined "the sternest realism with the most delicate poetic sense." He stated that "conventional words had passed from the Kansas settlers' vocabulary and conventional deeds from their lives." He also referred to the region as "a paradise for the lungs" and a "grand, grand country." But the two women made up their minds definitely to go there when they read that "one feels like business in this rare, radiant atmosphere. Nothing drags here. Everybody feels fresh and youthful and self-commanding." A place where there were no conventional words or deeds and everyone was self-commanding seemed like absolutely the *only* place to go.

To this end, they made the rounds of stores that might conceivably carry any item they might conceivably need in such a "rare, radiant atmosphere" where "respiration has the ease and freedom to make life a lasting joy." Charlotte, especially, liked to look at farm machinery and hardware. Lydia liked to make notes on Charlotte's lastest findings for the time when they might be able to purchase them.


As Charlotte swept in with the latest wind after one such expedition, she found Lydia, as usual, sitting by the small fireplace, poring over a sheaf of handwritten pages. "What's that in your hand?" she asked, already knowing the answer.

"My latest list."

Charlotte gave a mock groan.

"It's my very last one. I'm sure it is."

"You say that every time you make a new one," Charlotte teased, but as she settled herself on the sofa underneath a soft woolen throw, Lydia read her list out loud:

> pine for houses and walkway between them
> oak for floors
> nails for floors
> two hammers
> one hatchet
> one saw
> fifteen panes of glass
> one bucket
> four heavy doors
> sashes
> blinds
> plaster
> curtains for bedrooms

two extra blankets
eight cotton sheets
eight pillow shams
sill
floor joists
studs
roof rafters
shingles

"Can you think of anything else?"

"Did you mention door knockers and doorknobs?"

"We bought those in Paris."

Charlotte smacked her palm to her forehead. "I can't keep all this straight. Do not read me any more lists."

Lydia stood up and wrapped herself in the shawl that had belonged to Charlotte's grandmother. "Whose idea was it to furnish the houses with only new possessions? Who insisted we take nothing from our past?" she gently taunted as she twirled about the room, making the scarf wave around her.

"But *you* decided we had to design our own houses. I was perfectly willing to copy from a pattern book," Charlotte replied with a wag of her finger.

"Do I have the wrong two women? I could have sworn we both wanted to escape conventional forms of all kinds," Lydia quipped.

"Twin houses side by side and surrounded by large land tracts are not going to be considered conventional," Charlotte rejoined, as Lydia swirled over to join her on the sofa. She put her hand on Lydia's shoulder. "Just think, I not only acquire a fabulous twin house, I have already acquired an even more spectacular twin, who is willing to make thousands and thousands of lists."

"And execute them."

Charlotte gave a seated bow. "You win," she said.

"The nicest part is that neither of us has to win. We're in no contests with each other." Then after a pause, Lydia asked, "Do you have doubts?"

"No doubts, but I get a little frightened sometimes, even when I remind myself that Kansas is paradise. Don't you?" Actually, she often felt more than a little frightened. Even though her homesickness had diminished, Charlotte did wonder on occasion what on earth she was doing in such a strange place. How had this happened to her?

"If it weren't for you, I'd be scared to death," Lydia confessed. "I concentrate on all the good points and try not to reflect for long on the enormity of the task we've undertaken."

"Me too," Charlotte said and massaged Lydia's shoulder. "When I do get afraid, I calm myself by thinking about our houses." The houses illustrated how she saw the two of them: strong and united, unburdened by worldly considerations, independent yet honoring the same values, the same ideals. "We're going to generate something fine in our houses and in ourselves because together we have strength."

"And we'll live happily ever after? I worry that you . . ." Lydia broke off, her smile only partially concealing the twitch of anxiety around her lips.

"We'll live happily ever after. I promise."

Lydia put her list away.

**19** "I cannot get this trunk closed. Where are Norah and Sally? Sally!"

Charlotte ran into her friend's room. "You must calm down, Lydia. Come, let me help."

"We'll miss the train. We won't be ready."

"We have plenty of time. Here, sit on your trunk like a good girl."

Lydia climbed onto her bed and perched as ordered, but she couldn't calm down. "Samuel should be here by now. If he doesn't hurry, he's going to miss seeing us altogether."

"Didn't he tell you as much last night?"

"But I'm his *sister*. You'd think he would manage to see me off on the biggest adventure of my life."

"He did, Lydia. He came all the way to Chicago to say good-bye.

That's a lot of brotherly love. Scoot to your left a little more. That's it. Do you need anything else while I'm here?"

"Don't act so unperturbed," Lydia said, climbing down.

Charlotte laughed. "I'm only unperturbed compared to you." Now that she was fairly certain Sam wouldn't come, she could afford to relax.

Two days ago he had wired Lydia that he'd arranged a business trip to say good-bye and to expect him the next day. When Charlotte begged off joining them with the excuse of too much to do and then excused herself again last night, claiming fatigue, Lydia hadn't minded. Sam himself had found a way to circumvent today, and after this, he and Charlotte would be rid of each other forever. She was glad he'd gone to the trouble to come, however, for his good-bye would sustain his sister for a long while.

"Where is Frank Bailey?" Lydia asked as she peered out the window. "He's going to make us late."

"He'll be here. In the meantime, you need to put on your hat and gloves and hook up your jacket," Charlotte reminded her.

"I haven't even smoothed my hair."

"See what I mean? Now, really, Lydia, you must get hold of yourself, and I must finish my own packing."

"Sam *could* still come."

"He won't. He told you he wouldn't."

To Charlotte's relief, Frank Bailey arrived early. Though he might not soothe Lydia, he would distract Charlotte while she made a last-minute check of all their arrangements. Since last week, all of Lydia's lists had been worthless to them both. Instead, Lydia had run from one project to another, leaving Charlotte to oversee the final details in a systematic fashion. Fortunately Lydia's prior organization had made Charlotte's task much easier.

As she picked up her parasol, Charlotte noticed that her own hands were trembling. So that dreamlike calm she'd felt all morning had only been her way of dealing with the awesomeness of their undertaking. Maybe Lydia's straightforward anxiety was a better way, after all, to cope with the unknown world that waited for them. Nervousness was something one could see and thus control; calmness was another matter entirely.

By the time Charlotte joined them, Frank and Lydia were both pacing the lobby. "Everything is loaded," he informed her. Briskly he assisted them into the carriage, and Charlotte believed he was as skittish as Lydia this morning. Charlotte would miss him—his enthusiasm, his brashness, his energy, his dry humor—and she suspected Lydia, for all her complaints about him, would miss him also. He had been a good guide, instructor, and companion.

He had brought along a picnic basket and a bottle of wine for the train. He had brought maps of Kansas and a dozen railroad pamphlets. "Let me know as soon as you've chosen a spot. In fact, why not let me know where you think you want to settle? I can find out about it for you."

"Mr. Bailey, for the hundredth time," Lydia replied with amusement and, possibly, affection, in her voice, "we can take care of ourselves."

"Then why are you playing Pin the Tail on the Donkey? Where did you two get the cockamamy idea that you can spin around and *feel* when you've come to the right place?"

"We will already *be* in the right place, Mr. Bailey," Charlotte pointed out. "It's only a matter of *where* is the right place."

He groaned but gave up on that lecture as they proceeded to the station. Once there, Charlotte decided the bustle, the noise, the sheer expanse of it, excited and overwhelmed them in much the same way that Frank Bailey and Chicago had. Now I am leaving civilization, Charlotte said to herself as Frank escorted them to the train.

She watched a man shouting and beckoning with his arms as he dashed through the crowd. He'll be late, Charlotte thought before she noticed that he was running in their direction, *not* toward the trains. Running to them. And Samuel Benson, breathless, perspiring, his hair disheveled, stopped directly in front of Charlotte.

"I came to say good-bye," he announced, looking straight at her, and she did not even have the presence of mind to avert her eyes or to speak.

"A good thing, too," Lydia was saying, grabbing him by the arm. "Mr. Bailey wanted to meet you. I wanted to see you, and Charlotte's feelings were hurt."

Charlotte produced a halfhearted smile. So they stood there, the four of them, making inane conversation during their last few minutes in civilization. An appropriate end, she supposed. But when Frank pulled her aside, she was grateful and wondered why she hadn't thought to do that herself. Certainly Lydia would want a little time alone with Sam.

"If you need anything, let me know," Frank said to Charlotte. "It's no disgrace to ask me for help and advice."

She thanked him while covertly listening to Lydia plead with Sam to join them in Kansas.

"Be sure to get near water if possible," Frank advised. "Not too close, though; you don't want to get flooded out."

"No, we don't," she answered. Lydia's back was to her, and without really looking, Charlotte knew that Sam was watching her and Frank. This time she managed a particularly dazzling smile.

"If you won't move to Kansas," Lydia was entreating, "please come for a visit."

As Sam tried to avoid making a commitment, Charlotte lifted her face to his. He stopped in mid-sentence. "Alright, a visit," he said, without breaking eye contact with Charlotte even after Lydia threw her arms around his neck.

Remarkable, Charlotte thought. His eyes hadn't changed at all.

Suddenly Charlotte threw her arms around Frank Bailey. "Write us. Come visit. Don't be a stranger." Don't be a stranger? Wherever had she picked up that American expression? She took it as a good sign, however.

Stiffly Charlotte and Sam shook hands, and then Frank propelled her by the elbow up the train steps. She found herself waving and nodding her head.

Frank was shouting one last instruction to them: "Don't forget the underground springs. Get a dowser to help you find them. You'll need them!"

"I do believe Frank Bailey is going dotty on us," Lydia said, as they waved gaily, their arms around each other's waists.

Giddy with exhilaration, Charlotte laughed, then shouted to the world, "Here we go!"

20 Lydia carefully unbuckled the leather strap of the wicker basket propped on her lap. Just as carefully she removed two white porcelain cups, two saucers, two sterling silver demitasse spoons, and two white linen napkins, which she placed on the hatbox squeezed between herself and Charlotte. With the same care she lit the kerosene wick under the teapot.

This activity provided a distraction from the sameness of the landscape, which had grown less and less verdant. Soon after leaving Kansas City that morning, Lydia had begun to feel disoriented. The flatness, the vastness, was too strange, not of this world.

The intense concentration required for making tea—measuring precisely, steeping for exactly the right amount of time—showed in the fierce way Lydia sucked her lower lip, and only when she passed a cup of steaming tea to Charlotte did a look of triumph cross her face.

Though Charlotte murmured appreciatively and insisted that she didn't care a hoot—her newest American expression—for cream in her tea anyway, Lydia felt a twinge of disappointment, no more than a starling's flutter. Charlotte definitely did not understand the difficulty involved in preparing an adequate cup of tea under such adverse circumstances. Her eyes drifted back toward the windows and the miles and miles of undulating grass. She could go on watching the hawks and eagles swoop over the herds of antelope—more antelope than she had known existed—forever.

"No, no," Lydia commanded, "you must talk to me. I haven't gone to the trouble of preparing tea only to have you go dreamy again."

"I'm not dreamy, Lydia. I'm trying to take in our new home. It's quite the most extraordinary sight I've ever seen—as mesmerizing as looking at the sea. Remember our crossing?"

Lydia rolled her eyes. "You were always going out on that cold deck to gaze at God knows what, then running back in to tell me you'd just shed another skin." They'd begun referring in a gently mocking way to their inner probings as the "shedding of skin"—a phrase that didn't smack of earnestness, an attitude they deplored.

If they were going to convince others of the need for "essence," a visual image helped. "I think most Americans won't accept this concept because there's no empirical evidence," Lydia had commented on the ship one morning when they were both confined to their bed by the roiling ocean and queasiness.

"But they can accept the notion of ghosts and spirits?" Charlotte was thinking of the popularity of mediums.

"Yes, but they experience those, and ghosts are outside themselves. It's always easier to look outside, don't you think?"

Charlotte let out a sigh. "Right now the outside is pretty overwhelming. I feel the way I did on the ship when the terror and the thrill kept crashing into each other, don't you?"

"More so now than then," Lydia admitted. "You were on your way to the New World; I was about to face my old life again."

"So you see? This crossing is for us both."

"Yes, but I have shed quite enough skin for one day," Lydia said, touching her dry face. "The wind and dust are taking care of it for me." She moved farther away from the window. "This vastness is tedious. For that matter, so is the Atlantic Ocean."

Charlotte shook her head in disagreement. "Neither bores me," she replied as they continued to sway with the train, "but both make me uneasy. They seem to have no limits."

"I'm in a state of *confusion*," Lydia admitted.

"It is bewildering," Charlotte replied as their train pulled into a small station.

"Another tiny town," Lydia commented, "but they do break up the landscape." So far, they'd come across none that appealed to them enough to investigate to any extent. "Are there many more?"

Lydia threw up her hands. "Who knows? I've lost track of the towns. I've lost track of the days. I've lost track of the amount of skin I've shed. I've lost track of these stops."

They watched a couple of men jump from a freight car, a common means for husbands and sons to travel, the women had discovered. The rest of their family followed with the household possessions in passenger cars or wagons. Charlotte suggested that they stretch their legs, too.

"We haven't finished our tea," Lydia reminded her.

"Oh, Lydia, come! *I'll* make *you* a fresh cup when we get back."

Charlotte was already standing and Lydia followed, but her early suspicions had been confirmed: Charlotte did not fully appreciate the effort she had put into making the tea. How could she? She might be the daughter of a countess, but things like making tea and looking at grasses came much more easily to Charlotte. On the other hand, Lydia could think of nothing that came easily to her, so many wars she waged inside herself.


Still feeling the movement of the train, Charlotte looked around the depot. "Look, Lydia, the sidewalks are built high off the ground."

"To protect the ladies' dresses from the dust and mud," explained the conductor, who had overheard.

"What a civilized idea!" Lydia responded. She then pointed out to Charlotte an opera house and a newspaper office.

"You can see the latest New York entertainment in that opera house," the conductor told them. "Well, almost the latest. The railroads encourage towns on the rail line to begin ready grown. This one got a real good start."

The women agreed that the village looked prosperous, and it was not as windy as Chicago.

The conductor laughed. "You've caught western Kansas on a good day. Wind, it's got. And dust. In the spring you can hang your hat on the barn without a nail, and the wind will hold it there all summer." He laughed at his own joke, and they smiled politely, hoping that it was meant as one. "But this place has got a river," he continued, "which makes it a pretty good location, and there's stone in the ground, which makes for some fine buildings."

"Do you live here?" Lydia asked him. "You seem to know the area."

"I know the stationmaster, who knows everybody. This town didn't exist ten years ago, but almost from the beginning, a newspaper has made it easy to keep up with the goings-on around here." A man named Carl Huddleston, he explained, had bought the land from the railroad and marked the street corners with buffalo bones. Then he had banned cattle trains from coming here because he didn't want this to be a Wild West cattle town.

Lydia and Charlotte looked at each other. "How long will the train stay here?" Lydia asked.

"A good hour. There's a pretty nice hotel in the next block if you ladies want a decent cup of coffee. Might even serve you supper."

"At four-thirty?"

"Ma'am, supper comes early in these parts."

As Lydia and Charlotte strolled toward the hotel, they noticed "real buildings," the first they had seen since Wichita.

"Charlotte, do you suppose any other town will be as nice as this?"

"We can ask the conductor, but we've gone through an awful lot of Kansas towns, and this one is definitely the most progressive. Do you suppose it will be too . . . you know . . . too refined, Lydia?"

This question made Lydia laugh out loud. "Look around you." Together they took in the buildings. A few were made of the handsome local stone, but most were one-story constructions which, to Charlotte, resembled nothing so much as the sheds on her family's estate, except that there were no trees, no grass, not even as many people as there had been in her part of the French countryside.

Lydia nudged her. "See, even those stylish women over there are a good two years behind the fashion."

Charlotte, her old instinct winning out, critically scrutinized the hats, gloves, and parasols of three women getting out of a carriage. "More than two years, I'd say."

"I wasn't speaking Paris fashion, goose. I mean mopey old New York style, or even Chicago."

Charlotte smiled triumphantly. "And that's because they don't care about such trivia here. You were right, Lydia, Kansas is where we belong." She was about to say more when they came upon a creek that was bounded on both sides by newly planted willow trees. They stopped walking and stared at the water, the trees, and then each other. "We've seen so few streams and even fewer trees," Charlotte said. "Do you think this is a sign?"

"A good one," Lydia confirmed.

"It's too bad we've only just begun to look and can't stay." Charlotte shook her head.

"But we can," Lydia replied, clutching her friend's arm. "If we're to change, we should be spontaneous in our responses. You said so yourself."

"That was in Paris. We now have a plan."

"Our adventure is our plan, and Huddleston is part of our adventure."

Charlotte concurred, and the two women walked resolutely back to the depot.

George Akers, the stationmaster, assured them that Huddleston was a most progressive town. Outhouses were placed far enough away from the homes to prevent water contamination, and an ordinance required landowners to fence in livestock. Lydia, having noticed pigs and chickens and mules wandering at will in other towns, was relieved to hear that last bit of information.

The man also assured them of a suite of rooms in the hotel and offered to give them a tour of the countryside. Since they were too impatient to wait until the next day, he promised to close the station as soon as the train pulled out. He also let it be known that he was a dowser and could find underground water with the aid of his very reliable forked branch. The women looked at each other knowingly.

"I think we'll find underground springs here. This is another mystical pulling, I feel it," Charlotte whispered to Lydia, who nodded assent. Both had come to accept the notion that some mysterious force was drawing civilization westward—a theory to which many in Chicago, including Frank Bailey, subscribed.

By the time they had ensconced themselves in their new accommodations with their ten trunks and Norah and Sally, evening was approaching. The wind had picked up, but the women insisted on taking a wagon ride with George Akers before nightfall. The warning that rain was coming because the hotelkeeper's leg ached alarmed them enough to journey forth even if it meant returning after dark.

"Besides," Charlotte reasoned aloud, "what's the point of spontaneity if it can't be acted upon." This caused George Akers to look baffled, which made them giggle like young girls. That's how I feel, Lydia thought, like a young girl, like a whole passel of young girls.

"These are sand hills," George told them. "Only ones around Huddleston. Real good for grazing, if you're serious about raising sheep. . . ." His voice trailed off.

The hills, more like small mounds, really, interrupted the flat land, and for that Lydia was grateful. They would remind Charlotte of the rolling French countryside where she rode, and for that, also, Lydia was grateful. Lovely in their austerity outlined against the staccato clouds, these hills were different from anything else around.

"Turn in here," Charlotte instructed.

"No road there, ma'am."

"No brush, either. This wagon can do it," she said with authority. Reluctantly he turned to go where Charlotte had pointed between the two hills.

"A tree!" Lydia said, clapping her hands. "Charlotte, how did you know?"

"I spotted it before we came on the last hill. Now, Mr. Akers, fetch your divining rod. We shall go in search of water."

"Forgot it," he said.

"Then fashion another. There has to be a suitable branch on that cottonwood," Charlotte replied in her most polite voice, which brooked no disagreement.

Reluctantly Akers stopped his wagon and fumbled around until finally, with extravagant surprise, he produced his dowsing implement. In a state of awed agitation, Charlotte and Lydia scrambled down. Within minutes and within a few yards of the wagon his stick dipped down, and George Akers announced that he had discovered water.

Lydia pointed toward the north: "Let's also try over in that direction, just to be sure we aren't missing something."

This time he was insistent. "Rattlesnakes out there," he said, possibly thinking to scare them. "Can't see 'em good this time of day."

"If we sing, they'll go away," Charlotte told him, then turned to Lydia. "That's what Odile taught me when I was a little girl."

"Wolves, too," George stated.

"You have a gun, don't you?" Lydia asked.

"We forgot to bring guns," Charlotte said.

"I'm sure Mr. Akers can find us some tomorrow."

"Ladies, we have got to git back. They'll be sending folks out after us soon. It's way past suppertime, and I'm hungry."

The last remark registered. Of course they would return. How thoughtless. How badly they were behaving. Of course they must go.

"In one more minute," Charlotte added.

"As soon as we have come to some conclusions," Lydia put in.

The three sat hushed, waiting. As the night sky spread over them, the wind stilled to a low hum with only a high-reed sound coming from the cottonwood to remind them of it. The horses shuffled and a fox howled while frogs and crickets set about their night's business.

Finally Charlotte raised her arms. "The hill on the right is mine. The hill on the left is yours."

Lydia nodded agreement as she faced her hill and Charlotte faced hers. "You may take us back now," Lydia told Mr. Akers.

"Can we buy this land tonight?" Charlotte asked him.

"Anybody else, I'd say no—old Lester Goodwin can't be roused to register a deed after supper—but you ladies tend to get your way, I've noticed. If we leave right now, you might be able to talk him into helping you."

On the road Lydia asked, "Will our homesteads include all the hills?"

"I reckon so, though some have already been claimed."

Satisfied, Lydia leaned back. "Won't our gardens be lovely? People will come from all over to see such unusual gardens," she declared. "And twin houses with a walkway between them."

"To 'protect us from the dust and mud,' " Charlotte mimicked the train conductor.

"And any demons that might stray across our land," Lydia finished somberly. After that, they contented themselves with staring hard at the landscape whenever the half-moon slipped out from behind the clouds.

## 21

Charlotte first heard the rain in her dream, in which she wandered from one room to another, searching for a leak. Slowly she awoke, relieved to discover that the sound of dripping water came from outside the hotel. Though she was lying in an unfamiliar and less than comfortable bed, she was secure, content, elated.

Last night, amid great commotion, she had acquired 160 acres of land: Charlotte Duret the landowner. Charlotte Duret the shedder of skin, the searcher for essence, the liberator of souls, the liberator of her own soul.

When the door opened after a peremptory knock, she knew she'd been anticipating Lydia's arrival. Her friend, dressed and coiffed, was carrying a buggy whip and a newspaper as she bustled into the room. "I thought you'd never wake," she said.

"How do you know I am awake?" Charlotte asked, rubbing her eyes.

"Well, you *look* as if you're no longer sleeping. A cup of French coffee shall be your reward."

Charlotte sat up in the bed. "I need a reward after a night on this mattress. What is in it?"

"Norah told me it's stuffed with straw."

"Is this customary in Kansas? If so, my back will be ruined by the time we get our featherbeds. Should we order two more for Sally and Norah? We mustn't ruin their backs either."

"They seem to be satisfied with these, but I'll ask."

"Where did you get the whip?" Charlotte asked as she slipped on the bed jacket Lydia held out to her.

"If milady ever condescends to arise, I have a surprise for her."

"Tell me now, Lydia, for you know I want my coffee first."

"Even on your first day as a landowner?"

"Especially on this day. I must lie here and savor the image, roll it from one side of my head to the other and back again," she said, as Sally entered with a tray of coffee and rolls. "Did you know we have found a place to live?" Charlotte asked her.

"Yes, ma'am," Sally answered, never looking up, and Charlotte now regretted having asked the question. Lydia was forever reminding her that Sally was shy and any notice caused her embarrassment.

Lydia walked over to the window spattered with rain and commented on their good sense in venturing forth the night before.

"Luck was with us," Charlotte agreed. "And now we can spend the day making our plans—after I know the surprise."

"Ah, you've guessed it anyway."

"A carriage? You've bought us a carriage?"

"A buggy. A carriage would be too costly and grand—too much like our old life. Besides, I didn't see one. A horse is for sale, too, but you'd better look him over first."

"What time did you get up?"

"Hours and hours ago, before the rain turned into a deluge. It's later than it looks outside."

"The rain will be good for our crops."

"Yes," Lydia said. "And our flowers."

All morning the downpour continued, and the wind picked up with sufficient force to send sheets of water slamming against the mud streets, the sodden sidewalks, the wooden awnings, the steeped and flat roofs, the glass panes, and a few folk unlucky enough to be caught outside. All this the women watched with fascination from the shelter of their suite. "This is quite a temper fit," Lydia commented, and Charlotte quite agreed.

Since inspecting either their new land or their new buggy was out of the question, Charlotte snuggled under the covers of her bed while Lydia settled on top of them. Here in a dreamlike state they talked of acquiring sheep and planting wheat and alfalfa, of designing a rose garden, and of building their houses. This last topic consumed hours as they once again debated the placement of windows and storage spaces and flower beds.

Having finally resorted to consulting a pattern book for home designs, they staunchly refused to allow their houses to be exact replicas of someone else's ideas. Instead, they took an existing plan and embellished it to create "two truly splendid structures," as Lydia kept calling them.

Then Lydia remembered the local newspaper, still unopened and half forgotten. "I'll read it to you as you dress," she said.

With affection and good humor, Charlotte smiled at her friend, who sat straight, readying herself to read. "Do you realize how far we've come?" she asked.

"How could I not? Weeks and weeks of ocean and months in Chicago and—"

"Not that," Charlotte interrupted. "I mean how far you and I have come as *friends*. We read each other's moods, sometimes each other's minds. More important we're genuinely fond of each other's eccentricities, at least I am."

Lydia, also smiling, lowered the newspaper. "For my part, I have never felt such a sense of *belonging*."

"And, I've never felt so protected."

"Are they the same thing, you think?"

Charlotte shook her head. "Not really, but we serve each other's needs well."

Lydia picked up Charlotte's hand. "I hope so. With all my heart, I hope so."

"Yes," Charlotte answered, patting the hand on top of her own. But Lydia's eyes had reminded her of those of her brother and she had to turn away.

Downstairs someone played softly on a piano, and for a while they listened, until Lydia stirred. "You're right," she said. "We have done so much. Even though we've only begun our adventure, I already feel cleansed, more in charge of myself, more at one with the world." Then she laughed and added, "Especially when my world is mostly you."

"Soon you'll be able to include all of Huddleston, too." Charlotte said, opening her arms in an expansive gesture as she scooted off the bed to begin dressing. "So read to me of our fair city."

"Good news here immediately," Lydia announced as she scanned the front page. "It appears the government in Washington feels kindly toward Kansas—fifteen thousand dollars has been added to the agriculture appropriation bill " 'to investigate and suppress cattle disease.' "

"Does that mean sheep, too?" Charlotte asked, pulling her chemise over her head.

"Mmmn," Lydia responded absentmindedly as she continued to read, "but I've found other good tidings. Listen to this: 'The West has had its first victory over the East, for we are now entitled to more representatives, which will give us equal footing.' "

"I thought the war was between the North and the South. What is this East-West rivalry about."

Lydia shook her head. "I don't know. In the past I paid little attention to this sort of thing, but I expect we'll find out soon enough. Oh, but here's one that should make Samuel happy. Our nameless Washington correspondent reports that—and I quote verbatim—'The inauguration of President Garfield was the grandest and most important of any that has occurred in the history of our government.' "

At the mention of Samuel, Charlotte had tensed. Her own feelings aside, Lydia worried about him too much. "Find *us* another item," she said with only a slight edge to her voice.

"How about this one? The state of Nebraska has passed a women's suffrage bill. Now only the governor's signature is needed. Nebraska, you know, is right next to Kansas," Lydia explained, looking up.

Charlotte nodded her head, though she had not known that at all. "I'd like to vote. . . . Are you wearing your corset today?" she asked, holding up hers and trying to decide whether to forget it. Although one of their resolutions had been to give up corsets once they arrived in Kansas, she wasn't sure this should be the day.

"I'm wearing mine. I was thinking we should get a little better acquainted here first." She tapped the newspaper. "I think the vote is our best omen yet. It means this part of the country is truly ready to accept us on our own terms. Want me to help?" Lydia asked as Charlotte struggled with the corset.

"No. I've got to get used to doing more for myself. Read on."

Both women had resolved to do as much as possible for themselves, for soon Sally and Norah were going to be busy with two houses and a lot of land. Besides, they realized that part of *being* was *doing*.

The international news informed them that the rapid destruction of New Zealand forests had created a scarcity of timber, causing a climate change for the worse.

Charlotte protested, "But there are almost no trees here, and the climate is wonderful." As she spoke, they both turned toward the window, which was still being pelted by rain, and they laughed.

"Never mind." Lydia continued scanning the paper. "Here's news from France, but will it make you homesick?"

"Of course not, though I didn't expect to hear any except in letters." Satisfactorily dressed in her new light blue poplin, Charlotte sat down in the room's only chair, a brown cane.

"This article will make you sad, for they report that Le Printemps has burned. Twenty-six people were hurt and there was seven million francs' worth of damage."

"I'm sorry for the people; I have no nostalgia for the drapery establishment. More?"

"Yes. The paper says, 'Paris journals of all opinions express horror at the assassination of the czar.'"

"I have no nostalgia for the czar, either."

"One more piece about Rand County, Kansas—that's us—and we'll have Norah fetch us a bite to eat from downstairs."

"A good idea," Charlotte agreed, for their morning had stretched into afternoon.

"Indeed, this article will definitely please you." Lydia rose to her knees on the bed to read in a dramatic voice: "'Kansas now has one million sheep—one for every man, woman, and child—and has done this in a very short time. This record has never been excelled by any country in the world.'" Lydia put down the newspaper. "This must mean that Kansans like sheep a lot. I was afraid they would be biased toward cattle. Aren't we lucky?"

Charlotte went to stand by her. "Very lucky," she echoed. Clasping hands they decided to celebrate with a bottle of good wine and sent Norah to purchase it along with the food. Unlike Sally, Norah was not shy but remained rather surly unless left to do as she pleased. Since it was difficult to find help, they put up with her bad temper.

Norah returned empty-handed. "The man says they've already finished servin' dinner and there won't be more food until this evening 'bout five o'clock, 'cause they're shorthanded in the kitchen, what with the rain. He also says you can't buy wine in Huddleston. Says they don't sell no whiskey, either, not anywhere in this town."

Lydia and Charlotte looked at each other. "Can that be so?" Charlotte asked.

Lydia nodded yes and looked at Norah, who went on to report that these rules had been written into the town charter by Mr. Huddleston himself. No alcohol for three years, and that included business establishments. There were two years left to go.

Lydia and Charlotte looked at each other again. "We were excited and tired last night," Lydia said. "Maybe we should have looked a little more."

"Mr. Huddleston says the riffraff will stay away if there's no liquor," Norah explained.

"I don't care what Mr. Huddleston says. How can one have a proper meal without a glass of wine?" Charlotte asked.

"Two years isn't forever." Lydia squeezed Charlotte's shoulder. "And we'll tell everyone this is another experiment in our adventure. Complete sobriety," she said, chuckling.

"But I don't want to eat my meals without wine!"

"Just for now. When we move into our houses—"

Before she could finish, a knock on their door interrupted them. When they saw the wife of the proprietor, they assumed she'd come to apologize; instead, she scolded them for expecting meals in their rooms and thinking food would be available at any time they asked. "Such grand ladies as you are going to have to do some changin'. It'd be best to learn our ways as fast as you can," she warned.

"Oh, madam, we're not grand ladies at all," Charlotte said quietly.

"Quite the contrary," Lydia agreed. Just then the rain stopped. "What a relief!" she sighed.

"Yes," the woman answered as the sun came out. All three turned to stare through the now glistening water-streaked window.

"We might go for a walk and forget about food until tonight," Charlotte considered out loud.

"Still too wet for that," the woman said.

"Not for us. We'll stay on the sidewalk and investigate Main Street's merchants," Charlotte told her. The woman shrugged and turned to go.

"But will you tell your pianist that we've been enchanted by his music?" Lydia called.

Ethel Cannon—by now they had learned her name—gave them a hard look, but almost smiled. "That's me. I come by piano playin' naturally. My daddy had a good ear and a little training. I inherited one and he taught me the other."

"You are quite gifted," Charlotte said. "Your playing makes our stay here very special."

"Don't get too used to it. The rain kept some of the usuals away, so I had a little time, which don't usually happen." Suddenly she was out the door.

Charlotte turned to Lydia: "The poor woman. I think her life is hard."

"She's probably cross from too much work, and she's almost as shy as Sally, I think. Now let's go see our horse and buggy."

The horse was of mediocre quality—no proud legs, no sleek coat—but better than no horse at all, Charlotte thought, and she had missed his kind. She had missed horse smells. Touch. As she stroked him, she felt tears forming.

"Is he all right?" Lydia asked anxiously.

"Just fine. And the buggy is perfect for us," she said, swallowing hard.

For the next hour they wandered through the stores on Main Street, in the process meeting the druggist, the grocer, a clerk in a dry goods establishment, and the owner of a furniture store—the only one in town, he told them, unnecessarily. He assured them that soon there would be no hitching posts on Main Street. The country people liked them because they were a convenient place to tie their horses, but the ladies, he said, hated the odor as well as the summer flies they brought and the mud they splashed. "And the ladies are our best customers."

The druggist had mentioned a lecture to be given that evening in the Methodist church by a General Clamp on the subject of that great statesman Abraham Lincoln, and they decided to attend.

"Some Kansans began to fight the war against slavery several years before the real war," Lydia explained on the way back to the hotel, "so this place reflected all the hostilities of the whole country. A great number of pro-slave and anti-slave families settled here early, each group wanting to claim the territory as a state for their side. The anti-slave side prevailed but at a terrible cost. In fact, for a while this state was called "Bleeding Kansas.""

"But it seems so peaceful!"

"Well, a lot of these people are probably newcomers like us, but on the whole—and I imagine this is true here as well as almost everywhere else in America now—people are reluctant to turn to violence unless a matter of honor is involved." Lydia turned to Charlotte with a rueful smile. "Though matters of honor are in no short supply, unfortunately."

"I hope that will not be so here," Charlotte responded.

Looking forward to hot baths and warm food and an enjoyable evening, Lydia and Charlotte returned to their rooms. Their travels and the exertions of the last two days had begun to catch up with them, but still they were too excited to rest.

In their sitting room, on a small table placed in front of the fireplace, they found two large coffee cups filled with something other than coffee.

"I don't know the taste," Charlotte said, grimacing slightly.

"Whiskey." Lydia smiled. "I'd guess moonshine."

"Mrs. Cannon?"

"I expect," Lydia answered. They took another swallow.

After their baths and supper, they once more began talking about the differences already evident between their lives now and their circumstances in Paris. Lydia found herself telling Charlotte how much the work of those rebellious painters Degas and Monet had meant to her. Their play with light and lines expressed more of some hidden need in her nature than anything else she'd ever experienced, she confided.

"I had no idea," Charlotte replied, a little hurt catching in her voice.

"I didn't talk about it. I didn't even know how, but I went to look at the paintings again and again, hoping to discover what it was in me they touched," she said, then swirled and sniffed the moonshine as if it were brandy.

For a few minutes they watched the play of shadows on the wall, creating fantastic shapes.

Charlotte asked lazily, "And did you discover what you were searching for?"

"No. Finally, out of discouragement or fear—and I didn't know which —I gave up looking at the pictures."

"So now we will create living pictures, and through them you'll learn what it is you need to know."

**22** The next morning Charlotte practiced her English on Lydia. They discussed politics, crops, and the heavy rain. "We have seen . . . how do you say? . . . 'the deluge?'"

"That's how you say," Lydia assured her.

This was a more important practice session than usual, for at the lecture the night before a Mr. Benjamin Leggett, a cordial banker, had invited them to dine with him and his wife the next evening—tonight.

In spite of the muddy roads and an occasional snore from the small audience—small, they were told, because of the mud—the lecture had proved successful. General Clamp had entertained the band of Lincoln enthusiasts while enlightening Charlotte. More important from the two women's standpoint, the congenial people in the group had gone out of their way to welcome them, word having already spread of their arrival.

Mr. Leggett had been especially hospitable, and so had a French-woman, Madame Beauchamp, and her seventeen-year-old daughter, Geneviève, both of whom immediately befriended Charlotte. For her part, Charlotte made a point of drawing out this broad-faced, handsome girl, just returned from Saint Mary's Academy in Leavenworth, Kansas. Almost more American than French, having lived here most of her life, Geneviève had the kind of appealing spirit neither Lydia nor Charlotte could resist.

To their amusement the girl confided that at the convent the nuns had disciplined her once for taking a bite out of all the apples in the fruit bowl. In retaliation she had organized a protest strike in which every young woman began to wear her kid gloves inside out.

Later, as Lydia and Charlotte prepared for bed, they laughed again at Geneviève's escapade. "She was telling me her story when her mother joined us to say there's a Catholic church here, which will be a good place for us to meet people." Charlotte smiled. "I think she meant men."

"At any rate, we've found you a French family, and we now have a banker," Lydia said, feeling altogether triumphant, as they concluded that the new society of Huddleston was aesthetically pleasing, culturally satisfying, emotionally fulfilling, and socially liberating.

Reasoning that if one cleansed oneself of old forms, one had to reflect properly on the achievement, they devoted the afternoon to trying on clothes. As a result, unpacking their trunks became a game in itself: two girls playing dress-up on a rainy day. They lingered over each new dress, each one promising to reveal a new image, a new self, and possibly that ever elusive "essence." Having chosen to adorn their bodies with the most eloquent yet simple of dresses, they luxuriated in the feel of the honest wools and cottons, beautifully cut and tailored before leaving Paris.

Lydia tried on a white blouse and put a sliver of white lace around her neck.

"That's perfect! That's just right," Charlotte praised her, almost in surprise. They both understood that Charlotte had the better visual sense, her Frenchness benefiting her, but Lydia was catching on.

"Paris educated my senses. I learned disciplined spontaneity."

"Disciplined?"

"Yes. In the beginning I soaked in the glory of the colors and sounds, even the words, but all their intensity, and coming from so many directions . . . well, for me, it was like dealing with this Kansas wind—bending into it, going with it when you can."

"Staying aware," Charlotte said, understanding.

"But knowing there was only so much I could control. I had to learn to be comfortable with being unsteady on my feet."

"So your experience with Gabriel wasn't totally oppressive for you."

"Put that way, I suppose not. Touch, smell, sound, sight—if you truly come alive, then each experience leads to a keen appreciation of the other."

"But you were always in touch with your senses."

"I think so. Maybe that comes with being French," Charlotte tossed off lightly.

Somewhere along the way, Charlotte had become reticent on the subject of sex, perhaps in deference to Lydia's less than successful involvement with Gabriel. Since it was not a natural subject to Lydia's lips, she had paid little attention to Charlotte's own silence on the matter.

Now, rather timidly, Charlotte asked, "Do you believe that sating most of your senses makes up for ignoring another?"

"Oh, yes," Lydia replied, but she was not so sure at all.

In the end they decided on the plainest of woolen dresses, Lydia's ink-blue, Charlotte's oak-leaf green. Only the slightest of bustles protruded underneath these garments of wool so fine it might have been silk. Neither woman was so modest as to underestimate the effect the two of them together would create, but then, neither wanted to admit she cared.

They were dazzling, Mrs. Leggett declared, when Mr. Leggett introduced them to her and to a Mr. and Mrs. Brown. Lydia found herself standing by a decorative hand-painted pale green fishbowl, a good two feet wide and balanced atop a tall pedestal that was decorated with the same hand-painted shells and ferns displayed on the bowl. She had seen nothing quite like it in either Paris or New York.

Shortly, however, their host led them into the dining room, where an imposing table—turned out with china and crystal and illuminated by a cut-glass chandelier—came as a surprise. A huge sideboard filled with silver and crowned by a heavy gilt-framed mirror, forced Lydia into an even more fundamental reassessment of her surroundings.

If, however, all this suggested more than a simple existence, so did Mrs. Leggett's eyes, darting about, alert to something that had escaped her or from which she was escaping. Even after they sat down and Wallace Brown began expounding on the possibility of Huddleston becoming another Kansas City, Mrs. Leggett appeared only to be lighting on a word here and a gesture there.

"What with the increase in immigration, our county is going to do mighty well these next few years," Mr. Brown boasted. "The last couple have seen this place turn around, weather-wise and money-wise. You can make a lot of money on this land right now." Indeed, it turned out that Mr. Brown was a land speculator and had done very well indeed because the railroads and the eastern investors kept pumping money into the region.

"I noticed in the newspaper three separate advertisements by loan companies," Lydia commented.

"Those big money boys from the East know a good thing when they see it. The town can already support two banks—Benjamin here owns one of them—two doctors, a dentist, three justices of the peace, and five lawyers. And this is only the beginning."

"Don't get too carried away yet, Wallace," Mr. Leggett advised. "As you said, it's the cash from the East that's pumping us up right now, and I'm not so sure either Wall Street or the government in Washington knows what they're doing. Mrs. Fulgate and Miss Duret could probably tell us more about the mood in that part of the country."

Charlotte nodded to Lydia, who responded that New York and Paris appeared buoyant also, with everyone looking to the future and the West. There's a lot of greed, but there's also a sense of getting on with new ways."

"Nothing wrong with a little greed," Wallace Brown replied. "If you don't extend your reach, you get stuck in a rut."

"A little greed, maybe, but a lot of folks are going to end up land-poor, mortgaged to the hilt, if bad times come around again," Benjamin Leggett warned.

"Then will you end up with our money, Mr. Leggett?" Charlotte asked.

His response was only an uncomfortable laugh. If we were married to Mr. Leggett, Lydia thought, he wouldn't ask our opinion about the United States government, nor would he listen to our answers with the rapt attention both he and Mr. Brown are doing. Later she would point all this out to Charlotte, tell her that, were it not for their resolve, either of them could turn into a Mrs. Brown or a Mrs. Leggett—once beautiful, probably intelligent, but ignored. How much nicer, she would tell Charlotte, to enjoy such men and their attentions for one evening rather than be at the mercy of their moods for a lifetime. She worried inordinately, she knew, that Charlotte would one day leave, abandoning her like Herman and Gabriel or, for that matter, like Sam, though of course he would never truly desert her. And what was the question Mr. Brown was asking Charlotte? And was that really iced tea being poured into the cut-glass goblet?

"Sheep," Charlotte was saying. "We have already ordered them."

"Ordered them?" Mrs. Brown asked, her first words since the introductions in the hallway.

"From an entrepreneur," Charlotte answered.

"But I thought you said you didn't know very much about Huddleston," Mrs. Brown said.

"We know about sheep, though," Charlotte answered.

Mr. Leggett turned to Lydia. "Much of Kansas is devoted to cattle, and as you know, cattle and sheep don't mix."

Lydia nodded assent and suppressed a sudden desire to reach across the damask-draped, crystal-laden dining table to Mrs. Leggett's hand and soothe her enough to still her eyes.

"At any rate, Miss Duret, you've come to the right place. Old Carl Huddleston has banned cattle drives through this county, and firearms in town are prohibited."

"But why this quaint notion of his concerning wine?" Charlotte asked. "It is barbaric, really, to have wine unavailable, *n'est-ce pas?*"

"A wineless meal is one of the lesser barbarisms in this county." Mrs. Leggett spit out each angry word as an embarrassed quiet settled over the table. Her husband calmly assured her that they were all grateful to be in a place conducive to raising families.

Benjamin Leggett addressed his next remark to the newcomers. "Some of these cattle towns have a proliferation of saloons and are completely out of control," he explained. "Though you'll find good, upstanding citizens in those places, you can understand why the people of Huddleston are willing to sacrifice a little pleasure."

"Sacrifice a little pleasure?" his wife asked, her voice tremulous. She raised her napkin to her face in a futile attempt to hide what appeared to be an involuntary grimace.

Mrs. Brown pushed back her chair, went around to Mrs. Leggett, and took her by the shoulders. Her soothing voice seemed to hold the woman steady. "But of course, Emma, you've begun a new life now. See how beautiful your table looks. And your chandelier? Why, it makes the whole room shimmer."

Emma Leggett surveyed her table with a critical eye, then looked up at Mrs. Brown. "Mama would be pleased, wouldn't she, Roberta?"

"Yes, she would." Roberta Brown continued to stand with her hands on the distraught woman's shoulders.

The others waited in suspense while Emma Leggett drew herself up, visibly forced herself to focus on a dish of corn pudding, then suddenly produced a lopsided smile. "Do have some more of this corn pudding, all of you. I've made enough for an army, haven't I, Mr. Leggett?"

"I've never had corn pudding before," Charlotte said and held her plate for Mrs. Leggett to serve. "It's delicious."

When she started spooning up the pudding, everyone watched anxiously to be sure Mrs. Leggett's calm demeanor would last without Mrs. Brown's support. Taking no chances, however, Mrs. Brown began talking about the Ladies' Literary Society.

In the last year the members had read *The Europeans* by Henry James and a shocking novel by Zola, after which they decided that the reviews in *Harper's Magazine* were unreliable. Even so, she went on rapidly, the club was involved with more than literary topics.

This past winter they had discussed the China question and had agreed that the Chinese laborers should stay in Kansas. How else would the railroads continue to get built? But perhaps Mrs. Fulgate and Miss Duret would consider coming to their meetings sometime? Membership rules were strict, but on occasion new members were accepted and visitors were welcomed.

"We'd love to come," Lydia quickly responded. Fortunately she did not begin an argument on the merits of Zola. Education took time.

When Mrs. Brown, seemingly exhausted, turned her attention once more to her food, the men began to offer practical advice on what crops to grow and which trees to plant, in the latter case, hardy varieties to withstand the weather—locust, box elder, and black walnut, for instance. The more trees people planted, the men agreed, the more likely it was to increase rainfall—the moderate kind.

"Does this mean that yesterday's weather was a fluke?" Lydia asked.

"Hardly," Roberta Brown replied.

"Still, droughts are more likely," Emma Leggett added, making a real attempt now to enter into the conversation.

Mr. Brown frowned. "The weather is getting better. The more settled the land, the more settled the weather. Our real problem comes from the rabble-rousers, like the Farmers' Alliance. They'll stir up trouble with their whining about big business and big government and railroad monopolies. If you ask me, all this criticism is plain unpatriotic, maybe even ungodly."

"Ungodly?" Lydia echoed.

"I mean, if God hadn't been on their side pulling for them, those big business types wouldn't have prospered. They're the ones who've got God's ear, so to speak."

"They are closer to God than priests?" Charlotte wanted to know.

"Sure they are. No disrespect, but you don't see many men of the cloth faring so well."

"Oh, come on, Wallace. It's hard for me to think God is speaking to old John Boyd," Mr. Leggett teased.

"No, I mean the really high rollers. We'd all do well to listen to what God is telling them. Absolutely it is ungodly to question their judgment, now that I think about it; and those ne'er-do-wells ought to stop their crying."

"Are they sad?" Charlotte asked, taking Wallace Brown literally.

"Angry is more like it," Mr. Leggett replied gently. "They feel the railroads, to take one culprit, are impoverishing them with high freight charges and—"

"The railroads are our financial salvation, but some people can't get that through their thick skulls," Wallace Brown interrupted. "Sure, there might be some overcharging, but in the long run if the big boys prosper, we prosper; and you'd think everybody around here would know that by now."

"The fact is, there are some legitimate grievances that need to be redressed before the situation becomes explosive."

"I hope the situation is not like that of the workers in France," Charlotte said, getting slightly confused. "Street riots are abominations. The workers do not know how to behave. They become animals."

"Out here we're talking farmers, and they do know how to behave, so don't worry your sweet head about riots," Mr. Brown replied.

Lydia counted to five and smiled. "I would suppose her head needs to worry about much the same thing as yours, Mr. Brown," she said, pleasantly. My brother agrees with you on one issue, however: he also thinks it's possible to tame the weather just as we have tamed the land." Her remark drew hearty agreement from the others.

Yes, the right mixture of vegetation, technology, and good old-fashioned will would result in a more predictable, less extreme climate. Lydia's brother, an outsider, a disinterested party, had said so, and they had all read that this was so. Most important, they all thought it to be true, willed it to be true.

Now the men, feeling grateful to Lydia's brother and charmed by the homesteaders, assured them that everyone in town, would be willing to lend them a hand and offer advice on their farm. "Though you ladies might consider delaying construction for a while," Mr. Brown interjected. "Two good-looking, intelligent women like you will have your pick of gents for miles around. No need to bother with the expense and the trouble of building two houses." Although Mr. Brown had begun with a gush, he was now faltering.

"Yes, indeed, you are both too attractive to stay single," Mrs. Leggett cut in.

"But we want to stay single," Charlotte said, beaming. "We do not want such imperfect lives as marriage might afford us."

Lydia coughed violently and reached for her iced tea, hoping Charlotte would not mention the shedding of skin, even in a playful way. These people simply wouldn't understand.

"But you must want children. Every woman wants children," Mrs. Brown insisted.

"Children are . . . how do you say?" Charlotte turned to Lydia. "A *condition* of marriage, not a reason for it."

"That's one way to put it," Mr. Leggett answered for Lydia, who could tell he was as enchanted by Charlotte as every other man. "And on a certain level I can understand how you feel, but farming the land and raising sheep are two very good reasons for matrimony. That's hard work you ladies have set for yourselves, and it takes a whole family pulling together to make a go of it."

"We have friends to help—other women who feel the way we do," Lydia retorted.

"That is not the natural order," Mrs. Brown argued.

"There's a great case to be made for the sacredness of the family," Mr. Leggett put in.

"They die," Mrs. Leggett blurted out.

"What, Mother?" her husband asked.

"Children, you fool! Children!" Mrs. Leggett slammed the table with both fists before leaving the room.

When Mrs. Brown rose to go after her, Mr. Leggett raised his hand to stop her. "We mustn't indulge her in these outbursts. It will only encourage such behavior."

"She's been through a hard time, Mr. Leggett," Mrs. Brown answered, her tone more apologetic than accusatory.

"So have we all, my dear."

"Did I upset Mrs. Leggett?" Charlotte asked.

"People upset her," Mr. Leggett replied. "She hasn't been around them enough lately. I thought this evening would be good for her, but evidently it's too soon for visitors."

"Well, I think all these derogatory remarks about family life upset her," Roberta Brown said, her face a landscape of anger. "Emma has given up everything for her family . . . everything. The very backbone of this community—this state—is made up of family ties, family values."

As they had during Mrs. Leggett's outburst, everyone just sat there, not knowing how to respond.

"With everything else so different and changing so fast," Roberta Brown continued, "we're more dependent on our families than ever. They're just as necessary as good weather for crops or good wine for the table. In fact, the ruination of too many families has been liquor—drunken men useless to their wives and children. It's not a pretty sight and one we can ill afford."

Taken aback by the extent of Roberta Brown's fury, they all shrank into themselves until Wallace Brown rose and broke the silence. "Amos tells me the bridge is washed out toward Newton. Want to come help us tomorrow?" he asked his host as everyone rose from the table.

"I'll come, but there's a man over in Salina I've got to see first," Mr. Brown said.

After Lydia and Charlotte said good night, they didn't speak until they were back in their own quarters, where Lydia let out a long sigh. "People here read. That's a sign of some kind of intellectual life."

"Yes, but when people read and think, they form opinions not always of our choosing. That's the unfortunate side of intellectual discourse," Charlotte said with a faint smile as she unhooked Lydia's corset for her. "I do not think, however, of tonight's discourse as intellectual," she added softly.

Near tears, Lydia could only shake her head in agreement. Part of their problem, she knew, was that they both longed to belong in the world—so long as it was a world of their own making. The other world would not suffice, nor could they satisfy it.

"Will they ever accept us?" Charlotte finally asked, intuiting Lydia's thoughts.

"We won't live in isolation, I promise you that. I told you we would have a community of like-minded people and we will."

"These people don't appear to be inclined that way, do you think?"

"They're like the French, to whom prosperity and family have become everything," Lydia said. "It seems everyone everywhere has become bourgeois, no matter their background." She avoided using the term "aristocratic," a concept she and Charlotte had struck from their lexicon.

"Look, life's a little scary for everybody, and people tend to hold tight to what they've got," she continued. "These people aren't so set in their ways as either the French or the eastern Americans. They've already had to adjust, as Mrs. Leggett implied, even if her house didn't show it. Once you've changed a little, you can change more. We'll be good examples. We'll show them the attraction of other possibilities."

"But these women have no other possibilities," Charlotte pointed out, "and I'm not sure the men want any other kind of life. Maybe the young ones can be encouraged, Geneviève perhaps. We should concentrate on them and let them instruct their parents."

"These people will listen only if we're successful," Lydia answered.

"We didn't come here to bother with success; we came for the freedom to be ourselves."

"Men can have both. Why shouldn't we?" Seeing Charlotte's doubtful look, Lydia added, "Success will also ensure our independence—unless we want to pretend to know our place."

Head cocked to one side, Charlotte considered this before she spoke. "I am not sure about knowing our place, Lydia, but I do know we haven't come all this way to stay in our place. I would rather our own hogs to slop?"

Lydia laughed. "I couldn't have said it better."

**23** For Lydia and Charlotte, spring came quickly, a series of sharp, bright days enhanced by the budding of young wheat, the proliferation of tiny green leaves on cottonwoods, and, especially, the building of their houses.

Because of Benjamin Leggett's intercession and the fact that they were beautiful women alone, one of the two local building contractors had put them at the top of his list. During construction they even managed, with the help of their hired hands, to sow wheat, rye, and broomcorn, and to cordon off one-quarter of their property to be planted in trees, qualifying them for even more acreage under a government program. They had also, with the help of their dowser, dug themselves a deep-water well, taking advantage of their underground springs.

Every day they filled their buggy with seeds and supplies and journeyed out to oversee the progress of their houses and to plant spring onions, radishes, tomatoes, and peas in their vegetable garden. As soon as the basements were dug and covered with floorboards, they installed in Lydia's kitchen the most up-to-date coal-burning cookstove, boasting two ovens and eight top burners. Because the carpenters and field hands expected a substantial noonday meal, Sally and Norah cooked up large quantities of potatoes and flapjacks and stews and sugar-butter pies.

When Sally took to her bed one day with a fever, Lydia and Charlotte pitched in. Though Norah had to tell them "every little thing," as Charlotte instructed her to do, they treated the task as a game. Soon Charlotte became adept at turning flapjacks; Lydia took much longer trying to roll out the pastry dough for pies.

"The crust has got to be thinner or the inside won't get done," Norah tutored her. Lydia failed to pay attention, and the first batch burned. With grim determination she again started mixing dough, but try as she might, physical tasks didn't come easy to her. Paris had taught her a keener appreciation of the tactile, but her experiences were of a more aesthetic order. Inept hands didn't help either; holding a book was about all they were good for, she sometimes despaired.

Charlotte, finished with her cooking assignment, came over to help, but seeing Lydia—dough covering her hair, her nose, her hands, and a good part of her dress, since she had neglected to wear an apron—Charlotte could only laugh. "Look at her, Norah. We could serve her up as a pie." Norah went so far as to grant them a smile. Lydia, beyond exasperation, took a big mixing spoon of dough and dabbed it on Charlotte's face.

Charlotte gave a little squeal and Lydia dumped another gob on her forehead. As Charlotte ran around the kitchen table, Lydia chased after her, every now and again slinging another spoonful. Amid the whoops of laughter and cries of mock distress, they looked up to see, crowded in the doorway, five workers.

"There won't be no pies today," Norah said to the assembled group.

"It sure looks that way," one of the men said and grinned. "But this sight is worth the loss."

Charlotte and Lydia stood very still and then collapsed into a heap on the floor, their laughter ringing from the new walls.

In less than a month two identical houses, whitewashed and made of sturdy oak, had been miraculously raised. On the advice of their carpenter, they put up pitched clapboard roofs—the best kind to keep out rain. In high wind, though, they might get snow, he warned. The peaks of their gabled roofs faced each other, and a long, narrow door, fitted directly under the peaks ran down the length of the second floor, and opened onto a walkway, which connected the two houses. From these walkways, as well as their bedroom doors and the single casement windows flanking them, Charlotte and Lydia could extend their first good-morning greetings or their last good-night benedictions.

Directly under each upstairs door was another one, offering easy entry into the house. On either side of each door was a three-quarter-length window bracketed by blue shutters. Instead of the soft locally made red brick—Benjamin Leggett had predicted its deterioration—the underpinnings of both structures were built of imported stone.

"Those rocks will outlast us," Lydia remarked with satisfaction one dawn when they'd eagerly driven out before first light to see the latest progress.

"Don't say that," Charlotte replied.

"I mean when we die."

"Don't say that, either."

"I thought you weren't afraid of death."

"I'm not, so long as you don't talk about it."

"I wish it were that simple for me."

"And I wish I could make it so."

"You help," Lydia said and smiled. "That's what's important."

The front door, each facing onto her own property, had one small lintel that was the same blue as the shutters. The sides of the houses were graced with four tall French windows. Granted, both women welcomed sunlight, but they also liked the look and feel of such luxurious openings to their natural surroundings. Everything else, however, was modest and made of durable materials.

Charlotte rode through their property every day, surveying, inspecting, planning new projects. By the time the houses were completed and the surrounding structures in place, she had taught Lydia to fire a gun and ride a horse with confidence.

She also came to recognize the sound of the wind passing through a cottonwood tree and could for some few moments close her eyes and pretend this was another kind of reed instrument, sometimes the whole woodwind section of an orchestra. But music was the least of their concerns; they were too busy memorizing their new landscape.

In the future they planned to build separate structures to house an expanded staff, including a cook, a gardener, and hired hands, but for now they contented themselves with a large barn, a few chicken coops, and a privy located a little farther from the house than Charlotte thought necessary.

For the most part, however, they had few complaints. The walkway served them well, protecting their skirts not only from mud but from dust, too. The interior furnishings had fit, just as they imagined—a good thing, for they had spent much time designing simple, suitable furniture without one unneeded curve or ornament.

These pieces had been made to fit into a small suite of rooms, including a parlor, a dining room, and a small library. On the second floor of each house were two small guest bedrooms as well as a pretty, if small, boudoir, made cozier by a sloping ceiling and a soft honeydew green duvet. The same green was echoed in the tiny flowers stenciled on the creamy wallpaper. While the color schemes in the rest of the houses varied, Lydia and Charlotte were too fond of the tranquil green for either of them to give it up.

Their paintings, mostly watercolors in plain wooden frames, enhanced the rooms without dominating them. Their draperies of heavy linen hung beautifully; their bedroom curtains of simple white muslin billowed gracefully. Along with the plain furnishings, they prided themselves on their choice of stark white china and an unadorned silver pattern, a perfect reflection, they felt, of their new landscape.

They spent one gratifying afternoon arranging their whatnot shelves to reflect each other and placing their sconces at exactly the same spot on their walls. Midway through decorating, they took a break to enjoy the cloudless April day. Sitting on the edge of Lydia's porch, its long overhang protecting them from the bullying sun, they surveyed their new surroundings.

Buttercups covered the expanse of space directly in front of them, and about fifty yards on lay two of their newly plowed fields, protected by barbed wire—a valuable acquisition, they were discovering. Just beyond the fields the rise of a sand hill framed grazing sheep.

To their right, the land—sprinkled with waving grasses, larkspur, and other flowers of gold, red, and blue, whose names they did not yet know— sloped down to their small stream and the lone cottonwood, then on to the road. To the left among the sand hills stood the barn and other outbuildings.

"Isn't this the most beautiful sight in the world?" Lydia asked, swinging her legs over the porch lip. The lack of trees no longer bothered them.

Charlotte, hugged her knees and rocked back and forth. "We're the luckiest two people in the world. The very luckiest two."

"Knock on wood," Lydia cautioned, "though since we made our own luck, we don't have to worry so much about someone or something else unmaking it."

"Why, Lydia Fulgate," Charlotte teased, "you sound like our friend Mr. Wallace Brown when he talks about God and businessmen."

"I'm not saying we're in touch with God, if that's what you mean."

"Perhaps we are our own gods, then?" Charlotte asked. Both watched two sheep rubbing heads.

After considering the question another moment, Lydia responded, "If we choose to change our fate, we can, with the proper amount of courage and determination. If that makes us our own goddesses, so be it."

"I don't think Mr. Brown would disagree with you, but do you think that when we're successful, Mr. Brown will accept that God speaks through us, too?"

Lydia laughed. "He'd better! But when we're successful, they'll all listen to us." She half closed her eyes, shutting out the sun's glare and the thought of Mr. Brown.

Charlotte pointed out a white cloud traveling across the horizon. "It's all alone," she remarked.

"Do you s'pose it's lonely?" Lydia asked dreamily.

"Lydia, what if we're not successful? What if everyone here rejects us? Will that make you too lonely?"

"That just won't happen," Lydia answered, as she stood up.

"But if it should," Charlotte insisted, "would you be too lonely?"

Lydia brushed off the back of her brown calico print skirt and breathed deeply. "Not if I have you. And Sam. And our friends. But being alone, truly alone, frightens me."

"Me too."

"Yes, but you don't need people as much as I do." Lydia looked down at Charlotte and smiled. "It's true what you're thinking: I like to have people around, for reassurance more than anything. I cultivate only a few close friends, but I need to believe I have access to many in case . . ."

"In case?"

Lydia shrugged. "Oh, you know, in case something happens to the ones I really love." She held out her hand to help Charlotte make the little jump down from the porch to the ground.

"I think we'll both feel safer when we truly discover who we are,"

Charlotte said, leaning over to pick a buttercup, and then another. Lydia did the same. "You make a little fun of our inner search, Lydia, but I think that adventure will take as much or more courage and determination as this one did. Afterward we'll be afraid of nothing, including being alone."

Lydia started to protest: "I don't mean to make fun, I'm just not as—"

"That's it!" Charlotte interrupted. They watched as a gentle breeze played with the loose flower petals caught in its funnel as it scampered across the yard. "We know the wind moves those petals. The same with us. We drop some petals, scoop up others, and we see only the petals, but another force directs them. If we can only find that force and name it in ourselves, then maybe our petals will fall in the order we choose instead of dropping randomly."

Lydia hesitated a moment before asking. "What if we discover that our petals do drop randomly, that we only play havoc with them?"

They continued to watch the path of the petals and to listen to the hum of bees in the buttercups and clover and the distant bleating of a lamb until at last Charlotte said, "We must hope for more," and took Lydia's hand in hers.


For Charlotte, building a house, tending the sheep, and farming the land was the most fun she'd ever had in her life. Even her times with Papa didn't equal the headiness she felt when she and Lydia hung their first draperies or watched their first sheep waddle across a hill. Charlotte regarded this shared excitement and closeness as her best defense against the sadness and anger that sometimes swept through her, for she'd determined not to let her past devastate her present.

Fortunately her present was all-consuming. And on another day, a fitting kind of cloudless April day, after they'd placed their gowns and hats and shoes in matching armoires and cupboards, they really did become twins, their homes a manifestation of their own strong ties. What had started as a lark in Paris, a way to propel them into an unknown world, had become in the sand hills a necessity, Charlotte conceded. They had combined their strength and convinced themselves they could conquer any world they chose. The best of each got coaxed out of hiding.

Then one fine May evening, after the wind died down and the workers disbanded for the day and every object in their homes was where it belonged, Charlotte and Lydia set a narrow table and two narrow chairs on their walkway to commemorate the completion of the houses and the naming of their homestead: Twin House Farm. The name had required almost as much consideration as the house-planning.

Sitting in the peaceful moonlit night, enjoying an adequate wine from one of several cases Sam had shipped out to them, they talked of summer plantings and fall harvests. They considered beginning an apple orchard. Fresh fruit was grown only one hundred miles away, but the exorbitant freight rates made buying it too great a luxury for nearly everyone, themselves included. Eventually, however, their present gave way to their future when they decided to write their friends to come join them as soon as possible.

"They will help us charm this town," Lydia said. "Then if Sam would only come!"

Since Sam no longer seemed real to Charlotte, she didn't mind his inclusion, except as he affected Lydia. "Why not do our own charming right now?" Charlotte asked. "We should give a dance for all our neighbors and friends to show everyone what we're about. Let them see for themselves that we're no threat."

"I don't understand why anyone thinks we are, and I confess, I'm disappointed. I never thought we'd find such a conventional society."

"They're afraid we'll upset the order of things. They want stability, the same as we do," Charlotte said consolingly. They had come to taking turns reciting to each other their litany on the town's ways. "Just don't forget that with all their conventional ways, they aren't like our old world. They're not leeching off the rest of society. Here you are important if you produce, contribute, and we need to show them that we'll produce and contribute too."

"Then by all means let's hold a dance and impress everyone with our productivity!"

This prompted Charlotte to propose a toast to their forging of a new way: to two minds for twice as much wisdom, to two homesteads for twice as much land, to two houses for twice as much space. "The best we have to offer will be interchangeable; while the worst, with effort, will disappear."

As they surveyed their dunes from the vantage point of their walkways, Charlotte wondered if, when their friends came, they would be able to tell how much already they had changed.

"This is ours. Our very own," Lydia said, her voice filled with pride and wonder.

"Nobody can take it away from us," Charlotte added. "We are propertied women!"

Whereupon they rose for one more triumphant toast—to the propertied women of Twin House Farm.

24 Of all life's distractions, Lydia mused, a dance is one of the better. Standing under the walkway on this ink-blue spring night, she could hear above her the music and chatter and shuffling of feet. Clearing their two upper floors—hers for dancing, Charlotte's for mingling—had worked beautifully.

Whatever reserve the community felt toward them had been dispelled for this evening. In fact, this celebration was turning into the perfect way to repair the somewhat shredded garment of amiability between themselves and Huddleston's citizens. So far, the guests had expressed nothing but admiration for what they saw here. The women especially had been taken with the interiors of the houses. While the decor might not have been what they themselves would have chosen, they appreciated the style and taste that had gone into the planning: Lydia's unadorned sleigh bed facing Charlotte's, Lydia's Shaker rocking chair pulled to the same corner near the fireplace as Charlotte's, Lydia's painting of a horse facing Charlotte's painting of a horse. This last, the paintings, had been a sop to Charlotte on Lydia's part; Lydia caring nothing about horses. But then Lydia had her porcelain collection, which Charlotte didn't share.

If the women could be won over, Lydia was convinced, the men would soon follow, since they appeared more perplexed than condemning of two independent women. Though farmers and land speculators and merchants might not understand the wish for a simpler, possibly radical, life, they sympathized with the impulse to start a new one. And so knowledgeable and so curious had Lydia and Charlotte become about the price of real estate and the benefits of various crops that at times Lydia felt that these men didn't begrudge them their independence as long as they didn't give their wives too many ideas.

But this was not a time for fretting or calculating, Lydia decided, stroking the grand-mère's shawl and swaying her shoulders in time with the music. Given the finite nature of human endeavor and emotion, an evening's worth of goodwill should be delighted in and not compromised because it might lead to something more. Yes, an evening such as this deserved a certain weight beyond what it held on its own. Pleased to be a part of it—to be a part of life—she turned to join the dancing.

It was then she heard a moan coming from the barn. At first, unsure of its origin, she hesitated to investigate without a gun. As she stood listening in the clear, sharp night the sound came again. This time she recognized an unmistakable human cry and without any hesitation plunged into the darkness of the barn, where she found Geneviève Beauchamp in the arms of Leonard Majors.

For a minute it was hard to tell which of the three was more startled. A man of no curiosity and little means, this dull, hardworking neighbor was not at all suitable for the young French girl, whom he was evidently trying to seduce. Geneviève broke away and ran back to the dance, but Leonard Majors, smelling of alcohol and strong tobacco, stood there defiantly. What had possessed her and Charlotte to invite such a repulsive man?

"You should be ashamed of yourself," she said before turning around. "She's impressionable and not experienced. Leave her alone."

"That girl knows a thing or two more than you, I dare to venture, prissy miss."

Lydia stopped, and turned back toward him. "I know that men like you foul women with your filth." Her eyes had grown accustomed to the darkness, and she saw him looking her up and down. When he moved toward her, she stepped back.

"Oh, I'll marry her, missy. Don't worry yourself on that account," he answered.

"That account, sir, is exactly what I'm talking about, and if you see her again, I'll report this to her parents."

"You want her to get a beatin' within an inch of her life? Come on now, missy," he wheedled, his voice oozing with suggestion. His breathing had become heavier, and he kept staring at her breasts, causing her inexplicable shame.

"Stop calling me missy!" Lydia snapped, but suddenly she knew that she'd let him engage her too long, that the atmosphere had become charged, a dangerous intensity developing between them. As she turned away, he grabbed her arm and pulled her back. Before she could stop him, he kissed her hard on the mouth. She clamped his lower lip between her teeth as tight as she could.

He let go, raised his arm to strike her but ended up laughing. "You might be prissy but you've got spunk. Maybe you're not such a sainted figure after all." Now he blocked her exit.

"Let me go or I'll scream," she said. Her firm, clear voice belied the panic that was settling in. Both knew that no one would hear her if she did, and, worse, he was strong enough to keep her quiet. If I had my gun, she thought, I would kill this man, and he knows that, too. With a terrible certainty Lydia realized this only aroused him more. They stood in the darkness, hearing each other's breathing, hearing the music from a lighted world.

"Let's rejoin the others now," Lydia said in a sociable but stern tone, hoping to remind him of who he was, who she was, where they were. She picked up her skirts to go inside, prepared to scream and knee him in the groin if necessary, but in one quick lunge he had pinned her to the floor with his body. One hand covered her mouth, the other clawed her breast. Then suddenly his mouth crushed hers and his hands pushed up her dress and petticoats. Her fists slamming into him only excited him more.

"I would advise you to move away from 'er right now, or I'll be obliged to put this ax through your skull."

As Majors looked around, Lydia rolled free. The voice belonged to Norah O'Connor, and she was as good as her word. Ready to strike, she held the ax above her head, all the while keeping just out of reach of the man.

"Didn't mean nothin' by it," Majors mumbled as he stumbled away.

Lydia grabbed the ax from Norah and whirled toward her attacker. "You bastard! You bastard!" He began to run and she started after him, but Norah stopped her. "He ain't worth the bother of a killin'. Let 'im go."

As a shudder coarsed through Lydia's body, she dropped the ax and sat on a bench, putting her head down on her knees. Without a word Norah grasped her shoulders and pulled her over into her own lap and rocked them both back and forth. Lydia began to sob, the assault only partially explaining her sense of desolation. For a long while Norah held her, until finally she realized the woman was trembling.

Rousing herself, she asked, "If he hadn't stopped, what would you have done?"

"What I said—split his ugly skull right down the middle."

The ferocity of the response caused Lydia to smile. "Well, I'm indebted to you, and I'll try to find a way to repay you."

"I didn't do it for money," Norah answered sharply.

"Of course not. But I won't forget, and someday I'll make it up to you," Lydia said and rearranged her clothes to go back inside.

"Beggin' ma'am's pardon, I think you'd better tidy up your hair."

"And my eyes?" Lydia stepped into the light. "Can you tell I've been crying?"

"Say you got a fleck of sand in one, and you've been out here tryin' to get it out."

"You are resourceful, Norah."

"Have to be."

"You do, don't you?" Absentmindedly, Lydia began removing the pin holding up her hair. Without having thought about it before, for she hadn't cared enough to bother, Lydia sensed that Norah didn't really like her. "Why did you stop me from killing him, for surely I would have?"

"It would have ruined all this." Norah's arms took in the countryside.

"You care about it?" Lydia's surprise showed in her voice.

"Not the land. I don't go all mushy over sand and dirt like you people. It's more like . . ." She faltered, then resumed. "It's more like it has to do with the notion of women figurin' out different ways for themselves. My kind do it all the time in the cities. Domestic work, mainly. It's a good enough wage and better than working yourself to death in a factory or something worse, but it doesn't show in the world. This shows in the world."

They shivered in the cool night air, reminding Lydia that they each had to attend to their duties. Still, she reluctantly gave up the conversation.

"One more thing, Norah: I would rather we told no one about this incident."

"Never occurred to me we would."

Lydia seized Norah's arm: "And I will destroy him, Norah. One way or another, I will make him pay."

"Never occurred to me you wouldn't."

Upstairs was still filled with dancers and music and warmth. Immediately, Benjamin Leggett came to claim Lydia for the next reel, and to the fiddler's tune and the swishing of petticoats, she danced. And in the swirl of black cloth jackets and white lace and yellow silks and green taffeta, she let go of the terror she had felt in the barn and rejoiced in her salvation, thanks to Norah and her cooler head.

Where was she now? Lydia wondered and thought back to Norah's solace and the surfacing in herself of some shapeless unnamed need for maternal comfort.

Lydia's mother and grandmother had not been affectionate women, though her grandmother, most especially, had loved her. And Lydia had not expected much affection from anyone; at least, until this moment she hadn't suspected she did. But along with her tears there rose within her a lamentation for time faintly recalled and seldom hers when a child's world is made perfect by soft, enfolding arms, a time when trust should be complete.

What had moved Lydia to a place beyond memory was an instinct in Norah that allowed generosity and courage to overcome her grudging, hostile nature. And would they ever talk like that again? She had not known Norah had that many words inside her. Notions, too. As many notions as the rest of us, she thought. And enough wisdom to understand that Lydia's humiliation must remain buried in the privacy of night.

# 25

While the dance generated some goodwill, Charlotte and Lydia received no invitation to join the Literary Society, nor did the community hug them to its collective bosom.

This state of affairs didn't daunt them, however. The spring crops came up fresh and green; the sheep thrived; the hens fluffed their feathers and laid large eggs; the two cows gave forth five gallons of milk a day. A constant flow of sunny, windy days filled them with excitement and a sense of possibility, the wind adding to the rapidly moving images and events of testing, learning, building.

To free up Sally and Norah for other tasks, a temporary cook was brought in to prepare the midday meal for the field hands, but the amount of work required didn't diminish. Soon Lydia and Charlotte also found themselves washing and baking and cleaning and mending and gardening and milking and gathering eggs and shooting gophers. Then, impatient with the progress the men made in clearing and plowing and planting and fencing, the new owners took to the fields, breaking up sod and erecting barbed-wire fencing, and in short order they began to notice the men working harder.

"They don't want us to show them up," Charlotte commented, and she was right.

Although their house and their work thoroughly absorbed them, all this activity reduced their time for contemplation. Some evenings they did make time to read to each other, a habit they'd begun while crossing the Atlantic, but their physical exhaustion and need to discuss their various projects curtailed that favorite pastime too. Occasionally, on a rare rainy day, they would read *Jane Eyre* together and so enjoyed the book that they would push themselves to stay up late reading it.

One evening Lydia was reading the scene in which Jane discovers that Rochester has a wife, when she glanced up to find Charlotte weeping, her body silently shaking with sobs.

"I'm the one who succumbed to romantic twaddle, not you!" Lydia gently teased.

While she attributed the emotional outburst to Charlotte's fatigue, she knew that beneath Charlotte's abiding calm lay a core of anguish that she constantly fought. They could point more easily to—and laugh at—Lydia's agitation, and certainly her anxious moments stirred up an abundance of commotion; but in truth, Charlotte's depths were more worrisome.

When Lydia suggested they go on to bed, Charlotte stubbornly insisted that they continue and, indeed, kept them up long past bedtime, straining their bodies' endurance.

Intrusions from the outside world, of course, were not only inevitable but welcomed. At their urging, Mr. Leggett took them to a session of the Farmers' Alliance convention.

"These men won't know what to make of the two of you," he warned them as they approached the Presbyterian church, where the convention was taking place.

"Oh, but Lydia and I know what to make of men, Mr. Leggett, which is why it's important to observe their arguments firsthand." Charlotte genuinely liked Benjamin Leggett, but he kept missing the point where she and Lydia were concerned.

"Well, then, perhaps you'll be willing to enlighten me. I expect we're entering the Tower of Babel."

He gripped each woman's arm tightly as they walked into the church auditorium. "Just ignore the stares," he instructed.

But Charlotte and Lydia were too busy staring themselves to worry about the impression they might make. Men were clustered in groups, telling each other jokes, chewing tobacco, talking about crops. It was hard to imagine them intent on the alliance's goals, which included encouraging better agricultural practices and working together for more equitable tariffs and higher prices for produce.

"Some of them look awfully well dressed for farmers," Lydia said to her companions.

"Some of them are not farmers. Some are railroad men. Some represent boards of trade. Some, like me, are here because our banks or loan companies have a stake in the financial future of this area," Mr. Leggett explained. "And everyone is going to have a say."

And everyone did, though it was doubtful if anyone could make out the messages, which were on the whole disjointed, rambling, full of either nonspecific complaints or vague justifications.

Most felt the Republicans had given the railroads a lot of money for ties and grading but received only a fraction of the cost back from their investment. "Why should we subsidize the railroads? They're doing a lot better than we are, and they're gouging us," speaker after speaker said. Unlike the larger community, these people, on the whole, were anti-railroad, almost all believing that arbitrary freight rates were hurting them—it cost as much to haul from Kansas City as it did from Denver. In fact, one of the alliance's objectives was to resist the encroachment of the railroads and push for government regulation of them, and the consensus was that this could never be accomplished without a new independent political party.

"I can understand their antipathy to the Republicans, but why aren't the Democrats mentioned at all?" Lydia asked.

Benjamin Leggett explained that the Democratic party was still considered the southern enemy they had fought so hard against back in the 1850s long before other states got involved. Though almost everybody now voted Republican, this convention gave voice to the discontented. "They're ahead of their time, but they don't have a coherent program or take themselves seriously enough."

By the end of the day everyone, including Lydia and Charlotte, looked exhausted, if not defeated. The one thing the women had most desired to gain—tips on farming the land and raising sheep—had gotten lost in the debate. No agreement at all emerged on what crops were best suited for the area, when to plant the winter wheat, whether sowing deep or shallow had proven most successful, or what tools and outbuildings were really necessary.

These men were unknowing of themselves if not their needs, Lydia decided, her impatience verging on exasperation. She had to keep reminding herself that they were dissidents, even if in this case, the dissent had to do with carving their own niche into the system. At least they weren't passive or smug or absurdly greedy—traits that were all too prevalent these days. Yet she couldn't help wishing they weren't quite so vague in their discord.

"We could straighten them out in two days if they would let us," Lydia whispered.

"I'm afraid their saviors don't come in skirts," Charlotte whispered back.

"We're still learning, and not very well at that. The fact is, farmers as a group are pretty much loners who like to go their own way," Benjamin Leggett explained. "Even in the worst of times they have difficulty organizing, and this is by no means the worst of times.

"If you listen carefully under that rumble, they're a pretty optimistic bunch right now. They just want as much of their share of business as they can get, but they're not concerned enough to do much about it."

"You seem to be in sympathy with them," Lydia said. Although she knew Leggett to be a fair and compassionate man in many ways, she thought of him as primarily a banker and therefore in cahoots with the business establishment.

"They've got some legitimate gripes, no doubt."

"I think we'll do much better without the Farmers' Alliance," Charlotte said emphatically. "We are not peasants to rise up and take the land by force."

Looking puzzled, Benjamin Leggett turned to Lydia, who smiled and elaborated: "Charlotte's family has owned land for centuries, and she assumes owning land is owning business and government."

"Whatever you're saying about me, I quite agree, I am sure, especially if it is that I intend to own land on that order once again, this time without the help of kings and queens and feudal lords. We'll take ourselves seriously and teach these men to do the same."

Although the speeches had bored Lydia and Charlotte and they'd had to go all the way over to the Leggetts' privy every time they wished to relieve themselves, they agreed that the day had been interesting, if not instructive.

"We needed your cousin's trousers," Charlotte had commented to Lydia in front of Mr. Leggett late in the afternoon. The remark served to bring Lydia back to the pleasure in their own situation and remind her they were in this arena but not of it.

Again Leggett looked to Lydia for an explanation; this time she only smiled.

Before the spring was out, they ended up purchasing trousers of their own—overalls, which they ordered from Chicago rather than buying them in Huddleston. When the hired hands were around, they were careful not to wear them. Corsets they ceased wearing altogether except on special occasions, though there were more of those than they had expected.

To ingratiate themselves with the townspeople, they participated in community and church activities whenever possible, including card parties, dances, and ice-cream socials. At Easter, following local tradition, they gave small presents packed in egg-shaped boxes to a few of their neighbors. They talked of crops and fashions and recipes. They even talked of babies, about which neither knew a thing.

"I vaguely remember when Sammy was born," Lydia confessed one night to Charlotte after they returned from a community picnic. "I would sneak in and hold him when no one was looking, but I once dropped him on the floor when he wet his diaper on my favorite pink dress."

"I thought we came here to escape conventional living," Charlotte complained. "These people are as set in their ways as the French."

"But as you've pointed out, people here have a real opportunity to reinvent themselves, if only they weren't so certain about what constitutes right and wrong."

"Yes, that most of all."

"This state was not called Bleeding Kansas for nothing," Mr. Leggett said one afternoon. "It's unique in history as a sounding ground for the war that was coming, for people came here, both slaveholders and abolitionists, to stake out claims. The first battles were essentially fought in this state. Whoever won Kansas would win the war. The abolitionists won, but the cost was high for everyone, including the Negro."

"I know there aren't many former slaves around here, but those who do live here are seldom included in social groups," Charlotte commented.

"Not very often. During the war there was support for the Negro, but once it was won, old prejudices returned. The battle here, and almost everywhere else, had more to do with preserving the Union.

"Fact is, western Kansas is much more open to the different races than the rest of the state or anywhere else. We need everyone we can get to help make this place work, and we're not particular about what people look like or where they came from."

"I wish that applied to their attitude toward women as well," Charlotte said. She hadn't expected to feel so diminished by the disapproval she and Lydia confronted for failing to meet the expectations of others. Her mother's revenge continued on, for now the town's criticism cut the same way her mother's once had. Of course, over time, she'd trained herself to disregard most of her mother's castigations, or so she'd thought. Perhaps her reaction to present rebukes was only a recurrence of her earlier vulnerability.

"Independent women take some getting used to," Benjamin Leggett told her. Be patient. A lot of the locals are good people who fought valiantly for a just cause. But just causes sometimes create a self-righteous attitude."

"This conversation is very boring, Mr. Leggett," Emma interrupted, walking in with a pitcher of lemonade. "You must stop monopolizing these young women and find them some men their own age. If not, I'll take matters into my own hands."

But at young men their own age they drew an absolute line, and even Emma Leggett's enthusiasm, a welcome sign to all, was not enough to make them budge from their position.

"Do people think us very strange?" Charlotte, half teasing, asked Mr. Leggett.

"Yes, I'm afraid they do," he gravely responded. "And some people are out to make mischief for you."

His veiled warning made Lydia wonder if one of those people could be Leonard Majors, though surely he would have better sense.

"You are brave women, and people tolerate you for that reason, but don't push them too far," Emma warned. "You'll have enough tests as it is." For a moment her eyes and mind were as clear and sharp as the spring's early markings.

Since that first night at the Leggetts', they'd discovered that the couple had lost two babies within a year of each other and within two years of moving to Kansas. One had died of a high fever and the other had fallen out of a runaway buggy. At that period neither a doctor nor a midwife lived in the vicinity, and no determination of the true cause of death was ever made on either. (The thrown child had few bruises.) Over time this not knowing had come to haunt Emma Leggett as much as the deaths themselves.

After the second burial, her mother had moved west to comfort her, but that summer she had been caught on the outskirts of town in a brushfire, a common occurrence, and she too had died—in her case an agonizing death over a period of days.

Now the community built barriers around the town in the summer as protection from these wildfires, usually set off by lightning, but nobody could protect Emma Leggett from her own fires. Laudanum had helped for a while, but her neighbors were afraid she suffered from opium drunkenness, a malady from which more than a few women suffered. Mr. Leggett had finally put a stop to the laudanum through sheer will and the threat of death to anyone who supplied her.

She had improved and, thanks to the encouragement of Roberta Brown and other women, once again became active in the community and took a renewed interest in her house. Lately, though, she had begun to slip back from time to time into a world inhabited by ghosts, a world that Benjamin Leggett tried to ignore, since he could not control ghosts. Charlotte and Lydia sympathized with the Leggetts but rejoiced that, for the moment, the work at Twin House Farm had all but banished most of their own ghosts. The tangible world was quite enough to handle.

The next test came sooner than expected. In the middle of one of their first baling nights, when stars were everywhere and the sky was lighted by a full moon, Charlotte awoke to the sound of a sheep's bleating.

"It's that ewe who has moped around here all week," she said a few minutes later, as Lydia held the lantern on the way to the barn. "Tonight we learn about babies, I think."

"The poor creature! Her wails will wake God. Would a little brandy help her?"

"No time to go back for it. Maybe the wails will wake Sally or Norah as well as God."

"Don't count on it. Where are those damn hired hands?" Lydia asked, but they both knew the question was only a form of self-accusation.

Lydia hadn't wanted to put money into any more buildings or full-time employees, preferring to invest in farm machinery and more land instead. "It's not as if we've never seen a lamb born before," Charlotte said, trying to reassure them both.

"This is not a routine birth," Lydia answered grimly even before they found the mother in the light.

What they saw was not a pretty sight. The baby's head was out but twisted the wrong way, and its shoulder appeared to be stuck inside the mother. Not only was the bloody birth sac still on the head, but blood also oozed in a steady stream around the mother's vagina.

"Norah! Sally!" Lydia yelled.

"You soothe the mother while I try to extract the baby's upper body," Charlotte instructed.

"We don't know anything about this sort of thing. We have observed only normal births," Lydia pointed out.

"In France I once watched our stableboy assist in a difficult foal delivery," Charlotte said as she gently turned the head. "That foal was a beauty when she finally came."

She soon wrested free a shoulder, but the ewe seemed incapable of expelling the rest of the lamb's body. "A beautiful brown baby, that foal was," Charlotte said, still working, perspiration now appearing on her forehead.

"If I held the ewe and leaned on her shoulders, do you think you could pull harder?"

"We'll try this another minute."

"I think I hear the girls," Lydia answered, relieved to get help. She ran to the barn door and shouted for whiskey.

"With whiskey this mother might not contract at all."

"I don't care. She's suffering, can't you tell?"

"Of course I can tell, Lydia," Charlotte answered sharply.

"So tell me more about the foal," Lydia said to calm them both. When Sally and Norah appeared, Lydia had hold of the shoulders while Charlotte continued her struggle.

"Do you know anything about this?" Lydia asked. When no answer was forthcoming from the startled women, she yelled, "Then give this animal some of that whiskey!"

"With what, ma'am?" Sally asked.

"I don't know with what. Here," Lydia said holding out her cupped hand. "Pour some in here."

Before the action could be completed, a terrible bleat, then a gushing sound, came out of the writhing ewe. "Blessed Mary, mother of Jesus," Charlotte shouted in joy, but Norah and Sally screamed and clutched each other. Along with the expulsion of the baby and the birth sac had come the mother's complete entrails.

The four women stared in horror. After seconds that felt like hours, Charlotte asked for the whiskey bottle. She took several large gulps and instructed the others to do the same. "Now force as much as you can down her throat."

This, however, proved impossible, so Charlotte poured some over the grisly pink-white intestines splotched with blood and poured the rest over her own hands.

"Would you like to know the name of that foal?" Charlotte asked, her tongue heavy with dryness as she picked up the insides with her bare hands and began stuffing them back inside the bellowing animal.

"Yes," Lydia answered. "The name of the foal. And the mother's, too. What color was the mare?" She picked up the bottle and used it to help shove them farther in.

"The mare's face had a pretty white streak. . . . The uterus—which way does it go?" Charlotte asked no one in particular.

"Try the other way, ma'am. That looks more right," Norah answered.

"We'll need something to sew with," Lydia said.

"Baling wire. I'll get baling wire," Sally suggested.

The women took turns pulling the wire through the folds of the sheep while the others held her still.

"This should hold until the doctor comes tomorrow," Charlotte said, when finally the work was done.

Sally insisted on staying the rest of the night. Fortunately, they already owned a bottle for providing lambs with goat's milk, having had one recalcitrant mother who refused to nurse her offspring.

"What were the names of those horses?" Lydia asked Charlotte on the way back to the house.

Charlotte laughed. "I have no idea. But it's just as well. Trying to remember those names is what kept me going."

A medical doctor rather than a veterinarian paid a call the next day. "I don't know how you did it, but I think she's going to mend so long as someone tends her closely."

"No problem there. Sally fell in love with her last night. She refused to be spelled for fear we'd not do things right," Lydia said lightly. "Charlotte got us through the crisis, though, with her good sense and calm hands."

Charlotte did not protest. She and Lydia had passed some inner test of strength and skill. The spring had been kind to them. If there had been no time to search for "essence," they'd come upon something else of worth in themselves and now could rejoice in the arrival of their friends.

26 They all came at once, dressed for June in other worlds. Each, without consultation, had given her costume a great deal of consideration. Each had chosen white. Anne in her white cotton, trimmed with a navy collar, looked ready for punting on the Thames. Marceline, draped in gauze, was attired for a garden party at the Comtesse de Gramont's summer home. Isabelle had donned a robed ensemble befitting a convent novice.

Though still agonizing over ways to shed her skin, Isabelle looked instead as if she'd added more, only her large frame preventing her from total immersion in the flowing garment. With the same aplomb they assumed as they strode through the most elegant of salons, they descended from the train into the intense heat, dust, and wind of Kansas.

From Chicago on, dust had settled over their hair, their skin, and their clothes, including the white dresses that had been so carefully packed for their journey. Marceline declared she'd never seen dust in such variety and colors—red, beige, white—and in so many textures, from fine powder to pebbly grain. None of the women really minded, for they regarded the inconvenience as part of the adventure. All had received letters describing the building of the houses, the rigors of farming, the glories of waving grass and limitless horizons, the excitement of herding sheep, the joys of freedom. Compared to these dramas, what was dust or heat?

To accommodate everyone, Charlotte and Lydia had purchased a large two-horse carriage, and Norah brought the old buggy to carry the trunks. As their little procession made its way through town, Lydia pointed out the larger stone buildings, which included the banks, the Presbyterian church, and the new hospital, where surgery was performed with the help of kerosene lamps. Much to Charlotte's and Lydia's pleasure, the visitors duly noted each building and made approving murmurs.

Charlotte was happy to find the streets had been sprinkled to keep the dust down—not always the case. "And aren't our wide boulevards wonderful? You would never find streets like this in a French village," she said.

"Indeed not in a French village," Marceline replied wryly.

"And I'm glad there are none of those little froufrou shops that dot our French towns," Isabelle added.

Until she heard that remark, Charlotte had quite forgotten that every nook and cranny in France stayed well supplied with gorgeous, bountiful, colorful arrangements of goods even in places where there appeared to be no shoppers.

Done up in her white, if sand-dusted, gauze, Marceline looked more fetching than ever. She too was running from her past and, like Lydia, specifically from Gabriel de Rochefort. Unlike Lydia, Marceline did not so much mind his other affairs so much as his indiscretion in handling them, or so she'd written Charlotte, who passed the information on to Lydia.

After all, Lydia had gotten over the baron, and besides, Charlotte never kept secrets from her twin—well, almost never. Last week Frank Bailey had written that he planned to visit in the third week of July, and Charlotte hadn't yet found an opportune time to discuss this with Lydia. Not that Lydia was overtly antagonistic toward him, but she avoided all mention of him. Now that their friends were here, telling her would be easier, for she'd be in high spirits. Possibly she wouldn't mind at all on a day such as this, Charlotte decided.

Kansas had plumped and preened and cleared its skies to reveal a warm, glittering sun for all to see. It paraded owls, quail, pheasants, ducks, wild turkeys, and red-legged mallards. This was its glory time, and today the foxes and white-nosed rabbits and black squirrels saluted while the fields of wildflowers, summer grasses, wheat, and alfalfa displayed themselves to best advantage.

"After the turn in the road, you'll begin to see Twin House Farm," Charlotte announced, delighted that their own fields of alfalfa were already being cut and bailed. Charlotte wished she could describe to these women just what that harvest represented.

"We've produced this crop from start to finish," Lydia proudly informed everyone.

"And what will you do with it?" Anne asked politely. She was as pale and drawn as when Charlotte had first met her, but there hung about her, Charlotte thought, a sweetness that brimmed with melancholy.

"We'll feed the sheep," Lydia answered. "We're now in the process of carding their wool to be spun, woven, and sewn into duvets for everyone."

"Will we get to do that?" Isabelle asked, for she much enjoyed all kinds of handwork.

"If we ever expect to see them completed, I think we'd better," Marceline put in as she took in the landscape. "You can see so *far* here, can't you?" She sounded bewildered.

"But you've created paradise," Anne said, placing a trembling hand over her heart. "I've dreamed about this for months now, and it's more than I ever hoped or imagined."

"I have to warn you about the people, though," Lydia told her. "Everyone will go to great lengths to find you a husband. All the single men are looking for wives to do household chores and help them with the farmwork."

She and Charlotte then explained how, in many cases, they wanted someone to raise their children whose mothers had died during childbirth or from disease or exhaustion. Except for parties and celebrations, the women of Kansas never stopped working, even the fortunate wives with money.

"Yet no one can understand why we're not interested in becoming wifely chattels," Charlotte said.

"Worse than the French," Isabelle commented.

"Even so, women do have more rights here than in most places. We can vote in school elections, and there's talk of woman suffrage," Charlotte felt compelled to point out. "For the most part, women's efforts are recognized and respected."

"For the most part," Lydia repeated. "But take your first look at our twin houses."

To Charlotte they rose in austere splendor, the whitewash fresh, the windows sparkling without their usual film of sand. They reminded her of two ships greeting each other, reaching out to each other. As Anne said, she and Lydia had created a paradise. For the first time, however, she noticed just how stark these two houses, standing proud and tall, connected by their graceful walkway, might appear to eyes not startled by the wonder of any house at all. She also realized that this paradise, even now, decked in all its finery, offered up no lushness, no hundred shades of green or endless varieties of flowers and fields. Only the sturdiest flora survived here on this copper-hard soil.

Inside, as they were giving their friends the grand tour, Charlotte allowed herself to see her home as Isabelle and Marceline might see it: the rooms smaller than she usually thought of them; her library, a shabby imitation of Papa's; the bedrooms, with their sloping ceilings, confining— rooms that only a short time ago Charlotte would have considered servants' quarters. Norah and Sally slept in the basement, and the hired hands now stayed in an outbuilding. Even the comtesse would not have kept servants out there.

Could these visitors possibly understand that many very respectable families lived in homes that were no more than a shelter clawed out of the earth? Charlotte doubted it. Until she and Lydia arrived a few months ago, no one had explained to them about sod houses or dugouts, or even how resistant the land was to hoes and shovels. One had to labor over it unceasingly to force it to release its treasures. How could she explain to their friends that digging their cellars had felt like wresting a trophy from the earth?

Her spirits brightened again when Sally and Norah served them an evening's feast of local food—biscuits with blackberry jam, a fish pudding, veal cutlets with new potatoes that the Leggetts had given them for the occasion, apple dumplings, and ice cream made with their own cows' milk and their own hens' eggs.

Only after they assembled in her parlor for cigars and brandy, transported from France by Isabelle, did Charlotte feel the serenity of the houses restored to her.

"And how is the pursuit of life's mystery going? That matter we've not yet discussed," Marceline said, after her first sip of brandy.

"They seem to be well on their way to solving it," Anne commented.

"If we are, it's by indirection," Charlotte replied. "The world around us is reality enough for now."

"That may not be so bad," Isabelle said. "I was a little afraid of finding two otherworldly spirits that I would hardly recognize, far along some mystical path that I couldn't follow."

"Or worse," Marceline added, "two odiously good, pure women, who would bore us to death."

Anne laughed—her first real laugh. "Be assured that Lydia Fulgate is incapable of boring anyone. Lydia darling, forgive me, but at this very moment that expression on your face of both hurt and flattery is the quintessential you: a mass of contradictions and complications."

Lydia looked reassured and asked, with self-deprecating humor, "And you think there is nothing under these contradictions? That living close to the center of ourselves, in the country, which some see as God's testing ground, won't help unravel some of them?"

"And what's wrong with contradictions and complications? I quite love you as you are," Anne answered.

"Please do not disabuse me of the notion of transformation so soon. I've only been here for a few hours—days, if you count the train ride— and I like to think I have already made a change, Marceline said.

"I didn't mean to imply that there has been no change for the better," Charlotte responded defensively. "Lydia and I are both changed. It's simply that we haven't had a great deal of time to contemplate *meanings*."

"I assure you I'm starving for a diet of real life with meaning and purpose," Anne said in a more serious tone than the others had assumed.

"But if I do nothing more than enjoy a good cigar and a sip of brandy and gather ducks' eggs and learn to bake bread and sweat in the sunshine and answer to no one, then that is as close to a center as I ever have to discover." She suddenly laid her head back on the chair and gave a high, nervous laugh. "I've worn myself out with all my talk; I'm out of the habit." Even in candlelight her pallor was evident, and she looked exhausted, possibly ill.

"This has been a long day for all of us," Marceline said quickly. "We should rest in order to have strength enough to begin gathering those eggs and peeking under rocks for essence, or whatever it is we plan to look for tomorrow."

"Knowing you and your lazy ways, it will take all your energy just to stir your body by morning; your poor essence will have to wait a while." Charlotte replied.

"Please note, everyone, that I am only hurt and not in the least flattered."

Charlotte, delirious with happiness, wanted to hug them all. You've completed the dream, haven't they, Lydia?"

"Absolutely! So long as nobody strives for perfection. As Marceline says, the odiously good are insufferable, and already you're all about as perfect as I can stand you to be."

Lydia had risen and the others were following suit when Anne motioned them back down. "I have a surprise that I've saved for last." She fumbled in her pocket and produced a letter. "For you, Lydia."

"From Samuel," Lydia said the moment she held it, and instantly Charlotte's heady joy in the occasion vanished. After a cursory glance through the letter, Lydia burst into tears. "He's coming!" she announced, elation in her voice, on her face. "He is *moving* here."

# 27

On their first day they did learn to gather eggs—hens', not ducks.' Each retrieved one and each fried one, after being shown how.

The next day, they received instructions on milking cows, and while this did not prove quite as successful as the first lesson, each took her turn drinking some of the milk and churning the butter.

To no one's surprise, Isabelle proved to be the most apt pupil. In the second week of her stay, she and Lydia, hoping to catch trout for dinner, had gone to the stream, where they surprised a rattlesnake sunning itself on a rock. Remaining calm, Isabelle raised a crude bench they had with them over her head and brought it down precisely on the snake's head. She continued pressing down firmly even as the snake's body writhed around the bench so high it almost touched her hand.

"Be careful," Lydia kept repeating, as if there were any possibility Isabelle would be otherwise. Minutes passed before the snake's movements stopped. Then Isabelle, satisfied that it was dead, righted the bench and rubbed her hands together.

Looking at Lydia, she raised her eyebrows. "I can now state I have experienced an intense feeling," she said with something akin to nonchalance, "the snake's as well as mine."

Lydia threw back her head and laughed. Isabelle eased herself into life with more grace than anyone she'd ever known, and Lydia told her so. Brushing perspiration from her forehead, Isabelle glowed.

A week later Marceline was digging in the vegetable patch when she suddenly began shouting to all the world, "My hands are ruined! My hands are ruined!"

Lydia, who was breaking up sod in a field, dropped her hoe and ran toward the noise; Anne, baking pies in the house, dropped one and also ran. The rescuers found their friend sitting on the ground, crying and looking at her splayed hands. Lydia knelt beside her.

"They're swollen and *red*," Marceline sobbed, holding her red hands out for examination.

"What can we do?" Anne asked anxiously.

"We can put buttermilk on them to relieve the burning—if they are burning."

Marceline shook her head. "Who cares about burning! They are *red*! I've ruined my hands to grow some damnable things called mustard greens, and I am not ready to have ruined hands!"

Anne continued to look alarmed, but Lydia barely hid a smile. "Sunburn heals quickly enough. If you'd worn your gloves, as we told you to do, this wouldn't have happened."

"They are bleeding, too!"

"As I said, you should have worn gloves. Now go inside with Anne and have some lemonade and a little rest. Your hands will recover." Lydia and Anne assisted Marceline up by her elbows.

"They'll be freckled forever," she said as Anne guided her toward the house, as if her legs were the affliction. "And gloves are too hot to wear in this weather."

"Then don't work outside," Anne suggested sympathetically. "It's a wonder you don't have windburn yet."

"Of course I'll work outside. I shall not be vanquished, I assure you." Lydia and Anne shot each other a quick grin.


After the first few days Marceline had begun talking openly about Gabriel de Rochefort and their problems. Marceline hadn't seen him for months after Lydia's breakup with him. Later, when they ran into each other occasionally, usually somewhere in Isabelle's orbit, Marceline didn't take him seriously. Being of a practical bent, they understood the futility of pursuing each other and, as a result, became comrades of sorts. While not so intimate a confidante as Isabelle, Marceline did become someone whom Gabriel regarded as more than an object to serve his pleasure, or his purpose, thus he didn't necessarily view her as a potential adversary. As soon as he realized this, he fell in love with her. She was his first and only real love, he'd declared.

Lydia cringed when she heard this last, her vanity being such that she preferred to think him a cad who nevertheless had loved her for a while and in a way. All the same, she enjoyed the idea of someone giving him his comeuppance, as Granny would have said; and, evidently Marceline had done just that.

Gabriel went so far as to propose marriage, but Marceline wasn't for a minute willing to pretend that such a possibility existed. She became impatient when he persisted, but her stubbornness only whetted his desire. Once he even pledged fidelity, a vow she found amusing. Finally she fled to Kansas, for to love him was to invite heartbreak and poverty, she confided to the group. "At any rate, he began to bore me."

Now he wrote long letters to her and Isabelle imploring them to come back, complaining that they had deserted him. Isabelle conscientiously answered each one since, for all his foibles, she cared about her cousin. This Lydia understood all too well.

Surrounded though she was by friends, her heart ached at Sam's absence. But now he was coming, and she would find him a fine piece of land. In his last letter he'd written of his plans to move his family to Kansas before the end of summer.

Unwisely, she had not yet told Charlotte that he would arrive sooner rather than later, but there was still time, she reasoned. At the upcoming community lawn party Charlotte could absorb the news in a happy frame of mind. Later on, Lydia could assure Charlotte that Sam's presence would have no affect on their relationship. How strange to feel a silence growing up where Sam was concerned, but Lydia was afraid her friend didn't share her own enthusiasm about her brother.

Still, when he came, her life would be complete. She would have all the people she loved the most, her own house, her own sheep, and her own land. She knew just how lucky she was. And to think she'd almost married Gabriel de Rochefort.

The women sat on Charlotte's porch enjoying a whisper of a breeze and the late afternoon shadows dappling the dunes as they rocked and stitched pillow covers to stuff with sheep's wool. "Here, after only a month, we are new personages," Isabelle said.

"Some of us more than others," replied Marceline, whose hands had peeled and then healed and then toughened. Now, out of pride, she refused to wear her gloves, except when doing the most arduous task, such as pumping water from the well and carrying it to the house. For reasons none of the others quite understood, Marceline considered this duty truly onerous. Sally, who still seldom spoke but appeared more at ease, always offered to do it for her, thereby earning Marceline's everlasting gratitude. In fact, Sally was the only person who was never a target of Marceline's harmless but frequent barbs.

"Do you suppose we should buy ourselves those big straw hats that other farmers wear?" Charlotte asked no one in particular as they watched the last of a wavering golden sun and listened to their rhythmic rocking and the occasional croak of a frog.

"These bonnets do get close, don't they?" Anne sighed swatting at a mosquito.

"I want some trousers like the ones Lydia and Charlotte have," Isabelle said. "Riding horses and building fences would be so much easier. I would stop riding sidesaddle immediately."

"We have to be careful," Lydia cautioned, "or we'll get a reputation for being really strange."

"We already have that reputation," Charlotte said.

"Well, we'll change our whole image at that lawn party you told us about. We'll be so-o-o-o grand that they'll wish we would go back to being just strange," Marceline said, causing the others to laugh appreciatively.

"I don't understand why the people around here remain so suspicious of us," Charlotte lamented. "They should know better."

"I don't know why you'd expect more. Not one soul protested when the newspaper ran that notice saying, " 'dead dogs kill no sheep,' " Isabelle countered. "That's simply uncivilized."

"But the truth is most dogs here are a menace to sheep."

Norah, just returned from a trip into town, hurried up onto the porch. Before she said a word, they had stopped rocking, for she wasn't in the habit of interrupting their end-of-day conversation. "President Garfield has been shot not dead," she blurted out, wasting no time announcing her news.

"What do you mean by 'shot not dead,' Norah?" Charlotte asked. "Tell us slowly."

"Some demented man shot him in the Washington railway station, but he looks to be recovering, according to early reports."

"Violence abounds in high places," Isabelle said sadly. "First the czar and now the president of the United States."

"But he's not dead," Charlotte pointed out, having noticed Lydia's shocked expression and Anne's look of dismay.

Norah remained standing, shifting onto one foot and back while they talked of politics and crimes and President Garfield, about whom all except Anne and Lydia knew next to nothing. "Perhaps you'd like to refresh yourself, Norah," Lydia suggested when she finally noticed that the excited servant was still with them.

But more news was forthcoming: "Miss Geneviève Beauchamp is running away."

"Oh?"

"Yes. Here."

"Here?" About that time Geneviève came around the side of the house.

"What's happened?" Charlotte asked, going over to her.

"She's run away," Norah answered for Geneviève.

"They want to send me back to France," she said and began sobbing and explaining that her parents wanted her to have a proper French husband—a distant cousin she'd never known existed.

"I told her we don't have much room," Norah said, handing Geneviève a handkerchief. "We're full up as it is."

"Most certainly not that full up, Norah," Charlotte answered.

"I don't deserve all your kindness, ma'am, after what I've done," Geneviève said once she'd settled herself in Charlotte's rocker.

"You've done exactly the right thing," Charlotte assured her.

"It'll cause more trouble," Norah muttered just loud enough for everyone to hear.

"I don't want to cause more trouble. I'm sorry if—"

"But you've done the right thing," Lydia interrupted. For reasons that were unclear to her, she had not yet told Charlotte of the incident with Leonard Majors, and she certainly didn't plan to mar their present happiness with such a revelation.

"You'll be no trouble, Geneviève. Your parents have made a mistake, and we will help you explain this to them." Charlotte assured her.

"Do you suppose we could find her a marvelous young American at the lawn party, someone her parents can't resist?" Marceline asked.

"Someone *you* can't resist," Isabelle commented.

Lydia knew Norah was glaring at her. She knew exactly what the servant was thinking and what she would say to her later, and she knew, unfortunately, that they were in agreement. Therefore, Lydia did not look up again from her stitching until Norah had gone inside.

28 From miles away the brass band could be heard, and a bare outline of the lawn party had come into view on the horizon.

"There'll be dancing and croquet," Charlotte was saying. "We bought a set for ourselves, but our terrain is too uneven for playing."

"It's too hot to play croquet," Marceline complained.

"Once the sun goes down, you'll think you're in Paris."

Isabelle laughed at Charlotte's remark. "Listen to that! In so short a time, our friends have adapted to this climate so well that they think it's like Paris. I hope we can do the same."

"Soon the climate will adapt to us," Charlotte explained, ignoring the part about Paris. She'd grown tired of that comparison.

"Since that has not yet happened, I shall perspire whether I endure croquet or dancing. Waltzing to a brass band on a barren strip of land will not remind me of Paris," Marceline answered.

"But you don't want to be reminded of Paris," Lydia scolded. "Lest you forget, we're here to establish a new life, a different social order."

"Then why are we going to a dance?" Marceline asked, all done up in her white gauze garden-party costume. Isabelle and Anne had worn their white outfits also. These three once more made quite an impressive display —three graceful white swans clearly out of their natural habitat.

While Lydia and Charlotte wanted their friends to make a grand impression, this display of elegance was a little more than either had anticipated. Yet who had the heart to tell them so? Hoping to tone down the overall effect of their little group, Lydia had worn her pale blue cotton print, and Charlotte was dressed in light beige.

At the moment, Lydia was taking her turn explaining the folkways of a Kansas lawn party. Along with playing croquet and dancing, they would listen to a band concert, eat ice cream, and drink soda water with ice. "You'll see for yourself how unpretentious, how close to nature, these people are. While they're not yet enlightened, they can be taught," she finished.

Anne, smiling, spoke up: "So the weather, the land, and the people must be tamed." Her smile was elusive, as it had been since her arrival. Although she made a great effort to join in, the effort showed and she remained wan, withdrawn, skittish even.

Charlotte responded to her enthusiastically. *"Exactement!* We've made a good start on the land, but people require a little more patience. Now, remember, these men are determined to find marriageable women. They strike up conversations with strangers in the hope of getting a proper introduction to us." Even on the frontier, a man wouldn't dream of approaching without one.

"You seem to approve of that tradition," Anne said.

*"Mais oui.* One does not wish to banish all rules of civilized behavior; one only wants to seek a more perfect order."

The others nodded in agreement and settled back to anticipate the festivities looming ever larger and louder on the horizon.

The public grounds boasted gaudy banners strung from poles circumscribing the festivities, defying the vastness of the surrounding landscape. In one corner the band, the town's pride, in royal blue uniforms, played loudly and lovingly on a temporary platform. Charlotte now understood why the human race expended so much energy in erecting cathedrals and monuments and performing rituals in places also once godforsaken: one had to assert oneself or be swallowed up.

But this was no time for solitary reverie. She must help Lydia attend to introductions and attempt to graciously occupy herself and their guests.

Madame and Monsieur Beauchamp, she was happy to note, weren't attending. Geneviève had predicted as much but, on her own, had decided to remain at Twin House Farm, and the women had breathed a sigh of relief. They didn't need the visible reminder of that complication at this particular time. Charlotte could only hope the girl and her family had chosen to keep this whole matter to themselves.

Unfortunately, Ben Leggett dispelled that hope almost immediately. Drawing her aside, he politely asked for an explanation. When she told him how Geneviève had appeared at their door and how they felt they couldn't turn her away, he only shook his head in sympathy. "For your sake, the sooner you talk the girl into going home, the better for everyone. I don't need to tell you that this ill will is the last thing you need right now."

Only a few minutes later Ethel Cannon echoed his words after first expressing her regret, as everyone did, over the suffering of President Garfield, whose condition kept worsening. Ethel too was sympathetic toward Charlotte and Lydia, but even sharper in her criticism. "Geneviève's parents are hardworking, reputable citizens. It won't do to cross them, and you're having a hard enough time around here without borrowing trouble from the Beauchamp family."

Charlotte agreed but saw no immediate resolution.

Presently Isabelle, Anne, and Charlotte consented to play croquet with two other young women and five men. Charlotte rolled her eyes at Isabelle, as the women and men paired off. Of course, in France, Charlotte, too, had enjoyed flirtations on the croquet lawns, but she loved the feeling she now had of being above such silly diversions. Since her partner, a thirtyish man named Joshua, was proving to be adequate, the game promised to be fun. Playing against Isabelle was always good sport, and Anne also looked to be a superior player. Maybe the game would be a pleasant diversion for her.

Charlotte so wanted her friends to like these people, to feel comfortable in their midst, and to have those feelings reciprocated. If only everyone could see how differences enriched, why, there would be no trouble! She wondered if she could be imagining the coolness toward her and Lydia, but she knew better, of course. Ben Leggett and Ethel Cannon had confirmed their fears.

To Charlotte's annoyance, Joshua Lathrip, wearing his white shirt partly unbuttoned, exposing a neck and chest as red as Marceline's hands had been, struck up a conversation. He would not have interested her in her old life and certainly did not now.

"Are you as good at farmin' as you are croquet?" Joshua asked.

"Games are tidier, I've noticed."

To Charlotte's embarrassment, Joshua laughed out loud and pounded his mallet on the ground a couple of times. A few people looked over at them curiously, and she could only hope nobody thought she was flirting with the large-eared man, who had obviously cut his own hair. They watched while Anne positioned her ball close to Joshua's and two of the others hit mediocre shots; then he resumed his conversation.

"I've heard you're doing all right so far."

"So far," she acknowledged.

"Well, if you're of a mind to add to your acreage, let me know. Friend of a friend is a little too much in debt and needs to get out from under a whole parcel of land close by you."

"How close?"

"How interested are you? I mean, he don't want his situation known to the whole world until he's out from under. Makes creditors too nervous."

"I understand," Charlotte said. She hit the ball but failed to make the shot she'd intended—her first bad shot of the game.

Joshua smiled sympathetically. "Happens to everybody," he said a little too agreeably, annoying her that much more.

"*Oui, monsieur,*" she said, breaking her resolve to converse only in English. When her turn came again, everyone was watching the game, for the level of competition had heightened. She aimed her ball at Isabelle's, but missed her target. The crowd sighed audibly, Lydia too. Fortunately, however, Isabelle's partner bungled his shot and left Charlotte's ball in a better position than she could have managed herself. Another murmur went up from the still gathering crowd.

"Lucky break for us," Joshua said, following her to the sidelines.

She and Lydia had all the land they could handle—and afford, so there was no point in pursuing any conversation with him. Nevertheless she heard herself asking, "How much?"

"Ninety acres for only four hundred fifty dollars."

"Too much."

"The land's been cultivated. Good crop of corn ready to pop."

"So why the sale?"

Joshua took his turn. Unexpectedly, he did better than Charlotte had thought possible, putting them ahead of the others and causing Isabelle's lips to thin out. Isabelle tended to look serene; but, when her mouth got set just so, she meant to get what she wanted, and almost always did.

Joshua came back over to Charlotte.

"Good shot," she conceded.

"I don't think you're taking my land-sale proposal seriously."

"But you are not taking me seriously."

"As I told you, the owner is mortgaged to his ears. Bought too much equipment, lost part of a crop to a brushfire. Four-fifty is a good price, I'm telling you. Why the harvest he's going to get from that corn will be a sight to behold."

"Half."

"Cash up front?"

"Cash up front and we split the crop."

"You drive a hard bargain, lady."

Charlotte smiled but not sweetly. "Talk it over with your friend." Joshua walked away from her without answering.

Just as well, Charlotte thought. What had possessed her—the idea of acquiring more land or the thought of driving a hard bargain? And Lydia had been rooting for her to excel in croquet, unaware of the other game in progress. But then, Lydia was the one who was always claiming that land would gain them respect and independence.

When it was once more Charlotte's turn, she took her shot again, and then once more. Afterward Joshua ambled back toward her. "Could he have the money tomorrow?" he asked. He did not mention her last good shots.

"Next Tuesday," Charlotte said without a moment's hesitation, though she didn't know how she would put her hands on that much cash so soon. Smiling triumphantly, she looked over at Lydia, who beamed back. The croquet game was exciting. And Joshua was going to accept her offer.

Excited by the possibility of winning at croquet, Charlotte focused her complete attention on the court. She wished her father could see her.

He so relished a win of any kind. When she was a child, he would sweep her up in his arms whenever either of them scored a victory, be it at chess or cards or croquet. Unfortunately he hadn't seen her today, but Lydia had.

Anne didn't make her shot, but when Charlotte's turn came again, she hit the ball exactly as she'd planned to and won. Everyone cheered, surprising and pleasing Charlotte.

Joshua shook her hand. As the crowd broke, she strained to find Lydia. She had to tell her about the land and the price. Maybe Frank Bailey would help them. He'd be coming soon, though she still hadn't told Lydia about his visit. It was ridiculous of her to have waited so long, but she didn't like to mention anything that might displease Lydia. Well, now she could tell her everything at once.

She hoped Joshua wouldn't back out on the land deal. Without any doubt, she very much wanted that land. Moreover, she knew she would rather suffer Lydia's displeasure than give up the prospect of acquiring more land. For once she understood its lure. Owning land was more than simply ensuring independence or gaining respect. It was, as her family had discovered centuries ago, a sport—a way to assert oneself against the vastness of the earth. Oh, Lydia, my dear friend, she thought, in the last hour I've won two games. I hope you're pleased about both. Charlotte herself was elated; she had risen to this occasion.

29     Charlotte so looked forward to showing Twin House Farm to Frank Bailey that she went by herself to pick him up.

He did not disappoint—bounding off the train and into her arms and away in the carriage with the same virile energy that had captivated her in Chicago. On the way home she chatted easily about everything from the construction of their houses to the raising of sheep and crops, for he remained interested in what they were doing. Because of his familiarity with this part of the country—as far as she could tell, this familiarity extended to the whole of the United States—she took special pleasure in pointing out the nuances in their vista.

Already Charlotte had become accustomed to a landscape without trees, though in the beginning it had not been easy. But with few other sharp outlines, she became one herself, to herself, as a new strength emerged. Sometimes, however, she simply felt one with the earth, took on its colorations, its hardness, its resiliency.

Now she delighted in the surprise of hilly mounds, which provided a certain whimsy; in the magnificent grasses, whose unceasing movement became a kaleidoscope of movement; and in her sheep, though she was still learning to distinguish one from the other. Now she understood the importance and power of visual stillness.

At the gate she pointed to their houses. "We like to think of them as two proud fillies, each strong and independent, but made three times more effective when harnessed together by the walkway," she explained, and Frank nodded appreciatively.

Graciously he praised their accomplishment, declared their design extraordinary, noted all their efforts and expressed his appreciation of them. Even Lydia commented on his exceptional eye and artistic sensibility. As it turned out, she'd accepted the news of his arrival with equanimity, since she too had news of Sam's impending arrival.

And because Lydia was now involved in overseeing the building of Sam's house, Charlotte felt free to enjoy herself with Frank Bailey. Riding with him in the early morning across the flower-strewn land, feeling the sweaty horse beneath her, reminded her of her girlhood. Even then she already knew much about men and women, hate and rage, jealousy and the hardness of hearts; here she'd come as close to innocence as she could ever get.

But on this particular morning she didn't trouble herself about human frailty, instead she experienced the thrill of a good ride on a swift horse with someone who knew about horses and how to sit them and push them to their limit. As with horses, so too with the land; she now wanted to push it to do her bidding.

Eventually she pulled up short and after catching her breath, pointed to the flat open prairie in front of them. "We shall have all that," she said, "all that your eyes can see."

"You ladies are nothing if not ambitious."

"Lydia says our eyes are bigger than our pocketbooks. There's only one piece of property she's obsessed with owning, and it's not for sale. On the whole, I'm usually the more cautious . . . a little more, anyway."

Frank Bailey laughed. "Well, it's probably a good thing one of you tempers that ambition with a dose of reality."

"What is reality to one person is simply an obstacle to overcome to another."

He laughed again, but queried her in the voice he had used in dealing with businessmen when she and Lydia were in Chicago. "Can you afford to buy more sheep?"

Charlotte nodded her head. "But it's of no use to increase our flock without the land to feed them. You taught us that. I'm also sure that as we get to know this country better, we'll have even more ideas."

"Like speculating in land?" he asked.

"We don't wish to deal in real estate, Mr. Bailey, only farmers."

"I thought you agreed to quit calling me Mr. Bailey. I can't give a horse to someone who calls me Mr. Bailey."

She smiled. "I'm in no need of a horse, though I will try to remember to call you Frank. This mare has turned out to be much better than she appears. She and I do well together." Charlotte leaned over and patted her mount.

"She doesn't have enough fire in her to suit you."

"How do you know what suits me?"

"Because you, my sweet, are as clear as this day; only you don't understand that any more than you understand what suits you."

"Are we both agreed that the land suits me?"

"On that we agree. Land, however, is not sufficient to quench either your restlessness or your sadness."

"I'll be the judge of that," she said with a toss of her head and turned toward the house, switching more than necessary the mare she claimed so satisfied her.

"What did he say?" Lydia asked as soon as she and Charlotte could slip away.

"I didn't get a chance to ask him."

"But you've been gone all morning."

"It wasn't appropriate. Besides, he knows."

"How do you know he knows?"

"You go ask him."

"He likes you best."

"That's what I meant when I said that he knows. He's not stupid, Lydia. Of course, I went out to show him that piece of land we want to buy. We should both have gone. That's what we'd do under most circumstances."

"But he likes you best."

"And he knows we know that."

Lydia threw up her hands. "All right! All right! But all this knowing will not result in a loan."

"Why can't we borrow from Mr. Leggett's bank?"

"Because we don't want the town to know all our business. And we've already borrowed a good deal."

"You ask Mr. Bailey."

Lydia nodded assent.


When Charlotte crossed over to her house, she found Isabelle and Marceline in quiet but animated conversation, their heads close together. Upon seeing Charlotte they seemed to try to compose themselves.

"Come, join us, *chérie*," Marceline called out.

As Charlotte pulled up a chair, she realized that Isabelle looked distraught. What followed was a jumble of explanation and argument having to do with why Isabelle should or should not go somewhere, which kept relating somehow to Marceline and the baron as well as to the shedding of skin. Isabelle and Marceline talked simultaneously. The house rule to speak English at all times—a discipline the women had imposed on themselves—was abandoned.

The lifting of the language restraint lifted another restraint as well. Suddenly Isabelle began wringing her hands, her most uncharacteristic gesture yet, and then she and Marceline were crying. Charlotte cried too, her friends' emotion unleashing some vague, pent-up anguish of her own. So far, though, she had pieced together very little except that Oliver Whitman had asked Isabelle to go with him to a church social.

"Is that all?" Charlotte finally asked, afraid she'd missed some vital piece of information.

"He'll ask her to marry him," Marceline explained rather too patiently.

"How do you know?" Charlotte asked. Oh, God, now I'm doing it! she thought, instantly forgiving Lydia their earlier encounter.

"He has all those children and he's older and needs a wife," Marceline continued. "And have you seen the way he looks at Isabelle?"

"And he thinks I'm more likely to accept—more likely than the others in our group, I am sure."

"That's absurd! He's beneath you in every way. He is uncultivated, uneducated, un . . . un . . . un-everything!" Charlotte answered. "He couldn't possibly think you would be interested in such a proposal."

"But don't you understand? I might be. I don't know, and I don't wish to be tested."

Hearing that admission, Charlotte slumped forward.

"She wants what the rest of us want—land, an independent life, a chance to find her soul, but she's never had the other."

"I understand all that," Charlotte snapped, probably because she didn't understand it at all. How could she have been so oblivious to what was going on with her friend?

"But of course you must test yourself," she said. "We have to have the courage to face the weakest part of ourselves; otherwise we've no hope of uncovering any hidden wellspring." This pronouncement came with such authority that, no one, including Charlotte herself, questioned the wisdom of it.

She walked away, pleased with herself. Lydia would be proud of her, and Isabelle would come to her senses soon enough once she'd been exposed to the alternative. As for Marceline, what was she saying about Gabriel? Surely she couldn't be serious about going back to him. However, Marceline had arrived in Kansas cross with the world and, for the most part, she had stayed that way.

Isabelle had tried to explain Marceline's aversion to her new surroundings: "Marceline may not want to marry, but she certainly wants to seduce someone, and she has found no one here worth seducing."

"But after she comes into her own power, she'll have no need for seductions," Charlotte had assured Isabelle.

"There might not be enough time in the world for Marceline to achieve that state," Isabelle had answered dryly.

As soon as the summer crops were harvested and the new land deal finalized, Marceline's problems would be dealt with, Charlotte vowed. Now, however, she must concentrate on the problems of Twin House Farm and content herself with the company of Frank Bailey. To her regret, he would not be staying much longer.

# 30

"Let's be on our best behavior today," Lydia lectured as they stopped their carriage in front of the Browns' residence, where a stableboy took the reins from her. "Roberta Brown has a lot of influence in the community and the literary club."

"Tell Marceline," Isabelle said, as she, Lydia, and Charlotte were helped from the carriage.

"I did, but she thinks it's impossible to convince any of these people of a purer, simpler way," Lydia said lightly, rolling her r's for effect. "They certainly have as many conventions as anyone else. Maybe more."

"But they have more of an opportunity to open themselves once they are shown the way," Charlotte rejoined.

"Oh, Charlotte, stop being so defensive," Marceline scolded, having joined them in the middle of the conversation. While the other three signed papers, she'd shopped in the dry goods store. "We're not attacking your precious Kansans."

Isabelle eyed the three-story stone house they were about to enter. "This does not look like a residence belonging to people who are interested in discarding artificiality."

"Imagine, they visited eight countries just to bring back fireplaces," Charlotte said. "Their house looks like a poor man's European tour."

"Except that it takes a rich one to provide it."

"The Browns plan to show us what domestic bliss can produce and disabuse us of any notions we hold of superiority," Marceline responded.

"But we don't have any such notions. We're trying to escape worldly vanities," Lydia argued.

"Not everyone wishes to do so," Isabelle cautioned.

"In France, even a peasant's house has better lines!" Marceline felt obliged to point out.

Charlotte laughed. "What a snooty group of seekers we are!"

The tour came even before the tea, and all eight fireplaces were on it. Charlotte had forgotten just how boring Roberta Brown could be when she put her mind to it. She said, "The lineages of objects are so interesting, are they not?" and proceeded to list all of the noble families who had owned each piece. "What a delight to show this place to people of refined sensibility who can appreciate the workmanship from an old castle in Belgium," she said and then proceeded to give the history of the castle. However, there was something touching about the Browns, Charlotte decided, for they'd appropriated other cultures and made them their own, thus turning the result into something truly American.

At tea after the usual talk of the expected boom in real estate, the conversation turned to another topic of local concern, the horrible suffering of President Garfield. According to the papers, he was near death.

"Well, if he does die, they should immediately hang the man who shot him," Mrs. Brown said with vehemence. Though few around Huddleston objected to the idea of hanging, the fate of Guiteau, the man who said he'd been called by a divine presence to shoot the president, was another matter.

"An eye for an eye," Wallace Brown quoted.

"But if one of the eyes is blind?" Isabelle remarked. The Browns looked puzzled, but their other visitors glared at their friend, for they knew that Isabelle and Anne thought the assassin was absolutely crazy and not responsible for his acts, Anne arguing more strongly than Isabelle that control was not always possible.

The others argued against outside forces or irrational inner urges dictating a person's behavior. Marceline thought Guiteau was simply another man who chose violence as a way to make himself feel real. To her way of thinking, she and her friends had chosen Twin House Farm to experience raw emotions; Guiteau had shot himself a president.

"But will is everything," Lydia said, and the Browns nodded, as Charlotte and Marceline murmured their agreement. And Charlotte thought how nice it was to be able to show solidarity with the Browns.

"How nice to find women possessed of such good common sense and sophisticated taste!" Roberta Brown smiled sweetly before continuing, "But, my goodness, what a waste that people of such fine sensibility are not establishing families. We must all spread enlightenment to this part of the world. There's no more sacred duty for a woman than to devote herself to the perpetuation of domestic bliss."

"On the contrary, Mrs. Brown," Charlotte heard herself answering, "I think one should seek ways to make the spiritual manifest in our daily lives in whatever form suits one." She looked for approval toward Lydia, who nodded ever so slightly.

"But as Mr. Brown can testify, we women have a special duty to perpetuate the cultural and spiritual values we all hold most dear," Mrs. Brown insisted.

Lydia, who was having a hard time concealing her true feelings, became determined to answer courteously though truthfully, but Wallace Brown spoke first: "Yes, indeed, Kansas is a great place for all of us."

"Yes, indeed it is," Lydia echoed, relieved of the immediate need for truth. "And your fireplaces are splendid," she added.

For a few minutes the conversation flagged, and Lydia took advantage of the opportunity to question Wallace Brown on land deals and the efficiency of the land commissioner. As circumspectly as possible, she inquired into the commissioner's corruptibility and discovered that, indeed, he could be bought for a fair price.

"More than one foreclosure around here has been due to influence in high places," Brown fairly boasted. Satisfied that she may have found a way to get hold of Leonard Majors's land and drive him out of the county, she turned her attention once again to her hostess. This time Mrs. Brown was addressing the real reason they'd been called here, fireplaces notwithstanding.

They simply could not keep that Beauchamp girl a day longer, the Browns insisted. The child's mother was frantic, her father was furious, and the Lord knew he had a temper. But the scandal of it was the main reason to be rid of the girl. Bad enough to live such a selfish life, flouting family tradition and offending the sensibility of neighbors, but for them to corrupt a mere child, why, that was shocking! And all sorts of rumors were circulating.

The Browns didn't believe any of the stories, of course, Wallace quickly assured them, and Roberta agreed. Needless to say, Lydia and Charlotte were asking a lot, testing the tolerance of good people. . . . Here Mrs. Brown's voice trailed off, and her expression grew vague.

Lydia wondered if Leonard Majors had anything to do with the rumors, but whatever they were, she didn't want to know. She rose. She gathered her gloves and thanked the Browns for the nice tea and tour. Perhaps they could one day repay the favor. The Browns would then see firsthand how harmless, though joyous, Twin House Farm was.

As they filed out, each woman curtsied and gave a proper thank-you. To Lydia's amusement, Charlotte assumed the haughtiness that had served her so well in Paris. Little had they known she would need it again in Kansas.

**31** The morning of September 21, 1881, was to be devoted to bidding farewell to President James Garfield, the afternoon to welcoming Samuel Benson. So Charlotte thought of that September day as she drove to town with her friends.

Dressed in black, they assembled with the other mourners inside the Presbyterian church and listened as the minister offered up a long prayer for the soul of the dead president and the righteous punishment of his killer. After the congregation sang "The Star-Spangled Banner" and "The Battle Hymn of the Republic," the minister rose to ask God's help in ridding the land of Satan. "An eye for an eye," the minister read.

Silence brought Charlotte's thoughts back to the service as the congregation filed through the church doorway. They marched in cadence with the town drummer as far as the United States Post Office, Huddleston's main symbol of the federal government. As a bugler played taps, Charlotte felt a tingle. Pageantry moved her; patriotism moved her. Until the shooting, she'd paid little attention to President Garfield or his politics, but she identified with the nation and its loss, and she regretted the president's death. She had found the service immensely moving.

Although in some ways Samuel's arrival would be a relief, Charlotte didn't look forward to the afternoon. For weeks Lydia had driven everyone crazy with her preparations and worries. Would Sam like his house? Would he like his land? Would he like Huddleston? Kansas? Twin House Farm? Her list of anxieties stretched endlessly across the plain; her list of arrangements, even further.

Flowers had to be planted, a garden plot begun, woodwork repainted after the workmen left, windows cleaned, floors scrubbed, fences erected. May and their baby daughter, Belinda, would not be coming, and Sam would not even be staying in his house, but this did not faze Lydia. Sam would fall in love with his new home. She wanted him to have no second thoughts.

And when Sam stepped off the train, Charlotte wondered what all the worry had been about—her worry. Even with his beautiful eyes, he was nothing of moment. He held Lydia in his arms for as long as she wanted, gently teasing away her tears. The others wept as well, for the fulfillment of a dream is no small occasion. With its completion, loss begins; another marking, Charlotte thought.

Samuel shook hands with Marceline and kissed Anne. He put his arm around Lydia, and kept it there as she introduced him to Isabelle, Norah, and Sally. When he got to Charlotte, the last in line, he acted almost as if this were their first introduction. Of course, nothing had happened that night in the carriage.

For only one minute did Charlotte question her assertion to Anne as they'd argued last evening. Again, the subject had been Garfield's assassin and the exercise of free will.

"Keep in mind," Anne had pointed out, "that Guiteau thinks God wanted him to kill the president because he thought Garfield's 'removal' would heal the factions in the Republican party." On the other hand,

Charlotte had maintained that free will was an absolute, in which case, "responsibility for our actions lies with each of us." Now, for only one minute, she was not so certain.

"You see, Sam? Anne is just as bossy as ever," Lydia joked after his tour of Twin House Farm. Although he would spend only tonight here, having insisted on booking a hotel room for the rest of his stay, he did plan to store his trunks of valuable household goods in their basement. Anne had urged him to keep them in her room where it would be drier; Lydia argued that she could accommodate them just as easily.

He cupped their heads in his broad hands. "Come on, you two, I refuse to referee your grown-up fights."

"But they are not grown-up fights, which is why you're so glad to see us," Lydia replied. With that he gently knocked all three noggins together, then vaulted toward the house balancing a large box on either hand, leaving Lydia and Anne laughing, as he always had.

"What's so funny?" Lydia's grandmother had once asked on a snowy winter afternoon. The two girls were huddled together, lost in laughter over some remark Sam had made to them before going about his business.

Neither could explain their laughter to Lydia's grandmother, nor did it really matter, for what they sought was Sam's attention, whether in the form of approval or irritation. In return they showered him with their girlish giggles, which had the desired effect of secretly pleasing while patently annoying him. And so it is now, Lydia thought, watching her brother's wiry back disappear through her doorway.

Anne watched with her. "He's so proud of you," she said. "I hope you know that."

Lydia did know it. She saw Samuel's pride in her and could hardly wait to show off her newfound knowledge and skills. She was amazed at how much she'd learned—things that people around Huddleston took for granted, but which she'd had to learn and Samuel did not yet know.

Tomorrow they would show him his new homestead. She knew how eager he was to see it, but it was ten miles from Twin House Farm. Ten miles was the correct distance, she'd decided. Close enough for them to see each other regularly, but far enough for her to stay away from May, and far enough for Charlotte not to feel threatened by his presence.

Dearest Charlotte, so giving and understanding about most things, was clearly troubled by his arrival. Lydia regretted Charlotte's and Sam's formality with each other, but she would make sure he did not disturb the order of their lives. She would build trust between them. Right now she felt she could accomplish absolutely anything.

But on this day after one more sad good-bye, she wanted only to bask in Sam's presence, for at her bidding and against May's wishes, he had come, finally.

32 Lydia and Anne stood at military attention atop a windy mound some distance from the houses. With a jerky movement in keeping with the stiff stance, Anne positioned the butt of the rifle on her shoulder.

"That's right," Lydia encouraged. "Be sure the stock is firm against it."

Anne put the gun back down. "What is the stock?"

"That part you had on your shoulder."

"Well, why didn't you say so? Now I have to start all over."

Ignoring the comment, Lydia went on with her instructions: "Lower your head so that your cheek is on your thumb. No, no, *just* your thumb; your face mustn't touch the rifle."

"This is impossible."

"You won't think so after you kill your first rattlesnake."

"I mean all this," Anne said, using the rifle as a pointer as she gestured toward the landscape.

"Don't be reckless," Lydia adopted the same firm, determined tone she sometimes took with Sam and Anne when they were all children.

Anne wiped the perspiration from her forehead with a lace handkerchief. "This is October. Why isn't summer over?"

"It will be soon. They say a frost will come any night now."

Anne sighed. "I find it hard to imagine such an abrupt switch, though if 'they' say so, I suppose it's true."

Then once more Lydia guided Anne through the motions, and this time Anne fired.

"My God!" Anne said after the gun flew up in her arms.

"I'm sorry; I forgot to tell you about the kick. When it goes off, it kicks up, and then you must let it settle back down of its own accord."

"Like life."

"Try again." Lydia used her patient tone. She'd been trying to acclimate Anne to Kansas in stages, nudging her to discover the sense of freedom in the place. Anything, to bring back her old Anne, who was much too private a person to probe too far.

For a while Anne practiced as Lydia instructed. They had always fit well into each other's rhythms, and their absorption in the exercise caused them to relax. When a conversation did begin, they were back on familiar footing in a way that hadn't happened since Anne's arrival.

"What did you mean earlier—about this place being impossible? I thought you liked it here," Lydia said.

"I love it. Twin House Farm is the best thing in the world for me, but . . ."

"Honestly, Anne, I've missed nothing of my old life except Sam," she said, exaggerating only a little. "Seeing him makes me realize just how much I have missed him."

"He missed you, too."

"Did he say so?"

"Not in so many words—you know how Sam is—but he was forever fretting about you. He'd say things like 'Too much nature agitates her' or 'Too many sheep will impoverish her.'"

Both women laughed out of their lifelong affection for his familiar quirks. Growing up, he had snatched up their fears and apprehensions even before they could feel them, for behind that placid exterior lurked a worrier of the first order.

As young girls they had known well that he couldn't stand to see Lydia in trouble, and occasionally they had set out to excite his sense of responsibility, now and again provoking him to an outburst of anger, despite his usual good-natured equanimity.

One day Sam discovered them practicing escapes from Lydia's third-floor bedroom window in anticipation of future punishments. Whenever possible, Lydia broke rules, one of which most certainly forbade sliding down sheets from high windows. After they ignored his pleas to stop, he'd stamped off, angry, hurt. Only then did Lydia have a pang of guilt.

Yet if she had not provoked him in such ways, she might never have known how much he cared, or so she justified her behavior. Already he was learning to conceal his feelings. And if Anne had not been here to bear witness, Lydia would have no way to know his feelings now.

"I also missed you," Lydia said and brushed her own cheeks with the backs of her hands, pulling away from the strong emotion threatening to overwhelm her.

"Well, it was your letters to Sam as well as to me that persuaded me to come. He not only bragged about you, he liked to quote you on your 'Kansas joys.'"

Lydia felt herself blushing. To say she'd been exaggerating the ease and bountifulness of life in this place was to understate her effort by a good bit, though no more than the western romances and pamphlets she'd read before her own arrival. Nevertheless, this was her own beloved Samuel she'd misled almost daily in her letters. She hadn't even told Charlotte how much she embellished, or how often.

Charlotte would not have approved on any count. She didn't fully appreciate Sam the way Anne did. He took a little getting to know, and while he was unfailingly polite, he seldom revealed enough of himself to be of interest to any but those who already adored him. Regrettably he still held himself more aloof from Charlotte than from anyone else.

"See that groundhog, Anne? He and his cousins are making holes all over these hills. The sheep step in them and break their legs. Now take aim, slowly, and don't forget to use only the tip of your finger to squeeze the trigger."

Anne did as she was told. She remembered to cock the rifle, took her time positioning the butt on her shoulder, and got the fat, wobbling animal in her sights, but to no avail.

"It's the wind," Lydia told her. "You have to take the wind into consideration."

This time Lydia raised her own rifle, took aim, and hit the groundhog.

"In your letters you failed to mention the wind, Lydia, and the sand. Did you know that?"

Lydia did know, but rather than answer the question she asked another: "Have I done the right thing by bringing him here?"

"Sam came because he wanted to," Anne said and touched Lydia's elbow.

"But I encouraged him even after I knew . . ." Lydia broke off and slowly shook her head as she leaned over to pick off a sandbur. "The problem is, this land is hard, not so hard I can't handle it, but, well, *hard.*"

"Too much for Sam, you mean."

"Look at the men you've met around here. Sam isn't like them."

"Neither are you."

"But in my own way I'm as tough as they are. So are you."

"Sam is tougher than you think."

"I hope so," Lydia said, then made another confession. "One of the few things I do miss from my old life is the sight of forms against the landscape. Silly, isn't it? But out here if you don't count the hills or the sheep, you can go for miles without seeing a silhouette." Here she stopped, took aim again, and hit another groundhog.

She had never thought so much about shapes before, how much they defined her everyday world. She'd found herself hungry for buildings, trees.

"You were speaking of forms when that groundhog interrupted," Anne said, fanning herself as they walked.

"I think I was getting ready to explain my unreasonable attachment to the objects in my house—everything from this rifle to that exquisite Limoges box and my little figurines. I now see them more in terms of their shape than anything else, and looking at forms that way makes the lines of this gun as valuable to me as the lines on the box. I know artists see that way, but this has to do with my immediate life, and it turns my ideas about beauty and worth topsy-turvy."

"As it should be, dear Lydia, if we're to reinvent the world."

"But I'm talking your ear off," she said to Anne. In spite of their enjoyment of the October heat, they had stopped walking. "And you should rest before dinner."

Anne gathered up her skirt. "I'll race you," she challenged, sounding more like the old Anne.

"In one more minute. I've wanted to ask all summer how you really are. Why you came. Why you won't commit yourself to staying here. I do not ask these questions out of indifference, you can be sure."

"I know," Anne said. She turned her head toward the sound of geese passing over and took her time choosing her next words, which, for Lydia, were a disappointment. "If I could lay out before us the contents of my mind, then we could sort through and cast aside or put in order all that we need to deal with. On that matter I would ask your help—honestly, Lydia, I would, but this disturbance has to do with the contents of my soul, and those aren't easily examined."

"I hate it when you become enigmatic."

"I hate it, too," Anne said. "I can tell you this much: Kansas holds a great fascination for me, as does this whole business of shedding one's skin. But what I don't know is whether this place, these concerns, are fulfillment of my . . . oh, let's call it my soul's longing or—and please don't be offended—only the cleverly disguised distraction of rougher currents."

Lydia sighed.

"You think I'm sounding mysterious again."

Lydia adjusted the comb in Anne's hair. "We might just as well admit that you *are* mysterious, Annie. Nobody knows you better than I, and even I am often fooled into thinking that you're as composed as you appear to be."

Anne laughed. "I do appreciate the effort you've made *not* to ask where all my pieces are."

"It's taken a great deal of self-restraint," Lydia said, "to resist my natural tendencies."

"Never occurred to me you wouldn't."

Instead of racing, they now ambled toward the house, but Anne stopped again and turned toward Lydia. "You have to trust other people to know how to survive," Anne said.

"I trust you to."

"You can afford to because I'm not crucial to your well-being."

"Most certainly you are." Lydia took Anne by the arm and shook her gently. "What a thing to say! I love you, Annie."

"I don't mean you don't love me. And I know you want me to stay here. I just mean . . . Oh, never mind." Anne looked at Lydia for a long time, started to say something else, but instead linked her arm through Lydia's for the remaining yards to the house. Lydia continued to cradle the rifle, much as she might have held a baby.

*33* All winter the wind played its mounting descant to the women's fluted voices as they discussed finding one's soul, finding stray sheep, finding a place in the community, finding ways to pry up slabs of ice to boil for water, finding ways to combat the bitter cold, and finding the deep underground springs when the thaw did come.

The early mornings, frigid and dark, Charlotte saw as their real test, for the milking, the feeding, the egg-gathering, and the lighting of fires couldn't wait. Her pleasure came in returning from the chill, thin air to the smell of strong coffee and their own fresh eggs with hot biscuits, combined with a strong sense of virtue. The rest of the morning they would bake bread or go out looking for wild turkeys to shoot and hang in the shed they used as a meat locker. Sometimes they collected buffalo chips for fuel or shucked corn, often leaving Lydia to work over the accounts. After the noonday meal, they usually wrote letters, took walks, or rode the horses out to check on the sheep.

In late afternoon they settled around a fire with their handwork while one of them read aloud to combat the loneliness of early nightfall, which called forth past times when every evening provided an occasion. Isabelle and Anne had also taken to weaving; and the others, after a few stern lectures from their weavers, learned how to scour the wool properly in order to keep it from matting and turning into felt.

Whether weaving, sewing woolen comforters, or mending their mittens and mufflers, they would soak in the words and warmth and company of Shakespeare or Hugo or Sand, every now and again commenting on whatever passage had been read. Charlotte loved especially the long evenings spent discussing Henry James's *Portrait of a Lady,* for that gentleman, too, seemed to be wrestling with the problem of identifying a "self." It provided all of them some satisfaction that the critics and social commentators in the magazines were as divided on the issue as they were.

Of course, when the jury came back after one hour of deliberation to convict Guiteau of President Garfield's murder and sentenced him to hang, the debate over free will intensified. Although Charlotte felt many newspapers went too far in wanting to ban all use of the insanity plea, she did agree that justice, however nebulous a concept, had been served. She and Lydia both argued that if people relinquished their hold on moral responsibility by declaring themselves nothing but a cluster of impulses— and formed by other forces at that—then what was the point in talking about, much less looking for, a real self?

Anne countered that if they were nothing but rational creatures who could reason their way to self-mastery—Anne knew the Greeks better than the rest of them did—then this put them at risk of being slaves to whatever "higher reason" reigned at the time. Although Isabelle sympathized with this view, none of the others would concede Anne's point, whereupon she declared them too threatened by the loss of ultimate control, which was not theirs to begin with.

On that score, Charlotte knew her to be partially right; she even knew that the part of her which was determined to resist the idea of impulse as a controlling factor had something to do with her own fear of that possibility in herself.

Ready for lighter pursuits by evening, they liked to try their skill at cribbage or charades. Sometimes they put on plays for each other or acted out dramatic tableaux, at which Geneviève proved to be exceptionally talented. As often as not, Sally and Norah were invited as participants or observers, for they did enjoy an appreciative audience. Best of all, they enjoyed dancing and ended many nights that way, thanks to Marceline's bringing along her violin. Charlotte played the piano, albeit not brilliantly, she and Lydia had decided against buying one on the grounds that it reminded them of the after-dinner soirees they were fleeing; but these, however, were not the same at all.

The coming of Sam, and even May, had enhanced that much more the musical enjoyment of the group. When they occasionally made their appearance, Sam contributed a fine male voice while May added another violin. To everyone's delight, Sam and Lydia resumed singing duets as they had done since childhood. While Charlotte enjoyed their voices, she felt left out of their tightly closed circle—sufficiently left out that she sympathized with May.

As wonderful as Lydia was, Charlotte had no doubt that she'd have been a disastrous sister-in-law. Sam attended to Lydia in business matters, clearly found her more amusing than any of the others, May included, and generally assumed a protective stance around her. Charlotte understood their closeness; nevertheless, during the long winter months, even though Samuel was not around as much, she felt many twinges of jealousy. For all her affinity with Lydia, Charlotte knew she couldn't compete with Sam in terms of shared emotions and experiences. He was her real family.

This knowledge saddened her, for she had once felt such intimacy with Papa. Now Lydia was her one hope of regaining that feeling; yet she could never be the most loved person in Lydia's life any more than she would be in Papa's.

There were two interruptions of this winter idyll. One was the death of a young Huddleston girl, hit by a train as she played on the tracks, and the other was the unplanned return of Frank Bailey.

He roared in, stamping off snow and bubbling with good cheer, passing out Valentines for everyone, new books for Isabelle and Anne, new musical scores for Marceline, a porcelain goddess for Lydia's collection, a new saddle for Charlotte, a comb and brush set for Norah, and a set of hair combs for Sally. Everyone laughed with him, listened to his stories, admired the way he stoked a fire, butchered a deer. All the same, no one quite knew what to do with him, or he with them. Nevertheless, he stayed on for the better part of a week.

"So many women," he would say. "You'd think the bevy of you would have a civilizing effect on me."

"You are civilized, Frank," Anne pointed out one snow-clouded afternoon. "You just aren't tamed."

Whereupon he cradled her in his arms and danced her around the room. "Your sweetness will domesticate me yet," he teased. "And is that apple pie I smell?"

"Mine." Anne beamed. When he deposited her in a chair, her face flushed, her hair loosened about her face, she looked ten years younger and much healthier.

"Well, is it to be eaten or only smelled?"

"Unruly and greedy," she called over her shoulder as she left to check on the status of her pastry.

"Don't excite her too much. Our Anne needs to be quiet." Lydia spoke from her desk where she'd been making copies of a skit they planned to perform. By adding a little sugar to the ink, then writing, then layering with another sheet of paper, after which she dampened the whole thing and pressed it with a moderately hot iron, she could copy materials. The entire process gave her great pleasure, and she was always looking for excuses to use her skills.

"Is that why you think Anne came here—to find peace and quiet?"

"She came here to find a different life, a change of scene."

"She came here to escape a living hell, to be busy, to be engaged, to be excited."

"Did she tell you that?" Lydia asked sharply.

"She didn't have to."

"Mr. Bailey," Lydia said, laying aside her ink and iron, "I have known Anne since childhood, and I can assure you that I would know if things were as bad for her as you say."

"Open your eyes, lady! She's not recovered yet."

"I know that," Lydia said patiently as if she were speaking to a deficient child. "She's been sick. That I can tell, since I do keep my eyes open, thank you."

"She has all the symptoms of neurasthenia, for which the treatment is complete rest, and that woman has too much gumption to live like that."

Without answering, Lydia collected her sponge and papers and put away her ink. "Please tell Anne I have other things to do right now."

Filling the kerosene lamps in the front room, Charlotte watched Frank Bailey perform a mock bow as Lydia left. It would be so much more pleasant if she would be less edgy with him and he more tolerant of her. Changing Lydia would be difficult, but if Charlotte approached Frank properly, he might be amenable to a suggestion. Wiping her hands on her apron, she decided to talk with him about the matter right then. However, as she started in, she reconsidered. He stood at the window gazing out on the cloud-laden day, looking intently for something a million miles away.

**34** "But I have plenty of money of my own," Isabelle insisted, as they climbed down from their carriage.

They had come into town to sign a contract for the tract of land belonging to Leonard Majors.

"Once my parents despaired of my marrying," Isabelle continued, "they bequeathed me a most generous amount to compensate for this peculiar affliction of . . . what to say? . . . 'single blessedness?' By all means, buy the land. I don't think any of us will lose money on it, and I want to invest in the future of Kansas."

"It will be waiting for you when you decide to settle here," Lydia gently nudged. Of the three visitors, Isabelle had the fewest reservations about staying. Lydia and Charlotte took as proof her willingness to put up money for another spread.

It had taken Lydia all winter to arrange a foreclosure on Leonard Majors's land. The bribe to the land commissioner had taken time and money, some of which was coming out of Isabelle's loan, though she didn't know it. In fact, none of Lydia's friends, including Charlotte, knew why she'd insisted on acquiring Leonard Majors's property. Now so much time had gone by that she'd not only have to explain the Majors episode, she would have to explain about not having explained. Besides, she'd reasoned, why let her schemes cause trouble for anyone else? Lydia guessed that Norah had a reasonable suspicion of what she was up to, but Norah was different. Norah *should* know. Norah wanted vengeance also.

Lydia hated Leonard Majors, not only for what he'd tried to do to her and, in as corrupt a way, to Geneviève, but also for the insidious lies he'd spread about them. She was sure he was behind the rumors. But more than vengeance was at work: fear, too, for if Satan was loose in the land, as half the country's ministers claimed, then one of his lesser vassals was Leonard Majors. A vile bully, a sinister leech, a mouth sucking in and a hand smashing out—he was all that and more; but the danger came from his lack of any moral underpinning. He had no attachment to the world, including his own land, which he'd sloppily tilled. Sheep took more care. Well, for once she would heed the ministers and help God rid the land of Satan.

As Isabelle, Charlotte, and Lydia assembled in front of the wagonmaker's shop, Emma Leggett approached. While they were aware that their relations with the community had deteriorated over the winter because they were harboring Geneviève, Mrs. Leggett in her anger and false chirpiness suddenly brought the situation into sharp relief.

"Naughty ladies," she said, "you've been keeping much too much to yourselves. And all of Huddleston panting at your doorstep!" Her eyes raced from face to face or, more precisely, from forehead to forehead, as she didn't look directly at anyone. Her eyes racing, her veiny hands fluttering, an inner chaos threatening to erupt, she seemed to cause commotion around them all. She was one of those people, Charlotte decided, whose very presence could agitate a situation.

"Don't think you can get away with this uppity behavior. Out here you have to participate!"

"But we do participate, Mrs. Leggett," Charlotte answered her. "We very much want to be part of your community."

Lydia shook her head at Charlotte to discourage prolonging this conversation, but already it was too late. Emma Leggett was not to be denied.

"You've refused every invitation from every young man within one hundred miles of here. And they are perfectly decent men."

"But as you know, we want to be independent," Charlotte responded in a most reasonable voice.

"That's absurd. This"—she waved her arm—"this is all too *impossible* without a family."

"We are our own family," Charlotte insisted.

"Then leave other families alone. It's a disgrace, kidnapping that poor child, and if you think Mr. Beauchamp is going to put up with this forever . . ." Emma Leggett had to stop long enough to regain control. "I warn you, he intends to show you people a thing or two, get you off your high horses!"

Lydia took Charlotte's arm. "Please excuse us, Mrs. Leggett."

Abruptly Emma Leggett spun round as she had that night at dinner and left them standing in the street.

"She's bedeviled, poor thing," Charlotte said to Isabelle. "Must be the opium drunkenness again."

"Don't underestimate her sentiments, however," Isabelle answered. "She speaks for the community, and we are definitely a threat to this established order."

More shaken than they cared to admit, the three women proceeded to the bank to sign the papers on the Majors property. Though Isabelle had insisted on having a lawyer present—which, to their chagrin, neither Lydia nor Charlotte had thought to do—she carefully read every word of the contract and asked sharp, specific questions about every clause that struck her as the least bit vague. Her thorough grasp of the English language could still astonish her close friends; not even the lawyer matched her preciseness.

"I'm sure we can find someone here who is able to authorize this as the official deed and official survey. I understand false claims are quite common," she said. "We wouldn't want anything like that, I'm sure."

When she spoke, the men accorded her the kind of respect they usually reserved for their own sex. The combination of her largeness and her serenity caused people to take note, which she accepted as her due. Neither heat nor wind nor dust nor ignorance caused her to so much as raise an eyebrow.

Lydia was proud of her and, at the same time, shocked to find herself covetous of the authority Isabelle commanded. Not shocked by the envy but by the sudden recognition that what Isabelle came by with such ease was what Lydia had been striving for, one way or another, her whole life: an acknowledgment of her personage. She did not ask for admiration, only the right to be herself. Such a simple thing, really. The shedding of one's skin was nothing compared to this one single measure of a life well lived.

**35** The circus had come to Huddleston, and the entire household, Norah and Sally included, prepared to go. Only Charlotte, recovering from the flu, would stay behind on this crisp early spring day.

"You are certain you'll be all right?" Lydia asked as she adjusted her hat once more.

"How many times do I have to tell you?" Charlotte responded.

"We can leave Norah or Sally."

"Lydia, I'm fine. You are going for the day, not for a month."

"Don't do any work," Isabelle instructed as she too adjusted her hat. Lately Isabelle, the other women had observed, took more and more time with her toilet.

"I could stay here," Anne offered.

"I'm not all that fond of circuses," Isabelle said, "but the circus is only part of it. We have to participate in the community."

"All of us should probably should stay here. Those people will never like us anyway; I don't know why we bother with them," Marceline put in.

"Let's go before an argument starts," Anne said, taking Marceline's arm and ushering her out. A minute later, from her bedroom window, Charlotte watched as the women arranged themselves in the carriage while Norah and Sally climbed into the wagon.

On their way out, Lydia looked back and waved. She seemed especially happy these days, ever since they'd bought the Majors property. She had been determined to have it, and in the end, he'd been foreclosed on and she'd been able to pick it up at an extremely low price. Charlotte still did not understand her friend's persistence in this matter, but whatever the reason, their household had already benefited.

For the first hour Charlotte feared the quiet. It was often still in the countryside, but people were always about somewhere, even if they weren't heard or seen. This kind of silence was different—she was *all* alone, unless sheep counted, which they didn't. What counts, she thought, is human contact, any human contact.

She thought of her mother, but she certainly had had little genuine human contact with her. Charlotte wished she could remember her wet nurse. Should she matter? Odile mattered. She missed her. Her father mattered. A silly thought. "My father is no better than my mother," she said aloud. Those words so startled her that she immediately began looking for a task other than the mending she had set out to do, but she didn't really want to do anything that mattered. If the others could take a holiday, so could she. No one expected anything of her. They were not her mother.

She looked in the mirror. No, she was not her mother either. In fact, she had come to resemble her father even more—the same small, dark face, the high cheekbones. Well, what did she expect—bone structure didn't alter, did it? She leaned closer to the looking glass. Were those new lines on her forehead? At twenty-one, was she old enough to have such lines? Did Lydia have lines? Isabelle? Marceline didn't. Of that Charlotte was sure. Worse, to her astonishment, her hair looked limp and stringy, and the desire to wash it overcame her. Feverish or not, she did not have to suffer grimy hair. What had become of her that she'd let herself go so? She set about collecting towels and soap and water.

Luckily, Norah had brought in two pails of water before she left. Lydia would think her ridiculous to use it up for washing hair, but sometimes, Charlotte argued to herself, the soul needed to indulge a vanity. On occasion, it could provide a satisfying sustenance, for vanities were not always as trivial as others made them out to be.

The task of heating the water, while exhausting, perked her up considerably. She knew now she could have gone to the circus, but something in her had needed the silence, the cessation of all activity other than her own. The light breeze, the warm sun, the comforting song of a sparrow in the cottonwood—these small pleasures reinforced her sense of well-being. Not even in her time with Papa had she felt so much at peace, such utter contentment. Until this moment she had never had that in her life. The realization so startled her that she sat down to consider the implications. The move to this remote place, the renunciation of worldly attitudes seemed designed to allow her this one moment of solitude. If so, she had made the right choice, she concluded as she started to plunge her hair into the water.

But she'd forgotten to bring the basin. Norah—and Odile before her—had always provided the basin as well as the hands. She had not been nearly as independent that time with Papa in the countryside as she had thought. While the staff had been minimal, servants had nevertheless been available to do all necessary chores, including shampooing her hair. Her responsibilities had required little physical action and that at her convenience. A servant could easily pour Papa's wine or slice his bread.

She fetched a basin, and as she poured the water into it, tears unexpectedly flowed from her eyes, but she soon stopped them. She refused to ruin this perfect moment with thoughts of Papa. After all, he had driven her to this remote place to pursue an abstract goal in service of a vague need. And what was the need? The shedding of skin? And if emptiness was underneath, what then?

Besides, she could not wash her own hair properly. Because the lather hadn't come immediately, she had continued applying soap, and now she couldn't get rid of the stuff. She could not even get her fingers through the tangles. And if she were to rinse all night, the soap would never come out. Tears, soap, and water streamed down her face and stung her eyes. She removed her blouse, now sopping wet as well, and sat down, finally giving in to the crying.

Preoccupied with her hair and with her crying, she didn't hear the horse approach, nor did she hear Sam dismount and walk around the corner of the house. In fact, he was almost to her before she noticed him. In her surprise, she forgot she was wearing only her camisole above her waist and peered at him through her fingers and the mess of soapy hair.

"Charlotte?" he asked, as she stood up.

"Who does it look like?" she responded sharply and picked up her shirt to dry her eyes.

"Are you all right?"

"I am always all right, Samuel. I just happen to be . . . to be washing my hair." She choked out these last few words, knowing that if he looked the least bit sympathetic, she would cry again. She had never felt so sorry for herself. This man she did not even like anymore was interrupting her precious time alone, and she couldn't possibly have looked worse for him.

He stepped close and put his arms around her. He was a born comforter, she remembered, but she stopped crying and stood still, sensing as much as feeling the presence of his arms, the strong heart rhythm in his chest. Their lower bodies remained apart. For a time they stood that way, and at some point she knew they had both become aware of her bare shoulders and arms. When she did step back, she said simply, "I have too much soap in my hair."

"Lean over the basin," he ordered, his voice revealing none of the agitation in his face. She reached for her blouse, but he took it from her hands and put it back down, his eyes not leaving hers until he bent her head over the basin. His shadow fell over her left shoulder.

As his callused hands massaged her hair and rinsed and massaged again, her body became more relaxed and aware, the tension transferring itself from her muscles to her skin. They did not speak at all, but when he had satisfied himself that the soap was gone, he picked up the large linen towel and began to dry her long tresses. Still without a word, he took up her brush and comb, led her to the porch and placed her between his legs, three steps below him. With great patience he proceeded to untangle her hair, a few locks at a time. He brushed with the same rhythmic movements he might have used to groom a horse.

If she did not think at all, she reasoned, if she blocked out the sensations caused by the heat from his legs and groin, then she would not feel disloyal to Lydia. Because it was Lydia, not May, whom she felt she was betraying.

Again, when Samuel appeared satisfied, he stopped brushing, pulled her up, and examined his efforts in the glare of the sun. He turned her around slowly twice, and on the second turn he did not pretend to be interested only in her hair. She allowed this. And when he handed her blouse to her, she put it on and he buttoned it.

She stood where he had placed her long after he disappeared from view.

So this is what brought me here, she repeated to herself. Not solitude at all.

# 36

So engrossed was Lydia in setting out tomato plants in the May sun, she paid no attention to the dogs' barking when horsemen rode past the main road and turned onto her lane. Only when she heard Anne's hurried footsteps did she look up from her digging.

"Lydia, it's Geneviève's father and two other men." Anne spoke in a rushed whisper. "I've hidden Geneviève upstairs in Charlotte's room and told him she's not here. He called me a liar. I think you'd better come deal with this."

Lydia slowly got up from her knees and wiped her hands on her skirt. Just as slowly she patted her hair. "Tell Mr. Beauchamp I'll receive him in my parlor."

"What I'm telling you is that Mr. Beauchamp is not in a receiving mood. Those men won't even dismount or doff their hats."

"Very well, then," Lydia said, striding to the other side of the houses, "while I'm being indignant, you'd better warn the others to arm themselves."

"Are we to shoot the men?"

Lydia spoke calmly to Anne: "They will not take Geneviève with them."

"Monsieur Beauchamp is her father!"

"If he insists on barbaric behavior, he leaves us no choice but to act in kind."

Anne nodded and ran into the house. Lydia continued walking slowly and calmly. After her scare at the hands of Leonard Majors, she had resolved that no man would ever again frighten her.

"Can I help you, gentlemen?" she asked and did not bother to smile.

"I've come for Geneviève," Beauchamp said in French. His dark, sharp eyes redeemed his otherwise shapeless face.

Charlotte floated into the scene, or so it seemed. Until she appeared by her side, Lydia had neither heard her steps nor seen her.

From the looks on their faces, neither had the men. "*Bonjour,* Monsieur Beauchamp. *Bonjour, messieurs.*" Speaking rapidly in French, she told them Geneviève did not want to leave Twin House Farm, nor would Lydia ask her to leave.

She then suggested that both Beauchamp parents come calling and talk with their daughter and listen to her side. Had they listened in the first place, Lydia scolded, this situation could have been prevented.

When Beauchamp began to dismount, calling her a slut and referring to his daughter in the same way, Charlotte produced a pistol from the folds of her skirt. "I am a very good shot, *messieurs,*" she said in French, "and kneecaps are very easy targets."

"We are all good shots," Isabelle echoed from an upstairs window in which the barrel of a rifle was visible. A closer look revealed that windows in both houses contained either rifles or pistols.

Beauchamp's cronies looked at him for instructions. To be sure they also understood the message, Lydia repeated it in English.

"You will pay!" Beauchamp shouted, but his party wasted no time in leaving.

Only after the sound of hoofbeats faded into the wind did the women let out their first whoop as they converged between the houses.

"Did you see Charlotte handle that pistol? I knew we'd win when Charlotte pulled out that gun with the same calm she does a knitting needle."

"Well, knitting needles bore me, and I *am* a very good shot," Charlotte told them. "As a young girl, I learned to shoot moving rabbits!"

"Hurrah for moving rabbits!" Anne shouted, and everyone clapped.

Geneviève, however, broke into sobs. "I have caused you much trouble. I am a bad girl." With those words she wept harder, and no amount of reassurance comforted her.

"You're not bad," Lydia told her, "and you mustn't worry about your father. He will not hurt us, and he will not hurt you."

Charlotte put her arm around the girl. "But he is her father," she reminded the others. "Don't pity him too much, though, *chérie.* He would have no pity on you."

"I hate him!" Geneviève sobbed anew.

"Only sometimes," Charlotte said. "It is all right when you do. And it is all right when you don't."

Later that night, after Geneviève had gone to sleep, the others sat around Lydia's parlor in their dressing gowns, drinking the warm milk Norah had brought them, discussing the situation with Geneviève. All agreed that Beauchamp would be back, and all agreed that the community would side with him; however, no agreement existed on how best to handle the deteriorating situation. At one point, Lydia chided Charlotte, "I do think you mustn't torture Geneviève with sentimental feelings about her father."

"I wasn't *torturing* her. I was attesting to the perfectly natural reaction concerning guilt over disobeying—hating—one's parents. To pretend she doesn't have it won't make it disappear."

"To pretend something doesn't exist oftentimes enables it to disappear. To condone or even understand it is an indulgence."

The two women stared at each other, neither speaking. For reasons not quite clear enough to articulate, Lydia wished she could take back her last words, which had served as a slap, she knew, to Charlotte.

Just then Norah reentered the room with another pitcher of warm milk and broke the tension, although again, without regard for the appropriateness of her words, Lydia asked, "And you, Norah, what do you suggest we do about Geneviève?"

"She has to leave this house," Norah said, continuing to serve as she talked. "She'll bring more trouble than you can handle."

"We can't turn her out," Anne protested.

"No'm, but you can't keep her here, either."

"Are you suggesting she go back to her parents, Norah?" Lydia asked, then turned to the others. "Perhaps we could give her money to go someplace else." Just as they were ready to adopt that solution, Lydia surprised even herself by asking Norah what she thought of that idea.

"She's no good for that kind of life. Too soft."

"She was brave enough to come here," Charlotte countered.

"She'll fall in with men," Norah answered looking straight at Lydia, and Lydia knew her to be right. Only an unfocused woman would have had anything to do with Leonard Majors.

"We could put her in a convent," Lydia said.

"She's too strong-headed for a convent," Charlotte reminded her, "and I'm afraid she's not yet ready to separate completely from her family."

"Then we'll have to risk keeping her here," Lydia decided.

Knowing Norah had overheard everything, Lydia caught her eye and her response, a slight shrug. But then, Lydia was learning that Norah expected little wisdom from anyone but her very own self.

**37** It was decided: Lydia and Anne would attend the Presbyterian church on Sundays; Marceline and Charlotte would go to the Catholic Mass held once a month. "Religious rituals no longer interest me," Isabelle said and refused to go anywhere.

"We are not going for reasons of ritual," Charlotte countered. "We are going to repair our image in the community. We will don our most conventional, most demure dresses."

Publications these days were filled with warnings for women in the West to renounce European fashions and culture and to delight in the virtue of their provincialism. At first the women of Twin House Farm had been delighted with this view, thinking it reflected their own sentiments, but lately Charlotte had grown depressed with the plainness around her. Still, she was determined to wear the dowdiest, most staid dress she owned.

"Then I positively refuse to go," Isabelle answered. "This is rank hypocrisy, exactly the sort of conduct we have chosen to forgo."

"Never mind Isabelle," Lydia said to the others. "The rest of us will do our duty."

For her part, however, Charlotte was glad of an excuse to participate in the old rituals that had brought solace in her youth. She yearned to go to confession, not for absolution or because of a desire to take communion, but to tell someone about Sam, to say out loud that she replayed the entire afternoon with him over and over in her head until she sometimes wondered about her sanity.

She did everything she could think of to get Samuel out of her mind. She plowed, milked, mended fences, worked as hard as any hand on the place, and rode her horse for hours at a time. When Sam and May and their baby came to visit, which they did less and less, for May was pregnant again, Charlotte excused herself as soon as possible. When she and Sam were together, they were cordial but formal.

When Frank Bailey came through on a business trip, she resorted to flirting with him in the hope of diffusing the desire that tortured her daily. He had, after all, sent a horse as promised—a spirited brown mare she had promptly named Essence. That horse had lifted her spirits more than anything else in a long time.

But her flirting served only to upset Lydia, though she had said nothing about it. Fortunately, Frank was more amused than taken in by her ruse, and she ended up respecting his shrewdness all the more and liking him better, too. She wished she could talk with him. She didn't care that he was a man. After all, she had, until Lydia, only confided in Papa, as her mother had been impossible. Of course, she now had Lydia, who was everything her maman was not; though her friendship was of no help in this particular situation.

The congregation was still milling about the churchyard when Marceline and Charlotte arrived. As they prepared to join the group, Charlotte drew a deep breath and reluctantly walked into the glare of the sun and the twang of harsh flat vowels and sharp consonants. When she saw a friend of Geneviève Beauchamp, Charlotte walked over to her, for they had met on several occasions.

"*Comment ca va petite fleur?*" she asked. She was sick of speaking English, and before the girl could answer, Charlotte, began commenting on the weather, the service, whatever else came into her mind, savoring each French syllable with sensual delight.

The girl, momentarily overwhelmed by such effusiveness, soon began responding in kind. Marceline also joined the conversation, the three now chatting and laughing in the bright sun, quite forgetting to open their parasols or to lower their voices in keeping with the rest of the parishioners socializing in small groups.

When the girl's mother approached them, Charlotte, caught up in the expansive moment, sought to engage her in conversation also, but the woman pulled back. "Natalie, come at once. We must leave," she barked.

"But you must not blame Natalie," Charlotte said. "We are the ones detaining her."

"Obviously." The woman jerked her daughter by the arm and marched her to their carriage.

"What did we do?" Marceline asked Charlotte.

"We spoke French."

"We are French! They are French!"

"They are bourgeoisie."

"I had forgotten how bourgeois the bourgeoisie is." Marceline put her arm around Charlotte's waist. "Don't look so forlorn. I will speak French with you. I, too, am sick of the American words."

This last statement, coming as it did from Marceline, brought Charlotte up short, for in it she heard her own betrayal of the dream that she and Lydia were working so hard to achieve.

"We are not sick of this language, Marceline. These American sounds have vitality."

"They are harsh."

"That is part of the vitality. It is the same as the people. And we were just snubbed because of our melodic French?"

"They are bourgeoisie. You said so yourself."

"The French nobility, are they any better? French peasants, then? Those saints who tried to burn down all the beauty of Paris. No. Forget the French. America has given us her land and the freedom to accomplish our goal. That is all one can ask from a country."

As the priest began saying Mass, Charlotte started to relax. When the bells rang, a sense of peace flooded through her. The chants alone filled her with enough pleasure and longing to produce that dangerous state between joy and despair. She had not known how much she missed the church. Perhaps she should attend more often. Perhaps it would be good for her.

Lately she'd become more and more moody. Although who had not? Charlotte wondered. It was ridiculous to feel guilty every time she looked at Lydia. Nothing had happened between her and Sam that day. She told Lydia the truth: Sam came by and ended up helping her shampoo her hair. Lydia had been pleased to hear that her brother and her friend made some sort of peace between them.

As Charlotte looked up to see if the priest was someone she could talk to, she noticed Norah waiting in line to receive communion. How did she get here? Charlotte wondered. Then again, where else would she be if she was Catholic, this being the only Mass for twenty miles around. Though Charlotte couldn't remember with certainty, she believed she had heard that Norah was Irish, and now that she thought of it, she'd seen the servant cross herself often enough.

In this setting, however, Norah did not look like a working girl. In fact, she looked like nothing so much as one of Manet's models. She had caught her hair up in a chignon befitting any lady, and she seemed to have powdered her face, for her usually ruddy complexion appeared translucent in the sun rays spilling into the church.

Though Charlotte couldn't see Norah's eyes, she assumed they were blue. In profile she had a delicately turned-up nose and bow-shaped lips and a jawline that jutted out ever so slightly, but nonetheless fit exactly the proportions of the rest of her face. She looked neither surly nor belligerent, the two attitudes that were most characteristic of her, but her face showed spirit, a stubbornness, a determination to claim a life, a self of her own, independent of her station.

Charlotte reflected on the strangeness of heart-calls. There was no accounting for them. In order to keep her mind from drifting back to Samuel she concentrated all the harder on Norah.

Any one of these farmers would have been delighted to have the girl as a wife, though the last thing their little commune needed was to lose a pair of hands around the place, even a pair that could be as incompetent as Norah's. In this part of America there were many girls like her who had bettered themselves by marrying hardworking, spirit-exhausting men. Then again, why should Norah have to settle for that kind of life any more than the rest of them did? At Twin House Farm she worked hard, but no one had crushed her spirit.

Charlotte brought her thoughts back to the Mass just as the priest recited *"Ite, missa est,"* and she was sorry the service was ending. She rose with the others and made her way out of the church.

"We might as well leave," Marceline whispered. "No one looks especially friendly today. We've walked past four different groups now and not one soul has bothered to look up and smile, let alone speak."

"Everyone is preoccupied with this drought," Charlotte responded. Still, not having paid attention until now, Charlotte looked around the churchyard, and she, too, began to see that they were being snubbed.

Then she caught Simone Clarkson's eye and, with Marceline in tow, strode over to her even though they had never done more than exchange pleasantries before. Mrs. Clarkson had been a seamstress before moving to America and marrying. Even with eight children flocked around her, she managed a magnetic attractiveness and an attendant flirtatiousness.

"How are you, Mrs. Clarkson?" Charlotte asked in her most precise English.

Mrs. Clarkson would have none of that, however. She spent so much time in her dugout alone with her children, whom her husband had forbidden to speak French, that she was not about to forgo an opportunity to converse in her own tongue.

"Much better, if you don't count the crops. My three oldest children are of some real use to their papa now, and I'm taking in more and more sewing. What with all the crop failures, the ladies are having their old clothes altered rather than ordering new ones, and my reputation as a seamstress is spreading.

"I'll be glad to do some mending for you, Mademoiselle Duret. I don't care what they say, you are a kind person, and I hope only the best for you."

Charlotte thanked her and indicated that she did have clothes to be altered; all of them did. Flirtatious or not, Simone Clarkson had a dignity about her that poverty, an oppressive husband, and too many children did not diminish. Neither she nor the children looked as if they'd had enough to eat and unless the drought broke soon, the winter would only intensify the situation.

On their way home Marceline, picking up on Simone Clarkson's remark, asked what exactly "they" were saying about their group.

"How should I know?" Charlotte snapped, annoyed that Marceline could not resist making her point one more time. Just then she saw a figure in the far distance. "Could that be Norah?" she asked, relieved to change the subject.

"*Mon Dieu!* We forgot to offer Norah a ride!"

"She could have asked us," Charlotte pointed out.

"Norah is too proud. You know that as well as I do," Marceline scolded.

"Then she is absurd."

"That remark is absurd."

At last they had found a safe subject to quarrel over. By the time they caught up with Norah, they weren't speaking to each other.

"You should have waited for us, Norah," Charlotte began lecturing at once. Then she noticed Norah's face—angry, defiant, streaked with tears.

"What happened? Are you crying?" Charlotte asked her.

"No, ma'am, I'm just sweatin'," Norah, mumbled, wiping her sleeve across her eyes and dripping nose.

"You've been running, that's what's wrong. How else could you have gotten so far ahead of us?" Marceline said.

"Norah," Charlotte said, sharply this time, "tell us what is wrong."

But Norah stubbornly shook her head. "They're mean, those people."

"They were talking about us?"

But all Norah would say was that they were mean, and once she had seated herself in the buggy, she refused to speak at all. Charlotte and Marceline also rode in silence.

"I am afraid we have lost the community forever," Marceline finally said. "It is never going to accept us."

38 At the dinner table at noontime, over fried chicken, creamed corn, and summer peas, for all declared a fondness for good farm fare, Lydia noticed nothing askew as she and Anne described their Sunday morning. While no one at church had openly embraced them, they had not been exactly shunned either. The unpredictable Emma Leggett had simply ignored them. Roberta Brown barely spoke, but several others came up to Anne and, by default, Lydia, for brief conversations.

Anne, the women agreed, was their best community asset. They debated whether it was her reserved, gentle manner or her aura of absolute integrity that drew these people to her. Whatever, she neither threatened them nor incited hostility.

But they talked about Anne for only a few minutes because that kind of attention embarrassed her too much, and she managed to switch the subject herself by mentioning that another farm was for sale. A bargain, that's what Wallace Brown had said, too good to pass up. Lydia didn't know where they would get the money. (Later, she had decided, she would ask Charlotte what she thought of asking Frank Bailey to be a partner again, but with him she had to be careful, for she didn't want to encourage her friend's relationship with him. It would not serve Charlotte well.)

Barely had she relayed this news when Norah came in with a red nose and asked to be excused from serving. Before Lydia could protest— for they were without Sally, who had taken the day off to go to Dodge City—Charlotte had quickly agreed. Norah had been crying after church, Charlotte and Marceline explained. Since no one could imagine Norah crying, the cause must have been dreadful.

"It's my fault," Geneviève burst out. "Everybody in town is saying Norah's crazy and Lydia and the rest of you are weird. Eva Woods told me so in her letter last week. It's that Leonard Majors who's the cause of it. He told terrible stories when he left here, and all because of me." Geneviève cried into her hands. Charlotte handed her a handkerchief, and they all turned to Lydia, who said nothing.

"He says Norah tried to kill him," Geneviève continued.

"Norah tried to kill him?" Charlotte repeated.

"In a manner of speaking," Lydia murmured.

"And you knew this?"

"Of course, I did. If it hadn't been for me, Norah wouldn't have done it."

"What on earth are you talking about?" Marceline asked. "Norah tried to kill Leonard Majors and you drove him out of town?"

Lydia took a deep breath. What could she do? She had to tell, and so she began her explanation about Majors and Norah and the ax, about buying his land to get rid of him. She did not mention the bribe to the land commissioner. But Charlotte looked hurt, and Lydia could understand that. After all, Charlotte had had a right to know why she'd had this obsession with owning Majors's land. She had not questioned Lydia's willingness to do business with Wallace Brown even though neither of them trusted him. Worse, Lydia knew she had no satisfactory explanation to offer as to why she had withheld all this from her friend.

Perhaps her encounter with Majors had caused more lasting damage than she had realized. For months she'd hardly dared to think about it, and she certainly couldn't talk about it. There was shame—inexplicable, haunting.

Even as she told the story, she hurried on, rushing to tell her friends of her revenge. And they applauded her and thought her brave, but Norah had been braver. Norah would have killed Leonard Majors with that ax. She would have killed him sooner than a rattlesnake. Norah was the brave one. And Lydia got up from the table to find Norah and tell her so.

Later, when Charlotte sought her out in their flower garden, Lydia decided that her friends had mistaken one of her strengths for another, miscalculating her resilience. On Sundays, about the only time she had for this indulgence, she liked to tend their flowers. The hum of the bees, the blend of summer scents, the feel of earth crumbling in her fingers had already begun to soothe.

"Since the day has turned into one of confession, I have another for you—or rather, we all do," Charlotte began.

"In that case, shall I stand up or will you kneel down? It does seem we should be on an equal plane, so to speak," Lydia said, smiling.

"I'm wearing my white silk stockings," Charlotte said, embarrassed to confess her vanity. She helped pull Lydia up, and they walked toward the stream.

"First, I understand why you didn't tell me about Majors," Charlotte began. "I saw you worrying about my reaction to your news, but your instinct to protect Geneviève and Norah was a true one."

"I also didn't want such ugliness to intrude on our new life. I suppose I thought I was protecting you, but . . . I am sorry. I—"

Charlotte held up her hand. "Some secrets take a long time in the telling. That's all," Now she was the one who smiled, and as they walked along the stream, hearing a frog, swatting a fly, she reached out for Lydia's hand. When they came to the bench, Charlotte pulled Lydia down and wasted no more time.

"We thought you should know Gabriel de Rochefort is pressing to come see Marceline."

"That's an easy one. Marceline should refuse in no uncertain terms and then Isabelle should write him a letter of her own explaining that a visit is quite impossible. Marceline is sometimes weaker than she appears, I'm afraid."

"You don't understand. Marceline and Isabelle have already told him to stay away, but he says he's coming anyway."

Lydia jumped up. "But that really is impossible! He is not coming here. I may be over him, but I am not about to allow that bastard to set foot on Twin House Farm!"

"That's what I said also. The others feel the same way. But Gabriel is coming to Kansas no matter what we say. He maintains he wants to see this country. Of course Marceline and Isabelle could meet him in another part of the state." As Charlotte talked, Lydia began pacing back and forth. "You would never have to see him, but you do seem to have gotten over him, and Marceline . . . well, without the support of her friends . . . As you just said, she may not be as steadfast as she thinks."

"Oh, this is all so humiliating."

"Then that's the end of it." Charlotte stood up. "I'll tell them to make other arrangements."

Lydia sat back down. "Don't do that either. I don't want them to think he matters to me, and I certainly don't want *him* to." She slapped her knees and stood again. "It really doesn't matter, except that he . . . But why should I care now? And why should we lose Marceline because of him? No. Let him come here. Let him see what we have built. Let him see how unnecessary he is to the course of human events!"

"By all means let him come," she said to Marceline and Isabelle as they sipped tepid tea in the tepid air of Charlotte's parlor, darkened now to keep out the oven-hot rays of the summer sun. "I don't plan to be his best friend, but I will certainly be civil to him. We'll put him to work for a few days. That will do him a world of good."

"Imagine Gabriel milking a cow!" Marceline said, effectively releasing the tension.

Soon afterward, however, Lydia retired to her room with a headache brought on by working in the sun without a hat. Whatever had she been thinking? Yes, in the future she would be more careful, and no, she didn't need a thing for supper.

But when Norah knocked on her door with a glass of milk and cold corn bread, she gratefully accepted.

"Corn bread is good if you crumble it into the milk," Norah suggested, "but you'll need this spoon to eat it with." Lydia agreed to try it that way.

"I'm sorry the truth about Leonard Majors came out, ma'am. But it's no matter to us. What's happened ain't fair, but it mostly never is."

"I'm sure you're right, Norah."

"The important thing is not to chew on it any longer than you have to. Spit it out first thing. Justice is worth a fight, but it ain't worth a tear. That way is craziness."

"Sound advice and thank you." Lydia always found something so comforting and wise about Norah.

"One more thing," Norah said. "That Majors man and that baron aren't worth the energy it takes to raise your little finger. That's the truth of it."

"You remember that yourself, Norah. Those gossipmongering fools are not worth one of your tears. Not one, Norah. You believe me, too."

They embraced, and Lydia began to crumble corn bread into her sweet milk as Norah closed the door behind her. So what else could she do? She could plan a trip, that's what. When Gabriel came, she would leave. Everyone, including Norah, would be watching to see how she would handle him. Well, why shouldn't Norah watch, too? Everyone else now knew all of Lydia Fulgate's business.

But she would leave. She would take a business trip somewhere. To Chicago perhaps? She would ask Frank Bailey for money. Another piece of property would put the oafs around here in their place. With enough money, she could also bring in more sheep, another piece of farm equipment—every day there was a new invention on the market to ensure success, and the more of them they had, the sooner this place would become dependably productive. Let those fools say whatever they wished; they would soon enough have to pay attention.

But Norah was right. She must rid herself of bitterness. The next step was to replace its taste—extending Norah's metaphor—with something sweet, though maybe not quite so satisfying as justice. Second best would do.

*39* Acting on impulse, Lydia fled to Chicago when Gabriel de Rochefort's arrival became imminent. She had made reservations at the Palmer House and looked forward to spending a few days alone. As much as she loved the bustle of her household, she could use a respite from engaging, entreating, and responding.

Frank Bailey met her at the train station. She hadn't expected that. Or had she? She had, after all, informed him of her arrival time. And she had chosen for her traveling costume her most attractive suit, a light gray wool that allowed the blue lace collar of her blouse to show, calling attention to her eyes. She had not only donned her bustle and petticoats but had also retrieved her corset from the bottom of a trunk. And here she was, expecting and receiving a compliment on her becoming outfit. Frank Bailey had never complimented her before on anything, so far as she could remember; yet she had assumed this, his first, as her due.

She was also not completely surprised when he suggested she stay in his home. Naturally, she protested. How would it look—such an arrangement? As naturally, he insisted. They argued. He chided her for being prudish, wondering aloud why a woman who claimed to be an independent spirit could still be so worried about her reputation, especially when no one would know her whereabouts.

So here she was, sitting in his library smoking one of his Cuban cigars and sipping his excellent brandy (he knew her weakness for both), having just finished the best meal she had had since she left Paris, having confided to him her frustration over their rejection by the larger community, and having asked for and received a much larger loan than she had originally intended.

"A harvester will be grand," he was saying, "but don't expect gadgets to solve all your problems."

"They'll go far in that direction. Even Roberta Brown will be impressed." She rested her head against the high back of the upholstered chair, content enough to sit there all night, enjoying the smell and taste of the brandy and cigar and watching the smoke, more nebulous than clouds, as the clock on his marble mantel chimed the hours.

"By all means, you must impress Roberta Brown," he chided in a drowsy voice and put his head back, too.

"Don't make fun of me. Roberta Brown is important to the people part of our undertaking." She glanced over to see if he was watching her. He was. She discreetly rearranged her skirt to show her slipper, of a more delicate cut than she was used to wearing these days. "Roberta Brown has influence with the Ladies' Literary Society."

"Then do let us cultivate our Mrs. Brown."

Lydia smiled at him. "You could, you know—cultivate Mrs. Brown. She would positively swoon at your feet."

"Does that mean she's a woman of no taste, or are you paying me a compliment?"

She lazily rolled her head from side to side. "Decide for yourself."

"If I remember correctly, Roberta Brown is the one with the garish house."

"It's not altogether garish," she answered with just a hint of flirtation in her voice, flicking her ashes into the brass spittoon that stood between them.

"Whatever," he said a little too quickly. Was it possible she could fluster him? "She doesn't sound like anyone you or Charlotte would want to spend two minutes with. I can't imagine any club worth that price."

"You don't understand. These women are the cultural and intellectual heart of the community."

He leaned over to pour her more brandy.

"That's enough," she said, touching the back of his pouring hand with her fingers. She allowed her fingers to linger a few seconds longer than necessary, and she realized that he knew that, too.

This time it was she who quickly continued: "On the whole, these women seem to take the time to read and think more deeply than their husbands. If we can get them to listen, they could spread our message. Most of them, I'm sure we'll enjoy. In our part of the world they really are the purveyors of ideas."

"But why do you think you need any of them—Roberta Brown, the Ladies' Literary Society, or the town? You have your good friends, you have your brother, you have an active, productive life, and, from what you and Charlotte tell me, you are successfully discovering your . . . whatever it is you call it."

"Our essence, the same name as the horse you gave Charlotte," she said. "You know that perfectly well."

They stared at each other, Lydia silently reprimanding him, Frank accepting it. So there *she* was, brought out into the open. All night they'd both avoided mentioning Charlotte's name.

After all, Frank Bailey was the cause of Charlotte's moping around these days, and with every visit his feelings for her grew more apparent. Naturally Charlotte, flattered and a little homesick, could hardly help noticing how much more comfortable Frank Bailey's life was than theirs. Kansas meant heat waves, floods, winds, crop failures, dust, sand, and more dust. By comparison, Chicago might pass for paradise. Or Paris.

And here Lydia Fulgate and Frank Bailey were, holding each other's gaze that same extra beat that had come with the touch. "You don't understand," she said, disrupting the moment. "If we turn only inward, think only of ourselves, then we're indulging in the worst form of arrogance."

"None of you strike me as evangelists," he countered, resuming his amused, distant pose.

"We are, however. We want a larger world; otherwise, our situation will become claustrophobic. On the whole, we're a gregarious lot."

"Is it possible that you are imposing your attitude on the others?"

"I am doing nothing of the kind." She was relieved to find the old tension between them restored—a feeling that was much more familiar and easier to control. "As I said, our main concern is that we don't become so inward that we lose our sense of the world. I personally think isolation is not the path to self-discovery. That's as useless as spending all one's time acquiring possessions and besting the world." They glared at each other until the look again turned into something else. But he was not good for Charlotte. She would not be able to resist him.

"May I remind you," he said, "that my acquisitions are supporting your notions of upright behavior?"

"You are crude!" As they resumed their angry silence, Lydia noticed the chairs had been placed within touching distance of each other. She was not the first woman who had sat here, she felt sure.

"Well, since I've already insulted you," he said, "let me continue. You think you are practicing single blessedness, as I understand the term from Anne, but what do you think this missionary stance is about? You are still trying to justify your way of life by doing good—as you define it."

"That is a far cry more gainful than the squandering, sordid life you lead."

"And what makes you think my life is sordid?" he snapped.

"I can tell. I know about these things." There they were, glaring again. Glaring, staring, gazing. Their cigars had burned out of their own accord. The candle would be next. No, Lydia had played this scene before, and she was not about to repeat the performance. And there was Charlotte. Just being here was a kind of betrayal of her, Lydia couldn't deceive herself about that. Charlotte would not have done this—not without telling Lydia, at any rate.

She should excuse herself this minute, but not for Charlotte's sake. Frank Bailey was loathsome. *That* temptation had already passed. No, she should leave for the sake of the loan. If they hurled many more barbs at each other, the money would vanish. But he had just refilled her brandy glass. Not to be outdone, she took a sip.

"I'm glad to see you indulge in a few earthly pleasures," he said. "That's almost as great a relief as knowing you recognize a sordid life when you see one. I didn't know a woman of your delicate sensibility could identify such a thing. I had the impression you only thought about souls."

Her first instinct was to throw the brandy in his face and stalk out. She resisted. Instead she looked straight into his eyes and smiled. "Pleasures of the flesh can turn into treasures of the soul," she responded slowly.

Man of the world though he was, he couldn't quite hide his surprise, and she found herself enjoying his unease. "I thought you, of all people, knew that, Mr. Bailey." Her voice had grown quiet and a little husky, just as she'd intended. He appeared genuinely astonished that she was flirting. Perhaps her anger hadn't sobered up her quite as much as she thought.

Acting again on impulse, she rose and stood in front of him. "Perhaps you can teach me something of sordidness, and I can teach you something of delicate sensibility."

For one dreadful moment she thought he might reject her proposition.

# 40

"Tell me the truth, Anne. Did he try to seduce you too?" Charlotte asked.

Anne laughed.

"Don't be coy. Did he? Yes or no?"

"He flirts; he doesn't try to seduce."

"So he *did* try. I knew it! Gabriel de Rochefort always assumes a flirtation will end in the bed, and nine times out of ten he's right."

"I take it you were one of his disappointments."

"Yes, but he didn't try very hard with me."

"As I told you, me either."

"I can't understand why I ever found him attractive," Charlotte said, "or why Lydia fell in love with him."

"Or why Marceline still is," Anne added.

Using the excuse of an errand in town, they had settled themselves along the riverbank under a willow tree just out of sight of the stores and houses. They weren't likely to run into anyone out of doors, for the day was blustery enough to discourage all but those who were most intent on their duties, which Charlotte and Anne were not.

With Gabriel de Rochefort in residence, they looked for excuses to escape the household. When Lydia had suggested that she visit Chicago for a few days, Charlotte had been relieved. Now she wished Lydia hadn't gone, for her hostile presence might—how did Kansans say it?—might shoo him away. If he didn't leave, Marceline was doomed.

No matter that Marceline knew he was a hunter of the first order, one who abandoned his prey once captured. No matter that Marceline had even used his vice as a ploy in her game with him. When confronted with the full intensity of his charm, she was finding it hard to resist his entreaties.

After all, she'd told them, love can change a person, and maybe she was as special to him as he claimed she was—so special that she could transform him. And then she'd begun to express the tiniest doubt about her friends' motives. Could they just possibly be a bit jealous of such a great love? Perhaps they simply did not appreciate her enough, did not understand just how special she could be to someone like Gabriel. Had she and her friends become too cynical, seeing every encounter between a man and a woman as a giant contest with no rules? Marceline didn't say any of this directly, but she hinted and pouted sufficiently when the subject came up, as it did with greater and greater frequency these days.

"We must hold firm to Marceline," Charlotte told Anne, as if she were introducing a new subject.

"Since we can't lock her in her room, what's there to do?"

"Take her on a trip, that's what," Charlotte announced, proud of her solution.

"But where? And do you think she'll go?"

"We'll take her to Colorado. I know someone who has a summer place there."

208 · Kate Lehrer

"Somehow I don't think that would be Marceline's idea of sum-mering."

"Then we'll take her to Virginia. Don't you have relatives in Virginia?"

"None who have spoken to me since the South lost the War between the States," Anne said.

"We'll think of someplace. We have to."

This idea had so captured Charlotte that she felt lighter than she had in months. This was the answer to her own predicament. A trip would take her away from Samuel, give her back her own world. Lydia would under-stand the need to rescue Marceline. For support and company she would have Isabelle, not to mention Sam. Never to mention Sam, who just now appeared to be riding toward them.

"I thought these were familiar faces," he said after pulling his horse to a halt. So she had seen him in the distance; she hadn't just conjured him up out of perverse need. She watched him look around for a place to hitch his horse, watched him give up on that idea, watched him climb down anyway, watched him loop the reins around his hand. He put his arms around Anne and swayed her back and forth. If he puts his arms around me, Charlotte thought, I'll push him in the water or faint or tear his clothes off—none of which seemed like a promising solution.

"Charlotte." He bowed from the waist and kissed her hand.

That's all he said, she thought: "Charlotte." Yesterday he'd brushed her cheek with his lips. She hated it that he could perform such intimate gestures and still manage to appear impersonal. She feared the world could read her feelings for him even when she didn't acknowledge him.

"You two look like refugees from a love nest," he said, teasing, as they got up to walk along the riverbank with him. "Any word on Marceline's latest change of heart today?"

"That's the problem. Her heart is stuck at the moment, and there's not a change in sight. Charlotte has just proposed a trip for us as a means of getting her unstuck."

"A trip?" he asked, his neck muscles tensing. "For how long?"

"However long it takes to unstick a heart, Samuel. Any ideas?" Anne said without smiling.

A troubled expression crossed his face.

"If Lydia agrees, Anne and I will be Marceline's nursemaids, and we'll get a vacation, too," Charlotte added, feeling more in control now that Samuel seemed less sure of his ground.

"Knowing my sister, she'll think no fixing is possible without her." They all laughed at the truth in that statement. "So you'll have to stay here to run things." He said this with such happy boyishness that Charlotte forgave him for revealing all, and with such innocence. In the future, though, she and Sam would have to be more careful around Anne.

"Sam, we need to go into town. Why don't you ride with us?" Anne asked. "It would be a great help if you'd take Charlotte by the feed store, since I'd almost forgotten I promised to call on Emma Leggett."

Before Charlotte could protest, Sam agreed to join them. The ride into town was pleasant enough, with Anne bantering with Sam while Charlotte focused on the horizon. Anne jumped from the wagon as soon as they were in town and was off toward the Leggetts'. Just as quickly Charlotte scrambled down beside her.

"Anne, I'm coming with you." Charlotte had to walk rapidly to catch up with Anne.

"The two of you have to talk sometime," Anne said. "The tension between you gets worse by the day."

"How did you find out?"

"I've known Sam all my life. I've never seen him behave this way. Besides, he's pretty obvious. He sometimes goes for months without dropping by Twin House Farm, but now, with Lydia gone, he's there every day. He probably thinks no one else notices, but he knows *she* would. As children, Lydia convinced us she could read our minds. In the intervening years nothing has changed."

"You had no right to decide I should talk to him."

"Well, shouldn't you?"

"I'm afraid to."

Anne stopped and took Charlotte's hands in hers. "Then tell him that. Tell him he has to stay away for your sake, his sake, his children's sake. For everybody's sake.

"Listen, I always thought of Lydia and Sam as Siamese twins: nothing comes between them, and if it did, Lydia would die." Then Anne gave a rueful smile. "After killing whatever it was, of course. They sometimes let me into their secret hideout, but only because I've always understood their rules.

"You must understand that Sam could do more damage than any bad weather to what you and Lydia have built and fought so hard for. Tell him that, Charlotte. He's too besotted with you to think straight for himself."

"I am afraid," Charlotte repeated.

The two women—one American, one French—looked at each other in silence, each understanding, all too well, the frailty of resolve and the oppression of consequence. Then Charlotte walked toward the wagon and Sam.

**41** Last night it had made such clear sense. Something about Charlotte. Something about pleasure and treasures. Certainly something about brandy. But she had seduced Frank Bailey into his own bed. Or had he done the seducing when he invited her to stay with him? Had he known what he was doing? Last night he did seem rather amazed at her behavior. She'd been a little startled herself; still was.

She could hear him breathing. Resentment welled up in her. He should have had the decency to pretend last night hadn't happened. God, he was still with her! She opened her eyes ever so slowly, as if an abrupt move of her eyelids might awaken him.

"Good morning," he said, not only awake but staring at her as well. Quickly she shut her eyes again, knowing, even as she did so that it was too late to pretend to be asleep.

"How old are you?" he asked as if that were a perfectly normal question.

"Don't be impertinent!" she snapped and reached down to pull the covers up to her neck. "How dare you watch me sleep! Examining me like I'm one of your mares!"

"There are worse comparisons," he retorted. "In any case, you rate at the top of whatever form you choose."

She jumped out of bed. "Damn you!" she yelled and tried to pull the bedcovers around her. But she didn't know what to do next. Her clothes were nowhere to be seen, and she was having an awful time keeping the covers wrapped around both her front and her back. Her shoulders were bare. Her feet were bare. And that man was taking it all in, watching her every little movement. She'd never felt so exposed.

She had also never seen a room with so many doors. The idea of opening each one to no avail, making an utter fool of herself to his vast amusement, transformed her resentment into rage. He was refusing to let her forget her conduct last night. Without hesitation, almost without thought, she picked up a vase of flowers, threw it at him, and was gratified to see he'd stopped being amused.

"Whoa!" he roared, bounding out of bed toward her—completely naked, she noticed, just as he pinned her arms to her sides.

"Stop speaking of me as if I were a horse!" she yelled back. If she twisted out of his grip, the bedclothes would fall. If she let him restrain her, he would win. She twisted away and this time aimed a paperweight directly at his groin, but he lunged for her, knocking her to the floor before she could throw it. Struggling over the object clenched in her fist, he wrested it from her, then rose, turned his back, and tossed her the bedcovers without looking in her direction.

She noticed he had an erection. Indeed, a very erect erection—full tilt, so to speak. Herman would have been out of his mind with pride at such a feat, but this man was trying to hide it from her. Good! Let him rot in hell in just that state.

As he disappeared behind one of the doors, he pointed a hand toward another. "There," he barked, but for all she knew, he was only trying to humiliate her further by sending her away without her clothes. Or to expose her to his household staff or keep her imprisoned in that tasteless bedroom forever. This last thought was so horrifying that she decided to risk public ridicule rather than succumb. In one bold gesture, she threw open the door, only to find her clothes laid out carefully and a tub filled with warm water.

The cast-iron tub itself was a rebuke, with its oak rim and ornately carved cupids and gold-leaf claws—quite beyond anything she'd seen or wanted to see in this new life of hers. No doubt it was the latest advance in technology and design. Then again, though it might offend her, it would certainly offend the medical profession and all the others who still warned of the dangers of a good soak.

She did take comfort in seeing and hearing no one about. Maybe no one had heard their argument, either. Too exhausted to calculate, she gave herself over to the bath and the delicious feel of the warm water on her body—this body with its newfound power, altered forever by the night before.

Give Frank Bailey that much. He had shown her what she was capable of. At times becoming frightened by the intensity of her passion, she had begged him to stop. When he didn't, she begged him to continue, and when he did, she also begged him to continue. He had taken her out of herself, beyond calculation; he had turned her body into an instrument of bewitching sensations.

But she owned those sensations. They were hers now. He had even helped her to understand that: the power was hers to call up whenever she wished, with whomever she chose. For she had not for a moment thought she was in love. That treachery upon herself had ended with the loss of Gabriel. No, this was about tapping into her own power, her woman's power. She thought she understood a little better those Frenchwomen whose secrets she envied: they grew up accepting and knowing they possessed their own sexuality. They hadn't been taught to disown it or pretend it didn't exist, or to discover it and think something was wrong with them. To them it was not an outside force but something that resided in them, and now she had it, too. She smiled: she had also discovered an activity that her own hands could perform very well.

She took her time bathing, dressing, and putting up her hair. Although she was out of the habit of being assisted by a lady's maid—Norah and Sally having far too many farm chores these days to assist with anyone's toilet—she had expected one and had felt both relief and disappointment when none appeared.

She wished Charlotte were here with her to enjoy such a bath, to share in this little respite from sand and chores. On returning to Twin House Farm, she would do something wonderful for her friend. The money would make Charlotte happy, and she need never know about last night. Besides, this would never happen again. The guilt would go away, for what had happened had nothing to do with her beloved Charlotte. The guilt would go away.

Finally, when there was nothing to do but return to the bedroom, she steeled herself for a confrontation. Frank Bailey obviously could not be relied upon to behave like a gentleman. If by some good fortune he was no longer present, she would leave a note demanding her trunk be sent . . . but where? she wondered. She didn't want to go back to Kansas without money. She herself had no good contacts in the banking world, and already on paper she looked land-poor.

Imitating Charlotte's most queenly airs, she opened the bedroom door, hoping as she did so that he'd drowned in his bath—and left Charlotte his entire estate. Instead, Lydia found her cloak with a note pinned to it:

*Dear Mrs. Fulgate,*

*For the remainder of your stay, consider this your room, since you are so fond of so many of the objects found here. This evening we shall dine at eight o'clock, at which time we shall discuss the details of the loan you wish as well as the best approach to take. My carriage and my staff are at your disposal throughout the day. This morning did not, of course, take place.*

*With sincere regard,*
*Frank Bailey*

*P.S. If I am able to overlook your impulse to murder, I assume you are prepared to do the same. Your breakfast is waiting on a tray in the sunroom.*

It was arrogant of him to presume she'd stay, but she could buy herself a little time by leaving her trunk here while she took a carriage ride to sort out her plans and consider her options. Also she was hungry. She navigated her way to the sunroom and ate a delicious melon with still-warm toast. Then she comfortably settled in with her pot of coffee and the morning papers.

Even without the sun, the room was inviting enough; and the papers, with their gossip of the social world and the advertisements showing the latest fashions, absorbed her for more than half the morning. Besides, what else was she going to do? She knew she had few options, since she really needed that money.

And she wanted a new dress. At that moment she didn't care whether or not it represented the frivolous world or fit into her household budget. She wanted it, and she would have it. She had saved expense money by staying with him.

What did one more night matter? How else could she insure both the money and his goodwill? If she wasn't careful, he might try to take Charlotte away from her, adding spite to attraction—a combination that would certainly have appealed to her, had she been in his circumstances. For he would destroy them if he could, but she had the strength to resist him. Charlotte did not.

By dinnertime she had managed to work herself back into a civilized state with the help of a much-too-expensive royal blue silk dress, alluring and demure at the same time. Her vanity was such that she wanted Frank to desire her again, if only so that she could reject him haughtily.

When she entered the dining room, he had risen from his chair at the table, where he had apparently been looking over some papers. He had acknowledged her with a curt "Mrs. Fulgate" and a nod of his head, but he had not so much as extended a hand or looked at her with appreciation, or even recognition.

She returned his greeting in kind and went one step further by thanking him for the use of his carriage. He did her the favor of not getting that irritating amused look on his face, the way he sometimes did with her. In all fairness, she was as responsible, if not more so, for last night as he; and he'd been decent enough not to point that out to her. She allowed herself to relax a little.

When a butler appeared at the table to serve, she was even able to forget that he had possibly heard the morning contretemps. Say one thing for Frank Bailey, she mused: he kept his staff invisible until they were needed; she had seen no one until a maid appeared at the bedroom door to help her dress for dinner.

Say this also for Frank Bailey, she thought, as he laid out his strategy on the loan: he was able to behave as if they had no business other than business, although his apparent lack of interest vexed her more than she thought it would.

They both played their game so well that when they moved to the parlor after dinner and sat in front of the fireplace, it seemed the most natural thing in the world. When he offered her brandy and a cigar, as he would any business companion, it seemed like the second most natural thing in the world.

But when he suggested they retreat to his bed again, it was her turn to be surprised, though not angry. Perhaps the wine and the brandy and the heat and the cigar had dulled her critical faculties more than most businessmen's, she speculated, for how could they ever negotiate deals operating as she had these last two evenings?

"You don't even like me," she was obliged to point out to him.

"And do you like me?"

She considered. "Not much," she answered.

"It's our mutual dislike that adds such piquancy. Besides, I would be less of a trial to you than the man you're now running away from."

"I am not running away. I detest that man." Then she felt a pang. "Did Charlotte tell you about him?"

"Charlotte wouldn't. Does it surprise you that I have friends in Paris?"

"You shouldn't have spent the entire night in the same bed with me. Why didn't you go find another bed, like a proper gentleman?"

"That is my bed, remember?"

"You gave it to me."

He laughed, a deep, unreserved laugh. "I loaned it to you today, not last night."

"To stay in the same bed with a woman, actually to sleep with her, is so . . . *intimate*," she said. She was holding her brandy with both hands, and on her knees, which felt permanently locked together. Her cigar had gone out.

"Tonight I'll leave whenever you say, although I hope you won't say it too quickly."

She looked up at him. "And you will never tell anyone? Never tell Charlotte?"

Gently he pried her fingers away from the brandy glass. Gently also he pried her knees apart.

This night he told her she had beautiful lips, unspoiled, almost virginal. So beautiful, he repeated. Her lips! She didn't even call them lips. But he knew so many things to do there—so many things. Before they fell asleep she had agreed to stay an extra night. With him. In his bed.

"Marceline, how can you squander your dream for him?" Lydia asked upon her return from Chicago.

"It doesn't feel that way," Marceline responded lamely.

"Marceline! Honestly, now, weren't you happier before that man reentered your life?"

"I suppose so," Marceline mumbled.

"Do you really think that going back to France with him, succumbing to his entreaties, will bring you greater happiness? Do you really think that once he wins the game, he'll become more attentive to you?"

After Marceline left the room sobbing, Charlotte scolded Lydia for pressing her too hard. Perhaps she had. But someone had to save Marceline, once and for all, and the trip proposed by Charlotte and Anne would be only a holding measure at best.

Lydia stared down at the papers on her desk and felt a bit put-upon that she was the only one willing to do whatever was necessary to protect her friends, although she could hardly claim to have sacrificed herself to the whims of Frank Bailey for Charlotte's sake. Even as she was seducing him—or he was seducing her, however it had been—she had known in her heart that she was only trying to justify what she wanted by claiming he'd be bad for Charlotte. Well, she didn't regret what she'd done, and Frank Bailey had certainly erased any lingering feelings she'd had toward

Gabriel. Though she wasn't sure that what Frank had stirred up would serve her any better. She sighed aloud.

"Now, that's a sound I never thought I'd hear coming out of the beautiful Lydia Fulgate," Gabriel de Rochefort said as he approached her.

In a reflex motion, she put her arm over the financial sheet she'd been going over at her desk. What did he know of finances, anyway? And what exactly did she feel she needed to hide?

If he noticed her secretiveness, he didn't show it any more than he appeared to have noticed her rebuffs the night before. Instead, he asked if this was a convenient time to talk with her. He wanted her advice on some business ideas. Where could they go to have a little privacy?

"With all due respect, this house is no place for solitude," he told her, "and I say this as one who is no connoisseur of that state."

For the first time since she'd met him, he wasn't trying to seduce or charm her. More important, some shield, some invisible suit of armor, had vanished. This is the way he must be with Isabelle, Lydia decided. This is why she is secure in their mutual need for each other.

"Why don't you join me here?" she suggested. "No one will bother us, since I always growl when I'm going over the books."

Pulling up a straight chair, he straddled it and gripped its back with his hands. He began to confide how intrigued he'd become with Kansas and the possibilities it offered. He had no illusions that he could farm, but he believed himself capable of running a business. How much did something like a newspaper or a hotel cost? In some town other than Huddleston, would a saloon be promising? Or perhaps he could open a chain of opera houses like the new one in Huddleston, or be an impresario for an established chain. "There are fortunes to be made out here. What I don't know is how to go about making them."

"A good place to start is with land."

"But I told you farming would be folly for me."

"Buying and building houses wouldn't. Buying and selling land would not. This town was settled a dozen years ago when a man laid out buffalo bones for its boundaries—with the cooperation of the railroad, of course." For clarity's sake, she spoke to him in French.

Should she give him advice when it could mean that he'd remain in close proximity to Marceline, even if they did manage to rescue her this time around? She felt misgivings, but his enthusiasm reminded her of her own and Charlotte's. She also saw that he too had discovered how to avoid being forced to marry for money. Occupations unacceptable to his status in France became perfectly reasonable pursuits here. As he pointed out, they promised a fortune.

For a while they discussed possibilities, including one that would take him to Colorado. Evidently a lot of activity was going on there. When he responded positively to that suggestion, she became more enthusiastic. Just maybe she had found a way to help both Marceline and Gabriel. And why not aid him, she reasoned, for he could no more change who he was than she could.

"I've never felt I could do anything, Lydia, anything of consequence," he confessed.

"You hunt pretty well," she said.

"But that's my nature."

"Your nature will be the ruin of Marceline. You know that, don't you?"

"Her nature is like mine. I can withstand hers; she can withstand mine." He dismounted his chair and came to stand by her side. "Let's not quarrel over Marceline. Or over us. I'm sorry if I hurt you."

"*If* you hurt me!"

"And your motives were altogether innocent?"

She leaped up, ready to strike, ready to scream at him of the pain he had caused her. But in the end she simply stared into those eyes she had once felt could see into her soul. Now they struck her as vacuous. She noticed how his whole face curled into itself. His nose curled. His chin curled. Even his cheeks curled toward each other. Women must be mad to consider him handsome, she thought.

Contrite, he asked her forgiveness. When she didn't answer, he added. "I did love you. Do you believe that?"

"The difference is that you *knew* your love wouldn't last."

"I always hope."

She shook her head slowly. "No, you don't," she said, speaking from a wisdom she hadn't known she possessed, "and that is your torment."

He looked as if she'd exposed some grotesquerie on his body, a disfigurement he had successfully hidden. Lydia forced her eyes away from his face, but she neither moved nor spoke until Isabelle appeared in the doorway.

"I take it the two of you haven't kissed and made up," she said in French.

Lydia had noticed they all broke the house rule and spoke French when Gabriel was present—as she had done just now, she reminded herself.

"Dear cousin, it is reassuring to find your tongue as sharp as ever," he responded.

"My dear cousin, I speak only the truth. Should I come back later, or will there be a dead body if I make an exit?"

"Quite the contrary," Gabriel replied. "Lydia was advising me on business matters."

Isabelle for once had no response, not even a raised eyebrow.

"Your cousin the baron is thinking of becoming a Kansas business-man," Lydia said in English.

"In this life?" Isabelle asked, continuing in French. Isabelle, who was succumbing ever so slowly to her suitor's blandishments, cared more for her cousin and knew him better than all the rest of them put together.

"Why is it that only you women get to shed your skin? Why can I not do so also?"

"Yours is gorgeous as it is, *mon cher*."

"You see? You condescend to me. You refuse to take me as seriously as you take yourselves."

"We can't afford to take you seriously, my dear cousin, for you men have ultimate power."

"To be sure," he agreed, "but power, for the most part, is not worth much."

"It is when you don't have it," Lydia countered.

"Let's be graceful winners, Lydia, and change the subject entirely," Isabelle suggested. "As it happens, I interrupted your conversation so that you could be among the first to know that the opera house is putting on a production of *Alcántara,* which got fairly good reviews in New York. I think it would serve as a proper introduction to the town for Gabriel. He'll get a little of the flavor, and perhaps he will charm enough women to earn the rest of us some goodwill."

Gabriel put his arm around Isabelle. "And may I have the honor of escorting you, madame? That is, if you can part from your peasant farmer for one evening."

Isabelle flushed before returning his banter: "But of course, although I warn you I have many companions who will insist on accompanying us."

Lydia had noticed that Isabelle and Gabriel never flirted with each other. Rather, they were careful to meet on a ground devoid of rocks and hidden holes.

"Gabriel, won't you be in Cimarron by then?" Lydia asked. "He wants to look into a land venture there," she explained to Isabelle, who then looked from one to the other.

"What's going on between you two?" she asked, looking more amused than puzzled. But then, what did puzzle or surprise Isabelle? Lydia wondered.

"Mrs. Fulgate is consulting with me on how best to make my fortune, after which, my dear cousin, I'll assume my rightful place as your guardian."

As Isabelle walked out on his arm, Lydia understood with cold certainty that he had come to sabotage his cousin's courtship, although he was probably unaware of his own motives. Marceline mattered to him more than most women had, but Isabelle was not expendable. Indeed, if he was capable of loving anybody, it was Isabelle, who shared his history and asked nothing of him.

Lydia felt she'd discovered the secret of Isabelle's serenity. Isabelle loved Gabriel, and she knew, even if he did not, how much he needed her. Among other reasons, her sexuality didn't threaten him. Other women might come and go, but she would prevail, for she'd become mother, wife, and confidante—an indestructible combination that no fleeting passion could dislodge—at least not for long. He must have given up hope of luring her back to France, and had therefore come to find her. Isabelle would never really be alone.

Samuel had come, Lydia reminded herself. He needs me, too. In fact, she couldn't ask for a more thoughtful brother, or one who enjoyed a joke more with her. Even so, they kept themselves on the alert, for hazards abounded, and surefootedness did only so much good when the ground itself was shifting.

How long had she been jealous of Isabelle? she wondered. The knowing felt older than her awareness of it. But then, when had she ever before acknowledged that Sam had always guarded himself from her?

*43* Before the performance even began, Lydia felt the familiar tingle of anticipation. She liked beginnings best. She imagined the whole audience must feel the same way. Because of a fire, the theater had been closed for almost two years now, so its reopening was more than welcomed.

Of course, *The Doctor of Alcántara,* an opera about two lovers who were forcibly betrothed to others, bore little resemblance to *Roméo et Juliette.* And the auditorium, with its bare plank floors and hard wooden benches, could not be mistaken for the marble and gilt of the Paris Opéra. Nevertheless, a stage existed, and a makeshift curtain had been fashioned out of several American flags. Lydia had no doubt the music would be better than the town's brass band or their own improvised attempts at chamber music.

What she heard, however, allowed no time for any more agreeable thoughts. The small orchestra, supplemented by a few townspeople, was not in tune. The soprano missed her first high note by an octave, and the tenor did not remember either the words or the score. Lydia wanted to cry. Marceline did cry. Charlotte kept yawning. Anne kept rereading her program. Only Isabelle remained her usual unflappable self, but then, Isabelle had confessed to being tone-deaf. For her, enduring a disaster at the Huddleston Opera House might not be much different from enduring the interminable evenings she had spent at the Paris Opéra. On the whole, the audience appeared to sit in affable contentment, and from the remarks she overheard at intermission, Lydia inferred that they had enjoyed the performance.

Although a few people smiled and nodded as the audience spilled out into the foyer to await the beginning of Act II, the women were left to make discreet remarks about the music to each other. The clusters of murmuring operagoers did not invite them in, so they sank into each other until Roberta Brown joined them. Word was the Browns' Europe-eclectic house became grander and grander practically by the day. Word also had it that in an age of spending, Wallace Brown was spending more than anyone else around these parts; he was said to be into everything from railroads to sewage-treatment plants.

While they always treated Mrs. Brown with consideration, seeing her as a victim of her husband's pretensions and her own ignorance of better ways, tonight they positively fawned over her, delighted to welcome outside company.

They spoke of the horrible plight of their neighbor, who had accidentally run over his father with a wagon load of stones and of the tragedy that had befallen Mrs. King, whose arm had to be amputated because of an infection.

They spoke of the merits of the operatic production and of the agreeable ambience of the reopened theater and of how smart all the women looked. No one told Roberta Brown her truly held opinion or qualified her praise—unless "considering the limitations of time" counted. No one made even the slightest irreverent remark, although Roberta Brown might actually have appreciated one.

Words tumbled from them all, but if they had stood there all evening, words tumbling every which way, what more would they have learned about Roberta Brown than they already knew? Would the words help peel back the bland exterior that Roberta Brown used so well to defend herself against the world? Against her own scant self, too, for that matter?

"We miss you," Charlotte was saying.

Now, what gush of hospitality had possessed Charlotte to say a thing like that? Lydia wondered.

"Do come calling," Charlotte suggested, as the operagoers began to file back to their places.

At first Roberta nodded and smiled noncommittally, but instead of separating herself from them, she drew closer. "Mr. Brown won't allow me to visit you, I'm afraid. You are considered a dangerous influence around here. Your way of life is seen as too . . . *different*."

Roberta Brown rushed these last sentences together and scurried away as if afraid the women might pursue her.

Lydia spent the whole next miserable act plotting just how she could quash such nonsense. That she couldn't never occurred to her. When the next intermission came, she was ready. "Engage Mrs. Leggett in conversation whether she wants you to or not," Lydia instructed Charlotte. "I'm going to enlist her husband's help."

Benjamin Leggett didn't stint on his good manners with any of them. When Lydia asked him to step outside into the balmy night air, he acquiesced instantly. If he shared his community's disapproval, he concealed it. Lydia knew he respected her and her friends, whether or not he liked them, although she suspected he still did. They would need his respect and goodwill in order to overcome the rampant animosity of the other local people. Surely he could understand why they could not simply turn Geneviève out, and he certainly knew how malicious rumors about an innocent servant woman could get started.

"If you could help explain to the people of Huddleston that we aren't a threat . . ."

"Of course. Unfortunately, reasonableness is sometimes a scarce commodity, as you well know."

"As for Norah, she's quite bright and quite brave, and Leonard Majors is the scum of the earth."

"I don't think you'll find many around here who have a high opinion of him."

"Then why would they believe his malicious stories?" she asked, her frustration mounting.

Here Benjamin Leggett smiled. "You're even more the optimist than I took you for, my dear. They believe him because his lies suit them for now. Twin House Farm and all it stands for are a threat to their need for moral order as they perceive it. I can and will climb upon that stage and proclaim your innocence and worth, if you wish, but it won't do you any good." Then he said what she already understood: there was too much uncertainty in their lives—change was too swift; families too uprooted. "At any rate, the present good times can't be trusted. Whether any of us wants to acknowledge that fact or not, we know it in our bones," he concluded.

"I will not let bigots defeat me," Lydia vowed.

"Nor will I, if I can help you." He took her arm to lead her inside.

"Have you been to any more meetings of the Farmers' Alliance?" she asked as they joined Marceline and Isabelle. Benjamin Leggett clearly had determined to show solidarity with them.

He laughed. "Since the crop of winter wheat was good and the price went up, interest in the alliance has dropped off. Now they're all for high tariffs because they think it protects their prices. Reform doesn't interest most folks unless they're having an off year."

"A lady cannot be too careful," Emma Leggett was saying to Charlotte when she saw Lydia and Mr. Leggett reenter. Charlotte could not be sure just what Mrs. Leggett was referring to and decided not to find out. At least the woman was willing to talk to her, Charlotte thought, feeling most dejected.

"It's a shame your friend Mrs. Fulgate can't be more like that nice sister-in-law of hers. And the brother is very respectable, too. May Benson has asked us for Sunday dinner. Will you be there?"

Charlotte shook her head, thankful that it was time for the last act.

After the discordant music and the discordant conversations, the ride home was quiet. "I don't think this town is ready to shed its skin," Marceline offered, but no one took her up on the conversation.

The worst part of the evening for Charlotte, though, had nothing to do with their utter rejection. It had occurred when Mrs. Leggett mentioned Sunday dinner. Charlotte had felt as if someone had kicked her in the stomach. She had not been aware that Samuel knew the Leggetts. He would now sit down with May to entertain at the table. They would speak of their children and their crops, and he would not give one thought to Charlotte Duret. He would smile at May and praise her food and look fondly at her belly, already filled with his second child and have no room in his heart for Charlotte Duret. And he would speak of politics and the railroad and explain in his patient way that all the farmers needed was to band together to get better freight rates, and he would not once speak of Charlotte Duret.

And Charlotte Duret would continue her ride home in a suffocatingly hot carriage, accompanied by forlorn friends, and Charlotte Duret would also eat dinner on Sunday and speak of the high winds and speak of the beauty of the spring flowers and smile fondly at all her friends and want to die because Samuel had a life without her.

She was a fool. She had failed to protect herself sufficiently. Now it was too late, and all the pain of her life came to rest in her stomach, around her feet, and in her heart during that carriage ride home.

*44* "What would I do with it?" Norah asked, wrestling in the September wind with a white linen tablecloth she was trying to pin on the clothesline.

"We would farm it for you until your husband takes over," Lydia explained for the second time as she grabbed one end of the fabric. Ever since she had returned from Chicago with more money than she'd requested, she'd been trying to decide the best way to reward Norah for her help that night with Leonard Majors. So far, however, she was having no luck.

"Husband! I sure am not wantin' one of them."

"Oh, not a common one," Charlotte interjected. "We'll find you a regular . . . a . . ." She turned toward Lydia, who helped her out.

"A regular farmer," Lydia finished.

This whole idea struck Norah as so funny that she laughed until she had to wipe away tears. "I got no use for land and no use for husbands, and I sure got no use for a package made up of both a man and a plot of land, though I'm most grateful, most pleased for the offer."

"You'll make a better life for yourself," Lydia explained.

"Not one I notice anyone around here is making for herself."

"We already have a better life, Norah. You don't," Charlotte chimed in. She was trying to shake the sand off the wet pillowcase she had dropped.

"A better life with a dozen babies and a husband to answer to and enough work to keep three people busy? No, thank you, misses, I'd rather be right here with only four of you bossin' me around. At least you don't beat me and you don't drink." She paused and twisted her apron around her hands. "I am, for a fact, treated better than any married woman I ever come across back home, and I aim to keep it that way.

"As for the land"—she paused again to hang up a recalcitrant sheet —"I seen too many minds and backs bent all outta shape trying to coax potatoes outta Mother Earth to care 'bout doin' the same. In the beginning, I almost didn't come with you 'cause I hate what land does to people, just eatin' thems up."

"We don't grow potatoes; we grow wheat and alfalfa," Charlotte shouted over a strong gust of wind, speaking slowly as if to a partially deaf person.

"At least you can eat potatoes—till you starve to death anyway. Besides which, this land ain't fit for potatoes, wheat, or alfalfa, and if the drought don't let up, it ain't gonna do much for sheep or people, either."

"The drought will let up any day now," Lydia assured her.

"Them's pipe dreams this whole country has about changing the weather. The weather don't change none; it's just the people die off 'bout the time they figure that one out."

Norah's last words had a chilling effect on Lydia that transmitted itself to the autumn day. For all that Norah was an ignorant, unlettered girl, she had a wisdom about her at times; she had stared into darkness and pronounced it bearable. Did Norah laugh at the rest of them, Lydia wondered, as they wrung their hands questing for their souls, while all the time Norah held some truth unnoticed by the rest of them?

"All right, then, we could provide you with some sheep."

For the first time, Norah stopped working and wiped her hands on her apron. "I am most grateful, Miss Lydia, to you and Miss Charlotte, but I just don't want no sheep, no land, and no husband. Sure, I dream of something like this in a place that's green and wet, but I'd want all the money in the world to make it work, and that's what it takes—all the money in the world. But in this life without the money, I don't want the burden of any of it."

"Well, what do you want, then, Norah" Lydia snapped, "to be a servant girl all your life? I'm offering you something better."

"Beggin' pardon, no, you ain't. Now I get a bed I don't have to share with nobody. I get three meals a day. I get money enough to send to Ireland to both my family and the church with a little left over to spend on myself.

And it's you, not me, who has to pore over them books all night to be sure I get them things. When night comes, I sleep. When next year comes, I'll better myself, but not with a husband or sheep."

"Norah, you're impossible!" Lydia told her and walked away in exasperation, but Charlotte laughed.

Norah turned to her. "Please make Miss Lydia understand."

"She understands all too well. She's just annoyed because you weren't having any of her noblesse oblige."

"I'm grateful for anything she offers."

These words caused Charlotte to laugh again as she went in search of Lydia, who, over another load of laundry, was trying to sort out that part of Norah's contrary nature to be admired and that to be corrected. Certainly more about that girl needed improving than not, ignorant girl that she was. Still, she had something above and beyond a wish for self-reliance —for she didn't want self-reliance at all, not the way Lydia and Charlotte did. Norah had something more basic—a clear vision of her own spirit. Though wrong-headed, in Lydia's opinion, it was nevertheless her own, to a degree that none of the rest of them had achieved.

The days that followed convinced Lydia that she and her friends were all experiencing the same deep, aching of despair caused by unmet expectations. They were compelled, possibly for the first time, to confront the reality of their lives.

Thus, one morning when they had assembled for breakfast, Marceline's announcement that she was returning to Paris struck Lydia as unsurprising, even inevitable. That Geneviève had decided to go with her was only somewhat less expected.

"She's too embarrassed to tell you herself," Marceline informed them. "She feels she's letting you down. But she can't stand the pressure from her family and the town any longer. I think she also doesn't really embrace the idea of a life without marriage. She can't overcome her lifelong training in that matter, so the arranged marriage will take place."

"Unfortunately, Geneviève's decision comes as no surprise," Lydia said. What did surprise her—surprised them all—was the news that Marceline planned to leave without Gabriel.

"I now understand that my real longing is for Paris," Marceline told them in her usual quick cadence. "I miss its brilliance and beauty, its triviality, its soft decadence. Life here in Kansas is too harsh, too unrelenting. Gabriel became an excuse for me to do what I already wanted."

"In Paris will you be able to uncover that elusive self you've been chasing?" Anne asked gently, only half teasing.

"I don't even know if there is such a creature, but I do know that a part of me is frivolous and needs to be indulged."

"So what will you do?" Isabelle asked.

"I won't marry, if that's what you mean. I finally realized that my decision about going to France with Gabriel or staying here with you and remaining independent had nothing to do with going back and everything to do with remaining independent."

"Marriage is the antithesis of independence," Charlotte declared.

"So is this way of life, if one isn't careful," Marceline answered. "Don't look so stricken, *chérie.*" She put her arm around Charlotte. "I have a new sense of myself and of my power. I don't need to supplement it with a man or with an illusion I can't sustain.

"You see, I came here to redeem myself for a singular reason having nothing really to do with Gabriel or any other man." She put down her fork and folded her hands in her lap, an uncharacteristic pose. "My mother, my dearest French friend, was one of those barbaric Communard members that you so despise. As a teacher, she'd come into contact with Louise Michel and became an early advocate of women's rights, equality for all in education, equality for all in trades." As Marceline talked, her voice slowing down as she told her story, the room was completely silent.

"Yes, my mother did set fire to some of our most beautiful buildings, and she did pillage the homes of some of our friends, I suspect. Some of our other friends—Verlaine, Hugo, Zola—protected her as long as they could after the uprising failed; but one day she was rounded up in a large crowd of suspects by our most dashing soldiers.

"She and the others were herded off like the sheep we send to their death." Marceline faltered, then lowered her eyes, but she began again in a firm voice. "The soldiers taunted and poked my beautiful mother and then shot her in the back like a wild beast.

"Of course, some of the Communards set fire to Parisian treasures, and I don't deny that the murder of our worthy and revered archbishop was an outrage. I grant that there were atrocities on both sides, but the

Communards didn't engage in the wholesale slaughter of human beings. My mother was only one of thousands. Yet even today the buildings are mourned more than the people." Taking a sip of coffee, she paused. Relating her mother's story was clearly costing her.

"Afterward friends placed me in a provincial convent. Luckily I found a wealthy old marquis who was willing to marry me. He died two years later and left me very well off. When I finally made my way back to Paris, my mother's old friends continued to keep my background a secret. They knew I'd experienced enough sorrow. They also knew I had turned my back on all my brave mother stood for, indulged myself however I pleased. They forgave me.

"But I couldn't forgive myself. Only after I came here did I realize my overwhelming desire for expiation. Twin House Farm—all of you—offered me a chance to stand up for some of my mother's convictions, without ever confronting exactly where they came from and why I felt this to be necessary.

"As I said, I'm also self-indulgent, spoiled, frivolous—everything my mother was not. I cannot be just those things; neither can I be my mother. That's why I have to go back to find and face the whole of me in my own way, at my own pace." She looked around the room, then out the window toward the fields. "And with a greater degree of comfort," she added with a smile.

✦═◗ ◖═✦

45  The drought lasted well into October. It lasted so long that Lydia and Charlotte, in town on business, could only delight in the sudden rainstorm and didn't mind at all getting caught in their relatively unprotected buggy.

When the rain turned into hail and lightning, a night at Mrs. Cannon's hotel struck them as a lark, reminding them of their first days in Huddleston, especially since Mrs. Cannon promised to play the piano for them after supper. She, at any rate, still enjoyed having them around.

Her husband, along with the rest of the town, remained aloof. So late that afternoon when he approached them as they took tea in the hotel dining room, they were a little surprised. However, he wasted no time on amenities in stating his mission: "We need your buggy, ladies. River's up. Couple of families need to be moved to higher ground."

"Won't the mud make that impossible?" Charlotte asked, not especially eager to subject either her mare, Essence, or their buggy to the ordeal.

"Not if we get a move on," Cannon answered, his nostrils fanning in and out.

"But our buggy can't hold much," Lydia said.

The man cleared his throat, inspected his boots, inspected the ceiling, but all he finally said was, "Ma'am, can we use your buggy?"

Lydia and Charlotte looked at each other with the realization that, at last, they could redeem themselves with the town and, not incidentally, show what they could do. Suddenly energized by that prospect, Charlotte told the impatient man to wait while they fetched their wraps.

"No need for that. My cousin's son will drive your buggy. Could be too dangerous out there for a woman," the man replied, looking alarmed.

"Not these women," Lydia said. "We're not about to let some fools wreck our buggy or our horse. We go with the buggy."

"But we need room to haul possessions and people."

"We'll put everything on our laps. We're not so heavy. We won't weigh it down."

While the man was deciding what to do with them, they rushed out of the room and up the stairs. Quickly they slipped into their coats, tied their bonnets, pulled on their gloves, and ran back down. Cannon's cousin stood in the lobby waiting.

"So, here we are," Charlotte said cheerfully. "We will rescue your families."

The cousin looked at Cannon, who looked glumly back.


Excited by the challenge, Charlotte quickly became inured to the pelting rain flowing over their faces and bonnets and cloaks and whatever exposed surface presented itself. I am surface, Charlotte thought, lost in sensations.

For now I can be all surface and blend with the rain and the mud and this horse I love.

"Charlotte, do you think you can manage in this weather? Does this make any sense?"

"Of course it doesn't make sense, but we'll do as well as these men."

"I couldn't bear for them to ruin our buggy."

"I quite agree. If it's to be ruined, we'll do so ourselves."

"Something I can help with?" Ben Leggett called, approaching them on horseback.

"We're part of a rescue party," Lydia explained. "If you have a wagon, I'm sure you could join us."

As she finished speaking, Cannon came around the corner with a team of mules and a wagon. The cousin and his son followed with a team of horses and a buggy that was larger but of the same order as Charlotte and Lydia's. Ben Leggett looked from the men to the women as Cannon—somewhat sheepishly, Charlotte noted—explained their mission.

"But why the women?" Leggett persisted.

"It's our buggy they wanted to use, but they got us, too," Lydia told him.

"Surely there are other wagons around," he said to the men.

"We're running out of time, sir," Charlotte pointed out.

Though Benjamin Leggett's face was hidden by the darkness and the rain and his hat, Charlotte felt his eyes assessing them, the animals, the buggy. Without another word, he fell in behind Lydia and Charlotte, who in turn, fell in behind Mr. Cannon. When they got close to the river, however, Charlotte maneuvered their horse from one high spot of ground to the next. Benjamin Leggett began looking for a crossing. The houses were on the other side, they'd been told.

Twice he suggested crossing spots, but Charlotte rejected both, saying the current was too swift. The other men decided to try one for themselves, only to find that Charlotte had been right.

"I still marvel at how much you know," Lydia said.

"You forget I spent a good deal of my early life in the country and on horseback. I may not yet understand winds and smoothed-out land, but I do understand mud and swift streams. Aren't you having a wonderful time, Lydia?"

Lydia looked at her. "I think you aren't joking."

"Of course not. Look at the water doing somersaults. It's magnificent!"

Lydia laughed. "Only so-so magnificent, I'd say. I'm afraid we'll get stuck or ruin our buggy, and I don't know which would be worse, damage or humiliation."

"We'll have neither. Trust me," Charlotte said, and took her eyes off the almost washed-out path long enough to smile at her friend.

As they reached the first of the houses, the river narrowed, but the current was too strong to ford the crossing. A man, his wife, and a boy around the age of fourteen stood on the opposite bank, pacing back and forth in desperation as if expecting a boat, a bridge . . . a savior to materialize.

Then, one at a time, children began emerging from the house—a girl, who looked to be the same age and height as the boy on the bank, two more boys around eight and ten, a younger girl, and a toddler. All four of the older ones, as well as the mother, had bundles tied on their backs.

While the men shouted to each other and Mr. Leggett suggested the cause was hopeless, Lydia asked the hotelkeeper for a rope. Though his exasperation with the situation and his impatience with such a clearly ridiculous request tested his patience even further, he managed to reply in a civil tone that, yes, he had a rope; everyone had a rope.

As soon as Charlotte explained her plan, Ben Leggett nodded approvingly. In no time the man on the other side had tied a large iron skillet to one end of the line. On the fourth try he managed to fling it across the river. As the rescue party tied their end to the wagon and to the buggies, the man and an older boy tied the other end to a post holding up one corner of the farmhouse roof. When tested, the rope proved taut.

By now Charlotte and Lydia were standing with the men. The rain didn't let up, and Charlotte began to worry that the post on the other side wouldn't hold, or that the children wouldn't be able to navigate the crossing even with their parents' help. The older two, a boy and a girl, came first. The boy wanted to go back for another load, but the parents refused to give him their permission.

The two younger boys came next, one at a time, each gripping the cord tightly as the father made his way across with each. Once they got halfway across the river, Leggett took over, and the father returned for the next child. While the men steadied the horses, Lydia shouted encouragement and reminded them to hold on tight. Charlotte shepherded the children to the buggy. They allowed her to lead them but didn't take their eyes off the river and the rope.

The father was now bringing the little girl, but as he passed her to Mr. Leggett, she began crying and clinging to her father. When Leggett finally managed to pry her away and the father started back to the bank, the child panicked completely, twisted out of Leggett's arms, and let go of the rope.

Before anyone else could react, Lydia jumped into the water. "Here, here," she crooned, grabbing the little girl firmly. "I'll take you to your mommy. Do you want your mommy?" She kept talking until her words penetrated the child's fright enough for Lydia to persuade her to hold tightly to her neck. With the help of Leggett, Lydia, never ceasing her crooning, finished the crossing.

Though the water came up only to Lydia's chest, Charlotte hardly breathed until her friend was on shore. One misstep and she would have been swept away. Even Charlotte, who considered herself an especially strong swimmer, could not have fought the roiling current. Now that the worst was over, her eyes filled with tears of anxiety, relief, and pride; the emotions were overwhelming. Before there could be any real rejoicing, though, the rest of the drama had to play itself out.

This time, taking no chances, the father tied the youngest child tightly to his chest, and Leggett ventured all the way across the river to help keep the little one's head out of the water by occasionally lifting the pair ever so slightly by the father's suspenders.

The time it took to make each crossing had come to feel like an eternity to Charlotte—to all of them, she suspected. On this trip, the father struggled all the way to the other side before turning to go the entire length back again for his wife, who looked to be pregnant. Fortunately, the couple managed an uneventful passage. Then, and only then, did the little girl scramble down from Lydia's arms.

Somehow Lydia and Charlotte managed to pile the four younger children and their mother in with them. Their party and Leggett, the older girl on the horse with him, headed back toward town. The remaining men set out to find the other family.

The return journey proved slow and hard. Lydia had to get out and push the child-laden buggy as Leggett pulled and urged on Essence. The rain didn't let up. Neither the children nor their mother uttered a sound.

Charlotte had underestimated her mare, she realized. She underestimated Lydia, too, she confessed to herself. Glancing over, she noticed that Lydia seemed to be filled with pleasure and with a new confidence, as well she should be. In the beginning, Charlotte had enjoyed Lydia's depending on her to take charge of this dangerous situation.

Eventually, a search party arrived and relieved the buggy of most of its cargo. Several of the men escorted Lydia and Charlotte back to town. Once they were all safe in the hotel, the mother tried to express her thanks but was either too tired or too stunned. Only one clear sentence emerged from her mouth: "Did we get my skillet?"

The rain lasted for three days. The roads were washed away, merchants carried supplies to their attics, and citizens herded their livestock to higher ground, bunked with neighbors who had upper floors, and prayed for the rain to cease and the water to recede. Wetness attacked from above and below, all life pressed between it.

Lydia and Charlotte stayed close to the hotel, where the grim, gray walls grew soggy and a smell of mildew seeped through bedraggled curtains and worn-out carpeting. They hardly noticed. They were too busy enjoying all the attention that came their way. They accepted thanks and praise—with proper modesty, of course. They delighted in their own bravery. They imagined happy scenes of their future life with the townspeople, with their friends, with each other. Experiencing all the freshness of their original optimism, this time they knew they would triumph.

# Part Three

# 46

"Imagine! A wedding at Twin House Farm! I never thought we would have one," Marceline said.

After three years away, she had come back for the ceremony and brought the wedding dress, an elegant white satin with a two-inch high collar and a lace-ruffled bib that extended to the waist. It was, without doubt, the grandest wedding dress that had ever made its way to Huddleston. Marceline had insisted on the best for Sally, who was marrying Will, Marceline's former groomsman.

"Do these sunflowers look all right?"

Charlotte stopped fussing with her bouquet of black-eyed Susans to eye Marceline's arrangement. "Fluff them up a bit more," she said and sighed. "I wish we had white flowers. A proper wedding should have white ones."

"What white flower could survive this hot wind? I don't know why Sally and Will chose August, anyway. Besides, these yellows and golds are lively. But the crops—has the wind burned them badly? I was so excited to see all of you that I forgot to pay attention to the fields."

"We've been lucky; we've had enough rainfall to temper the scorching winds, and the winter's disastrous blizzard left the ground with long-lasting moisture," Charlotte answered, amused that Marceline's staccato conversations were the same as ever.

"You've been lucky in lots of ways, I'd say." Last night Lydia and Charlotte had told her that they were close to being the largest landholders in the county, and they'd boasted about the general prosperity of the region, proudly showing her all the new buildings and houses in town.

Charlotte smiled. "Only if land and sheep are the measure."

"They've brought peace of mind and independence, haven't they?" With her apron, Marceline wiped water drops from the table.

"Independence, surely, but peace of mind?" Charlotte considered for a minute. "I suppose that, too." In truth, she'd been too busy to think much about it, but she did know the land brought her comfort and provided her with solitude.

The town had prospered without her participation; it had grown and expanded and built a roller rink and organized a polo club. She infrequently took part in its activities and then mostly for Lydia's sake. Lydia still needed circles upon circles, but they had learned to accommodate their differences with good humor.

As she snipped a leaf here, cut a stem there, she conjured up her own internal landscape of fields and sheep and sand hills, and this picture gave her contentment. Riding all of an entire afternoon on Twin House Farm, attending animals, tramping about the crops, following the path of a brown thrasher from cornfield to cornfield—these pastimes brought her enduring satisfaction. So much so that Sam Benson had gradually become a pleasant dream rather than an urgent reality. Both of them had worked to reach that point, and the sadness, when it came, did not break their hearts. Anne's awareness of the situation had helped Charlotte to feel less alone in her plight.

When Isabelle came in to dust the furniture and sweep the floors one more time, Marceline instantly began teasing her: "This wedding is good practice for us, Isabelle, since we shall get to plan another for you soon."

Isabelle blushed and dusted furiously. "Damn sand!" she muttered.

A week earlier a squib had appeared in the *Huddleston News* informing the town that Mr. Oliver Whitman had bought a new suit and had hinted that its purpose had to do with a marriage. At the time, the women had joked a good deal about it, and Isabelle had emphatically denied any such arrangement.

"I have no intention of marrying Mr. Whitman," she had wailed. Her friends believed her, which was why they took the matter so lightly.

Charlotte realized how much she'd missed Marceline—her jaunty mouth, her wary instincts, and underneath all that, her caring, which was more poignant because she had such a hard time showing it. Yesterday, when she'd told Charlotte that her papa didn't look well and that her maman was as formidable and unforgiving as ever, she'd been as tender as Charlotte had ever seen her.

Well, nothing could be done about Maman, and as for Papa, Audrey was to blame—Audrey and her father's dissolute habits, Charlotte had argued. But Marceline had been gently insistent about how ill he looked, and fear—cold and insurmountable fear—sliced through all their words.

Then Lydia, thinking she smelled the wedding cake burning, had hopped up from her chair, and everyone had followed her to the kitchen. Their fear was forgotten, as they busied themselves with decorations for the cake, which had not burned, thank goodness! It was as extravagant as any French pastry chef might have conjured up.

Just as well they'd been interrupted. By the time Charlotte did have a chance to digest what Marceline had said, she was able to convince herself that Marceline was an alarmist. Although by no means a robust man, her father was strong as an ox. Besides, he would have told her himself if he was really sick.

"I would remind you three that the wedding starts in two hours," Anne chided, interrupting Charlotte's reverie as she sailed through the doorway. "Marceline, please go help Sally with her dress. The rest of us have no idea how that newfangled bustle and hoop fit together. And *all* of you have to get ready yourselves. Hurry!"

These years had been good to Anne, too. Not only her body but her whole being had plumped out. She laughed now. Her eyes had a slightly mischievous quality, as if she held some great joke that the rest of the world didn't share; her sweet disposition no longer included docility as one of its components.


So here it was, the wedding: Sally, transformed in her gown and veil; Will, looking every inch the Kansas gentleman. Clothes are good levelers, Lydia thought. Standing with the rest of the bridal party, out of sight of the guests, she straightened the folds in her green silk dress and listened to Mrs. Cannon doing a fine job with a Chopin prelude.

On cue the wind had died down and the shadows of the houses fell, just as intended, on the wedding party and part of the surrounding yard. After the ceremony, the ceiling fan and drawn shades would make the parlor bearable for refreshments. Or they could come back outside. Without doubt, the setting they had created for the bride and groom had been worth the effort.

They had constructed a railing for the walkway and decorated it with tree branches and summer flowers as a backdrop for the ceremony. Sally and Will and the minister would look as if they were on a small, pretty stage up there. The railing lent a nice touch, gave their houses more substance. Lydia wished they'd thought of it sooner.

Isabelle had pieced together a muslin runner, which was flanked by pews facing the walkway and bridal party. The pews and minister they'd borrowed from the Methodist church. The piano had been one of those unexpected and too-generous gifts from Frank Bailey. "You ladies need this whether or not you want it," he'd written in his note. And, as usual, they were thoroughly enjoying his beneficence.

Lydia wished he were here today to see how well behaved Twin House Farm could be when it set its collective mind to it. Of course, he'd view the whole proceeding through his sardonic eye, but she'd grown rather used to that.

When he came through now, as he did infrequently, she no longer pretended indifference. This lack of indifference and her feelings of disloyalty to Charlotte, though, kept her out of Chicago and out of his bed. She couldn't afford to admit Frank Bailey into her life.

After working and struggling to create the kind of life she and Charlotte wanted, she wasn't about to sacrifice their effort to satisfy a moment's desire, unruly as it sometimes was. Their work was still in process, naturally, but the scope, the contours, had arranged themselves. She turned to smile at Sally, who looked ready to faint. Maybe the dress, elegant as it was, wasn't quite suitable in this August heat, which was now unmitigated by wind.

Life would be different without Sally, who had become an integral part of Twin House Farm. Over the years she'd learned to take the initiative when called for; but, unlike Norah, she probably would be better off married. And Will was a fine young man.

During her long stay in Kansas, Marceline had never had any luck in locating him, but she received a letter from him on her return to Paris. He had done well, he wrote. He'd gotten himself to Dodge City and was hired on to teach French and arithmetic to the son of a local merchant. For this, he owed Marceline a debt of gratitude for her own efforts in tutoring him and for giving him enough money to stake himself. This he now returned in the envelope, explaining that he now clerked in the family's store, a position he had assumed after the young son died of a heat stroke. As evidence of Will's ambition, he had stayed away from the rough element and joined every club in town. "That is the way to get ahead," he'd written.

Since Marceline knew that Sally had relatives in Dodge City, she relayed the information to all parties and one thing led to another. Sally still had the fewest words of anyone they knew, and that was saying quite a lot in a region inhabited by many unskilled in the art of conversation. When she gathered her courage and announced her engagement, all of Twin House Farm became involved in the wedding plans. Within hours the women became mothers and Sally their only daughter. Like mothers who might reject certain conventions for themselves, might assume themselves strong enough to withstand all manner of vicissitudes, these mothers insisted their daughter wear the mantle of conformity. How else to ensure her happiness?

Without delay, all of them, including Norah—Marceline had not yet arrived—proceeded to Dodge City to inspect Will and to judge his prospects. They had to see for themselves that Will was indeed an upstanding citizen of the infamous cow town, and they came away impressed with his accomplishments and also with the forward-looking nature of the town itself. Boasting a streetcar, it had begun the construction of a canal to irrigate the countryside in dry years.

However, with some degree of smugness and no proof whatsoever, the women of Twin House Farm had come to believe that their own land was already well irrigated by the great subterranean flow. They planned to tap into those underground currents if the rainfall ever became too scant again, a condition they didn't worry much about. Yet they did think a canal for Huddleston worth mentioning to Ben Leggett.

Will, with some trepidation, had insisted on hosting a proper tea for Sally's "mothers," and understandably, the women had caused quite a stir among the more respectable citizens of Dodge City's "Gospel Ridge." They had donned their finery for the occasion and seen to it that Sally was adorned appropriately. They wanted it understood by all that Sally would never be alone, that, if necessary, they would be protectors to contend with. Not that they mistook her shyness for lack of pluck, but she was without guile. One needed a certain amount of artfulness to survive any institution, be it a business, a club, or a marriage. With their help, though, Sally would do well as a wife; her nature was suited to marriage.

Sam Benson's was not. Today, for instance, sitting upright in the rented pew, he looked ready to bolt. Today even his indomitable rectitude could not mask his misery. He never mentioned it; but Charlotte saw him chafe often enough, recognized in him some unquenchable restlessness that matched her own.

Lydia watched Charlotte walk down the aisle. Too bad that Marceline had upset her with the news that her papa looked ill. They had harvest time ahead, so Charlotte had not mentioned going to see him. She probably wouldn't have gone, anyway; she was too happy here. Lydia had done everything she could think of to see to that, for Lydia could not endure another loss.

Paris was beguiling. Who knew that better than she? Unfortunately, this knowledge led to an irrational fear of Charlotte's returning there. Or perhaps her anxiety was not so irrational. After all, had not her own mother and father gone off for a holiday, a lark, and never returned? Who was to say this couldn't happen to her again?

But it was her turn now to be a bridesmaid. All of them were bridesmaids—all of them mothers. In a few moments the Methodist minister would speak, and he would ask who was to give this woman in holy matrimony.

When that moment came, Lydia, Charlotte, Marceline, Isabelle, Anne, and Norah took a step closer to their daughter and, with one voice, announced, "We do."

47 On awakening, Charlotte dashed over the walkway and through Lydia's door. "I no longer dream in French," she announced to Lydia, who was pulling up her overalls. "I think I haven't for a long time, but today I caught the dream before it escaped. I tricked it."

"Good for you on both counts," Lydia answered and slipped the last strap over her shoulders.

"Yes, but you're ready for work, and I'm not even dressed."

"Take your time. We've got plenty of hands out there. Speaking of which—"

"The hands, you mean?"

Lydia nodded. A few days ago she'd broached the subject of laying off a few field hands and investing the saved money in sheep and land. They hadn't done too badly financially this year, although crop prices were down and freight fees were up. The town was still growing rapidly, however, and the general mood was optimistic; better things were to come, the slump in the economy was only temporary, and weather patterns were changing for the better. It only made sense to keep investing, Lydia had argued, even if it meant sacrificing a few more hands around the place.

Charlotte, in a more cautious mood, had put her off, but now, seeing Lydia's eagerness, she acquiesced in good humor. "Why not? Just don't tell Ben Leggett our plans. He thinks we're overextended as it is."

"Sam does, too. In fact, since we're cutting back instead of borrowing, we don't have to tell anybody," Lydia said.

"A deal," Charlotte agreed as she eyed Lydia in her work attire. "Too bad Marceline left again. She'd think you as smartly turned out as you were in your cousin's trousers."

"She'd think that for about fifteen minutes. It's going to be another hot day in the fields."

Charlotte grinned. "Knowing Marceline, she wouldn't have lasted that long; she'd have found a way to avoid actually working. Speaking of which . . ." Without finishing, she ran back to her own house to dress.

All that sultry, windy, cloud-gathering morning they harvested the last of the October corn, but during their noonday break Charlotte announced to everyone a new revelation: "Since I came to America, I'm no longer afraid of catastrophes."

"If you mean the pox," Isabelle said dryly, "I think there's a reason for that."

The others laughed, and Charlotte agreed. "But that was only the worst of many disasters I worried about. Today, for instance, we're going to have a bad storm—a fire-setting lightning storm—or perhaps a tornado, but I'm not worried."

Lydia looked around her. "We'll have a shower this afternoon, that's all. The sky seems darker because it's October."

"No, it will storm," Charlotte answered, not letting her annoyance with Lydia show. How could she live here these years and not read the sky better? These skies—their light, their threat, their teasing, their danger— had been foreign to both of them when they arrived. But, over time, how could one not learn?

Abruptly, Isabelle, who appeared not to be listening, proposed a glass of wine to celebrate the end of the harvest.

"Wouldn't tonight be more fitting?" Charlotte asked, annoyed now with Isabelle, too.

"Isabelle doesn't make frivolous suggestions," Anne instantly pointed out.

And so with the wine came another farewell. At first, what Isabelle said didn't register with any of them. When she repeated herself, they all responded at once: "What do you mean?" "Go where?" "Does this mean you're marrying Oliver Whitman?"

Waiting for an answer, they fell silent and watched their friend, her thick plait dropping over her right shoulder, her strong, still hands atop the table, her serenity deeper than it had ever been. Whatever her quest, it had ended.

Or had it ever begun? Charlotte wondered. Had she always possessed a secret that escaped the others? Have the rest of us only sought to achieve what Isabelle was born knowing: the essence of selfhood? Charlotte wondered when Isabelle had learned to be silent.

Now she was talking of Gabriel and Colorado and opportunities abounding. With Gabriel? In Colorado? She was not marrying Oliver Whitman after all. But . . . Gabriel?

"He writes that he has plenty of room in his house, so I shall stay there with him. He misses my French," she said as if that explained everything.

"What will become of you?" Lydia asked.

"*Become* of me? Nothing will become of me. I will always be *me*—here, there, wherever—but I prefer being with Gabriel."

"He'll be an inconstant companion," Charlotte said, almost in a whisper.

"Not to me," Isabelle answered. "The other women never count for much for long." Noticing Lydia's face, she amended, "Excluding you, of course, Lydia. And Marceline."

"Not excluding us at all, my darling Isabelle," Lydia said, taking her friend's hand. "Only my vanity allowed me to hang on to that illusion as long as I did. Part of me always knew better."


Isabelle had been clever: the afternoon's work was too important to dwell on her information. Almost before the bottle of wine was finished, they had to be back in the fields. By now no one disputed the possibility of a late day weather disruption. What they hadn't counted on was a visitor.

About an hour before the storm broke, a man appeared carrying an eight-inch piece of iron pipe. "Lookin' for my uncle," he said as they were finishing up the last cornfield.

"I'm afraid he's not here," Anne told him.

The man, in his forties, stubby, redheaded, and with more freckles than hair, would not accept that answer. Even when all insisted—after a description that sounded much like their visitor—that the uncle was not about and never had been, the man persisted.

Finally he explained, with only a minimum of exasperation, that he understood they had not seen his uncle. "He died here. That's what. A rattler killed him. I've come to commune with his spirit." He held up his pipe. "I don't go 'round carryin' this heavy pipe for nothin', you know? I'll stick it just as close as I can git to the spot where he died. He'll speak; I'll listen."

With that, they all escorted him to the presumed spot. Storm, tornado, fire—whatever might happen—could not possibly equal the exultation this man might experience.

"Next time we'll ask him to have his uncle help us locate our underground springs," Lydia whispered.

They asked him to stay for dinner, but he was too disappointed not to have found his uncle. "Gone, I'm afraid," he'd told them. "Can't imagine it's heaven, though."

They were disappointed he hadn't stayed, they had wanted to know what it was he needed to hear from this uncle who had not made it to heaven.

"Perhaps he's looking for his essence," Charlotte quipped. But something good had happened today, she reminded herself: she had dreamed in English. "Perhaps he could take Isabelle's place," she added—lightly, she thought, and lightly her friends took her comment, until she fled the table.

Later, in her bed, she recounted again her good fortune: her fears had vanished; her friends loved her; her land soothed her. She thought of how far she'd come. Yet she continued to cry, not sure her mourning had to do with the loss of Isabelle or of the French voices in her dreams.

*48* Charlotte saw Samuel Benson walking down the sand hill toward her. Fearful of hurting the injured lamb she was holding in her lap, she did not rise to greet him. Until he was upon her, she continued to stroke the lamb and make consoling sounds.

"His leg is broken," she said, pleased to have something as tangible as a lamb to speak about.

Sam squatted beside her and gently examined the distended leg. "It's bad. Give me your gun, and I'll take care of this for you."

"I didn't bring one."

He frowned, and Charlotte had to resist a desire to kiss his furrow line. He should always be happy, she thought, and I could make him so.

"You really shouldn't wander this far from the house without some sort of firearm," he reprimanded her.

"You did."

"Yes, but I'm a man."

She laughed at his remark, one that would normally have infuriated her. Coming from him, however, it delighted her.

With a smile she answered him: "Well, I'm a woman and—"

"I've noticed," he interrupted, then laughed at himself.

She liked it this way, when they were almost easy with each other. Months could go by without his awakening her desire—desire combined with dread and urgency. Although the two of them were usually careful to keep their distance, sometimes that didn't feel quite so necessary. She gently placed the lamb on the ground, but continued to stroke its neck.

"Then maybe you've also noticed that whatever attacks women out here attacks men as well," she said. "This country is no respecter of sex, sir."

"You win," he said as he stood up, putting a little distance between them. He held out his hand for her to stand also, but she shook her head.

"I'd better stay with the lamb." She wanted more than anything to walk back to the house with him, just to walk as any friends would do. And what's so wrong with that? she asked herself, but she already knew the answer.

He reached into his back pocket. "Before I forget," he said, "Lydia says to tell you she'll be delayed in town. She's sent along a letter for you from Marceline."

With this news, she leaped up, forgetting the necessity of staying away. He handed her the letter, but suddenly, without having made any conscious decision, she was in his arms. Her mouth found his neck and face and lips and tongue. She had her hands on his belt when a bleat from the lamb startled them both, that lamb a signifier of their reality. In one instant they were apart.

She tried to pin back her fallen strands of hair, but her shaking hands made it difficult. Sam finished the task for her. "Are you aware of how much time I've spent on your hair?" he asked, an affectionate tease in his voice.

Unexpectedly he took her hand and kissed it, saying, "I'm sorry. Just so sorry. So sorry. So in love . . ." And he was on his knees, his head buried in her skirt, his shoulders heaving.

She stroked his hair and stood in the quietness of his anguish for a long while until he regained control. But once composed, he assumed his most formal eastern manner, and Charlotte knew her heart would break even before he spoke.

"I assure you this will never happen again," he said with great conviction, and she knew he would keep his word. As for her, she'd become mute. Would she remain mute? she wondered. And in French, too? Was she French? Was she crazy?

"Go back to the house," Sam ordered with uncharacteristic gruffness. "I'll take care of the lamb." She did as she was told.

Charlotte knew he would use his knife. He would wait until she was well out of hearing distance of the final bleat before he did his "taking care of." That was why one mustn't be "taken care of," for if one allowed oneself to be taken care of, one eventually would die—an additional reason why the choice she and Lydia had made, to remain independent, was correct.

Besides, she had proved, first with Maman, then with Papa, that she could survive alone. All she needed was the land. And Lydia—a better friend than any Frenchwoman had ever been, a better sister than any she could dream of, a better mother than Charlotte had known existed.

So once and for all she would banish Sam from her thoughts and heart. In the beginning, had she not wanted to know him better in order to know Lydia better? Had she not loved him because he embodied so much of Lydia? But love of Samuel had turned into a betrayal of his sister.

"Did Sammy find you?" Anne asked. "I wasn't sure which way you'd gone but didn't think you strayed too far. Shall we ask him to stay for supper? I've shot enough birds to feed an army. Must be migrating—the birds. It's a shame Lydia's running late, for I planned to make a soufflé. Now I'm baking a pie. Soufflés won't hold." She turned to show Charlotte the unbaked piecrust, perfectly formed. "Nice, huh? And to think that if I hadn't come here, I'd have spent my life cross-stitching just to occupy my hands."

Anne set the pie down and wiped a smudge of flour off her nose. "But where is Sam?" Anne came closer to Charlotte. "I think I'm getting nearsighted. Yes, I must be."

Suddenly Anne stopped babbling and looked too knowingly as she said tenderly, "Maybe hearing from Marceline made you a little homesick. That's perfectly understandable." Anne patted Charlotte's shoulder. "Why don't you lie down until supper? I'll send Sam along home. He's already seen Lydia in town, anyway. What we need tonight is a nice, cozy meal, just us women."

In her room, Charlotte took the letter from her pocket. She heard Sam's and Anne's voices but could distinguish their words. With no energy left to open her mail, she pocketed it again and lay down on the bed. She would, of course, be all right again, she knew that. Wounds healed. Who knew that better than she? Sam would stay away now. She knew that, too. And this last acknowledgment caused her to curl up on her side, where she fell asleep. She had not wanted to hear him take his leave.

*49* When Charlotte woke to the sound of laughter, she first thought it was Sam's. When she realized it was Lydia's instead, she felt relief. Without so much as smoothing her dress or hair, she followed the sound of Lydia's voice. Lydia would take away the flattened feeling that had settled on her.

I will do nothing more to feel guilty about; I will not betray Lydia again, Charlotte told herself as she made her way to the voices in the kitchen.

"Hurry up, slowpoke," Lydia said. "I have lots to talk about, and I'm starving."

This remark annoyed Charlotte out of all proportion. Largely due to Lydia's appetite, they now ate as early as the farmhands, no longer waiting until a civilized hour. Charlotte found the custom boorish and did not care if this made her seem like a snob. Already they had given up so much— no music in months, no charades in years. But this wasn't Lydia's fault, Charlotte chided herself. Anyway, most of the time she relished her life and wouldn't trade it for anything or anybody.

"Charlotte, don't look so glum. I've got all kinds of news for you—a whole new investment idea."

"Free, I hope."

"Not free but *very* profitable—so profitable that we won't ever have to worry about money again. We'll actually have cash in hand for a change, but most important we can get rid of our debts forevermore. Who knows? Maybe we'll be able to afford more land, more sheep, new equipment— everything!"

"Can we hire back our help?" Charlotte asked. Since she and Lydia had begun economizing, their workload had tripled. I'm tired, that's all that is the matter with me, Charlotte decided. This afternoon wouldn't have happened if I hadn't been so tired.

"Sure. We'll be set for life," Lydia responded enthusiastically. "And we'll set you up, too, Anne. You'll never have to depend on your uncle's stingy allowance again. I promise."

"Don't do it for me," Anne said, taking the pie out of the oven. "I'm perfectly happy as we are."

"Me too." Charlotte agreed, looking at Lydia, who was bursting with excitement over her scheme. "So what is this road to paradise?"

"We invest in railroad stock. There's a trunk line coming right through Huddleston, and now is the time to get in on it, according to Wallace Brown."

"And where do we find the money for the getting-in-on-it part?"

"The fabled Frank Bailey. His moneymen always come through," Lydia announced.

"That's because he is one," Anne remarked.

"Maybe we should wait to see what actually happens first," Charlotte suggested, not wanting Lydia to go to Chicago. Over the years their roles regarding Frank Bailey had changed, primarily because Lydia had turned into their business agent. In the beginning Charlotte had somewhat resented being displaced; now it didn't bother her. Nevertheless, at the moment, she didn't want to be without her friend—or to share her with Frank Bailey.

"Then it'll be too late," Lydia replied, slightly exasperated.

"Maybe this discussion should wait until tomorrow," Anne volunteered. "Charlotte looks awfully tired, and she hasn't eaten a thing."

Dear Anne, who understood everything. But then, she would. She knew Sam almost as well as Lydia did, and Charlotte felt herself to be transparent at this point. The wonder was that Lydia had never noticed.

"Would you like me to take a tray up to your room?" Lydia asked, suddenly all solicitude. "You're not coming down with something, are you? We've plenty of time for this conversation. For now you should go to bed."

But Charlotte did not know which was worse: to be alone with her thoughts or to wear a mask throughout the evening. She looked to Anne for guidance.

"Go lie down. You can always join us later," Anne suggested. "Or you can eat some of my pie while reclining on your puffed bed pillows. By morning you'll feel better."

Charlotte turned to leave, but Lydia, as an afterthought, asked if Marceline had related any good gossip from Paris.

Charlotte pulled the letter out of her pocket. "I was saving it for all of us," she lied, since Lydia would never understand how she could have forgotten about one of their favorite treats—receiving their friends' letters.

As she prepared to read it aloud, she caught a mention of her father in the first paragraph. She continued scanning: "Your papa is sick . . . wants very much to see you . . . loves you."

Charlotte handed the letter to Lydia and sat down. Her legs had failed her. "Do we have the money for me to make this trip?" she asked as soon as she could summon the energy.

Lydia hesitated before she spoke. "Not ready cash."

"So, Lydia, you must go to Frank Bailey after all," Charlotte said, looking up.

"I'll go immediately," Lydia answered and kneaded Charlotte's shoulder.

Charlotte made herself reread the letter and was glad she had. Her apprehension lessened. "It doesn't sound that urgent, but I'd like to go before the spring planting starts."

"He could just be having a bad spell. It's probably best to give him some time to recover," Lydia assented.

"Yes, I agree. It doesn't sound nearly so bad as I thought the first time I read it."

"But it would be well to have a plan in place," Anne insisted.

Suddenly despair overcame Charlotte.

"He'll be all right, *ma chérie*," Lydia murmured.

"This is my punishment," Charlotte mumbled.

Lydia lifted Charlotte's face in her hands. "Don't be ridiculous," she scolded. "You are our one pure heart."

# 50

Lydia looked down at her breasts, still full—"voluptuous," Frank called them—but she'd already begun to pay the price of hard work and age. In a few years she knew they would sag unmercifully, sallying forth only with the help of corsets. Frank, however, would not be satisfied with examining them in such a bound-up state. Would he want them at all once time's steady pull had taken over?

The question caused a tightness in her chest, for she could no longer pretend she was only using Frank Bailey for her own ends. She also could not pretend she loved him; rather, her body was drawn toward his with no object other than to sate a seemingly insatiable appetite. With Gabriel she had her first hints of this voracious creature within her and had found fit to name its importunings "love." With Frank, she could call upon no such innocence.

This time they hadn't even bothered with preliminary amenities. She had walked into his house in the middle of the afternoon. He had called down to her from the top of the stairs. He did not receive her in his study or greet her at the door. Instead, in front of the servants he beckoned her up, the way he might a common strumpet.

She had wanted to kill him for that humiliation, but murder was an unaffordable luxury. She wanted his money too much. And what lay in store for her behind his bedroom door, she wanted that also. So, refusing to be shamed, she had gone to him and they had made love. And then again. And once more.

Rays of the late afternoon sun fell across his legs as he stood at the foot of the bed, assessing her. With a smile he uttered his first words since she had climbed those stairs. "Your body does not cease to amaze me."

She proffered one breast, but he laughed, shaking his head, "I can't," he said. "Haven't got the strength to raise my little finger."

"It's not your little finger I want," she replied as she scooted over to allow him to sit on the edge of the bed.

"So what *do* you want?"

"You know," she answered coyly.

"I know that at this moment sex is not uppermost in your mind. I can always tell when your eyes turn to the rest of the world."

She started to protest but stopped herself. Why did she continually underestimate his shrewdness concerning her?

"Four thousand would do," she said.

He whistled through his teeth. "One thing about you, Lydia Fulgate, your wants aren't small."

"I need four thousand," she repeated, only this time somewhat impatiently.

"May I ask *why* you have this handsome sum in mind?" He asked, as he took one of his dressing gowns out of his wardrobe and put it around her shoulders.

Touched by the gesture, she remarked on this small act of thoughtfulness but also couldn't resist commenting on his usual lack thereof.

"Today you earned my thoughtfulness."

"And my four thousand?" he retorted.

Let him believe she was only there for the money. Served him right, she thought.

"Don't I deserve an explanation as to why you would like—or need—that kind of money?"

She began telling him of the opportunity to wipe out their debts and ensure their future by investing in a certain rail stock. She also confessed that they were overextended at Leggett's bank, which was, unfortunately, pretty overextended in loans itself.

She did not mention Charlotte's need of money for a return to France. After much thought, Lydia had decided to ignore that issue. She didn't believe for one minute that Charlotte's father was either sick or dying. He was a user, and he was simply ready to use his daughter again. Even Charlotte, after her initial shock, hadn't seemed too alarmed, had even urged Lydia to take a few extra days off to relax.

But Frank was continuing his probe: "Other than my money, what resources do you have?"

"I could sell some land directly to the speculators; but by the time I paid off the interest and the mortgage, we'd be left with very little money and less land. With your help, we can hold on to the land and improve it. We've got room for a few more sheep, too, and we don't lose money on them. In fact, as soon as the weather improves, we'll be in fine shape."

"Stop that idiotic talk about the weather. It's not going to save you."

"But your money will." She was pressing hard, a tactic that could make him balk.

She did need to make improvements and add a few more sheep. She also wanted more land, which she regarded as a long-term investment in the future of Twin House Farm. Mostly she wanted the railway stock to secure their current assets. Their debts were much greater than she'd let on to anyone, including Charlotte. They owed Wallace Brown a lot more than she was willing to admit, and high freight rates, bad winter weather, and overzealous purchasing of farm machinery had taken their toll.

"I've made some mistakes," she confessed out loud to Frank, "but now I've found a way to correct them."

"Are you sure you shouldn't unload some of that land?" he asked. He lit his cigar, then stretched out in a chair, his body already betraying his decision to acquiesce to her demand. "One more blizzard in Kansas like this year's and the state's livestock industry will be wiped out."

She sat straight up, now perfectly willing to oblige his need to make her work a little harder. "We fared as well as anyone, everything considered, and I've brought my books with me to prove it to you."

Actually, she wanted him to see the books in case she had overlooked some pertinent detail. His assessment of their situation could be helpful, for he did have long and varied experience in the world of finance. She also wanted to show off a little just how much land they had acquired. Soon they could be the largest landholders in the county. She liked that and was proud of it although she wouldn't say as much today. Not with the loan in question.

"Do we have to look at the books now?" he asked with more amusement than irritation.

Shaking her head, she lay back on the pillow. Of course, she thought, he knows exactly how eager I am to discuss all this with him. In which case, she wondered why she bothered, after sex, with the civilities. Neither romance nor friendship affected their equation.

Education, however, did, she decided as he got up to bring her the satchel of papers. He seemed to enjoy schooling her in business and farming almost as much as he did in sex; and in all subjects he proclaimed her an apt pupil. Herman, she now realized had not been adventurous or sophisticated in his lovemaking. He had not been without skill, perhaps, but his range was narrow. The same limitation did not remotely apply to Mr. Bailey.

"You're looking mighty Cheshire cattish," he said, interrupting their silence. "Are you pleased with the afternoon, or are you merely certain that the money is forthcoming?"

"Both," she answered, then added, "especially this afternoon," for he'd never before sought any kind of assurance. The idea of his needing approval deeply satisfied her.

"Why do I always feel that half of my money goes to your brother? Don't look so shocked. You know that thought has occurred to you."

"You're wrong about Sam. He refuses to take anything from me, and I learned years ago to offer him nothing, else I offend him."

"Good for him! I didn't think he knew how to protect himself from you."

She threw a pillow in his direction. He picked it up and replaced it behind her back. "See?" he said. "You're relieved you can't offend me."

She leaned her head back and grimaced. "I do get tired of worrying about every little thing I say to Sam. He just gets edgier, though I see very little of him these days."

"Do both yourself and him a favor: stop taking his pulse and stop counting his visits."

"And you stop telling me how to act with my own brother."

"Somebody needs to tell you before you drive him away. He needs breathing room."

"I'm not what's driving him away!"

The words were more vehement than Lydia intended.

Frank didn't reply, just stood there puffing on his cigar.

"May is the problem," she added lamely, not sure that was what she really believed. "She drives me crazy talking about their little family or the dresses she's forever ordering from New York. She lets me know how well she and Sam are doing and implies it's because they haven't tried to gobble up all the land in sight and that she's the reason they haven't. She resents everything about me. I really cannot stand that woman!"

He laughed and sat down beside her. "Why wouldn't she resent you? For starters, you act as if their children had no names or sex. And these are your brother's children, too."

She looked up at Frank. "I have no *hold* on him any more," she blurted.

He gently shook her shoulder. "Is it necessary for you to have a *hold* on him? Can't you trust the world to stay in place without your monitoring it all the time? You feel you've got to provide for both Samuel and Charlotte in case either falters, and you always expect they will."

Thinking of the money he was lending her, she restrained herself from pulling away.

"Stop pouting," he said.

"Stop reading my mind," she replied, and turned over, by way of suggesting a massage.

"That's more like it," he teased. "Not every encounter with me has to be adversarial."

"I'm not aware our encounters are adversarial."

"You mean you haven't noticed that about us?"

"Well, certainly not in bed," she replied.

"In bed, too—during the first course and after the meal."

"That leaves us amicable for the main course and dessert. Why are you complaining?" But she knew he wasn't. She knew he had enjoyed the afternoon as much as she. A wonderful day altogether, she thought, as her eyes began to close. She must be careful how she handled the money situation with Charlotte. For a while, she would have to keep it to herself, find some way to hide it; otherwise Charlotte would feel obligated to go to her father. But now it was time for a nap.

"Are you listening to me?" Frank asked, startling her back to wakefulness.

"Of course, I am. I'm just drowsy."

"Then are you drowsy enough to agree?"

"Of course," she answered, having no idea what she'd consented to. However, it couldn't be much; Frank made no real demands on her.

"Good! Rest for now, though we'll eat soon in order to make an early start in the morning."

Suddenly alert, she forgot she was supposed to know what he'd said. "Where are we going?" she asked.

"The same place I mentioned five minutes ago—Michigan."

"For how long?"

"As I told you five minutes ago: three weeks."

"I can't possibly stay away for three weeks. This is a busy time at home."

"Not that busy. Besides, Charlotte is the real farmer. She'll get along fine."

"But what will I say?"

"You're resourceful. You'll think of something. Tell her it's the price you must pay for the loan," he said.

Lydia knew he meant it exactly and hated him for wielding his power over her. Yet she truly wanted to go with him, to spend three weeks cut off from the world. And Charlotte had suggested she stay on for a while. In fact, she'd seemed strangely relieved at the idea of Lydia's getting away for a few days. Maybe they both needed a little break from their routine. She still had Anne for company. And Twin House Farm would survive without her.

"We can wire the money to the bank immediately if that's what you're worrying about," Frank told her.

Since she dared not tell him about Charlotte, she assured him the money could wait. He would still give Charlotte anything she wanted, Lydia knew that. She also knew she could never make him understand why her friend's wants and needs were two different matters.

Besides a return to France was out of the question. Charlotte wouldn't be happy there. Though she might be seduced by its trappings into staying, she'd lose not only her dearest friend and companion, but her very soul as well.

In her telegram to Charlotte, Lydia simply said she had been delayed and a letter would follow. In her letter—for she really didn't trust the telegraph operator—she explained that she'd failed to secure a loan and that Frank Bailey had arranged for her to accompany him on a business trip, which promised good possibilities for investors. In the meantime, she wrote, she would miss her dearest friend.

The only thing Lydia felt guilty about was not returning sooner. But in the long run, this trip would benefit both of them.

*51* So here they were, Charlotte and Anne, attending a meeting of the Ladies' Literary Society in the company of virtuous wives and mothers, and feeling something akin to acceptance by them. Well, perhaps not acceptance exactly, but certainly not exclusion, either, or alienation, the state she and Lydia had sometimes experienced around these women even after they had been asked to join this club. Charlotte was sorry Lydia had to miss the meeting because of her trip to Chicago.

Joining the club had not produced the results they had hoped for. While most of the members were sincerely interested in better educating themselves and bettering their community, they weren't particularly interested in simplifying their lives—in fact, quite the opposite—or pursuing an inner path. Instead, they clung to most of the values they had grown up with and saw no need to mold their lives into new forms. For most of these women, life in Huddleston had already required enough reshaping of old expectations.

Tonight, however, promised to be different, according to the hint Mrs. Randolph E. Sargent, the club's president, had dropped to Charlotte a few days ago. Indeed, as soon as the meeting was called to order, a debate ensued over whether or not to debate the subject of women's voting rights.

Mrs. Randolph Sargent explained that for the first time in several years, women had a good chance of being given the vote. Although many men were helpful and supportive, many others had to be shown why woman suffrage was needed. Therefore, clubs like theirs all over the state needed to educate the general public. As she talked, Charlotte wondered idly if anyone—perhaps her husband? her children?—ever referred to her as anything other than Mrs. Randolph Sargent.

"They know why we want to vote, which will be the reason we're denied suffrage," rejoined Barbara Moore, a usually diffident woman.

"If we speak out, the men will listen," another woman chimed in.

"This club shouldn't be the forum, though. Some of our husbands already believe the Ladies' Literary Society is going to lead to the moral breakdown of the family."

A few women laughed, but Mrs. Moore continued her objection: "To have this club sponsor that debate would only confirm their suspicions."

"So?" a Mrs. Owen asked.

"So they might forbid their wives to attend."

"If my husband finds out that some of our members are suffragettes, he won't allow me to come." This last came from a younger woman whose voice was little higher than a whisper. "He doesn't approve of women using their brains in too serious a fashion," she went on. "He's been told that the energy a woman uses in thinking diminishes the energy in her reproductive organs."

"My husband believes that too," another woman confessed. "And he thinks the right to vote will be a corrupting influence and take time from family duties. He'd be horrified to think I'd consider such a matter here."

"You must assure him that we don't speak of these things in this club," Mrs. Randolph Sargent ordered.

"But that would be a lie," another young woman countered.

"I would remind you that we can adjourn this meeting of the club and in the future will not call it to order until we have sufficiently disposed of this matter. Thus anyone who wants could show the minutes of our meetings to her husband with complete impunity."

"But is this not deceitful?"

Mrs. Randolph Sargent's great bosom and imposing voice, in tandem, rose to the heavens as she announced, "We do not engage in deception. We engage in higher truths."

Even the doubters nodded assent to this declaration. Nevertheless, Mrs. Moore would not be put off. "Whenever we've invited our menfolk to these meetings we've been careful to keep the discussion light, with funny verse and lots of jokes."

"And plenty of flowers and a smattering of music," someone else put in. Again the group laughed.

Mrs. Sargent rapped her gavel for order: "We don't plan to use wives for the debate." With these words all heads turned toward Charlotte and Anne, who turned toward each other. "Don't forget that Miss Duret and

Mrs. Fulgate saved some of our families through their courageous acts during the flood," their president declared, "and Miss Cunningham is well regarded for her many acts of Christian kindness."

"Whom do we debate?" Anne asked.

"We shall let you know soon," Mrs. Randolph Sargent proclaimed.

Charlotte and Anne looked again at each other. Charlotte wished Lydia were here to help make this decision. Adding to Charlotte's confusion was the realization that Mrs. Randolph Sargent was very much like the countess—as she had taken to thinking of her maman—not so much in looks as in demeanor. In fact, nearly everyone in the room reminded Charlotte of someone back in Paris, a realization as disconcerting as it was absurd. Maybe it's because of my father, she thought. I have worried about him so much that I've transposed Paris into Huddleston. Or was it the other way around? Gradually she became aware that the women, including Anne, were waiting for some response.

Finally Charlotte thanked them for the honor but told them she was not yet an American citizen. She wished she hadn't come to this meeting. She felt that she and her friends were being sacrificed, for the debate was bound to stir up animosity, and they would be the ones to suffer.

Possibly reading her thoughts, Anne spoke of "the grave, perhaps hazardous responsibility entailed," and agreed only to take Mrs. Sargent's suggestion under advisement, especially since Lydia was out of town.

"Mrs. Fulgate's position will be one of total support," Mrs Sargent said firmly, "and rest assured, you have ours. This matter is therefore closed. In the meantime, the club will study the definition of citizenship, going back to the Greeks. An in-depth study of a subject is essential and provides what we as members are most lacking—discipline and concentration." Again Mrs. Randolph Sargent rapped her gavel.

Charlotte felt much as she had when the countess ordered her about: rebellious but reluctant to challenge—until that parting challenge. Well, she'd done that, had left her home, her family, her country—all because of a father who had turned his back on her and now mocked her with his dying, if he *was* dying. What if even that was a monstrous trick, one more fraudulent ploy on his part?

Without waiting to be recognized, Barbara Moore abruptly stated that while she still wasn't sure this was what they should do, she appreciated "our friends' willingness to stand up for the rest of us." Then one woman after the other stood to pledge her support of them. It was a fine moment, one that Charlotte wished she could share with Lydia.

Barbara Moore reminded Charlotte of one of Papa's cousins. Why had she not seen the resemblance sooner? In fact, in this setting—and discounting the earnestness, the drabness, the endemic weariness here— these women prompted each other, vied with each other, scoffed at each other, needed each other, demanded of each other in the same way her aunts and cousins and Parisian friends did. Did this mean these women were no more redeemable, and that she was no more redeemable, in this society than in the other? Had she freed herself of the one group only to be bound now by the other? These new entanglements, though, didn't confine her in the same way. Except, of course, the one with Lydia.

But why was Anne standing? Charlotte wondered. Must she stand also? Had she become so preoccupied with her own thoughts that she had missed some cue while nodding and smiling. A childlike panic rose inside her; missing cues was a dangerous game. Anne smiled at her. Everyone was smiling at her. Charlotte smiled back and looked to Anne, who whispered to her that the meeting was over.

"Are you all right?" Anne asked as soon as they were out of hearing.

"Yes, yes. I'd been daydreaming and lost the thread of the meeting."

"You looked distraught. Does the idea of a debate upset you?"

"A little, but Lydia probably won't mind, and it's in keeping with what we've always said we wanted—an enlightened attitude. Anyway, I may be in France when it occurs."

Anne hugged Charlotte. "I'm sure you will be. I'm sure Lydia will make that journey possible for you."

Charlotte burst into tears. "Oh, Anne, do you understand? Without Papa, France will not exist for me at all."

Since leaving Chicago, they had been traveling on a luxurious barge along the waterways—up to Michigan and now down to Saint Louis. As a result, their mail was late catching up with them, and there was a lot of it.

Lydia had been writing daily out of guilt over her duplicity regarding the Paris money and staying away so long. In the meantime, Charlotte dutifully answered each guilt-written missive out of her own sense of contrition over Sam.

"But why has she agreed to this?" Lydia asked Frank as she waved one of Charlotte's letters in front of his face. "How can we convince anyone to grant women voting rights? This will just make us the focus of more animosity. Anyway, we have a hard enough time figuring out what's right for ourselves these days, let alone anyone else."

"I didn't realize you were still in the soul-searching business," Frank responded before taking a puff on his cigar, stretching his legs out on the leather ottoman in their stateroom.

Lydia glared at him. "You know perfectly well we are. Don't be sarcastic."

"I was merely surmising. It seems highly unlikely that anyone who puts so much energy into acquiring land has much time left over for higher pursuits."

"Don't be so damned condescending. That land enables us to have higher pursuits—or lower ones, if we want. What's wrong with trying to shape a future to suit ourselves? Because we're women, is that a sin?"

He tried to pull her onto his lap, but she resisted. "Point conceded. My only rebuttal is to ask if you're sure what it is that still suits you?"

"Yes! No." She pushed his legs to one side and sat down on the ottoman, her chin cupped in her hands. "I don't know what suits us anymore. Nobody told us that life in Kansas would be so hard."

"I tried," he said, "back there in Chicago."

She shook her head. "You have to experience it to understand. Nothing prepares you."

"Let me rephrase my question: Are you still pursuing your original goal, or has the search itself replaced the goal?"

"The latter, by necessity. I know that. But only for the short term, until we're secure."

"You will never be secure."

This time she let him pull her onto his lap.

"A debate! What has possessed her!"

"The spirit of the times. Now, tidy your hair or whatever you do. We've got to see a man about a train. If you're going to invest in rail stock, this meeting could be useful to you."

"It's the spirit of the times," Frank repeated two hours later, speaking to a partner of his in a rail speculation venture. The context was the rapid migration to western lands and the equally rapid disappearance of white pine close to Michigan's waterways. They were debating the best location inland for trunk lines to haul that timber.

"We'd better take action while there are trees left to cut and before disillusionment sets in."

"You're such a pessimist, Frank Bailey," George Sanderson said. "There's no earthly reason why this boom won't go on forever."

"There are many earthly reasons," Frank countered. "Mrs. Fulgate comes from Kansas, and she can tell you it ain't no picnic there right now."

"Mr. Bailey is referring to the crop failures and stock losses due to a siege of bad weather," Lydia said to Sanderson. "However, I happen to believe that this temporary blight will be corrected if enough diligence is applied to the problems."

"Mrs. Fulgate is an optimist," Frank said.

"A necessity for life in Kansas," Lydia responded.

"Mrs. Fulgate speaks sense," Sanderson said, smiling at Lydia for the first time as if she were a person instead of an ornament.

Lydia had almost forgotten what it was like to be treated as an appendage. This trip, unfortunately, served as a reminder and reinforced her conviction that she and Charlotte had set out on the right course.

Although her conviction needed no reinforcement, she knew, only her justification for denying Charlotte the money for a trip to Paris did. But Charlotte had to be saved from unwise decisions, Lydia reasoned for the hundredth time. As soon as they left this stuffy room, she would see what she could do about saving Frank Bailey from one, too.

Later, on their way to inspect a parcel of land Frank hoped to turn into a summer resort, she began, "I don't trust George Sanderson."

"He certainly turned into an admirer of yours."

"Not soon enough. The very fact that you took me with you should have caused him to take note in the beginning."

"Anyone looking at you should do so."

"I'm serious, Frank."

"I am, too. On this trip, you're my intelligence gauge. When someone dismisses you, I assume he's not going to outwit me. That means I can discount George Sanderson as any kind of danger and use him for my purposes. Since he has more contacts and more experience than I do, he'll be helpful in this particular enterprise."

"I'm glad I can be of service."

"Oh, you are. Of much service."

But Lydia didn't pick up on his remark, and instead expressed doubts again about Sanderson.

"I'm more astute than he is," Frank assured her. "I can handle a man like that, believe me."

"Astute is not always wise."

He laughed out loud and threw his arm around her shoulders. "I could say the same to you, Lydia Fulgate."

"What happens when all the trees are gone?"

"The forest turns into a prairie, which turns into a settlement, which feeds and houses people and provides them with opportunities like the ones you have had."

"If that's so, then why speak of disillusionment?" she asked.

"Because there are more dreamers than dreams fulfilled. You've had some experience with broken dreams already."

Lydia thought of those who had packed up and moved on, even during the good times. "But I've achieved my dream," she finally said.

"With my help."

"With your help," she conceded, somewhat grudgingly.


They borrowed two horses and rode to an inviting spot along the river, where they sat entranced by the water's hypnotic flow. "My river looks paltry compared to this one," Lydia said after a long, peaceful silence.

"This river can be wicked when it gets out of hand."

"So can mine."

"So can you."

"Is this a lecture whose point I'm missing?"

"I'm just reminding you that we're the main source of the chaos in our lives, not natural disasters or even society in general; and neither well-meaning causes nor other people are going to save you from yourself."

"Looking for spiritual rebirth is not a cause."

"The way you go about it, it is. You'll never let go of your own devils if you keep denying their existence, I don't care how many rebirths you go through or how many people you think you can save, even if those people include your friend and your brother."

"Why do you always bring up Sam? Are you jealous because we're close?"

"I feel sorry for the poor bastard, I've told you that. You've given him no room to make his own mistakes."

"Did I interfere with his marrying May? Did I?"

"May suits your purposes fine. She's no threat to you—as both you and your brother know."

"Don't speak to me like that!" she yelled and scrambled to her feet.

"Lydia, calm down."

Quickly she mounted her horse. He grabbed for her reins: "What the hell . . . ?" But she galloped off before he could finish. Let him worry about her. Let him feel some consternation—if he was capable of any emotion.


Having waited until the last minute to return to their stateroom, she found Frank stretched out on the bed asleep, his boots crossed neatly at the ankles, his hands crossed on his chest, his trousers as crisp as ever. He was the picture of nonchalance. Without a moment's hesitation, she picked up a large pitcher and poured water on him, then turned for the door. He woke sputtering and gasping, and leaped for her. While scanning the room for some kind of weapon to defend herself, she felt him release her arms, the tension of the moment disappearing with his dawning realization of what had happened.

He reached for the hand towel. "It's refreshing to see you won't put up with ill treatment just for money," he said calmly.

She drew back her fist and slammed it into his temple hard enough to make him stumble backward. During the seconds it took him to regain his balance, she scooped up his jacket and pistol and threw them out the porthole.

"Get out of here," she yelled, as she tried to shove him toward the door. "Get the hell out of here!"

"Lydia, I'm sorry," he apologized. "Calm down, please. I'm sorry!" He wouldn't leave, nor did he allow her to, but he made no effort to stop her pummeling until she picked up his walking stick. Then he restrained her until she fell exhausted on the floor, where she continued to cry. At some point he placed a pillow under her sobbing head and a blanket over her body. Later, after dark, she slept.

When she awoke, he was on the bed, smoking. She knew because she first smelled the cigar, and upon opening her eyes, watched its red tip, the only light in the room, traveling from his face to his belly. She lay still a long time, giving herself a chance to sift through the emotional debris. He must have noticed a change in her breathing, for in a while the cigar, still lit, stopped moving; she sensed his body straining to pick up any movement from her.

"Are you awake?" he finally whispered.

She answered by shifting positions.

"I went too far," he said. "I apologize. I admire your spirit, and I respect your courage. Those are the reasons I lend you money, and I hope you know that.

"I'll go whenever you like. It's your very nature that I love and admire, but sometimes I want to destroy it. I'm not good for you, Lydia. I deluded myself into thinking—hoping—that perhaps I was."

Silence again while the cigar continued to provide the only light, the only movement. After a long time, she crawled the few feet to the bed. The cigar no longer glowed. With his hands under her arms, he lifted her up beside him.

At first light they slept awhile, then made love again. Slept again. As the morning came on, someone would occasionally knock on their door, wait a few moments, then go away. Sometimes, when they heard the footsteps subsiding, they came together before drifting back to sleep.

In early afternoon they had their breakfast brought to them, along with two fresh pails of water.

"We both knew you had to go back, anyway," he said as she poured them another cup of coffee. "You're feeling too guilty about leaving Charlotte."

Although he had no way of knowing the extent of her guilt, his perceptiveness always amazed her. "I should never have agreed to stay away so long."

"I made it a condition."

She placed her hand on his. "I wanted to come, Frank. I needed the excuse—your condition."

He watched her as she began packing. They would dock in Saint Louis before dinner, and there he would put her on a train to Kansas. Except for that last exchange, both had held on to their silence.

When Frank did speak again, it was to say, "Charlotte is not your child, Lydia. She's an able-bodied adult, as able as you. She and Sam do not need you to be responsible for them."

She saw it was with some effort that he forced himself to say this, so she responded as honestly as she could: "Sam needs me more than he shows, or even knows. I've made sure of that. From the time I was a little girl, I needed somebody to need me. My parents didn't seem to, so I did everything I could to make my brother love me."

Frank came over to where she stood, so still, a dress folded precisely over her arms, and tried to put his arm around her.

She shrugged it off. "I don't want pity," she said. He started to protest but instead sat back down.

"I feel responsible for Charlotte for many reasons," she said, "some of which I don't wish to discuss. She's going through a hard time personally, and she trusts me to take care of her. The least I can do is go back to look after her. I'm trying to do what is best for her, but . . ."

Lydia squeezed her eyes shut to keep from crying. She did not desire pity, and she did not deserve it. Nor could she believe him when he said that she, of all people, did not need to "make" herself loved.

As she waved good-bye to him from the train that evening, she knew that she could never trust him, for he was even more skittish than she and could not have withstood her vulnerability. She also knew that she had never been more honest with anyone in her life, herself included.

5 3  It was Norah's birthday and Lydia had returned—two good reasons to celebrate, Charlotte reminded herself, as the women gathered in the kitchen to prepare the birthday feast.

Charlotte had volunteered to make the cake—a black cake, it was called. As Anne browned the pound of flour, Charlotte laid out the other ingredients: one pound each of butter, sugar, citron, and blanched almonds; two pounds each of currants and raisins; a half pound of figs; twelve eggs; one teacup of molasses; one glass of brandy; one tablespoon each of mace and cloves; two each of cinnamon and allspice; three each of ginger and grated nutmeg. Then she added two teaspoons of cream baking powder to the flour and one of soda to the brandy.

Most of the ingredients were gifts from Frank Bailey, who knew how scarce and expensive such delicacies as figs, currants, and almonds were in Kansas. Lydia had brought them back with her from Chicago as a surprise. Also the deluxe coffee grinder and the carpet sweeper—"a miracle appliance," Norah had pronounced, upon trying it out. Charlotte had acted more enthusiastic than she felt, largely because she understood how upset Lydia herself was with her failure to obtain funds, not only for the farm but for Charlotte.

The new gadgets did amuse and please her, and the thoughtfulness of the gesture—a gentle reminder of their reason to persist—had touched her. But she'd been disappointed beyond words. She had counted on seeing

Papa. She still did, she realized. Every day she expected money to come through; Lydia had told her it might, had said not to give up hope entirely.

Lydia had come back distracted, sometimes distraught, and given to saying things like, "We have to get on with our lives" or "We have wonderful lives." These remarks came out of nowhere and appeared to be uttered for her own benefit as much as Charlotte's. While she'd expressed reservations about the literary society's debate, she had agreed to it readily enough. In fact, it hardly seemed to register; nothing did, for long, and she didn't mention Frank Bailey at all. Charlotte only hoped that her friend's distress was only temporary.

"Careful with that sharp knife, Lydia," Anne was cautioning, for Lydia was cutting chops from a calf—one of their own, which they'd planned to raise for milk before the calf broke her shoulder. They had decided to eat some of the meat at this evening's birthday celebration.

Although Norah had chosen to sit in the kitchen with the other women while they prepared her meal, they wouldn't allow her to help. With everyone baking or peeling or chopping, the kitchen was warm and cheery. Another pleasantry to be thankful for, Charlotte noted as she finished meticulously rubbing the fruit with the browned flour.

The knife Lydia was using on the calf carcass glanced off a bone and careened onto the floor. "Anne is right," she scolded. "You've got to be careful there. That calf is not Leonard Majors."

At that remark, Lydia and Norah both laughed, prompting Charlotte to ask: "So, Norah, when are you ever planning to use your reward?" Since she refused the land Lydia and Charlotte had offered, they had given her a cash settlement instead, with the stipulation that she had to use the money for her own benefit and not give it to her family or her church. Knowing she felt the same way about marriage as they did, they were determined to improve her lot themselves, even if that meant losing her for Twin House Farm.

"Maybe next year or the next I'll start a dry goods store over in Dodge City. Sally says that between the bad element and the good one, there's plenty of demand along that line for primping women who like clothes and such. She says she'll help, too, in between babies; and Will's got no objections."

This announcement surprised them all, but they reacted enthusiastically. As they rolled out dough and peeled potatoes and boiled bones, they constructed a new business for Norah. "And if worse comes to worst around here, we can all come join you," Lydia said and smiled.

"Twin House Farm never comes to worst," Norah answered fervently.

"No, it doesn't, does it?" Lydia said, obviously heartened by Norah's inconsequential remark. "It survives. We survive! Bedbugs and fleas and all!" An infestation of both had all but overtaken them in the last few weeks, the only hope of their diminishment being a solid winter freeze.

Lydia suddenly laughed and turned to Charlotte. "Remember when we almost fainted at seeing animals butchered at the stockyards?"

"We were such sissies then," Charlotte said, giving the fruit mixture one more hard stir before putting it in the oven to bake for four hours.

"But no more. We mustn't lose sight of the fact that we've done what we set out to do. We must never forget that." Behind the words was an echo: be happy, Charlotte, be happy. So Charlotte smiled.

**54** As it happened, the news of her father's death reached Charlotte on the second day of the new year. It was a relatively painless death, Audrey assured her. Too weak to write himself, he had asked Audrey to convey his love and regret to his dearest pussycat. Her last letters to him had been very important, had extended his life a little longer, Audrey generously reported.

Charlotte read the words over and over; then, unable to bear the finality of the message, she wadded up the letter and tossed it into the woodstove. Eyes closed, she lay on her bed and counted her breaths. So Papa was dead. At least the wait was over. In the end she could not help him any more than he had helped her. But the letters had been important. Audrey had said so. "Important"? Was that the word Audrey had used? She shouldn't have destroyed the note so soon.

She should have gone to see her papa. No matter what had happened later, he had been the only protector she had ever had; he had tried to keep her safe from her mother. Had it not been for him, she would have been too intimidated ever to stand up for herself. He had loved her, and his love's reflection had been instilled in her.

But what good was the grieving now? She had grieved for years already. She had to save her energies for the future. For Twin House Farm. For Lydia. Oh, yes, Lydia—the only one who had ever come close to accepting her as Papa had. She shuddered to think she'd once come close to losing Lydia by violating the charmed circle that surrounded her and Sam. Where would she be now? He couldn't help her. He had his life. Only Lydia in all the world cared enough.

With great effort, she pushed herself up to sit on the edge of the bed. Then she tidied her hair and went back across the walkway to Lydia's house. It was going to be a cold night. She had to help melt ice for morning, round up more fuel, tend to the chickens. How lucky she was to be so busy that there was no time to grieve. If only she weren't so tired, so very, very tired . . .

The next morning Charlotte awoke to find a fine sheet of snow covering her bed, the sheepskins she had tacked to the cracks in her ceiling were unable to withstand the accumulation. By noon they could tell from the size of the rapidly falling flakes and the gale force of the wind that this would be a blizzard of significant dimension. After the initial worry, however, spirits in the two households lightened, with Charlotte reflecting the gaiety of her friends.

They'd had a great deal of experience in dealing with these conditions, especially after the storm of the year before—the worst ever, some said. If the clouds looked especially laden, they would house the horses and the chickens and herd as many sheep as possible into Lydia's basement, easy enough, for they'd constructed an earthen ramp leading down to it when they built the house. Everyone else moved into Charlotte's for the duration, thereby saving on precious coal and cow chips and avoiding the worst of the smell emanating from Lydia's basement. They put out plenty of feed in the barn for more sheep, just in case the snow kept them housebound a day or so. Starting in October they had put aside extra provisions for just such emergencies.

Since they'd taken every possible precaution and since there wasn't much work to be done, they used the time as an excuse to bring out their violin and guitar and favorite books and plays. They read aloud to each other and sometimes attempted to perform a play. They even managed a game or two of charades and pulled out the puzzle Frank Bailey had brought them during one of his visits. When they did venture to open a shutter, they could see nothing but snow, Lydia's house curtained off entirely by the lashing whiteness.

"I hope Sam has enough sense to stay inside," Lydia said to Charlotte as their eyes scanned for any landscape.

"He wouldn't go out, Lydia. He knows better than that. Doesn't he, Anne?" They had put on several pairs of woolen stockings as well as coats, gloves, scarves, and their warmest dresses. Charlotte could wear her black cashmere without giving explanations.

"Sam will take care," Anne consoled them.

"Of course he will," Lydia said, smiling now at Charlotte. "You mustn't worry about me. I don't plan to spoil our own fun."

Charlotte quickly managed to compose herself, hoping she masked her own anxiety about him. On the whole, she had held very well to her resolve to keep him out of her life, could go whole days without thinking of him. Then she sometimes hated him with all the fierceness that had earlier gone into her loving.

But all that was over now. Ever since the snow began, she had felt nothing at all; she had been as one with the snow and its silent, icy, numbing splendor. Now her father was dead, and for her, Sam was dead, too. She did not intend to see him again. But she had to know he was living, breathing, *somewhere*. Or was it her father she meant? Was the numbing splendor of the blizzard driving her mad?

On the fourth day of the storm, when snow and wind had reached a chaos of whiteness, she awoke to the sound of her father's howling. Quickly opening the shutters, she could see nothing but the dizzying flakes. A drift of snow blew into the room.

"For God's sake, Charlotte, close that window!" Lydia shouted from the bed. For warmth the three had slept together with their clothes on.

"Don't you hear someone calling to us?" Charlotte asked.

Lydia sat up, listening intently, but shook her head. "It's that hideous wind, or maybe it's the uncle's spirit," Lydia joked. "You remember, the spirit that the man with his pipe was looking for. Now, please close up, Charlotte, before we freeze to death or get buried by snow."

Anne had not opened her eyes but seemed to be listening. "A bad dream?" she suggested.

"It was not a dream," Charlotte said. "I heard somebody."

"This blizzard is enough to upset anyone," Lydia said, stretching over the bed to light a lantern. "Come back to bed. You're shivering, and you look terrible."

"This snow is driving me crazy!"

"It's the wind," Anne corrected, eyes still closed. "The wind will drive us all crazy if we're not careful."

Lydia jumped up. "Then let's be careful. We'll splurge with hoecakes and sausage for breakfast and follow it with a dance. We'll take turns dancing and playing."

"A dance in the morning?" Charlotte asked.

"Why not? A little music to drown out ugly howls," Anne responded.

"We'll teach Norah the tunes so we can all dance," Lydia insisted.


That day they danced and read stories aloud and sang their favorite arias from Verdi and Offenbach and Gounod—acting them out, of course. They made elaborate plans for a spring garden. That evening Charlotte felt more like her old self, felt consoled by the love and care Lydia and Anne gave her. That night she slept, and with no bad dreams, no unexplained howls.

The next day they danced again. The day after, the snow stopped, and a day after that they cleared a path to the barn. Two sheep had died. The women counted themselves lucky to have lost no more. Only for one brief instant did Charlotte consider the two sheep lucky. To be frozen out of pain and want did not strike her as an unnecessarily high price.


Snow came again the next day and the next and intermittently in the same fashion for the rest of the month, and intermittently they danced, though they gave up acting altogether. Only the reading brought them any real solace, but never once did they discuss the evolution of their souls or the notion of their essences.

In spite of days of utter stillness, Charlotte grew no closer to any revelation of truth than before. Then again, when was the last time any of them had expected a truth, some vision, to be found through nature? Far from a good to be tapped, that mighty force had become an enemy to be reckoned with. They had said as much to each other over the last few years, although never too directly. Not now, either. Not even on days when entombment in the snow seemed a possibility. By now every room had a sifting of snow over its surfaces.

The whiteness and cold continued to reinforce Charlotte's lack of feeling, but she did not slip into gloom. That first day of dancing had saved her from some deeper slide. But the abundant real concerns did not engage her. They lost sheep daily now. Coal and cow chips and daily provisions were meagerly apportioned. The gathering of ice to melt for water became a more and more arduous task. It was impossible to be really warm.

To conserve energy and the need for food, the entire household lolled around the stove. Norah alone refused to give in to the lethargy, and she took a keen delight in the reading. In fact, because of her, they read only fiction. Norah's pleasure in stories was so great that the other women enjoyed obliging her. "I know lots of stories," she'd say, "but no one ever bothered to write 'em down." Sometimes they persuaded her to tell one of her own.

The landscape, transformed into a white coverlet, had lost its familiar contours, distancing Charlotte that much more from physical reality. She could not imagine seeing a green field again and began to understand how much she'd come to depend on both the dunes and the flatness, the colors and smells of the seasons, for solace. She missed the touch of the earth, the roll of it beneath her feet, the feel of it between her fingers. She came to think she might recover when the snow melted and she connected to the earth again. She came to think the snow would never melt.

To her amazement, the thaw did eventually begin, and the shoveling out started in earnest. Early on, Lydia had to be dissuaded from setting forth to Sam's, with Anne repeatedly arguing that he would come to see her as soon as he possibly could.

"But his horses may have died. His babies might be sick. *He* might be sick." This last thought always put Lydia into a complete panic. "I've got to go!"

"He'll come as soon as he can," Anne would answer firmly and knowingly.

Charlotte knew that, too, but the knowledge meant nothing to her. She had buried Sam and her father in the whiteness. Not bound by any emotion, she wondered if she had found her essence after all. If so, why had she bothered?

For several days they didn't clear the walkway between the two houses. No one was staying in Lydia's, and the space between, in shadow most of the time, had hardened into a sheet of ice. Soon enough, they told each other, it would begin to melt, and then they could spread out again. In truth, they derived comfort from the coziness of their cramped, temporary arrangement.

Charlotte knew Sam would arrive any day and the knowledge drove her one morning to begin shoveling a path between the houses where the snow proved most pliant. Rather than stir up painful memories, she would retreat to the other house.

Enjoying the repetition of vigorous movement, she went about her work alone. In a while, Anne joined her. Soon after that, not twenty-five feet from Charlotte's front door, they came upon the body of a man lying face down in the ice.

"He's too small for Sammy," Anne said almost at once.

Charlotte nodded. Even with a heavy jacket and hood on, he wasn't big enough to be mistaken for Sam. Charlotte summoned the rest of the household to help cut him out of the ice. His face set as if determined not to give in, his mouth agape, he looked as if he were still in flight, running from hell.

"It was his howl I heard," Charlotte moaned. "His cry." Sinking into the snow, she put his stiff, ice-circled head in her lap. "I could have saved him. I was so close. I could have saved him." Not taking her eyes from his face, she continued to clutch him.

"Come inside, *chérie,*" Anne said softly. "We don't know him. Come, now." But Charlotte couldn't move.

"Charlotte, get up," Lydia ordered. "You can't help him now, and you can't stay out here. I mean it. Come along."

Charlotte looked up. "My father is dead," she said.

Lydia squatted beside her. "We don't know that," she said tenderly.

"We do," Charlotte replied and shook her head. "It wasn't worth speaking of, with everyone so busy and happy."

"Oh, my Charlotte, I'm sorry. I'm so sorry," Lydia intoned, cradling Charlotte's head in her hands. "You should have told us. I should have. . . . But please, *chérie*, please get up now. We're turning blue. Come inside."

Through the rest of the day and all of the night, Anne and Lydia and Norah took turns sitting with Charlotte, who continued to stare straight ahead, trapped in a vision of death. At dawn Lydia persuaded her to drink some brandy—a lot of brandy. "I have buried my two loves," she said to Lydia before she fell asleep.

When she awoke, she heard the drip of ice melting; and her own tears began to fall and continued to flow every day until she could see the soil again. Every day she cried on waking, and every night she cried herself to sleep. She had let her father down and could not be forgiven.

She shed tears for her father but also for her mother—and for Sam. She shed tears for herself and for all that she had lost—her entire world, except Lydia, who would not forsake her. Lydia would not so much as leave her at night until sleep had come.

Then one morning Charlotte awoke to discover Lydia asleep in the chair beside her. Charlotte gently shook her friend's arm. "Lydia," she said, "I'm better. I know it. I have buried my ghosts now."

Lydia stretched and rubbed her eyes. When she had taken in what Charlotte had just said, she smiled.

"This spring let's plant the most beautiful of gardens, Charlotte. We will build ourselves a kingdom. We'll not give in to howls."

# 55

The plan was this: Anne and Lydia would hold the sheep steady. Charlotte would snip away the wool. Norah would gather it into bundles. So far, only Norah had become adept at her task. It took an hour to wrestle their first ewe to the ground. Another hour later Charlotte had nicked the ewe four times, including once on her teat. This last nick caused consternation all around, especially to the ewe herself. Lydia and Anne secured the animal more tightly in their arms as the noon sun, mitigated only slightly by occasional clouds, glowered fiercely down on their proceedings. Charlotte still had half the chest to go.

"She's dying!" Lydia suddenly screamed.

"Move her head. She could suffocate on her back—as you know," Charlotte barked impatiently and wiped perspiration from her forehead with her sleeve.

Lydia, having withheld her criticism of Charlotte's technique until now, responded in kind. "Our crew would have done at least three sheep by now."

"I'd remind you they've been doing it all their lives. We have not."

"But our shears are English Sheffield steel, the very finest. I would think they would speed things up."

"This year's fleece is beautifully greasy. I don't believe it's ever been better," Anne said.

"Thank you, Anne the Peacekeeper," Lydia replied, her sarcasm only thinly disguised.

"There's no need to be uncivil to Anne," Charlotte scolded.

"I could shear," Norah finally offered. "Back in Ireland I used to do a little of this."

"*Mon dieu,*" Charlotte answered crossly. "I'm good with my hands! If Anne and Lydia would only hold this creature still! Maybe you can help them."

"She's frightened. It's impossible to hold her steadier," Anne snapped back, abruptly dropping her role as peacekeeper.

"But this sheep knows us. They all know us. Why would they be frightened?" Lydia asked. Just then the half-shorn animal wriggled out of their clutches, and Charlotte threw the clippers down.

"We have chosen an idiotic way to save money. If we hadn't had to have the most expensive harvester and the newest McCormick reaper, we could afford to have proper help around here," she growled and stomped toward the house.

Anne and Norah looked toward Lydia, who shrugged. They were becoming accustomed to the unpredictability of Charlotte's dark moods since her father's death.

"If the two of you will lay her shoulders and back on my legs . . . No, no . . . like this," Norah instructed and grabbed the animal's hind legs to bring her down. Then the three, as if on cue, redoubled their efforts to shear the wool.

Without Charlotte's bad humor, they relaxed and even began to laugh at their incompetence and inefficiency. As it happened, Norah did do a fairly adequate job of clipping, working in long, smooth strokes, following the contours of the sheep's body. When she came to the next teat, she suggested singing. "Sometimes they're sensitive, and a little tune helps."

Anne began singing "Baa, Baa, Black Sheep," and Lydia and Norah joined in as a round. If the singing didn't soothe the ewe, it improved the performers' spirits. Lydia kept glancing toward the house, but Charlotte didn't reappear.

After completing the shearing, Anne suggested they take a break. Covered with sweat and the odor of sheep wool, Lydia, Norah, and Anne sat down at the base of the sand hill, and Anne adjusted her sunbonnet to better shield her face from the sun and flies.

"Where's that fabled Kansas wind today?" she asked. "It would provide some relief from the stench and the flies, probably the heat, too."

"I ain't never heard of a place that don't have trees for shade, 'cept where barbarians live," Norah said.

Anne laughed. "Well, we were looking for an alternative civilization; maybe we got an alternative *to* civilization instead."

"Oh, no, ma'am. I didn't mean disrespect where you ladies are concerned. You're the most proper, real ladies I ever worked for. Even out here, even right now, you are proper ladies to the core. Highfalutin ones are puny imitations of your likes."

Lydia would not condescend to Norah by exchanging glances with Anne, but she couldn't resist asking why her knowledge of sheep had never come up until now.

"To tell the truth, ma'am, I don't much like thinkin' about my old life. Thinkin' of my mama makes me sad, and thinkin' of my daddy and brothers gets up my dander, 'cept for one little brother I kind of liked. He don't have a chance in hell, though, but to grow up like them other men."

Lydia thought back to the night when Norah had been prepared to kill a man, and she realized now that Norah would have performed the deed with some degree of pleasure.

"Besides which," Norah went on, "I don't much like things to do with land or animals. Both suck out all your strength and joy, just keepin' em goin'. Before you know it, they've used you up, and they're not even grateful. They don't give nothin'." She ended with some bitterness.

Lydia stood up and brushed off the back of her skirt. Norah was lecturing her, of course, cautioning her. "But we'll triumph, Norah. We shall. Now let's get back to your barbering skills."


The three worked on although, Lydia noticed, not with the earlier enthusiasm. She would give Anne a little cheering up later and remind her that Norah was notoriously pessimistic about everything. With the passing of time, Anne had become her old self, but Lydia remained watchful for the melancholia that had enveloped her when she'd first come. After their first and only discussion of her troubles—over six years ago now—neither had brought the subject up again. But whatever her problems were, the rigor of their life and the love of their friends seemed to have dispelled them. Anne was more subdued than she had been in her youth, but she could now also laugh once again with abandon.

And how touching, Lydia thought, that Norah should speak of joy, for even a lament on its absence signified an acknowledgment of its existence. What on earth had she meant about their being "ladies to the core"? Over tea she would ask Anne what distinctions existed between the ladies of Twin House Farm and "highfalutin ones."

"I have no idea," Anne replied as she and Lydia and Charlotte sipped their late afternoon tea and nibbled the shortbread that Charlotte, clearly in a better mood, had baked. She didn't quite apologize for not helping with the shearing, but she was certainly putting herself out to be useful now.

"Perhaps highfalutin ladies don't have content compatible with their veneer, so they strike her as hypocrites."

"Or empty."

"Or both," Anne joined in. "But would you then say, Charlotte, that we fare well with Norah because we dropped many of the forms that don't fit our lives? Wasn't that one of the reasons we all came here?"

Charlotte hugged Anne. "Oh, Anne, once again you've reminded us what we're about. We need that from time to time, don't we, Lydia?"

Choked with gratitude for Anne, Lydia could only nod in agreement. Anne, her oldest and wisest friend, had considered exactly the impact of her words on Charlotte and waited until she could ease her reminder in among Charlotte's own thoughts. As well as anyone, Anne understood the importance of timing.

It contrast to the earlier rift, their evening meal was festive and spontaneous. They talked of their hope for more late spring rain, and they gossiped about the Browns' ever greater social pretensions at a time when everyone knew how overextended they were. They spoke once again of the literary society as a vehicle for change. One of the women had even asked Anne what she thought of "Building Character through Adversity" as a topic for discussion, once the upcoming debate on women's voting rights was over. Anne had assured her the women of Twin House Farm had done just that.

They laughed, and Charlotte's laughter encouraged Lydia to give her a friendly nudge: "Charlotte, why not change your mind and come with us to the christening tomorrow? May will be busy and won't bother us. A small party would be good for you." Taking silence as a positive sign, Lydia added, "And Sam would be so pleased to see you. He always asks after you." Unfortunately, these last words did not have the desired effect, for Charlotte descended instantly back into the murky center of her despair.

"You go to the goddamn christening and pray for all their goddamn stinking souls. As for me, I'll save my prayers for our land while I stay home and work, work, work!" She slammed her palm down on the table. "If I'd wanted to attend parties, I would have stayed in Paris." She left the room with Lydia and Anne gaping at each other.

"She has certainly got the knack of English," Anne finally said.

But Lydia could not rise to the humor. "What happened? A few minutes ago she seemed just fine."

"She's going through a difficult time." Anne had taken up her embroidery, a means she'd always used to console herself during disturbances.

"She was coming back to us. I could feel it," Lydia insisted.

"Give her time."

"No. Time to indulge herself is the worst thing we can give her. No," Lydia repeated, rising to her feet. "She allowed herself to slip as soon as we brought up a subject not to her liking."

Anne looked up from her needlework. "She's not in the mood for parties or family gatherings. That's all. Even you can't help her right now, Lydia. You did your best. She knows that. Come, finish your wine." Anne patted the seat of Lydia's chair.

"Did you notice what happened?" Without waiting for a reply, Lydia continued, "I mentioned Sam, just mentioned his name, and she flew into a rage. She's jealous of him, you know; she thinks he takes too much of my time. She is not like you. She doesn't understand that Sam and I are extensions of each other."

"She understands," Anne said quietly.

Lydia shook her head vigorously. "If she understood, she wouldn't hate him so much. She would love him too, as part of me." Taking another sip of wine, she suggested, "Maybe you're the one to talk to her about this. Maybe she would take advice from you better than me."

This time Anne put her work aside and pressed Lydia's hands together between her own. "You must let Charlotte resolve her own problems with Sam. As her friends, the best we can do is respect her right, and her wish, to grapple with them in whatever manner she chooses."

"We have to try—" Lydia said.

"We have to go to bed," Anne interrupted and rose to stoke the fire. She picked up the lantern, and Lydia obediently followed behind her.

As they began climbing the stairs, Anne stopped and turned to deliver a final message, one that she seemed to have thought about for a long time: "We can't chuck Charlotte under the chin or tickle her feet or tell her a funny story to make her happy, the way we did with Sammy when he was little. We can't make such tricks work for him anymore, either. They never did, really, because we couldn't change what made him sad in the first place. We hardly know what causes our own sadness or how to change it, let alone anybody else's."

Lydia gently tugged Anne's skirt. "You and I don't indulge ours, Anne," she said softly, affectionately. "That's why we're stronger than the others."

For a moment Anne's eyes engaged Lydia's in an unspoken admonition before she turned to finish the climb.

56 Some said the huge turnout, including quite a few people from as far away as ten miles, showed not so much an interest in the question of women's voting rights as a need for distraction from the woes besetting the area. So much damage had been done, so much wreckage needed repair, so many crops required planting that spring was well under way before anyone thought of the debate again.

For Lydia and the other women involved, this was no mere distraction, however. This was a struggle for the very soul of the community. Lydia, especially, had come to see it as a way to validate the vision she and Charlotte shared in the beginning. They really could create another kind of world, one in which they wouldn't feel quite so isolated.

As the participants assembled on the stage of the opera house, Lydia inspected the men's panel, which included a judge, a minister, and a farmer. They weren't, so far as she knew, as smart as the women, but she wasn't sure that mattered, since all the judges of the debate were men. The other side had refused to consider any woman at all in that role.

She caught Charlotte's eye and acknowledged her thumbs-up. Charlotte looked distressed, however. Maybe she had picked up an undercurrent in the audience that Lydia had not yet sensed. A moment earlier Sam had sought Charlotte out, but she had practically turned her back on him. Now Lydia despaired of their ever being friends.

And he had looked despondent, although now he too gave Lydia an encouraging salute. The winter had taken its toll on Sam, and now he faced a drought. May had even dropped her self-satisfied stance. Perhaps Frank Bailey would help him. Sam needed outside encouragement—and money, of course.

And where *was* Frank? It had been months since she'd had a letter from him, an occurrence she hadn't expected.

"Time to begin," someone called out to all the participants.

Lydia barely had time to close her eyes and take a deep breath before the polite applause began, first for the moderator and then with the introduction of each debater, the men receiving a substantially larger hand than the women.

What followed felt like a slow-moving bad dream.

Lydia, Anne, and Mrs. Sargent made their point about the need to accord to women the same basic rights as men and to give women an equal voice in the affairs of the community. "Basic justice calls for no less than our voices also being heard," Lydia said. Women desired to serve, to advise the community in the same matters that men did, and benefits would come from such service.

"If a woman's wisdom and virtue are good enough to serve and guide our families, then why are they not good enough to serve our community as well?" Lydia remembered one of them asking, although she could not remember which one. The three of them knew each other's lines and arguments so thoroughly that who said what became incidental.

All the club women were aware of the need to state their opinions without sounding strident. A great number of Kansas men had supported women's rights as well as the temperance movement for years, but even these fair-minded, honorable men needed to be handled gingerly. An emotional appeal would confirm their assumption that women were unreasonable; too much deference would suggest that women were weak-willed. Too much boldness would be the most damaging stance of all—a direct threat and a blatant challenge to existing authority.

As Judge Holland was pointing out now, the authority here invoked was no less than that of God, country, and the entire governing structure of Western civilization. He left it to the Reverend Mr. Rumsdale to explain why giving a woman a public voice defied the teachings of the Scriptures.

Both men spoke in such reasonable tones and with such a good nature that Lydia found herself wanting to agree with them despite their unreasonable language. How could anyone not want to comply with the wishes of such fatherly, kindly men? Who in her right mind would wish to deliberately invoke their wrath?

For they refused to play to the rowdies in the audience, refused to raise their voices or otherwise posture to the thundering applause that greeted their every point. The judge and the minister left it to Clement Riggins, "a humble man of the soil," as he kept referring to himself, to rouse these elements to new levels of zeal.

When Riggins spoke of the inevitable chaos wreaked in the natural order by such unnatural acts as a woman participating in public forums, he got applause, whistles of approval, huzzahs. When he contented himself with speaking of the destruction of the family and the collapse of Western civilization caused by women wanton enough to flaunt their talents—alas, so meager!—in public, he received shouts of "amen" amid the clapping and now boot-stomping of these usually somber, hardworking, taciturn men.

When they responded to the women's reasonable statements with catcalls and boos, Lydia suspected they were venting their anger, frustration, and despair over their lost cattle and crops, the low price of what they sold, the high price of what they bought, and the government's favoritism toward railroads—to name just a few of their grievances.

The men's disillusionment was almost complete now. They had been good citizens, had followed the business leaders, for were they not God's true representatives? They had invested their faith in them only to find these latter-day priests to be men just like them, just as unable to cope with the rapid changes in technology and the brutal weather. They needed to control something in their lives—if not the weather, well, then, at least their women.

Along with a certain pity, Lydia felt scorn for those men. They will all clear out of Kansas before we do, she thought. They will give up sooner.

These sentiments did not console Lydia when she herself was jeered.

Angry, humiliated, she felt her face flush but managed to remain composed and clear-headed. She could tell that nearly all of the women agreed with her, as did a substantial minority of the men, some of whom nodded encouragement, even smiled.

In fact, most of the men had not responded to the debate one way or the other. Underneath those polite exteriors, what did they really think? Did they have any clue how complex these problems were? Did they understand that the anger turned on the women at this moment would eventually turn on them, whether they deserved it or not? The smug looks on those polite faces made her doubt that the men realized how much disillusionment had set in, just as Frank had predicted.

Suddenly Emma Leggett was on her feet, pointing her finger at Clement Riggins. "Scoundrel! Scoundrel!" she yelled. "Shame on all of you men. And a curse on you, too." She had turned to include the most obnoxious cluster of male boosters, who became church-still. "Do not treat us this way! We wipe your filthy noses and have your babies and seed this barren land and dust your wretched houses and dust and dust." Here her voice trailed off, only to come back in a bellow, "We have no chance to rest!" She hammered the air with her fist, then became still again, opened her frail arms wide, palms upward, and ever so softly but distinctly cried out, "And the babies die."

Anne was the first to find her legs. Gently, quietly, she led Emma Leggett to the stage steps, where Ed Leggett now waited. The winter and his troubles with the bank and with Brown had aged him, had crushed his proud spirit. And now this: his beautiful wife was no longer able to control her demons.

To a man, the judges pursed their lips, clasped their hands, and withheld their compassion while Emma Leggett raved. They left the stage to pass judgment on the debate during a short intermission. The three male panelists, with extravagant politeness, excused themselves to go outside for a smoke.

Lydia joined the other female panelists in the far corner of the stage. "Whatever else, we must remember we have enlightened a few people," she declared to them.

A few minutes later a mild-mannered man pronounced the judges' verdict: "Resolved: Although the women of Kansas have no right to vote, they do have the right to unhampered freedom in tending to their homes without the worry of needless outside responsibilities."

Lydia's deep-down sense of defeat came as an unwelcome surprise.

**57** Lydia showed Charlotte the account book one more time. While Charlotte studied their records, Lydia stared out the window at the early morning clouds streaking the sky. It was to be another beautiful day after all, a good day to plant; but that was a mixed blessing, for that meant yet another day of no rain.

"You see?" Lydia said. "Like the others around here, we have become land-rich and cash-poor. Now we've got to find a way to unload some of our property."

"Unload it?" Charlotte asked.

"Yes. Sell it. Get rid of it," Lydia answered sharply.

"I understand the term, Lydia," Charlotte answered carefully, trying to keep her voice from rising. "It's the concept that I find difficult. Besides, who would buy it?"

"There must be some outsider at least as gullible as we were when we set out. We just need to advertise in places where nobody has ever heard about western Kansas weather."

"What if you talked to Frank? Could he appeal to those investors who finally came through for us? He could point out that a little more money would save their original outlay."

"Charlotte, wake up! They're not going to help us." Lydia took a breath to restrain her impatience. No reason to get upset with Charlotte because that bastard Frank Bailey had disappeared. Charlotte didn't know why he should have stayed in touch or, for that matter, that he was out of touch. His visits had always been erratic. In a more reasonable tone, Lydia continued. "Nobody is going to help us. Anybody who knows anything knows this land isn't worth a damn. People are leaving this area, not coming in."

The drought had persisted all spring; whereas blizzards for the last two winters had nearly obliterated the cattle industry, this drought of the last few months had wiped out most of the crops. Still, Charlotte could not give up the notion of willing abundance from the land. With enough prodding and pulling and pushing, the land and the elements would yield up their bounty. The secret was to hold out, to remain as tenacious as the wind—one elemental force against the other, her cunning against nature's. She had come to believe she would find her essence—if indeed she had one—only in outwitting the world around her.

To this end, she insisted on taking one more look at the account books. Although Lydia let out an impatient sigh, she sat back down to answer any questions, explain every number. Finally she said, "Now do you believe me? Everything in these books shouts bankruptcy." Lydia pounded the black ledger for emphasis.

"You're sure Mr. Leggett's bank won't help?"

Lydia smacked her head. "I forgot to tell you the worst piece of town gossip."

Charlotte leaned back in her chair and folded her arms across her chest. "Get on with it," she said resignedly.

"Well, there are lots of rumors, but all that's known for sure is that Wallace Brown is very ill and possibly dying," Lydia began her story. His family had been granted permission to close off the street in front of his house. "That area is as hushed as a tomb," Lydia reported. "The curtains remain drawn; no visitors, not even servants, are allowed in his room. Roberta Brown does everything for him."

"How terrible for them," Charlotte said.

"How terrible for us," Lydia countered, as she arranged Charlotte's grand-mère's shawl on the back of her chair. "Evidently Wallace Brown is so broke that Ben Leggett had to lend them the money to pay their insurance premiums to secure the family's future." It turned out, Lydia explained, that the Browns had known he was sick long enough ago to give Ben Leggett time to make some business arrangements for them.

"All of his ventures went broke?"

"All. We're not the only ones who will lose money because of him."

"What does it mean for us?"

"That we can't use the ventures as collateral for a new loan. It also means Ben's bank might be in trouble. That's what some think. It had a lot invested in Brown's enterprises."

"What happened to all those railroad magnates and East Coast financiers Brown was supposedly so friendly with?" Charlotte wanted to know.

"They disappeared along with all the railroad trunk lines that were supposed to be coming into Huddleston," Lydia answered. Without thinking, she threw the shawl over her shoulders.

"That means our bonds are worthless, too."

Lydia nodded her head in confirmation. "It looks that way."

Charlotte hesitated, then asked the hardest question of all: "What about Sam?"

"He's in worse shape than we are."

Charlotte pushed back from the table and rubbed her eyes. "All right, then. We'll help ourselves."

"What do you mean?" Lydia asked, getting up to pace the room.

"If we cannot borrow from the bank and we cannot wrest a living from the land, we find another source of money."

"You're talking in riddles."

"Lydia, how does Norah make ends meet?"

"You want us to become *servants*?"

"*Courtesans* is closer to the mark."

Lydia sat down and stared at her friend. "My God!"

Charlotte laughed. "Don't look so horror-stricken. We wouldn't *really* be courtesans, but we would open our houses for the entertainment of affluent gentlemen—only those of a certain station, naturally."

"My God!" Lydia repeated. She pulled the grand-mère's shawl tightly around her.

"We could offer them genteel surroundings in which to gamble, imbibe, and look at attractive women. Nothing cheap or tawdry, of course. It would be a salon, really."

"A saloon, really."

"Why are you so negative about this? How many choices do we have?"

Lydia jumped up again and threw her arms in the air. "Here we are after all these years, finally attaining respectability in this community, and you want to mock the values that are the very foundation of this place."

"Think back to Paris. Is there one woman in this town whose company we would have chosen then?"

"We were snobs. We would have been better off knowing any one of the women of Huddleston than all those fine French ladies we traipsed about with. In fact, it would behoove you to remember that those pretentious Parisians were one of the reasons we fled to this place."

"So we now aspire to another set of pretensions." Charlotte could not keep the sarcasm out of her voice.

"At least their pretensions don't have to do with whom you know or where you come from, and they are trying to better themselves. However misguided they sometimes are, they are seeking knowledge."

"Not knowledge of themselves—that was to be our pursuit, as I recall."

Lydia seated herself once more beside Charlotte and propped her elbows on the table, hands clasped. "Don't you understand? Our quest for self-knowledge was as frivolous as our former concern with going to the right parties."

"Yet you want us now to conform to the standards of a different but equally wrong-headed community."

"I simply don't want us to alienate ourselves entirely. That kind of isolation is overwhelming to me at times," Lydia confessed.

"You've said yourself that this place accepts success. Trust me, we'll remain respectable." Charlotte knew she was not being quite fair. She agreed with most of Lydia's arguments and repented a little when her friend wearily rested her head on her folded arms.

"What do you want us to do?" Lydia mumbled without raising her head.

"I want us to keep all this land in production. We can do that by gouging anyone who has two cents left in his pocket. We'll make this the plushest place in these parts, and we'll even run a carriage to and from the train station. Our establishment will be *très élégant*. All those British lords who spend their days fox hunting will be delighted to spend their evenings in such a refined establishment."

"Do you suppose they have any money left?"

"They certainly act as if they do, and their part of the state hasn't been hurt nearly as badly as ours. This won't be so bad, I promise. Look on it as another adventure. We'll take on new roles for ourselves. Who knows? We might even invent a different Lydia and Charlotte, perfect ones this time around."

"Do you honestly think we can bring this off?" Lydia asked.

"*Mais oui,*" Charlotte exclaimed. "But only long enough to regain our solvency, after which we'll be able to buy ourselves lasting freedom—and restore our good name, if that's what you want."

"I want our friendship to be restored, Charlotte. We're drifting apart."

Charlotte shook her head vigorously. "Not apart, just drifting, but that's as bad." She looked around the room. "Do you think Norah will mind serving so many?" Lydia asked.

"She'll oversee the other servants and get a portion of the tips."

"What will we do?"

"Act charming."

Lydia smiled. "If we can remember how."

"We can if we remember our goal is to purchase our liberty. Do you realize we have more freedom here than women anywhere? That's worth a little more sacrifice and hard work, be it of a different order."

"The community is not so restrictive, after all?"

Charlotte smiled. "I had to persuade you of the *rightness* of my argument. So long as the townpeople don't stone us—and they won't—that's all I ask."

They spent the rest of the night making plans, their earlier enthusiasm returning. For the first time in a long time, Charlotte felt in control of her situation. Before dawn she confided in Lydia a new dream: breeding horses. "Only after we get the weather righted, of course."

"Of course," Lydia assured her.

When Anne came down for breakfast they eagerly laid out their new plans and did not understand when she failed to share their excitement.

# 58

On the front porch of her brother's house, shaded by an overhang, Lydia rocked and watched Sam's baby crawl on a pallet. May bounced their toddler on her knee. Belinda, their oldest child, played with a doll on the steps. Today was Sam's birthday, and May had finally succeeded in setting up her little domestic drama for public display—the public consisting of Lydia and Anne.

That, at any rate, was how Lydia saw it, and she now wished she hadn't allowed herself to be lured onto May's turf. It was just as well Charlotte had refused to come; she wouldn't have enjoyed this and would only have added another note of disharmony. Lydia had enough on her mind today, for the news Sam was about to receive wouldn't please him.

When the baby began to fuss, Anne scooped him up in her arms. "He looks just like you, Sammy," she said.

"He has my father's eyes, though, doesn't he, Samuel?" Sam seemed to struggle to understand his wife's question. "Samuel?" May repeated sharply.

He had always been a dreamer, but Lydia had watched him withdraw from his surroundings these last few months. She might have taken some pleasure in watching him withdraw from May, but he had turned away from Lydia, too.

Anne and Lydia glanced at each other, but Lydia hadn't quite gathered her courage to tell Sam and May about her new plans. Instead, she launched into the latest local gossip: "Rumor has it that Wallace Brown may not be dead. A husband of a cousin of George Akers swore he spotted him in Florida."

"How could that be?" May asked. "The Brown family cordoned off the street. The whole town practically shut down on his behalf."

"But no one has seen him. We simply accepted Roberta Brown's story that he was ill," Lydia replied.

"Now people remember that the doctor was out of town during the three days leading up to his death and hadn't seen him for several days before that," Anne explained. "The doctor recalls he hadn't had a good look at Wallace Brown in over a month because of the drawn curtains."

"The last time I saw Roberta Brown she told me she'd just sold the house and most of their furniture, and that was only a few weeks ago," May parried, implying that the very fact she knew Roberta Brown somehow made it impossible for her to be a party to scandal.

Lydia enjoyed informing her that four days ago, while half of the town was attending an ice-cream social on the other side of the river, Mrs. Brown slipped away with the children and the rest of their possessions. "She didn't pay off one single creditor, though she had cleverly given them all a pittance when she sold the house, a good-faith offering, which everyone accepted as a sign of her good intentions."

"I feel sorry for Ben Leggett," Sam said. "He's lost his money and his friend twice."

"No, the first time he lost a friend; the second time he lost a business partner who betrayed him," Anne suggested. "In any case, I've heard he's a broken man."

"Speaking of partnerships," Lydia began, knowing it was time to get on with the news from Twin House Farm. Though she rather enjoyed anticipating May's shock at their plan to set up a gambling palace at Twin House Farm, she dreaded Sam's reaction. Still, his own situation was bad enough that he would surely understand her troubles. Only the bequest of a small inheritance from May's aunt had gotten them through this hard year. Also, Sam had contented himself with his original 160 acres—a wise decision, although earlier it hadn't struck Lydia that way.

Now she wished Charlotte had come to help her explain their plan. Her arguments and enthusiasm were quite convincing. Although she and Sam got along no better than ever, she would have been more persuasive, and if anyone had to suffer his disapproval, it might as well have been Charlotte.

As it turned out, "rage" was a more apt word. At first Lydia had been slow to notice how upset her brother was. She'd been pleased with the presentation she made to May and Sam. She was pleased with her reasonableness, pleased enough to take a little more credit for the idea than she deserved.

She even began to think she had made some headway with Anne, who had been uncharacteristically withdrawn ever since she'd been informed. And May was every bit as scandalized as Lydia had guessed she would be. Unfortunately, Sam's reaction was much like May's, only worse.

"This is the most damn-fool cockeyed thing you have ever come up with! I forbid you to do it!" He slammed his fists on the arms of the weather-worn rocker in which he was sitting.

Lydia, taken aback, resorted to a childish defense: "It was Charlotte's idea."

Leaping to his feet, he started pacing. "I forbid her, too!" he roared. "I will not have the two of you befouled in such a way."

"Forbid" Charlotte? "Befouled"? Maybe Sam was a bit unbalanced these days. The very idea of his forbidding Charlotte anything was preposterous, and Lydia told him so. For a moment she saw something akin to hatred in his eyes. He looked ready to explode; instead, he turned to Anne. "How can you allow this?" he demanded of her.

Lydia held her breath and hoped Anne would not use the occasion to express her own disapproval.

Anne said nothing, however. Absolutely nothing.

Sam turned his glare back on Lydia. "I will not tolerate this. As your brother I will not allow it." He wagged his finger in front of Lydia's face.

He had never spoken to her like this in his life, and she restrained herself from answering. Clearly, whatever she said would only make matters worse. Anne's tactic was the right one: wait silently. His anger had to die down sometime.

May looked as alarmed as the other two women. "Shall we open your presents, Sam? The children have something special for you." For a moment, Lydia actually felt grateful to her sister-in-law.

"To hell with the presents!" he shouted, and slammed his fist so hard into the side of the house that Lydia was afraid he'd broken his hand. Without another word he strode off toward the pasture.

"I have never seen him like this," May said, accusation in her tone.

For once, in front of May, Lydia was not defensive. "I had no idea," was all she could say. May unfortunately was right: Sam had never before responded to anything in this way. Although Lydia had assumed he wouldn't embrace the idea, she did believe he might eventually be amused, that he might even admire her resourcefulness. Before today she could not recall one time in their lives when he'd been censorious of her.

Coming to stand next to the rocker, Belinda patted Lydia's hand. "Daddy is angry," she said.

"Not at you," Lydia answered, and looked down into eyes remarkably like her own.

In the end, Anne went to find Sam, who returned to apologize and assure Lydia that he understood her plan was one of necessity.

"What did you say to him?" Lydia asked Anne during their carriage ride home.

"That he should stop carrying around the world's guilt."

"Guilt? If he has any fault, it's sanctimoniousness."

Since Anne looked straight ahead and didn't respond, they rode on in silence, a more and more common occurrence with Anne these days.

When Lydia felt she would burst with dejection, she blurted out her question: "Did you tell him you also disapprove of our idea? You haven't said so, but I know you do. You've been perfectly horrid to me lately."

Anne did not hesitate before responding. "I'm sorry you feel that way, but I've got a lot on my mind, too. I shall leave for Washington, D.C., as soon as the summer harvest is over. My cousin Mary and her husband have asked me to move in with them. Mary has developed a bad case of arthritis. She could use some good company, she says, and assures me the capital is a lively place to be. I made up my mind a while ago but didn't want to leave you while I could be of help."

"Moving to Washington is a ridiculous idea, Anne. Just because you're peeved!"

"This has to do with what is best for me. Listen, Lydia, Twin House Farm saved me. When I came here, I'd been having weeping fits, not wanting to get up in the morning, some days not getting up at all. I didn't want to eat and couldn't sleep. Even before all that, I'd begun to feel disconnected from everyone and everything around me.

"The doctors finally suggested I could be cured by going to bed and ceasing all activity, including reading—in other words, by resting all the time. Even if I got better, they said, I was to throw myself into domestic work alone; under no circumstances was I to use my mind. In my state, I had no desire to do anything anyway, so I took their tonics and their advice. Nothing, of course, helped. My only pleasure came from reading your letters and imagining your life.

"Then one day I realized I'd never get better in that prison I'd created, that my problem had resulted from my lack of understanding of what kind of life suited me. That's when you were generous enough to ask me to come here. I started making plans because instinctively I knew this would be the place to define myself. Everything you and Charlotte talked about, I'd wanted too. But now it's time for me to move on."

"Why didn't you trust me enough to tell me all this sooner?"

"Trust had nothing to do with it. I didn't want to be treated as an invalid—I'd had enough of that—and you would have fretted constantly over me, thinking all the while I wouldn't notice."

"Anne, don't go," Lydia pleaded. "This new plan is only a means to take us back to where we all want to be. You know that."

"I also know that turning Twin House Farm into a gambling establishment is a travesty of everything we've stood for. You will be catering to men in a most demeaning way!"

"But they won't have power over us. They won't own us."

"You'll still have to please them."

"You heard what I told Sam earlier. You know we have no choice."

"You had plenty of choices. There was no reason to continue borrowing money and investing in land and bonds. You and Charlotte started defining yourselves by the amount of land you owned. And how is that different from identifying yourself by means of the clothes you wear and the plays and parties you attend? Whether it's your standard or that of others', what is left of significance after you've lost your soul? No, greed alone has caused your financial ruin."

"We had our investors to think about. I was doing what I told them I would. I was just trying to make sure once and for all that Twin House Farm couldn't be taken away from us."

Something about the way Anne stiffened and went silent made Lydia dread whatever she meant to say next. The clop of the horse, the rumble of the carriage wheels, even the occasional cry of a hawk sounded ominous to Lydia as her anxiety grew, taking precedence over self-pity. In one day, her two oldest allies—Sam and Anne—had turned on her. Lydia would have burst into tears but for the fear of unleashing Anne's anger again.

Though it did erupt, this time Anne's words were slow and calculated, every sentence recited to the turning of the wheels. "The money you borrowed came from Frank Bailey, not from a group of investors."

Lydia's mouth and throat were so dry she couldn't swallow. As in a bad dream, she could barely get out the words: "How do you know?"

"The Randals are old friends of my family. Mr. Randal is on the board of the Chicago bank Frank uses."

This is not happening, Lydia thought as they rode along. I will wake up and this day will be erased.

Then Anne spoke the words Lydia dreaded most to hear: "You had that money when Charlotte needed to go to her father."

Drawing the horse to a halt, Lydia tried to explain. "What if Charlotte had not returned? Paris is so enticing and life here is so hard. Surely you can understand. I could not bear the risk of losing Charlotte." She did not want to lose Anne, either.

"Please don't go," Lydia entreated again, clutching Anne's arm. "Give me a little time to come up with the money. The land isn't worth anything now, but I'll sell it as soon as I can. I swear it, Anne. We can have our dream again."

"The dream disappeared long ago. You and Charlotte are too driven to notice. We overstayed the dream." Anne said nothing more but looked down at her arm, still clenched in Lydia's fingers.

Lydia removed her hand. "I'm sorry," she said. "I'm sorry about so much." Then she asked, "You won't tell Charlotte, will you? About Frank lending me the money, I mean."

Anne turned to her: "What goes on between you and Charlotte is complicated enough already."

Lydia smiled in relief. "But you'll see, I'll make it up. You need a little vacation, that's all; and when you return, you'll find everything fine. We'll go back to simplifying, searching for *true* purpose. If it's within my power, I'll save Twin House Farm without trampling on our dream. I promise you, Anne."

Lydia put the horse into a trot. Yes, a vacation for Anne, she thought, not dwelling on why she felt that Anne was so crucial to their enterprise.

The idea of Anne as the only stabilizing force merely flitted through her mind. She had so much else to think about. She had to find a way to pull everyone back together—even if that meant approaching Frank Bailey once more.

As much as she hated him, she could endure the humiliation of crawling back to him after his complete rejection of her. She would beg him, if she had to. She would do whatever was necessary, for she had the strength to right her world. She had no other choice. Now that her betrayal of Charlotte had been exposed to the unforgiving prairie sun, Lydia felt scorched, withered, forced to stare at her shame in the mirror. Her only hope lay in the reclamation of their dream, and for that she must now tap into an underground spring, make use of that mighty subterranean flow. She might not be a dowser, but she had it in her to will water from this barren earth.

**59** This time she would meet Frank Bailey in the hotel dining room; their encounter would be very proper, very public. She had no idea whether he had received her notes, and if he had, if he would come.

"In Chicago on November 2. Will dine at Palmer House 12:30," her telegram had read.

She wanted him to understand that this trip was strictly business, that she had no intention of starting things up again between them. If she hadn't been desperate for money, she would never have come.

Of course, he mustn't know that. Of course, he would already know that. Else she would not be here. Else she would have had too much pride. She had not expected him to disappear so completely, to abandon her.

These eighteen months had aged Lydia. He would notice that, too; it was the first thing he would notice. She touched her hand to her hair. Twelve thirty-five by the wall clock. How long should she wait before ordering? She'd seldom eaten in a public dining room. Would a woman be allowed to eat alone?

"I shall order for myself and my companion," she informed the waiter when he appeared.

Maybe Frank was dead, she thought. If she didn't want money so badly, she would have wished for just that! The waiter brought her soup; Frank's, too, at her instruction. "I'm expecting him any moment," she explained. At least she would not starve, she consoled herself, as she sipped her consommé.

When the waiter sought to clear both dishes, she waved him away. "Mr. Bailey will want his soup when he arrives. But bring our trout. He can catch up all at once."

"Madam, his food will be cold."

"Then cold it will be." She dismissed the waiter with the back of her fingers. "He prefers cold food," she called after him. By now she was sure Frank Bailey was not dead or indisposed. He simply wanted to humiliate her. Again. . . .

Halfway through the fish course, at one-fifteen, he walked through the door. She knew this, although she forced herself not to glance in his direction. Until he sat down at the table, she continued to eat her fish, paying him no attention.

"I hope you like the wine I chose" was all she said. She smiled. Think of the money, she told herself. Money.

"You could have given me more notice," Frank complained. "I was in Canada, for God's sake! I took the first train. I've only just arrived."

"All the more reason to try the wine. And the soup. It's delicious."

"It's cold." He twisted around impatiently. "Where's the waiter?"

Relieved that she could still fluster him, she wiped her lips. He hadn't noticed the lines in her face after all. "I told him you prefer cold food." She smiled again.

"Stop smiling. We both know you'd like to kill me right now."

"You explained why you're late. I'm flattered."

He had resigned himself to eating the cold soup. "I haven't explained why I haven't been in touch for so long."

"You had no obligation to me. Quite the contrary. It's I who am obliged to you." Pleased with herself, she smiled again.

As she and the wine began to take effect, he smiled back and, without complaining, cut into his trout. "But I do prefer my beef heated," he told the waiter and winked at Lydia. The rest of the meal went well. He explained his ventures in Canada and Colorado and caught her up on his Michigan lumber project. She, in turn, told him about the Browns and her voting rights debate, all the while keeping his wineglass filled, all the while laughing at his stories. That was easy to do, as he told good stories. She did too, and he laughed appreciatively.

He waited until after dessert to ask, "Why all this reasonableness and charm? You are not a forgiving woman. Obligation or not, I should have stayed in touch."

She took a moment to compose herself before saying, "I need money."

"That I assumed. The question is, how much?" His tone was as pleasant, as businesslike, as hers.

"Ten thousand dollars."

"Out of the question. I can't get that much right now."

"I'm prepared to offer my part of the farm as collateral. I'll sign it over to you if it would help." He now knew how desperate she was, but she had no choice really. "I would like to keep the house."

"In other words, you're willing to sacrifice all your worldly goods except your house and its elegant furnishings in order to protect Twin House Farm?"

"Yes."

"I'm touched by your noble sentiments; however, I would point out to you that your land is not worth two cents."

"It will be, someday."

"Not in our lifetime."

"I am sure it will, Frank. The blizzard and drought were flukes. People are still moving in," she said, though she wasn't sure this was true. "Soon we'll have the land under control."

This time his laugh was hard-edged. "You can't still believe that! I never understood why you bought *sand* in the first place. It won't hold crops. No wonder people were willing to sell you as much as you wanted as cheap as you wanted."

"It's not all sand," she said, but decided to forgo the argument. "I have to have that money," she repeated and forced herself to tell the truth about their financial situation. She explained Wallace Brown's straits and the pessimistic rumors about Benjamin Leggett's bank. "I'm afraid they might foreclose on the land deals in the hope of salvaging something. Then Leggett will resell to speculators for a lot less than it's worth, though he won't believe that. He's so out of touch with what's really happening, he'll convince himself that reselling is his only alternative.

"He's too understanding—it's one of the reasons he's in trouble now. And one of the reasons he'll have no compunction about calling in the note. He'll still be able to regard himself as a good Christian gentleman," she told him and proceeded with her confession. The more vulnerable she appeared, the more receptive he became.

"I thought the newest mechanical implements would give us control over what are still essentially uncontrollable elements. They made us feel better for a while, but they can't change the laws . . ." She paused before grudgingly admitting, "And they can't change the weather." She took another deep breath. "So I now want to drill for those underground springs —to protect us, whatever the weather," she went on hurriedly. "That and paying off the loans would save Twin House Farm."

He shook his head in wonder. "You have more harebrained schemes than I do. Woman, won't you ever learn?" He slouched down in his chair, ordered two brandies for them—Lydia's to be served discreetly in a demitasse cup—and waited until they appeared before he resumed the conversation.

Lydia also waited, calculating.

"What else are you willing to do?" he asked, not looking at her.

She took a breath. "Go upstairs with you."

He looked amused. "I never knew that was a hardship for you."

"When you humiliate me, it is."

His face turned red. "I had that coming."

"Well, whores should expect no better, should they? Isn't that what I am? You give me money, I sleep with you. That is our arrangement, is it not?" She took pleasure in his hurt. She hated him with all her heart.

It took him a while to answer: "The stakes are higher now for both of us. You have a greater need for this money, and I'm going to have to do a little sleight of hand to get it for you. As I said, cash is not readily available for me at the moment."

"This time I'll be more grateful—and humble." She added, "I mean it," in case he thought she was being sarcastic.

"This time you will have to marry me."

In one gulp she finished her brandy. "You couldn't be bothered enough to write to me or visit me for over a year and now you want to marry me? Are you completely out of your mind? We've never pretended to be in love. Most of the time we don't even like each other. You abandoned me. You humiliate me. You . . . you . . . Do you think I'm out of my mind as well? Give up my independence for you? I can't stand the thought of you!" In order for him to hear her, she had leaned so close that their noses were almost touching.

He spoke in an equally hushed voice. "I'm only interested in acquiring that which I can't have. Power excites me even more than sex."

"You are a coward," she hissed. "You stayed away because you are in love with me. That gave me control."

" 'Gave' is the correct tense. *I* will have control now." By this point they were both whispering.

"Only if I marry you."

"You will."

"Twenty thousand."

"All right."

"Also, no one is to know we're married, and we shall continue our present living arrangements." She paused. "Except that I'll come here more often."

Abruptly he leaned back and smiled. "You drive a hard bargain."

"I loathe you," she said serenely, also leaning back.

"I'll order champagne."

She shook her head. "If you do, I won't be any good to you upstairs. I'm sick enough already."

"Then don't let me keep you. By all means, repair to your room. I'll fetch you in the morning and escort you to the ceremony."

He pulled back her chair, and she took slow, deliberate steps to the doorway, cursing him for not escorting her. Cursing him, period. She would pay for having drunk so much wine, but her step was steady. And she had the money, plus enough to help Sam. She would pay, though. She despised Frank Bailey. Strangely, however, she felt disappointed that he didn't come upstairs.

# 60

Charlotte brought the galloping horse to a halt and began to scan the rise until she caught herself. She expected no one, looked for nothing.

My spirit is as parched as this landscape, Charlotte thought, and could find no tears to relieve the misery. Loneliness rode her these days as hard as she rode her horse, her hour-long journeys never relieving the sense of loss. Anne had gone to Washington; Lydia was away, and Sam, too.

How was it possible to miss someone you never saw and didn't miss so long as you knew he was near? Charlotte wondered. Just because he'd gone to Colorado should make no difference. She had heard him reassure Lydia that he was only looking into investment opportunities.

She could still hear those words "investment opportunities" roll out of his mouth, maybe because they were the last words she heard him speak. She also remembered her last glimpse of his face, his eyes scanning the yard, his thin blond hair hanging damp on his forehead. After that, she'd moved away from her window and stayed hidden in her room, crouched down beside her bed like a cornered fox, barely breathing until she heard his horse's hoofbeats retreat.

He had been looking for her, she knew, but even mute, she no longer trusted herself in his presence in front of Lydia. Anne had understood all too well the danger, and Charlotte had been profoundly shaken by her warning and its implications. Instead of feeling relieved when the one witness to their duplicity left, however, she'd felt worse. Anne's knowledge authenticated her feelings.

Her eyes came to rest on the shadow of a white cloud drifting across the late autumn-red pasture. This treeless wedge of earth never failed to comfort her, even in her isolation, for this landscape was hers alone, without the ghosts of her parents to haunt her. They had never experienced this place. She owned this, and the ghosts had no part in it.

She had been created anew out of this landscape. Not the way she'd originally planned, perhaps, but the effect was nevertheless powerful, abiding.

Comforted by these thoughts, she turned the horse toward her house, grateful for the pleasure these roads gave her. They had remained dusty, what with no rain, but she hadn't even minded that. Soon Lydia would be back; and if Lydia could borrow money, Anne might come back, too.

Norah sat on the walkway, legs swinging, rifle resting on her lap.

"He's snoopin' around here again. I saw him from the barn, but when I got up close, he'd gone."

"Did you check the horses?" Charlotte asked, a shiver running through her.

"He wasn't that close to 'em. He hugged the road in that field up there."

Charlotte rode off in that direction but turned back after a quick search. Ever since Leonard Majors had been sighted in Wichita, Norah kept spotting him, usually when she was by herself. If Norah weren't so practical and sensible, it would be a lot easier to dismiss her apprehension as unfounded, but she wasn't given to imaginings.

Wherever Majors was, he probably knew who had purchased his property, thereby also learning why it had been foreclosed on in the first place. Charlotte feared more for Lydia than for herself, and she feared for Norah, too.

Charlotte turned to her. "Would you join me for dinner? I think hash will taste better if we share it with each other."

Norah looked shocked. Charlotte was a little surprised at herself. Still, she couldn't bear to sit down to another meal where the only noise was the sound of her own chewing.

"You must get lonely, too," Charlotte said.

Norah shook her head. "Not so, but I reckon human companionship would make that hash edible."

——◦——

Norah ate self-consciously, as if afraid to take a bite at all. To put her at ease, Charlotte began to talk. "Maybe tomorrow I'll ride out and kill some pheasant. It's nothing like we had in France, but it would be a change from this stuff."

"Yes'm."

"It's too bad the buffalo are all gone. One big buffalo would last us for a long time around here. We could put enough meat away to last all winter. My father probably wouldn't have approved. After all, the dumb beasts are such easy targets, and above all else, he was a sportsman. Actually, he saw all life as sport." Charlotte shook her head and waved her fork.

"I never understood that when he was alive. But then, there were a lot of things I didn't understand. For instance, I'm a lot more like my mother than I realized. I managed to mask it from myself. You don't know my mother, Norah, but she is ruthless and unforgiving. I am not so forgiving either. In my own way, I have as much strength as she." Charlotte wiped her mouth and gestured with her napkin toward Norah. "Strength," Charlotte went on," is not a bad thing, as you know yourself, for you are strong, too, Norah, aren't you?"

Norah answered that she supposed she was, and it was a very good thing for both of them.

"Yes," Charlotte agreed absently for she had returned to thoughts of her mother. "And when I want something, I'm pretty determined to have it, regardless of the consequences—Twin House Farm being the prime example. Unlike my mother, though, I do have limits," she said, thinking of her fairly successful resolution to stay away from Sam. "Here, have some more hash." She pushed the pot across the table. Now that she'd started talking, she couldn't seem to stop.

"Maybe tomorrow we'll put the linen cloth back on the table. Just because Lydia and Anne are gone is no reason we should let our standards slip. Somehow it just didn't seem worth the trouble, you know? I mean, all that washing and ironing just for me."

"Yes'm."

"Do you ever wonder what it must have been like when the herds came through here? Every time I see a buffalo wallow I wonder. Spooks me a little, knowing how quickly things change."

"We still burn their shit," Norah said.

Norah's remark caused Charlotte to pause a minute to ponder the propriety of turning this into a two-way conversation. "Yes . . . yes, we do, Norah." Again she hesitated, then added, "And were there buffalo in Ireland?"

"Not that I ever heard of. But I never heard of much of anything livin' there. Where I come from makes Huddleston look grand."

"Do you miss your family?" Charlotte asked, suddenly interested in what Norah's life had been like.

Norah thought a minute. "I miss my ma, but she's it."

Charlotte banged her knife on the table. "I'm the same way, but I don't even miss my mother." Then she considered. "I do miss Odile sometimes. She looked after me. My grand-mère did as well, but she's dead."

"If they're good, they die," Norah said with such assurance Charlotte found herself agreeing. She also found herself disappointed when there was no longer any excuse for remaining at the table.

In fact, she'd felt so cheered that she began to feel a little optimistic about their finances. "I think I'll get out Lydia's wretched account books," she announced to Norah, "just to be absolutely certain we can't find another solution to this money crisis. Then Lydia could come back home." Now that Charlotte had identified with her mother's verve as well as her flaws, she felt a resurgence of her own vitality.

Of course, the need to borrow money wasn't the only thing keeping Lydia in Chicago, Charlotte acknowledged as she opened Lydia's desk drawer looking for the ledger. Deny it as she might, she knew Frank Bailey played a part in the delay. They must think her a fool. Then again, Lydia didn't always give the complexities of life their due. She knew better, but her temperament wouldn't allow her to face the conflicts—it was all too unbearable for her. Charlotte not only forgave her but envied her this obstinancy.

Charlotte pulled out an old perfume-scented lace handkerchief of Lydia's. That smell, so much a part of Lydia, suffused Charlotte with happiness. She missed Lydia and wanted her home. Holding the handkerchief in her hand, she continued to search for the latest ledger. Surely Lydia wouldn't have taken it with her. Charlotte tried another drawer.

In the third drawer she came across a jumble of letters, and began idly glancing at the envelopes. Not one of them was from Frank Bailey, she was relieved to see, in fact, all were letters she remembered Lydia receiving. At the very back, however, was one from an unfamiliar Chicago bank.

Rationalizing that the contents might pertain to a new loan, an avenue Lydia possibly had forgotten existed, Charlotte pulled out the letter. She found a perfunctory note informing Lydia of a loan for $10,000.

Trying to recall this transaction, Charlotte looked up. The money from the investors, of course. It had come in a period when she had been despondent and forgetful. Then she noticed the date: a month before her father died.

Her hands trembling now, she looked at the ledger from that period, but no $10,000 showed up until months later. By then she noticed that it was $10,000 with interest. She scrambled again in the drawer until she found another letter, this one announcing the transfer of funds to the Huddleston bank and thanking Lydia for her business.

Charlotte stared at the piece of paper until her candle began to flicker. Searching around the room for another, her eyes lighted on a display of Lydia's precious porcelain figurines. With a wave of her hand, she swept them to the floor.

"Everything all right?" Norah called as she climbed the basement stairs.

"All right," Charlotte answered, her voice constricted and thick. She picked up one of the shards of porcelain and began to slash her grand-mère's shawl, thrown over the back of Lydia's chair. With some effort, she ripped and cut until the shawl was in shreds. Quickly she stuffed the pieces into the trash bin. "I'm going back to your house. We can share the light if you'd like," Norah said, emerging from the basement.

Charlotte had forgotten that Norah was sleeping at her house while Lydia was away. She pulled herself together and followed Norah over the walkway.

"Nights are right nippy now."

"Yes," Charlotte answered.

"We're gonna need a fire soon."

"Yes," Charlotte answered again.

———•◦•———

Charlotte sat for a long time by her window, staring out at the darkness. Then she began rearranging her furniture, her pictures. By morning she had moved every item in her house to a new location. She hadn't so much formulated a plan as been possessed by some inchoate compulsion.

With the first light, she began draping her furniture with sheets and rolling up her rugs. She was just finishing when Norah walked in.

"What in the world, ma'am!"

"Could you tell me, Norah, where Lydia said Mr. Sam had gone?"

"Colorado, ma'am. But, ma'am—"

"Where in Colorado?"

"Pueblo."

"Thank you, Norah." Charlotte stepped back to survey her work. Satisfied, she turned back to Norah. "I'll be leaving this morning. For how long, I don't know. I'll leave money for you. Can you manage until Lydia returns?"

" 'Course I can."

"Bring in help if you need to. Johnny and some of the other hands will surely be glad for more work."

"Don't worry 'bout nothin' here. Are you all right, though?" Norah looked more stunned than upset. Charlotte had no idea how she herself looked—or felt, for that matter.

Within twenty minutes she was packed and Norah had hitched the horse. They made one stop at the bank and then proceeded to the train station. Charlotte insisted that Norah not wait around and did remember to thank her for the basket of food.


The man who opened the cabin door did not have a face she recognized. For a moment she could not get past his reddish beard. Framed by the doorway of the cabin, the man continued to stare at her unbelievingly. Charlotte stood very still, as if posing for a portrait, and began to study his eyes, which reassured her.

"Samuel?" she asked, still a little tentative.

Very slowly he reached out to touch her cheek with his fingertips. "You are real?" he asked. As she nodded yes, he folded her in his arms.

# 61

Lydia had stayed away too long. She knew that, and this time could think of no excuses to give Charlotte. None that either of them would believe. Days, then weeks, had gone by in a blur while she thought of nothing but punishing Frank Bailey for marrying her.

She had insisted on a honeymoon—"You might as well get your money's worth," she had taunted him. So they had ended up in Birmingham.

"It's a lot warmer than Chicago," he told her. Of course, he had business there.

He had always liked showing her his enterprises, and grudgingly she acknowledged that she enjoyed seeing them. Here he was involved in the iron-ore boom. "Look at this," he said, as they watched smoke rising from one of the iron mills. Fifteen years ago this had been nothing but a big cotton field.

"Only fifteen years ago," she repeated and marveled.

Every night she would meet him more than halfway in lovemaking— sometimes tender and pliant, sometimes demanding and bold, but always filled with demons that insisted on release. She had missed sex a lot more than she'd let herself know and wondered if she was depraved to want it, *crave* it, as she now did. Too embarrassed to ask anyone, she still didn't know if other women became as aroused as she had with Frank Bailey since the very beginning, though she hadn't always admitted that to herself, either. She tried to keep him from knowing just how much she desired all that they did in bed together.

In the daytime, when he was not educating her, she would be polite, cold, filled with loathing. She was addicted to both the days and the nights. Perhaps one of her selves would kill him, perhaps the other, or both in combination. She was obsessed with notions on how best to drive him mad, but he determined to last her out. Only when they could ignore the external world no longer did they return to it.

Norah waited for her at the train station, a sign that Charlotte was probably in a sulk. Well, that wouldn't last much longer when she told Charlotte about the money. She had only alluded to it in a letter she had written from Birmingham saying Frank had contacts who might come through for them.

After that, she had put Charlotte, along with the rest of the world, out of her mind—even Sam, although she had written to him, too, to suggest good news for all of them. Actually, she had written him two more letters, for his anger during her last visit had been more frightening than anything she had ever experienced.

Once Frank had come upon her writing to her brother. "Is the cost of keeping your brother and his family really worth the price you've paid?" he had asked, leaning over her shoulder.

She stiffened. "The price I've paid is for my independence."

"Strange idea of independence," he replied before walking away.

Nevertheless, she felt triumphant.


Only as they were turning into the road to Twin House Farm did Norah deliver the news.

"What do you mean, she's gone? Where?"

"She didn't say. Just up and left." Norah pulled to a halt. "She went a little crazy, maybe. Broke some of your things, too."

Lydia jumped down and ran inside; Norah followed. "I decided to leave it be," she explained, "so you could see for yourself. The porcelain was all over the floor, so I did sweep it up into a pile."

Lydia, however, was more interested in the disarray of her papers. "She did this?" she asked, already knowing the answer. She didn't need the confirmation of the bank's letter. She already knew the answer to all of it.

Well, perhaps not quite all of it. She sat Norah down and made her go over everything once again.

"Well, to start with, she's been most lonely—riding for hours and hours on end, or holing up in her room. Don't think me cheeky, but we was losin' her to some dreamworld. Then one night she asked me to eat with her, and she started talkin' to me like maybe I was you. Next thing happens, I hear a crash in here, maybe two, three hours later. She says everything's fine. We have a pleasant enough chat goin' back across.

"Morning comes and I hear her bangin' things shut. She asks me to take her to the train."

"Does she say anything else?"

"You know, the part about me lookin' after things. She thought you'd be back any time. That letter you sent from Birmingham hadn't come yet. She worried some 'bout leavin' me enough money and gettin' me some help, but I told her I'd manage. I mean, she was enough of her right mind to think of them everyday things. Tell you the truth, she hadn't been much use around here anyway."

Lydia controlled her impatience. "Anything else?"

Without looking at her, Norah answered, "She asked the name of the town where Mr. Sam had gone."

"Sam?" Lydia could think of no reason Charlotte would contact Sam. Unless she wanted to tell him what I'd done, Lydia thought, so he could punish me, too. "Did she post a letter?"

Norah shook her head and looked straight at Lydia: "She's most crazy about him. I figure that's what flipped her over."

Lydia let out a harsh sound meant to be a laugh. "Charlotte? She can't stand my brother."

"Yes she can, ma'am."

Lydia shook Norah's arm. "How do you know this?"

"It's all over both of 'em most of the time."

Lydia leaned back and put her hand up to massage her temple. "I never noticed." She spoke quietly now.

"I don't think you were meant to."

They sat there staring at each other until Lydia asked, "Did Anne know?"

"Unless she was blind, and she's not. Now, how about a cup of tea?"

Lydia looked up. "Yes, tea." Norah turned to leave. Lydia called her back: "Norah, how could she do this to me?" She began sobbing. Norah walked over to Lydia and lifted her head up. Lydia buried her face in Norah's stomach, much as she had the night Leonard Majors attacked her. "How could she? I try so hard, but I lose them . . . I lose them."

"Miss Charlotte was driven by the devil. It's hardly her fault."

Lydia straightened up and blew her nose on the handkerchief Norah handed her. "My brother was all I ever had." She shook her head. "I was never sure about Charlotte." Lydia knew she was saying too much, but she had this urgent need to share her thoughts with someone. She was sick of keeping silent. In the end, her secrets had done her no good. She still had lost control.

"You see, I couldn't trust Charlotte. She was fickle, like my mother, not strong, like me. None of them are. Except you.

"You see, I had to protect Charlotte. Sam too. They just aren't strong. I can't live without Sam."

"He'll be back. He's got a family."

"He won't be mine anymore."

"You had him for a long time."

"Not long enough, Norah. Not nearly long enough."

 At the expense of her pride, Lydia lied to May. Never would she have believed that Lydia had come just to pay a social visit. Instead, she pretended to think Sam had already returned and let her sister-in-law give her information about him.

May didn't gloat, however; maybe she also understood that they were no longer in competition. "He sent word he's snowed in by an early storm, but he expects to dig his way out before Christmas." She looked up from shelling peas. "I doubt that he minds."

Lydia found herself in the strange role of assuring May that he would mind—another lie in May's favor, but based on something akin to pity.

"Just so he gets here before the cold weather really sets in," May said. "I'll go mad if this winter is as hard as the last two."

"Those were just a fluke," Lydia tried to reassure her.

Belinda walked in. "Luther's crying. I pat his bottom but he cries and cries."

"Tell Pauline to see to him."

"She's feeding the chickens."

"Could I do something?" Lydia asked and instantly regretted the offer. What if May let her help?

"You could finish these peas while I see about the baby."

Relieved, Lydia readily agreed. Peas she could handle. As May put them in her lap, Lydia noticed how weary the woman looked. Fine lines had appeared around her eyes, and the translucent pinkness of her chin had become permanently chapped. Although she still wore her hair piled in small curls on top of her head, she had traded her too-elaborate costumes for plain dark cotton dresses. In not too many years she would look as old as Emma Leggett.

Even the room had aged; the fabrics and carpets had faded, leaving a bedraggled re-creation of a New York parlor, a conceit May had insisted upon. Now sand and dirt were embedded in the upholstery and no amount of cleaning would remove them. Besides, cleaning was pointless, for the next day's wind would blow the dirt right back in.

When May returned, Lydia was talking to Belinda, whose expressions were Sam's exactly.

"Daddy says we're look-alikes."

"I was thinking the same thing. You look just like your daddy when he was young."

Belinda giggled. "Not me and Daddy," she corrected. "Me and you."

"And so you do," May said. "Run along, Belinda, and find Pauline."

Belinda pouted. "I found Lydia."

"*Aunt* Lydia. But grown-ups are talking now." The little girl obliged only after looking to Lydia in the hope of a reprieve.

Lydia didn't want her to go, but she didn't feel she could interfere. She wondered if talking to all children was this enjoyable. "I'll come and find you before I leave," Lydia promised.

Left alone with May, Lydia couldn't think of anything else to talk about. This was the first time she could ever remember the two of them sitting alone together. She was glad she had peas to shell.

"You've been in Chicago?" May asked.

"On business."

"That's what Sam said. I think he'd heard from you once before he left. He's received two letters since. I didn't send them on, because I kept thinking he would be back."

Lydia nodded. May picked up a basket of mending and in a moment continued talking. "I wasn't sure if I should open them. I don't usually open his mail, but I thought something important . . . I didn't, though."

Their nervousness was just coming out in different ways, Lydia realized. "Mainly I wanted him to know I got a loan. We won't have to compromise ourselves, after all. I told him that in the first letter. The other two weren't of any real importance."

"He didn't tell me about the loan." The surprise must have shown on Lydia's face, for May elaborated. "He doesn't tell me much. This is not a very . . . talkative household. If it weren't for the children . . ." Her voice trailed off.

"All done!" Lydia held out the peas. "These look tasty." She found May's foray into intimacy unsettling. She had no desire to hear of the desperation in her brother's marriage.

"Why don't you stay and eat dinner with us? Belinda would love it."

"It's kind of you to ask, but I've taken enough of your time already."

May shrugged. "I guess I've lost the knack of keeping company."

This new role of beleaguered woman irritated Lydia even more than May's haughty airs used to. She wanted to shout at her to put some pride in her backbone. "You've got enough to do as it is without an extra guest," she answered instead. When she saw the disappointment on May's face, she relented. "On the other hand, I'll be going back to an empty house myself. . . ."

"Then it's agreed. And you'll stay the night."

"Norah would worry too much. If we eat soon and I ride hard, I'll have daylight most of the way home."

"Norah?" May asked. "Where's Charlotte?"

Lydia thought the question a little too disingenuous. "She's visiting Isabelle in Colorado." For a while Lydia had actually entertained this notion, but then a letter had arrived from Isabelle with no mention of Charlotte.

"Maybe Sam will get to visit with Isabelle. He always liked her."

"Colorado is a big state," was all Lydia could think to say. She now regretted her decision to stay, but Belinda's squeals of pleasure at the news changed her mind again.

Then Lydia set about, for the first time, playing the role of aunt.

## 63

In Charlotte's dream, a woman—bedraggled and exhausted—sat mutely in a hallway as a man walked by on his way out the front door. A baby and several toys blocked his exit. Rather than step over them, he turned around, lay down, and curled up on his side.

She awoke with a sense of unbearable sadness and shook Sam out of a deep sleep. Finally, still half asleep, he stirred and threw one arm over her hips.

"We have to go back now. It's time."

Without opening his eyes, he drew her closer. "I know," he said. Hours later, when they left their bed, he helped her pack.


On a map Sam found Isabelle's place and led Charlotte to her. In order to anchor their memories, they had sought out Isabelle as a witness to their time together. That was three months after Charlotte had come to him.

During those months they had remained silent much of the time, each moment too precious to fritter away with words of no consequence. On some nights they poured out the anguish of their past, in order that the other might know as fully as possible all that could be brought to their present. One afternoon Charlotte discovered that she had tried to be a part of Lydia in order not to realize herself and told him this also.

Not once did they speak of their future until they sat together at Isabelle's kitchen table for one final cup of coffee, which she had discreetly arranged for them to have alone in an empty house. (Unable to separate, he had stayed on three unintended days.) For a long while they sat in their customary silence, imprinting for eternity the memory of their existence together. For the first time, he asked her plans and so she told him. He promised to leave her alone, forgetting the history of their resolves. He tucked her hair behind her ears and thanked her for loving him and left her sitting there, sitting at Isabelle's kitchen table staring into her coffee cup. He looked as dazed as Charlotte felt.

But I have it now, she thought. Whatever else happens to me, I have my capacity to love. I know intensely the wonder of hungry lips between my legs and the equal wonder of a dahlia petal on my face. I am rescued from chaos.

When Isabelle came in much later, she found Charlotte still sitting there, her coffee untouched. For a minute they simply looked at each other, tears in their eyes. Then Charlotte smiled—a radiant smile—at her good fortune to have loved a man who was not afraid to love back. She was blessed to know the exquisite deliciousness of being alive!

If their arrival had surprised Isabelle, she hadn't shown it. Nor had she said she suspected as much. Isabelle's early observation of matters of the heart had taught her discretion as well as amused resignation.

For her part, she still glided through life, seemingly no more ruffled by the conflicts and emotions of having a baby and living with Gabriel— who, as always, was constantly in search of money and women—than she had been by the gossip and glitter of Paris salons. Gabriel had changed in one way: he would not accept Isabelle's money. That made life harder but it also made Isabelle feel essential and loved.

She admitted to missing their enclave. Life in Colorado was more isolated. "But I'm so busy I hardly have time to dwell on the past. The present inhabits me completely. Besides which," she said, laughing, "I have taken to conventional life as easily as any French shopgirl." Only Isabelle, Charlotte thought, could thrive on such unrelenting labor.

She spent a week in Isabelle's loving presence before announcing that it was time to go home, not realizing that Isabelle would take "home" to mean Paris. When they cleared up that misunderstanding, Isabelle did not question the decision nor did she ask how Charlotte proposed to live in such close proximity to Lydia and Sam. Charlotte had no clear idea herself, but she was now living by instincts, not ideas.

She had punished and loved and been punished in return, these experiences had created a fundamental shift in her being. She knew she was past redemption, but she was resigned to this state, which made her free in many ways. If one can follow one's instincts—not abstract concepts of right and wrong—one can always survive. She wondered if this was essence—to lose all pretense of reasoning, to act without care or regard. She did not have the moral energy to hope not.

"*Je t'aime*," Isabelle said when Charlotte left, bringing tears to Charlotte's eyes. Isabelle was not given to such sentiments.

*6 4* Lydia had taken to her bed. A terrible fever had seized her on the ride home from May's. Possibly because the cold night air chilled her through, or because she was already run down, or because she once again despaired of fulfilling her dreams, she had succumbed violently and for a long time.

Her nightmares were frightening: Sam, Frank, and Charlotte would take turns mocking her—laughing, jeering, pointing at her. New York and Paris floated somewhere beyond realization. She found no relief.

And for the second time Norah saved her life. Norah fed her, sponged her forehead, wrapped her in wet sheets, kept the farm running. She also sent word to May, because Lydia, when she was not delirious, was terrified that she had transmitted this "poison," as she called it, to Belinda.

Fearful that Lydia might be contagious, May did not come in the beginning, but she later paid two visits, the second with Belinda in tow.

"Daddy is coming home," the little girl informed her aunt, and Lydia experienced both relief and dread.

May brought a bottle of Lydia Pinkham's and looked almost girlish.

"I could have told you your husband would never run away—not for good and not for long," she wanted to say, but she didn't. Instead, Lydia took the medicine, as May expected and became light-headed from the high alcohol content. Then she lay back and waited for something to happen.

**65** As soon as Lydia heard the wagon, she knew Charlotte had returned. She heard Norah take her suitcase and heard a man's voice say giddap and heard Charlotte's thank-you, addressed to either the man or Norah.

By now Lydia's strength was returning, but she refused to look out the window or move from her bed. She would have welcomed the return of the fever and for a while convinced herself that indeed it had come back. All plans of action had failed her, who had always thrived, one might say survived, on action. During the whole of her convalescence she had not come up with one satisfactory solution to her dilemma.

Had she been a man, she reasoned, she would have dueled and been done with it, and she did on occasion have a vision of herself challenging Frank Bailey. In the scheme of things, however, although she was his wife, he was incidental to her daily life. Charlotte and Sam were not.

This last thought occurred to Lydia again when she heard a loud banging. She thought she might be dreaming, for she knew some hours had gone by since she heard the wagon. During the long, silent wait, save for the bleat of a lamb or the cluck of a hen, she had drifted in and out of sleep or reverie; to her they had come to mean the same.

With the next loud pounding, her curiosity finally propelled her out of bed. Moving the curtain just enough to see the front of Charlotte's house, she discovered Charlotte on the crosswalk, her small back even thinner than usual.

With one hand Charlotte held a board across her upstairs entrance; with the other she hammered a nail through the board into the doorjamb. She dropped the next nail, and as she stooped to pick it up, Lydia caught a glimpse of Charlotte's profile, including the three nails she held between her lips.

Even with tensed lips and hair pulled back severely, her face almost emaciated, Charlotte looked more beautiful than ever. It is love, Lydia thought. They love each other. They know love. But only two words escaped her: "Without me."

Fury suddenly flowed through her. "She is using all of the lumber!" Lydia said to no one in particular.

With no more thought or words, she threw her heavy coat over her robe, scrambled for her boots, and went outside to seek hammer, nails, and lumber of her own. She felt slightly light-headed from so much unaccustomed activity but decided she was in better health than she'd thought—either that or she was just too angry to care or notice.

Lumber, being a scarce commodity, proved not so easy to come by, Charlotte having already confiscated the only two loose planks on the place. Lydia had to resort to ripping a loose board from one of the outhouses. She took an ax to one plank and would have put Norah to searching for more if she could have found her.

She marched out onto the crosswalk with her two boards and, deliberately keeping her face turned away from Charlotte, hammered the first nail with all her might, barring entrance to *her* house. Sensing Charlotte watching, she hammered in the second nail with more vengeance. Suddenly each bang felt like a blow for righteousness and vindication.

Charlotte had not counted on Lydia's retaliation, nor had anyone asked, could she have said exactly what she was counting on. Certainly not Lydia's ability to wield a hammer so skillfully. That had always been Lydia's weakness: she couldn't execute half the half-baked schemes she came up with. She had no aptitude for physical labor and would have been a hopeless failure left out on her own.

Yet here she was, whacking that board with all the skill of a master carpenter. She had even been deceitful about that, though Charlotte would not give her the satisfaction of noticing.

Determined not to finish second, Charlotte used a ladder to make a trip to the shed where Lydia had gotten her wood. There she raised her and ripped off not two but three more boards. Not to be outdone, Lydia followed suit. This so enraged Charlotte that she chopped out four more before she began carrying them back.

Since access to the crosswalk from the houses had already been cut off, they heaved each board up and then were forced to use the ladder to climb back up. Charlotte was quick enough to locate the ladder and angry enough to maneuver it herself. Lydia had to resort to the use of a barrel and to the indignity of heaving herself on it and scrambling from there up to the walkway.

With renewed energy they both hammered and sought new sources of wood. By unstated consent, they gave up on the outhouse and attacked instead the sheds and chicken coops. Long after the boards were secured and long after all of the nails were in place, they both continued to hammer as if their lives depended on it.

When Lydia could no longer gather strength to pound another time, she flung her hammer down and turned around. "You have ruined my life," she shouted, and with the shout came an involuntary sob.

Charlotte remain composed. "You betrayed me."

"The sooner you leave, the better!"

"I'm not going anywhere."

"After what you've done?"

"So you didn't betray me, is that what you're saying? You never gave a damn about me, anyway. We are all just substitutes for Sam, aren't we?" By now Charlotte was shouting, too.

"You stole him away from me!"

"He is not a possession. You cannot possess people, Lydia. You cannot."

"And you cannot stay. Get out of here. You will not destroy this family."

Charlotte lowered her voice, but the anger in it remained. "I will never leave. You still don't understand! I love this place. Twin House Farm can't be possessed either, but I shall abide on it." This she shouted, with fist waving.

Whereupon Lydia took the ladder down, only to return minutes later with a saw. With no logic whatever behind her, she began sawing through the walkway.

The last word of this day, though, belonged to Norah, who came rattling up in the wagon. When she saw what they had done she halted abruptly and gaped at one door, then the other, and back again to the two women standing in midair, hands on their hips.

"Jest git yourselves down from there this minute," she yelled in a tone she had likely used with her younger brothers and sisters. "I mean it, now. Git down!" she repeated.

Lydia resumed sawing, however, and Charlotte went back to hammering. In a very few minutes, Norah shot a pane of glass out of one window in each house. Now it was their turn to stare at Norah and her rifle.

"You're gonna look like fools come winter, and I'm gonna keep shootin' till you both git down!"

This time they heeded her words, which was just as well. With only a little more time and effort the walkway would have been sawed in half, and Lydia would have fallen with it.

66 Both women stayed on out of spite. Neither would admit defeat. With the onset of winter they grew accustomed to the silence, the tension, the hatred. Their enmity sustained them.

When spring delivered them a tornado whose darkness and destruction reflected exactly their own emotions, they exulted in its fierceness, its uncontrollable violence. Charlotte watched from her basement window and regretted civilization's need to tame nature's unbridled fervor.

Lydia considered it miraculous that the houses and animals were not destroyed. That Charlotte's barn should blow into her yard with only a few boards missing, she considered fate's great good joke. She refused to return it to her.

The spring was wet. The spring was good. The spring produced an abundance of crops and feed for the lambs. The spring restored belief in the viability of farming as a means of power. The need to secure the future of Twin House Farm had not diminished in either Lydia or Charlotte, and in that effort they cooperated—through Norah.

From the moment she had stopped their feuding, she'd become their intermediary, their negotiator, their referee, their scold. Norah divided and assigned their chores. Norah hired the extra hands when spring came and made the final decision on the number of sheep to buy, the amount of acreage to put into feed and into wheat, the amount of money to spend replacing or refurbishing equipment. Norah kept them sane, provided with each with her only companionship.

On days when one or the other was being especially childish, she would threaten to leave, to start her life anew in Dodge City. She told them this feud couldn't go on forever. But both knew she would not desert Twin House Farm, not yet. Both women had lost their sense of time and felt this was forever.

They went into town as seldom as possible. Neither attended social events, though they were not often invited. While no one in Huddleston knew quite what was going on in those houses, everyone knew life there had changed, and not for the better. A few had run into Leonard Majors over in Wichita or Caldwell. He had stories to tell, and who was to say he wasn't right. At any rate, for Charlotte and Lydia the town had become an abstraction, a Greek chorus taunting them but, finally, not touching them.

Neither woman saw Sam—his choice as well as theirs. If May knew what had come between her husband and his sister, she did not reveal it. On occasion she would bring Belinda to visit Lydia. Also on occasion Oliver Whitman would call on Charlotte, who tolerated him only because she knew that Lydia found him repugnant. Charlotte had once been re-pelled by him, too, but now she hardly noticed his presence.

It was Oliver Whitman who told her that Ben Leggett's bank had failed. A few weeks later he reported that Leggett had reimbursed out of his own pocket all bank depositors who'd maintained a balance of one hundred dollars or less, effectively wiping out his remaining savings. She was heartened to think there was honor left somewhere in the world.

On one occasion Norah returned from town with a letter for Lydia from Frank Bailey. By accident she dropped it on Charlotte's floor along with a few supplies; by accident she failed to retrieve it before going out to feed the chickens. Quite unaccidentally Charlotte steamed it open.

> Lydia,
>
> Permit me to apologize for all the humiliation and aggravation I have caused you. Permit me to concede that on two counts you have been right: I did stay away because you held a power over

me; and George Sanderson did swindle me, as you predicted, and as a result I have lost most of my material possessions.

Since those possessions ensured my hold over you—not the only one, but the only one you will grant me—and since I plan to find Sanderson and kill him, honor still being an excuse for violence, I release you from your marriage contract. I am releasing you because otherwise I would destroy you or you would ruin me; such is our need to control and dominate, especially each other. Now, this part shames me most: I believe that I possessed an almost imperceptible urge to ruin what you and Charlotte had built between you. I'm not sure why, except that I was incapable of giving—or receiving—devotion. As you already know, you are well served to be rid of me. You may contact my lawyer at your convenience. I will, of course, take care of any expenses accrued.

I admit that killing Sanderson will give me greater pleasure than anything I have done in a very, very long time, including humiliating you. Contrary to strongly held public opinion, killing is a connecting force, a validation of our commonality with the universe. As you have now discovered, nature is no more benign than we are.

My belief that dominating so many different worlds would give me something, make me something, has turned out to be as futile as your belief (knowing you, it still continues) that you can will the climate to become docile. Unfortunately, you can will nothing of any consequence. I kept trying to tell you that, but never recognized I was doing the same thing.

Please know that I love you—unsuited though I am for such a condition, as unsuited as you. Had a Garden of Eden (still your idea of Kansas, no matter how much you moan) existed, perhaps we would have had a chance. As it is, we are doomed. I confess all this with sadness—did you know I was capable of such?

Please send Charlotte my best regards. No. Send her my blessing, whatever that is worth. You cannot accept it, but she understands life better than you and understands you better than you. I would tell you to trust that about her, but you do not trust—usually to your credit.

*If, however, for one minute you can trust someone other than yourself, listen to me: don't allow yourself to be consumed by some infernal dream that you approach the Holy Grail for, my dear Lydia, you are not remotely close to it, and possession of either Sam or Charlotte won't be worth the price you're paying.*

*Do not fret over us. We are part of what is happening in this country. We don't abide by the old rules; we can't. But our way is costly, too. You fight paying whereas accepting that cost as part of the bargain would be more profitable to you. Then who am I to say, you ask. In your more reasonable moments, you know.*

*With utmost repect, F. Bailey*

*P.S. Was it worth the effort never to call me Frank?*

*If Charlotte had succumbed, would I have been deeply satisfied? Or was I always seducing you, understanding full well the competitiveness (you would call it protectiveness) in your nature? That, dear Lydia, will always be a puzzlement.*

Charlotte did not bother to reseal the envelope.

Nor did Lydia bother to respond to Frank's letter when summer, in its abundance, produced a cornucopia of rattlesnakes and Charlotte's mare Essence, was felled by a rattler's venom. Within hours, the horse's head had swollen to three times its size. Lydia knew this because she heard Norah's scream on discovering the demented animal.

Lydia watched as Charlotte appeared, watched as Charlotte went back into her house and came out carrying her rifle, watched as Charlotte raised the weapon and shot the horse directly between the eyes, watched as Charlotte sank to her knees and bowed her head into her skirt. Lydia did, the next day, return the barn to Charlotte.

In late summer, coyotes became more of a problem than ever. Distraction and lack of interest had hampered the women's efforts, desultory at best, to keep their population under control. As a consequence, Charlotte awoke one morning to Lydia's screams. Since by now any display of emotion was unthinkable, she rushed in her nightshirt toward the screams, as did Norah, as did the hands employed to finish up the summer harvest.

In a field away from the houses they found Lydia writhing on the ground, clasping her knees to her chest. For one brief moment Charlotte felt as if she were plummeting into a bottomless pit. Then, noticing a prostrate sheep, she felt only agony. Their ewe, their miracle, the symbol of their wit and courage had been mostly devoured. Only the beautifully marked head and some bones and intestines remained. A coyote, indistinguishable from all the rest, had tortured and mutilated its prey beyond salvation.

Lydia looked up, tears streaming from her eyes: "You want essence?" she yelled. "Well, here it is in all its glory!" As Norah instructed and comforted Lydia, Charlotte walked away.


Though neither walked away from the houses, they still waited for something to happen to make forever end; but what the reckoning would be, neither could have predicted. When it came, they would know.

When it did come, the price was high. And it was Norah who paid it.

When the reckoning came, Lydia was out picking corn in a field close to her house. When it came, Charlotte was examining the hoof of one of the lambs. When it came, they had no inkling of danger, for they had become half dead to the world and thus to danger. Later, neither could even remember hearing the horseman approach. Who it was did not concern them; Norah would see to him.

Both heard Norah's voice as she shouted to the caller on horseback, "Whoa, there, mister!" When they heard her cock her gun, they turned toward her voice. Lydia, standing amid the high corn, did not see the end of forever, but he had her in his sights. Charlotte, from atop a nearby sand hill, saw that it was Leonard Majors and cursed herself for having forgotten to carry a gun. She started running toward the house. If Norah could hold him off for three minutes . . . only three minutes.

But he, too, had heard Norah cock her rifle and turned his aim on her. He did fire first. Of that Charlotte was sure; she would testify to it later. His bullet ripped through her neck. Charlotte could tell that immediately, for Norah's blood gushed from the large artery that led straight to her very wise brain and that very large heart. Her movements were like those of a hen whose neck has just been wrung. That is what Charlotte saw also.

Lydia saw only Leonard Majors fall underneath his horse. Later the coroner would testify that the horse literally bashed his brains out, and Norah's two bullets in his fat gut had not killed him. But what did that matter? What would anything matter ever again?

Charlotte and Lydia had surely killed Norah with their pride and their greed. Evil and sin were no longer abstractions to be argued over in front of a cozy fire, and responsibility was not something to be analyzed on a late summer afternoon. Yet their hearts had hardened so that they could not forgive each other. If they did that, Norah's death would truly have been in vain. Each would have to admit total culpability.

That night Sam came for Lydia and the Leggetts for Charlotte. But Charlotte would not leave Twin House Farm. After the hearing, Lydia traveled to Washington, D.C., to visit Anne. "We can sort out our lives later," she told Charlotte on the day of Norah's funeral, held without a band or a chorus or a march from church to cemetery.

Both knew they would spend the rest of their lives sorting through the events of the last few weeks; they had only begun paying the price for the death of this woman who had, in the end, loved Twin House Farm more than they.

**67** By fall, while Charlotte had not forgiven herself or Lydia their transgressions, her struggle to keep Twin House Farm viable with a scarcity of cash and help absorbed every waking minute. In effect, she sentenced herself to hard labor. She saw almost no one, but from time to time Joshua Lathrip, when his own work permitted, gave her a hand with the unrelenting tasks. Having had to sell his first farm, he understood what she was up against.

In turn, she began to liken herself to the Joshua Lathrips, Ethel Cannons, Leggetts, and Beauchamps. All had come to Kansas looking for something better. All had embraced, in various ways, change and advance. Yet ultimately none could control or predict the outcome of his personal transformations, including the infrequent advent of prosperity. Both the accomplishments and the failures worked against the very entities everyone was trying desperately to hold on to.

Not quite grasping all the aspects, Charlotte discerned an inherent conflict in the engagement necessary to make something of themselves, to count in the world, and in the search needed to find something lasting, not of the world. The women of Twin House Farm, she saw, were not the only ones in Huddleston who dreaded insignificance and sought deeper meanings and a feeling of realness. For the most part, the townspeople chose to cling to family or church or possessions, while the women of Twin House Farm chose each other, the shedding of skin, and the possession of land. The difference was subtle, but the danger of corruption in all was ever present.

As the year progressed, Charlotte thought she'd forgotten the terror of passion, but Sam's reappearance disabused her of that notion. He arrived as Lydia's emissary to negotiate a settlement: he would buy out Lydia's share of Twin House Farm and rent to a tenant, provided Charlotte approved. She agreed on the condition that Lydia never return to Kansas, for her treachery had run too deep for forgiveness or even mercy. Sam accepted her terms.

He made love to Charlotte. Afterward, racked with guilt, he apologized, cried, made love again, apologized again. Thus would it be, always, Charlotte knew. She did not mind. She had hardened her heart, although not against Sam. How else could Lydia exist for her?

As for Lydia, she accommodated herself to life in the nation's capital and came to understand, ever more clearly, what enormous forces had arrayed themselves against them and how dependent they'd been on whatever haphazard and indifferent relief Washington and the country's industrial giants provided. For a while in Kansas, she had almost convinced herself that Twin House Farm could be self-sustaining, once the finances and weather were under control; but nature wouldn't submit to control any more than Lydia herself did. This nugget of self-knowledge had been the costliest of all her lessons.

Her year, one of the last of an extravagantly promising decade, had held nothing but loss. Although Sam supported her through the ordeal of Norah's death and wrote weekly, Lydia sensed an irreconcilable rupture between them. Charlotte had replaced her in his heart. (Lydia had faced honestly her too close attachment to her brother.) Yet only Lydia's own treachery had driven him beyond reach. So she had lost them all—Sam, Charlotte, and Frank—forever.

Shortly after receiving that last letter from Frank Bailey, she'd filed for divorce, although the marriage no longer signified her betrayal of Twin House Farm and Charlotte. But the filing had been harder for her than she'd ever imagined, even knowing that Frank had been right: he and Lydia couldn't survive each other's temperament. He would always remain elusive—need to get away, fight the intimacy until it once more drew him back, an untenable situation for her. She needed closeness; yet she herself was elusive, not comfortable with the strong emotions that Frank Bailey could elicit from her. She recognized that, too.

She and Frank had been too much alike. All she hated in herself, she saw reflected in him. They destroyed, they savaged, smug in the knowledge that they could work their will. No wonder they'd been drawn to each other. No wonder she had resisted his pull. As vital, as buoyant as he was, his pull toward darkness was the greater. He had always tried to tell her that, had given her up because he could not protect her from his havoc.

In the end, his sacrifice was for nothing. George Sanderson—in many ways not unlike Frank, but filled with deceit, not of bountiful spirit —had triumphed. The lawyer sent her a letter informing her of Frank's death in the duel and of the inheritance left her; it was not grand, but it was enough to ensure her independence. Frank had put that in his will: "I hope this is enough to ensure Mrs. Fulgate's independence. Please apologize for me if it is not."

But Lydia didn't grieve for her losses. Nor did she throw herself into the life of the city, except on those occasions when she found someone who understood the plight of those she'd left on the Plains. Instead, she read voraciously, walked endlessly, and did good works as her penance.

Although separation and randomness still petrified her, simply enduring had made her stronger and more self-reliant than ever. She had discovered she could survive emotionally alone, the only blessing of the year.

For a year Lydia's house sat waiting for an occupant, but none came. May wrote that Sam hadn't been able to find a suitable tenant. Lydia suspected he hadn't looked, did not want to inflict a stranger on Charlotte. Shortly after May's letter had arrived, Sam wrote that he and May planned to move to Twin House Farm themselves and sell their own home. He'd been offered a reasonable sum for his house, and it made sense to accept the offer. Since Charlotte was planning to sell her own home, he would farm both spreads and build a new house on the property, some distance from the twin houses. Charlotte's upcoming marriage to Joshua Lathrip was left to May to report in her next letter.

"Can you imagine?" May wrote. "He's so far beneath her. She wouldn't have deigned to invite him to a party, let alone a wedding—anybody's!"

In Sam's follow-up note, he told Lydia that Charlotte had given permission for her to come back long enough to sort through her possessions and attend to certain papers having to do with joint acreage and livestock. Lydia immediately wrote back that he was welcome to keep anything in her house and sell whatever he didn't want. As for signing papers, she had already given him power of attorney.

She didn't post her letter that day or the next, however. On the third day she tore it up. On the fourth, she wired that she would arrive within the week to finish up business.

Sam met her at the train station, looking healthy but older. In a year he had aged a lifetime, she thought, removing her glove to touch his face. "I love you, Sammy," she said, unable to check her emotion.

He smiled and leaned down to kiss her cheek as he put his arm around her. "A good thing, too, since there's only one of me and one of you." She came close to joy; someday Sam would forgive her.

They would go to his old house for dinner. May and the children could hardly wait to see her. Lydia, in turn, could hardly wait to see them. She'd had no idea that she would miss Belinda so much.

The signing was to be in the morning at the Leggetts', neutral surroundings, everyone agreed. In effect, Ben Leggett would act as an impartial adviser and judge of sorts. Though he was failing badly, all parties trusted him.

Lydia asked Sam about Emma Leggett. Now that she was here, she was at a loss as to what to say to this brother-stranger, for Charlotte, the one forbidden subject between them, was the only one either had any interest in.

So he told her of Mrs. Leggett's remarkable recovery. The more adversity pursued the Leggetts, the more Ben Leggett weakened, the stronger his wife grew. She involved herself in community activities, saw to a good many of their affairs, had a focused look in her eyes. Yes, Emma Leggett had pulled herself together. And Isabelle and Gabriel had just had another baby. Did Lydia know? She nodded yes. She and Anne had kept in touch with Isabelle. And, yes, Anne was fine. She was working too hard on her good causes and in caring for her invalid cousin, but Anne was thriving in her own way.

Sam seemed happy to hear of Anne's well-being, though Lydia conceded that this was only speculation on her part, for what did any of them ever really know of Anne? Even Lydia, who saw her most days, had only a sketchy knowledge of what went on in Anne's head, and maybe that was for the best. Anne had a lot to teach her about boundaries, though Lydia was still not an adept pupil.

And, yes, it was true, as she had written, that Washington was as indifferent to their troubles as everyone in Kansas suspected. Sam said he'd always known that but the people here were at fault, too. They wanted to do everything on their own, without interference from anyone, including their neighbors. Yet there was no way to fight the storms and droughts and insects alone. They had to be part of something larger, but they clung to the myth of complete independence. In his outrage, Sam turned to look at Lydia, and both grinned. He hadn't changed. He still cared about the world and its frailties.

As they crossed the open fields, the day leaped at them in shades of gold. Lydia saw field after field of goldenrod, sunflowers, yarrow. Even on this cloudy day, the sun shone through enough to reflect all the honeyed tones singing from the dried grasses, the wheat coming in, the weeds shooting up, the turning leaves on the cottonwoods. "I had forgotten how glorious . . ." Filled with ache, her voice faltered. "When it's on its best behavior," she finally added, more as a reminder to herself.

She put her hand on his. "I need to see Charlotte first."

"That's not the plan," he answered, looking straight ahead.

"I have to see her, Sam. She cannot marry that man."

"She's going to."

"Why don't you stop her?"

He turned toward her: "By what right?" he barked.

"Please, take me there."

"She won't like it," he replied, but she could tell he would give in. This was their last chance to save Charlotte.

**68** As arranged, Sam remained in the carriage. Without waiting to be asked, Lydia stepped inside the house as soon as Charlotte opened the door. She didn't object but remained standing by the door and only reluctantly allowed Lydia to engage her in conversation.

Afraid to broach the subject of either the approaching marriage or the state of Twin House Farm so soon, Lydia did as she'd done with Sam—she spoke of friends. Had Charlotte heard that Sally'd had a baby? Charlotte knew that and knew that Sally held out hope of opening a restaurant. Neither mentioned that the restaurant would be the one that Sally and Norah had talked about. They never once mentioned Norah's name.

Lydia then moved on to Marceline. Had Charlotte any news of her? Isabelle had written Lydia about rumors of Marceline's traveling extensively in Italy and Germany with a woman companion.

After finally suggesting grudgingly that they sit down, Charlotte volunteered that Geneviève had sent a letter reporting that Marceline had paid her and her husband a visit but seemed dismayed at the domesticity of the scene and quickly fled. Geneviève herself was not particularly happy,

she had confessed, but believed she'd come to the right decision for herself. The other way—the Twin House Farm way—took too much courage,
too much toughness. She was not cut out for such a life. Charlotte volunteered this, too, but she sat upright on the edge of her chair, ready to flee
at a moment's notice. Lydia remained in that same pose, hands clasped
tightly in her lap, but she relaxed a little.

"I suppose that could be said of me, too," she remarked. When
Charlotte didn't answer, she went on. "Of the two of us, I thought it would
be you who'd succumb, but you proved me wrong."

"I didn't give up my country and my way of life for a whim—to leave
as soon as the dream tarnished."

"I didn't think ours ever would."

"All dreams tarnish. How could you not know that?" Charlotte
sneered.

So it was begining, Lydia thought. The amenities over, she joined the
issue abruptly, bluntly. "Charlotte, don't stay here. Get out while you still
can. Times are going to get harder and harder here."

"I don't want to get out. I never have."

"But there's no dream left. What we had was always a mirage. We
saw what suited us, and now you're paying the price of our arrogance and
cocksure belief in progress at any cost. We got caught up in ownership and
in the belief in everlasting progress. We got caught up in other people's
hunger. We even got caught up in their conventions without ever knowing it.

"That last part was mostly my fault. I know I worried too much about
what people thought, no matter on what terms I justified it. I even wanted
people to conform to my way of thinking! I was as much a part of what we
decried as anyone." She was half afraid that Charlotte would throw her out
before she'd had time to make her case.

"I'm not trying to excuse what I did," she went on, "or what you did,
either. I am saying that we worked against enormous forces: nature fought
us; society censured us; friends left us. We were so alone. We were scared.
Only a miracle could have saved us."

"Only miracles save anyone. You should know that by now."

"Look, Charlotte, I plead guilty. But we both betrayed our dream, and
the roots of that betrayal were in the dream itself. Like most others around

here, we thought we could control anything: the community, the weather, nature, and especially human nature. And for a while and to an extent we did; but we couldn't control our own nature, not even when times were good in other ways. We were guilty of false pride."

"That's the least we're guilty of," Charlotte retorted.

"I submit," Lydia said slowly, "that marrying Joshua Lathrip is no way to expiate your guilt."

"I'm under no such illusion."

"Then under what illusion are you marrying him?" The question came out more sharply than Lydia intended.

"Unlike you, I didn't come here for a dream, but for a life. I intend to marry. I intend to stay on the land."

"But you will not be on *this* land. You'll give up Twin House Farm, so why—"

"I forfeited Twin House Farm the day Norah was shot," Charlotte interrupted. "It's this region I love. It possesses me, not the other way around. Which piece of land isn't important."

"I was never wise enough to understand that," Lydia confessed.

Charlotte relaxed a little. In a more conciliatory voice, she continued: "You see, I love the tension—the not knowing if spring will bring a flood or a drought; or winter, a blizzard; or the summer, a plague of grasshoppers. It's a grim game, I admit, but I thrive on it, and I no longer care if I'm trying to best God or my mother or the world."

"But if the besting ceases?"

Charlotte shrugged her thin shoulders. "Then the game is up, isn't it?"

"Don't say that!" Lydia cried out. "What about your essence?" she asked, hoping to elicit the old magic in that word just one more time. "How can you give that up?"

"My life *is* my essence. Thanks to you, I gave up the last of my ghosts. My essence is simply what I do, what I *choose* to do. That's why I can stay here. That's why I can marry. My essence doesn't *depend* on my external life; it *is* the external life I choose for myself. We kept looking in the wrong place—way down deep or way up high, for whatever wasn't ordinary; we forgot that ordinariness is what makes the rest work.

"You never understood that, Lydia. Your past defeated you. You relive your old patterns over and over. You don't trust anybody, including yourself. You kept thinking fate would trick you again—it usually does—but there's nothing to be done about it."

Emboldened by Charlotte's openness, Lydia suddenly implored Charlotte to come back to Washington with her. "For however long," she quickly added, seeing Charlotte's startled look. "Or, if you can't do that, let me give you some money to make a start somewhere else. When Frank died, he left me some. I could split it with you. Remember those second chances that once meant so much to us. I still need that sense of possibility. So do you. If you stay here, that will be gone."

"You use possibility as distraction from the tension of life, Lydia. You refuse to accept the inevitability of different pulls. You're still looking for one great, satisfying answer." To Lydia's dismay, Charlotte's scorn had returned.

"Oh, Charlotte, don't treat our hopes so harshly."

"You're the one who expects too much out of life. Out of people!"

"I made a terrible mistake. I don't want you to make one, too. I want you to get out of here. Don't throw yourself away. I can't bear it," Lydia pleaded.

"I'm not throwing myself away. No one dominates my spirit. Life in this place is too difficult to worry about romance, and that's fine with me."

Staving off a sense of defeat, Lydia decided to try one last argument. "Earlier you mentioned my ghosts, and maybe you're right. But marrying a man who will use you up even as he idolizes you—isn't that similar to the situation between you and your father?"

"That's ridiculous."

"Why? We both know that I was a kind of substitute for your mother. I even look like her."

"Why are you bringing this up now?" Charlotte interrupted, all the suppressed anger suddenly surfacing. "Indeed, you *are* like my mother! You're the one who began the betrayal. You both ruined my life. You both needed to control me. What I wanted was of no consequence. You are both selfish monsters!"

"I was sometimes a selfish monster, and I'm sorry. As I was saying, however," Lydia continued, determined to make this one last case, "but I was most often a good mother to you, as you were to me. I know that wasn't all of it. I like to think I was special to you in and of myself."

"You were," Charlotte answered simply.

Lydia took a deep breath. "The important point now is that you see what you're doing. You think you're free from your past because you've been strong enough to reject the world's falseness in ways that I haven't. And you are strong, Charlotte, stronger than I in many ways, but to do this to yourself . . . Well, it's a terrible price to pay to keep a father around."

"That man is nothing like my father," Charlotte said. The contempt in her voice for "that man" chilled Lydia to the core.

She looked down at her hands, fighting the constriction in her throat. She entwined her fingers, pulled them apart, entwined them once more. She had only one more ploy, but she had not been prepared to use it, had not thought she could. When she looked up, tears filled her eyes. "What if . . . What if . . ." she began again, "I gave the money to May and the children, took them back to Washington with me, took care of them. You and Sam could make a start somewhere else—someplace that's *possible*."

"You are now offering up Sam as a sacrificial lamb to save me?" Charlotte asked incredulously.

"To save us all."

"No. To save yourself! To assuage your guilt. To make me forgive you and to make your brother grateful to you and indebted to you for the rest of his life. To have his children and his wife need you because, God knows, you want to be needed. And what do you think that arrangement would do to Sam—honor-bound, code-driven Sam? You underestimate your brother. He couldn't leave his family, and if he did, he'd grow to hate me." Charlotte's voice, rising, came out harsh and shrill, and Lydia experienced the words as blows.

She shook her head in protest and defeat. "My ideas felt to me like a relinquishing rather than . . ." she said quietly, her shoulders slumped. She had seen her offer as a selfless gesture beyond her limitations. She had hoped to remember it all of her life and know she'd been capable of one true thing. "Never mind," she mumbled, too weary to attempt the unexplainable.

"Don't you know your brother well enough to know he's not prepared for consequences the way we are!" Charlotte taunted, refusing to let go. "He's not that strong."

"He's strong enough to suffer the consequences of loving you. He's capable of that," Lydia managed to answer.

Charlotte's stare seemed to go right through the door, to the carriage where Sam waited. Her voice softened. "In that way, yes." She brought herself back to the room. "But leaving his family would destroy him."

"So you're going to sacrifice yourself instead?"

"I don't see my marriage as a sacrifice."

"Will you concede that I might be right? That you haven't given up your last ghost?" Lydia couldn't seem to let go of the argument herself, she realized.

"The one that keeps me a child, you mean? Do you really believe that? I concede nothing. Look at me. Look how far I've come."

"I have. I know. And you're wise—wiser than I, stronger than I. But in this one way you wrong yourself." She added obstinately, "Joshua doesn't have to be like your father to serve your purpose."

"What about *your* purpose—in withholding our money, in marrying Frank Bailey? What exactly were you accomplishing with that marriage? Withholding the money makes some perverted sense, but the marriage—"

Lydia seized Charlotte's hand. "We were about to lose Twin House Farm! In the end, I had to marry him," Lydia interrupted.

"If you believe that, then you're lying to yourself," Charlotte replied quietly, and Lydia recognized the truth in those words.

"Good-bye, Lydia."

They both looked down at Lydia's hand, which held tightly to Charlotte's, but there were no more entreaties. For another moment neither of them withdrew. Then Charlotte said a gentle but final good-bye.

Lydia, dazed now, nodded absently, needing only to leave. Unlike Charlotte she no longer had the stomach for besting life. She felt utterly defeated, as bereft as she'd ever been.


Lydia climbed back into Sam's buggy and could only shake her head. She wished she could comfort him, but she had no words of consolation. Like Charlotte, Sam was brave. He embraced the whole of life, Lydia thought. She had not been courageous enough to open her heart that completely.

Except for moments of escape or diversion, she would never still the longings, that much she knew, but perhaps she could learn to accept them. If Charlotte was right, then only through embracing that tension could she embrace life. Perhaps that was the secret she'd been searching for all along.

If so, she'd have to give up looking for beginnings and learn to live with the messy ambiguities that always followed, make herself face those monstrous pressures that kept the spirit from growing static. Yes, with enough determination, she could do just that.

It would not be a happy time, of course, but one must not give up on dreams. Past dreams, present dreams, future dreams—the time frame didn't matter any more than the dream itself. What mattered was the ability to dream, for to dream was to pray. Otherwise all became loss, and unhappiness folded itself around you. That was what Lydia had come to believe.

Charlotte watched as Lydia climbed into the buggy with Sam. She watched until the buggy turned out of their lane onto the main road back toward town and the train station. She stood there listening until she could no longer hear the rolling of the wheels. She did not know what to call her feeling for Lydia. Besides, a thought without form did not exist.

# Acknowledgments

The story of Charlotte and Lydia is fictional, but the inspiration came from the lives of two real women who met in Paris in the 1880s and did, in fact, build twin houses on a Kansas prairie.

Many people, through the gift of their time and talents, helped me bring this book to life: John Ferrone was there from beginning to end with advice and encouragement; Erik Tarloff provided astute readings with hilarious notes in the margins; and Jim Holland generously shared his vast knowledge of the period.

I also want to thank Mary Lynn Baker and Kathy Roach of the Reno County (Kansas) Historical Society, as well as Kris Gali, Duane Schrag, Rose Brooks, Pat Mitchell, Anne Renwick, Barbara Raskin, Jim Dickenson, Dick Brown, Sandra Day O'Connor, Louise Mellon, and Maya Gorman for a variety of assistance that ranged from the literary and historical to the more practical—helping me understand how to shear a sheep.

As always, Shaye Areheart, my friend and editor, guided me through the journey of this book. Cheering me on, making suggestions, and supporting me were my family. And an everlasting debt of gratitude goes to my husband Jim, who continues to bolster my spirit and my efforts.

# About the Author

KATE LEHRER is the author of *Best Intentions* and *When They Took Away the Man in the Moon*. A Texas native, she lives in Washington, D.C., with her husband.